Andy McDermott is the bestselling author of the Nina   &
Eddie Chase adventures, which have been sold in over 30 cou   s
and 20 languages. His debut novel, *The Hunt for Atlantis*, was his
first of several *New York Times* bestsellers. He has also written
the explosive spy thriller *The Persona Protocol*. His latest thriller
series begins with *Operative 66*, about a government assassin who
finds himself hunted by his own side.

A former journalist and movie critic, Andy is now a full-time
novelist. Born in Halifax, when not travelling the world researching
locations for his novels he lives in Bournemouth with his wife
and son.

Praise for Andy McDermott:

'Adventure stories don't get much more epic than this' *Daily Mirror*

'*Operative 66* is an action-packed thrill ride . . . twists and turns
that will keep you guessing at a blistering pace that never lets up'
Adam Hamdy

'A writer of rare, almost cinematic talent. Where others' action
scenes limp along unconvincingly, his explode off the page in
Technicolor' *Daily Express*

'If Wilbur Smith and Clive Cussler collaborated, they might have
come up with a thundering big adventure blockbuster like this . . .
a widescreen, thrill-a-minute ride' *Peterborough Evening Telegraph*

'True Indiana Jones stuff with terrific pace' *Bookseller*

'Fast-moving, this is a pulse-racing adventure with action right
down the line' *Northern Echo*

'For readers who like hundred mile an hour plots' *Huddersfield
Daily Examiner*

'A rip-roaring read and one which looks set to cement McDermott's
place in   *vening News*

By Andy McDermott and available from Headline

Standalone Thrillers
The Persona Protocol
Operative 66

Featuring Nina Wilde and Eddie Chase
The Hunt for Atlantis
The Tomb of Hercules
The Secret of Excalibur
The Covenant of Genesis
The Cult of Osiris
The Sacred Vault
Empire of Gold
Temple of the Gods
The Valhalla Prophecy
Kingdom of Darkness
The Last Summer (A Digital Short Story)
The Revelation Code
The Midas Legacy
King Solomon's Curse
The Spear of Atlantis
The Resurrection Key

ANDY McDERMOTT

OPERATIVE 66

HEADLINE

First published in 2020 by
HEADLINE PUBLISHING GROUP

First published in paperback in 2021 by
HEADLINE PUBLISHING GROUP

1

Cataloguing in Publication Data is available from the British Library

ISBN 978 1 4722 6379 7

Typeset in Sabon by Avon DataSet Ltd, Arden Court,
Alcester, Warwickshire

Printed and bound in Great Britain by Clays Ltd, Elcograf S.p.A.

HEADLINE PUBLISHING GROUP
An Hachette UK Company
Carmelite House
50 Victoria Embankment
London EC4Y 0DZ

www.headline.co.uk
www.hachette.co.uk

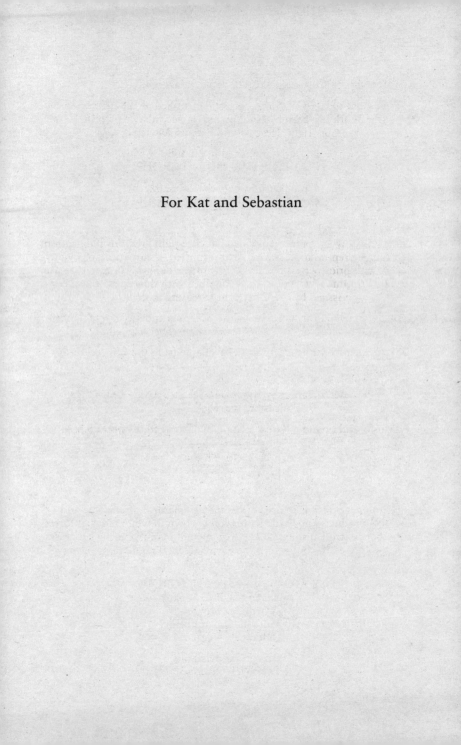

For Kat and Sebastian

CHAPTER 1

Alex Reeve ran into the darkness, alone.

He darted across the derelict railway track. Beyond the line was rough woodland. Reeve hurried into the cover and crouched, listening.

Just the hiss of rain. He waited silently for a full minute. Still nothing. He surveyed the woods. No lights, no movement, no voices.

No enemies.

Reeve allowed himself to relax, fractionally, and took out a small red-lensed torch. Three rapid flashes back the way he had come. He had been the canary, testing security near the military base's perimeter. If he'd been spotted crossing the railway, there would have been a response by now.

Three more figures scurried across the track. The glow spilling from the industrial buildings behind them highlighted their weapons. Like Reeve, all wore dark camouflage gear. Balaclava masks covered their heads, only eyes and mouths visible.

'We all clear?' asked the largest newcomer. His voice was echoed in Reeve's radio earpiece; all had throat mics.

'Wouldn't have signalled otherwise,' Reeve replied. The big man, Mark Stone, made a dismissive sound.

The smallest figure – a woman – gestured uphill. 'Pylon's up there.' Deirdre Flynn's accent immediately revealed her as Irish, despite her work to soften it. 'Let's go.'

Reeve led the way into the wood. After fifty metres, they reached a structure: an electricity pylon. 'Flynn, can you climb it?' asked the velvet-voiced Harrison Locke. The skeletal frame was bounded by barbed wire four metres up.

'Give me a boost,' Flynn replied.

She slung her AX308 sniper rifle. Reeve moved to act as sentry while Stone and Locke lifted her. Sharp *snips* from her wirecutters, and the obstruction was clear. Flynn clambered up to the first cross-beam. From there, she swung to a ladder and began a more rapid ascent.

Reeve was already continuing up the slope. 'I'm going to the fence.'

He soon reached his first major obstacle. A chain-link fence three metres high marked the base's outer boundary. He was near its corner. One leg headed west, the other south, parallel to the railway. The industrial lights revealed detail within the darkness. Concrete posts at regular intervals, razor wire topping the chain-link. A pole stood set back inside the corner.

His gaze went to its top. Cameras stared down at each leg of the fence.

A brief chill – had he been seen? But he was in cover, and unless the lenses were fish-eyed, out of frame. Were there any more?

He looked eastwards. Nothing but trees. The base's perimeter was close to two miles around. In dense woodland, covering it completely would need hundreds of cameras, dozens of observers. Too expensive. He wouldn't be spotted.

He hurried to the fence and lit his torch. The red beam both protected his night vision and was hard for cameras to pick up. He checked a post. If the fence were electrified, the wires would need insulators . . .

A small plastic peg jutted from the far side. He moved the torch. A fine, taut metal line ran between the posts.

A warning system. Low-powered, but contact would alert the base to an intruder.

Reeve was prepared, though. He took out a pair of insulated crocodile clips connected by a coiled wire. Next came wirecutters. He began to snip through the chain-link.

Flynn's voice crackled in his earpiece. 'I'm in position. I can see most of the base.' Reeve didn't respond to her. If she had anything to report, she would do so—

'What can you see?' demanded Stone, East End accent strong.

'No immediate threats.' Flynn's faint impatience quickly vanished, replaced by crisp professionalism. 'The main complex looks quiet – the rain's keeping everyone indoors.'

Reeve's cutters severed the lowest link, and he carefully peeled the fence open. 'What about patrols? Dogs?' Stone asked.

'I see torches to the west,' Flynn reported. 'In the open, near the witch's house.' The team had used commercial aerial and satellite imagery to map the facility. Various structures had been given nicknames; this was a red-brick building in a clearing.

'Coming our way?' Locke asked.

'Yes, but not fast. Looks like a routine patrol.'

'Fucking great,' muttered Stone. 'Reeve, you hear that?'

'Yeah,' Reeve replied. He carefully attached the clips to the electrified wire. Another snip, and the alarm was severed. No distant sirens, no floodlights flaring to life. He laid the connected cable flat on the ground. The gap was now clear to traverse. 'I'm through. Going in.'

He manoeuvred his silenced UMP-9 submachine gun through the hole. Then, with infinite care, he brought himself after it.

He cleared the severed wire's ends by several inches. Collecting his gun, he stood and surveyed the slope above. The only thing moving was the rain.

'In and clear,' he reported as he set off. 'Taking the east side.'

'Roger that,' Locke replied. 'We're coming to the fence.'

A new voice through Reeve's earpiece. 'We're almost there,' came the clipped tones of John Blake. He and the last team member, Craig Parker, were in a car. They were using deception rather than stealth to enter the base.

'Flynn, can you see 'em?' asked Stone.

'Not yet,' she replied. 'The road's behind trees.'

'We'll be there in one minute,' Blake said. 'Cover us, won't you?'

Flynn didn't reply, but Reeve knew her rifle would already be raised and ready. Her overwatch position covered most of the base, including the main gate. If Blake's bluff was called, she could snipe the guards to aid his escape.

Reeve moved on. Lights became visible through the trees ahead. He was nearing the facility's northern outbuildings. He consulted a map; in his memory, not on paper. Another fence ahead, but merely to separate structures from woodland. It ended sixty metres to his right. He angled towards the opening.

'We're turning on to the entrance road,' said Blake.

'I see you,' Flynn responded. 'Got you covered.'

'Gate guard's coming to meet us. Going silent until we're inside.'

'Or we have to run,' added Parker, with wry humour. Like Reeve, a hint of his natural northern accent remained, though Liverpudlian rather than Mancunian. The vocal training to anonymise the team members could only go so far.

Reeve halted. If things went wrong, he might need to abort the mission. A glance back to check his escape route. It was clear. He looked ahead again. About thirty metres to the fence's end—

Someone came around it.

Two men, glistening wet ponchos over camouflage gear. Both carried assault rifles. A patrol.

Coming towards him.

CHAPTER 2

Flynn stared unblinkingly through her rifle's scope. From high on the pylon, the main gate was just visible over a rooftop. Blake and Parker's car slowed as it approached the barrier. A man emerged from the guard hut. Another stood inside its doorway, reluctant to step into the rain.

She shifted the crosshairs between them. The man outside was fully exposed. An easy target even from this range. His companion, though . . .

Tricky. But she could do it. Her sharpshooting skill was one reason she had been recruited. The first sign of alarm, and both men would be down. Two seconds was all she needed—

A voice in her earpiece. Reeve. She instantly knew his situation had changed: he wasn't one for chit-chat. 'Another patrol coming out of the east ingress,' he said. 'Thirty metres away. I'm taking cover.'

Flynn muttered a silent curse. The car stopped, the guard walking to the driver's side. One hand was near his holstered sidearm; the visitors were unexpected. Her crosshairs tracked him. 'Reeve, do you need help?' She could target the patrol – if she abandoned her overwatch of Blake and Parker.

'No.' Certainty in the curt reply.

His decision. Her attention returned to the guard. The

car's window wound down to reveal Parker at the wheel. Passes were presented, Parker indicating his companion. The guard shone a torch, reacting to their rank insignia. Parker wore a lieutenant's uniform; Blake a colonel's.

The guard became visibly more deferential. But their arrival was still unscheduled. He called to the man in the hut, who retreated inside. Flynn tensed. Target lost—

Blake, his torchlit face a half-moon behind the windscreen, spoke. His expression didn't convey fear or blustering anger; rather, patronising impatience. A senior officer's attitude, which, considering his past career, was no act. Flynn could guess what he was saying. First would be a pointed reminder of his rank. Then annoyance at being held up after a long journey. *What do you mean, you weren't expecting me? I want to talk to the watch officer. No, do you really want to drag him out in the rain? I'll see him myself.*

The guard was torn between following procedures and obeying a superior officer. He called out again to the other guard, who reappeared. Flynn's sights found him once more. If they were going to challenge the intruders, it would be now . . .

One final exchange – and the second guard shrugged. *Your call.* He went back into the hut to use the telephone. The first man spoke to the car's occupants, then withdrew. The gate rose. Parker's window closed, and the car drove into the base.

'We're in,' Blake said a moment later.

Flynn had already turned to find new targets. It took her only a second to spot lights moving away from the east ingress . . .

Two men, already partially obscured by tree cover as they walked into the woods.

Heading for Reeve.

Reeve watched the men approach through leaves. He was three metres off the ground, left arm hooked over a branch. Both feet were wedged against the tree's trunk, holding him practically horizontal.

He hadn't been seen. There was no urgency or alarm in the men's movements. It was a routine patrol . . . which by sheer bad luck was coming straight towards him.

The bough would obscure him until they were a few metres away. Even then, he could be missed. The rain would subconsciously deter them from looking up. They might walk right under him without noticing.

If they *did* notice . . .

His UMP was still in his right hand, held against the branch. Both for concealment – and instant accessibility. He could eliminate both men in a moment.

But only if he had to. Some team members would already have shot them without a qualm – Stone, certainly. Probably Locke and Blake as well. To Reeve, though, that felt . . . *sloppy*. He had a specific target; he would eliminate that target. Anyone else would come into his sights only if they posed a threat.

But the threat posed by the two approaching men was rising.

Torch beams swept lazily over the wet ground. One man spoke, the other responding in amused agreement. Only three metres away now. If either looked up, they would see him.

Dull footsteps grew louder. One metre – then their heads passed an arm's reach below—

They walked on.

Reeve remained still. He would wait until they were at least thirty metres clear before moving—

A sharp *thwack* echoed through the trees.

One man jerked in pain as something hit him. His companion exclaimed in surprise—

Reeve had already reacted to the bullet's impact, whipping his gun around. Even firing one-handed from an awkward position, at this range he couldn't miss. The suppressor reduced each of his six shots to a muffled thud. Three rounds into each man's back, and both fell.

He dropped from the tree. 'Flynn,' he growled. 'I told you I didn't need help.'

'I was covering your arse,' came the reply. 'They were going to find you.'

He quickly checked the two figures. 'They'd already gone past. But now they're both dead, and sooner or later someone'll realise they're missing.'

'So just speed things up,' cut in Stone.

'Which means more chance of making mistakes.'

Before the Londoner could reply, Blake cut in. 'We're at the administration building. Going inside.'

'Better get your backside in gear, Reeve,' said Stone. Annoyed, Reeve resumed his journey, moving more quickly.

He soon reached the fence's end. Beyond was an expanse of wet tarmac between large warehouse-like buildings. Shipping containers and a few vehicles were dotted around. Nobody was in sight.

'I'm at the east ingress,' he whispered. 'Starting the search.'

He moved through the yard. More buildings came into view, vans parked at unlit loading docks. Still no activity. He crouched behind a forklift. His target was somewhere on the base. But where?

It was unlikely to be here. All the nearby structures were logistical in nature. Few had interior lights on. Another check of his mental map. What had looked on aerial imagery like operations buildings were to the south. Sticking to the shadows, he headed in that direction.

Stone and Locke passed a firing range in the woods and continued south-west. 'There's the assault course,' said Locke, crouching amongst bushes. Beyond an access road were several prefabricated buildings and Portakabins. Between them was the physical training facility; a useful landmark.

'Not as fancy as ours,' Stone noted with faint amusement. 'Okay, the main buildings are on the far side. Let's find our man and pop him—'

Locke let out a sharp hiss: *quiet*. He dropped lower. Stone swore and followed suit.

A two-man patrol walked along the road towards them. 'Must be the ones Flynn saw,' Locke whispered.

'I thought they were down by the witch's house,' growled Stone. 'Deirdre, you fucking bog-ape, you're supposed to be keeping watch.'

'I don't have fucking X-ray vision,' came Flynn's irate reply. 'They went into the woods while I was watching the main gate. Oh, and Stone? Fuck you.'

'Yeah, dream on.'

'Shut up,' hissed Locke. Stone gave him a dirty look, but fell silent.

The patrol ambled along, torch beams sweeping with disinterest over the roadside. One brushed Locke, but with his form broken by camo and shadows, he went unnoticed. Then they passed, continuing eastwards.

A wordless look between Locke and Stone . . . and they rose.

The big Londoner brought up his submachine gun. Locke, however, drew a matt-black carbon-fibre combat knife. He cleared the bushes and advanced cat-like for several steps – then rushed.

One man heard his footsteps and turned. Red flowers burst open across his chest as Stone fired. Locke was on his companion before he could react. The knife sliced through the air to find his throat.

Stone jogged up beside Locke. 'You're dead, arseholes,' he told the fallen figures, before addressing the other man. 'Why didn't you just shoot 'em? Would have been safer.'

Locke returned his blade to its sheath. 'I like to keep my surgical skills honed.' There was no humour in his voice. Stone let out a faintly unsettled half-laugh. They dragged the men into the bushes, then continued into the main complex.

CHAPTER 3

Flynn watched Stone and Locke disappear behind a building through her scope. 'Christ,' she whispered. She had shot the patrol to protect Reeve, but this? They had acted purely for their own enjoyment.

But what was done, was done. 'Locke, Stone, I've lost line of sight.' She could no longer provide cover. 'I'm coming down. Reeve, I'll catch up.'

Reeve's acknowledgement was terse. She started back down the ladder.

Parker stopped outside a modern block at the heart of the base. 'Looks like someone's waiting for us.' A figure was silhouetted behind glass doors. 'Think you can fool them?'

'Of course,' Blake replied. 'It helps when you know the lingo.' Parker began to get out, giving him a quizzical glance when he didn't move. 'Play the part, remember? I'm the colonel, you're the lieutenant. Now, hold my umbrella. I don't want to get wet.'

'Posh bastard,' Parker growled under his breath. He rounded the car and raised an umbrella before opening the door for Blake. The taller man stepped out beneath the cover. He made a show of straightening his uniform, then started for the entrance. Parker flanked him, keeping him dry.

The waiting man was the watch officer, a youthful captain. He greeted Blake with a salute, but remained wary. 'We weren't expecting you, sir,' he said, after brief introductions.

'You should have had the notification this morning,' Blake snapped. 'Where's your office? I've had a long and tedious drive, I need a coffee.'

'This way, sir.' The captain led the way. 'In here.'

Two junior non-commissioned officers were inside, both rising as they saw Blake's uniform. He acknowledged them, then surveyed the room. An administrative office, which in daytime would house nine or ten staff. 'Are you the entire night shift?'

'Yes, sir,' said the captain. He went to a coffee pot. 'If I may ask, sir – why are you here?'

'It's about your VIP guest,' Blake replied.

The other men seemed confused, apparently out of the loop. The captain, though, nodded. 'Ah, I see. You're here to meet him?'

'In a way.' Blake glanced at Parker. 'We're here to kill him.' They both drew suppressed handguns.

The three men stared at the weapons in bewilderment. One of the juniors let out a nervous involuntary giggle. 'I assure you, we're quite serious,' Blake said, before his voice rose to a bark. 'Now get up. Into the corner. Move!'

'Ah – do as he says,' the captain told the other two uncertainly. They backed away, Blake advancing to cover them.

Parker went to one of their computers. 'Still logged in. That makes things easier.' He sat and produced a USB drive, plugging it in.

'What are you doing?' the captain demanded.

'Quiet,' snapped Blake. 'Well? Can you get in?'

Parker ignored him. The USB mounted, and he double-clicked on a file. He waited for a program to run – then pushed a button on the flash drive. A window appeared. 'I'm in. Got access to the base's network.'

Locke's voice buzzed in his earpiece. 'You bypassed the security?'

'Yeah. Now, wait.' Parker typed rapid commands. A list of numbers scrolled up the screen. 'We know his laptop's MAC address. I'm checking if it's on the system. If he logged in, I'll know where he was. If he's still logged in, I'll know where he *is*.'

'To the building?' asked Blake.

'To the room.'

'How long will it take?'

'Couple of minutes.'

Blake gave his prisoners a mocking smile. 'I should have let you make me that coffee.'

Reeve ducked around a corner as a van approached. It stopped near a loading bay. Nobody got out, but he saw a pale light in the cab. The driver was making a phone call. Needing to continue unseen, Reeve continued behind the building. The perimeter fence stood before him, running parallel to the railway line.

'Reeve, I'm through the fence.' Flynn. 'Where are you?'

'Behind a pale green prefab on the east perimeter,' he answered, slipping southwards. 'There's a guy in a van outside the front.'

'Wait for me. I'll be with you in three minutes.'

Reeve frowned in impatience. 'We still need to search for the target.'

'Parker's on it. He'll tell us where to look.'

'And what if he can't find him?'

Flynn made a sound of annoyance. 'Just wait for me, for Christ's sake.'

Reeve reached the building's far end. A large, blank-walled structure rose ahead, crates and pallets piled outside. Head around it towards the base's centre, or keep following the perimeter?

He chose the former. The target was more likely to be near the heart of things. He moved along the green building's side to check the roadway beyond. The van was still stationary, lights on. Staying in the shadows, he scurried to the larger structure and surveyed what lay beyond.

More industrial-looking buildings, trees, a couple of parked trucks. A car drove along a road sixty metres distant, but soon passed from sight.

Nowhere that seemed an obvious place to find his target. Maybe he should see if Parker could locate him after all . . .

He was about to withdraw when he heard something. Distant, the wind carrying the sound.

A helicopter.

Civilian aircraft would generally avoid flying in these conditions. So it was probably military. And he was in a military facility.

The team's objective was to eliminate the target before he left the base. They had expected him to depart by road. But if he left by air . . .

The faint rhythmic thudding reached him again. Still some distance away – but now fractionally louder.

He was about to warn the others when Parker spoke first.

'I've got him,' Parker crowed. 'He's logged into the base network a few times. Last time was . . . less than ten minutes ago.'

'Where?' asked Blake, eyes not leaving his three prisoners.

'The communications centre. Near that big open field.'

'He's leaving in a chopper,' Reeve cut in urgently. 'I just heard one. I think it's coming in.'

'There's an airport ten miles away,' objected Stone. 'It could be going there.'

'You want to risk it?'

'Reeve's right,' said Blake. 'It'd be just like that bastard to sneak out under our noses. Everyone head for the field – it's got to be the landing zone.'

Stone was still argumentative. 'Who fucking put you in charge?'

'Would you rather keep playing hide and seek in the rain?' suggested Locke. 'We're on the way.'

'Parker, let's go,' Blake ordered. Parker retrieved the USB drive and stood.

The captain watched as he headed for the exit. 'What about us?'

'I'm afraid,' Blake told him mildly, 'you failed your security test.'

His gun thumped three times.

Parker regarded the aftermath. 'Bit harsh. They were just doing their jobs.'

Blake smiled. 'Did you want to waste time finding rope to

tie them up?' He followed Parker to the door. 'We'd better get moving. We have a flight to catch.'

Flynn followed Reeve's route into the main complex. She stopped at a corner. The van Reeve had mentioned waited ahead, headlights reflecting off wet tarmac.

If she crossed in front of it, she would be seen. She back-tracked. The helicopter's clatter was now discernible above the rain. Coming closer.

She returned to the east ingress. On entering she had gone left; now she went right. A long rank of parked military trucks greeted her. She hurried past them and peered out from behind a building.

There was the green prefab. She went to the next corner, checking the loading bays beyond. The van was still station-ary, but now she could pass it unseen. 'Reeve, I'm almost with you,' she said, as she crossed the open yard.

'I've already gone,' came the reply. 'I'm heading for the field.'

She stopped, hesitating before turning back. 'I *told* you to wait for—'

'Hey! You! *Halt!*'

Two burly men were approaching from the south, fifty metres away. Both were armed, rifles snapping up. One broke into a run as the other crouched to target her. 'Drop your weapon!' the latter yelled.

She couldn't reach cover before being shot. And if she fired on one man, the other would get her. 'Reeve, I need help,' she hissed.

*

Reeve was cutting through a darkened parking lot when he heard Flynn's plea. He ducked between two trucks, considering his options. She was at least a hundred metres back. 'How many men?'

'Two. One's running right at me.'

His decision was instant. 'I can't help you.'

'*What?* You bastard, we're supposed to—'

She stopped talking, instead pulling her rifle's trigger. A man's muted cry – then Flynn herself gasped in pain. A thump as she fell to the road's hard surface. 'Jesus, *fuck*!' she moaned, another man shouting in the background . . .

Then nothing.

'Shit,' Reeve muttered. But there was no way he could have reached her in time to intervene.

And the mission always took priority. Every team member knew that. Including Flynn.

He moved again. The alarm would be raised at any moment. The helicopter was now clearly audible.

His target was about to escape.

The thought spurred him on even faster between the darkened buildings.

CHAPTER 4

'Shit, Reeve was right,' said Stone, as he heard the incoming helicopter. 'How far to the field?'

'Two hundred metres,' said Locke. 'Across the main road.' The base's centre was bisected by a two-lane roadway.

'Past all the buildings with fucking lights on, you mean.' Beyond the road were numerous blocks of living quarters.

'Down the back, through the trees.' Locke led the way, sprinting across the road. Stone followed—

Alarm bells rang, followed by an urgent, raucous klaxon. 'Balls,' spat Stone. 'Flynn, you stupid Mick bitch! They know we're here.'

He raced after Locke as floodlights burst to life around the base.

Blake and Parker ran from the administration building. The dark expanse of the field was off to their right. They hurried towards it.

'There!' Blake shouted. The helicopter was coming in from the south, descending quickly. He followed its track, predicting where it was going to land. The field's northern edge. 'Move it.'

Headlights appeared, a car coming between two accommodation blocks. 'Must be him,' said Parker.

The aircraft dropped heavily on to the grass. The car stopped. A figure ran from it towards the helicopter.

Parker raised his gun, but the man was already shielded by the fuselage. 'I don't have an angle.'

Stone and Locke raced around the accommodation blocks to the field. The helicopter, rotors whirling just below take-off speed, was ahead. A cabin door slammed shut.

Locke sent three rapid shots at the fuselage. All hit the side window. Stone, however, fired on full-auto – at the cockpit. The curved windshield erupted with bullet impacts.

A pause – then the shrill of the engines dropped. The rotors began to wind down.

Stone gave his companion a triumphant grin. 'If you can't hit the passenger, hit the driver.'

'We still need to hit the passenger, though,' Locke pointed out. Someone scrambled from the aircraft's far side.

'I see him,' Blake reported over the radio. 'Firing – damn it!' The car surged forward, skidding around to shield the running figure. The man ducked behind it and leapt inside.

Stone and Locke fired again, but the car set off despite taking multiple hits. It fishtailed on the wet ground before powering back the way it had come.

'Come on!' Locke barked. 'We might intercept him on the main road.'

'We'll go after him in the car,' said Blake.

Locke and Stone reversed course. The alarm was already drawing a response. Several uniformed men emerged from a building to the west. More would follow.

They passed the nearest block, crossing a secondary road. Stone looked along it in case the target was coming their way.

Instead, he saw rapidly retreating red tail lights.

'Target going east,' he reported. 'He's getting away.'

Blake and Parker reached their car. 'I'll drive,' snapped the former. He set off before Parker had closed his door.

He reversed at speed, whipping the wheel around hard. The car skidded into a J-turn, coming completely about. Blake controlled it with practised ease and powered from the car park.

Parker wound down his window and readied his gun. 'Where is he?'

'Should be coming from the left – shit!' A van rushed out of a side road ahead – from the right. Blake swerved to avoid a collision as it tried to block them.

More lights flared in the rear-view mirror. No sign of their target's vehicle. 'The situation's getting rather dicey,' he said. 'If we don't take him right now, we'll need to bail out.'

Parker squinted into the blowing rain. 'Still can't see him.'

Blake glanced at the mirror again. The headlights were in pursuit, coming fast. 'Stone, Locke, I'm coming along the main road,' he said, accelerating. 'The mission's blown – time to leave.'

The escaping car was still nowhere in sight. 'Fuck!' Parker snarled. 'Where the hell's Reeve?'

*

Reeve had run behind several buildings. He emerged just in time to see Blake and Parker's car shoot past. Two more cars and a van raced after it.

He stayed in the shadows. Where was the target? If he had gone east from the accommodation blocks, he should be in sight . . .

Headlights came on across the road.

Reeve felt the thrill of discovery. The target's car had pulled in behind the last block and switched off its lights. Its occupants had gambled on the attackers assuming they were fleeing through the base. Instead they had hidden, waiting for the military forces to drive the intruders away.

A good gamble. But one they had lost.

The car started towards the road. No rush. They thought they were safe. Reeve waited until it reached the junction – then ran out into the open.

The driver saw him. The car accelerated, turning hard on to the wet road. Reeve brought up his UMP and fired. Shots burst across the windscreen. The car charged on for a few seconds – then it veered across the road on to a lawn. It slewed around, right side facing him, and stopped.

Reeve raced after it. Movement in the car's rear. He ducked, angling to go behind the stationary vehicle rather than straight to it.

Gun raised, he scurried to the left-rear door – and threw it open.

The interior light came on. The man inside had his back to him, a pistol in one hand. He had expected Reeve to come to the closest door. His head turned—

Reeve fired three shots into his back.

A pained cry, then the man slumped. Reeve checked his face. It was the target. One mission objective completed. Now for the other. Where was his laptop?

An impact-resistant briefcase on the floor. The weight felt right for a laptop and charger. A closer look. Combination lock. No way to check easily what was really inside. A decoy?

No. It was wet. The target had carried it through the rain. Confident he had his prize, he backed out of the car. Over the clamour of alarms he heard another vehicle approaching. Enemy forces would be here any second.

He sprinted back across the road. Headlights to his right, but he was behind the building before the car stopped. He ran, weaving through trees towards the perimeter fence.

It was designed to prevent people scaling it from outside. From within, it posed less of an obstacle. He shouldered his gun, then quickly climbed a concrete post. Coiled razor wire awaited him at the top. He mashed it down with the briefcase and scrambled over. A gasp as a blade cut his calf, but the wound was superficial.

He dropped down on to the slope below. At its foot was the railway. He hurried through the trees towards it. Shouts from behind. Had they seen him climb over?

The voices spread out, his pursuers moving along the fence. They hadn't spotted him. It wouldn't be long before someone noticed the crushed razor wire. But by then, he would be gone.

Reeve reached the line. Buildings rose past fences and walls on the far side. He rapidly scaled the nearest barrier. Small industrial units lay beyond, silent and dark. He hurried through a yard and ducked behind a rusty container.

Debris crunched underfoot. He took out his torch. The ground was littered with broken wood and discarded junk.

Reeve put down his gun, then removed his camouflage gear. Nondescript civilian clothing was revealed beneath. The balaclava came off, exposing short mousy hair and a youthful, angular face. The discarded camo covered the rifle. Recovering the briefcase, he returned to the yard and headed east.

He soon reached a street. A few cars and vans were parked along it, but no one saw him emerge. He walked quickly, away from the base.

Radio chatter told him what had happened. Blake and Parker had collected Stone and Locke before crashing through the gate. Blake was an expert driver, soon losing their pursuers. Now all talk was anger and recriminations, fury at their failure. He was not surprised when Stone loudly blamed everyone but himself. Parker and Blake for losing the target, Flynn for getting caught, Reeve for disappearing—

Reeve smiled, then cut in. 'I'm here,' he said. 'The target is down, and I have the briefcase. Mission complete.'

'*What?*' Stone's bark almost overloaded his microphone. 'How the fuck did—'

'I'm going dark. See you at the rendezvous.' He removed his earpiece and throat mic and pocketed them as he continued.

It took several minutes to clear the industrial estate. Factories gave way to low-rise apartment buildings. Few people were out in the rain, but Reeve still avoided any close encounters. He made his way to a van parked on a side street. A check that nobody was watching, then he entered via the driver's door.

Faint condensation inside the windscreen revealed that he wasn't the first to arrive. He sidestepped between the front seats into the darkened rear.

Someone sat on the bench seat along one side. He looked up at Reeve.

It was the man he had shot in the car.

'You killed me, Alex,' said Tony Maxwell, sounding affronted. Then he grinned. 'Well done.'

CHAPTER 5

Once the rest of the team arrived, Maxwell took the van's wheel. Their first stop was the industrial estate so Reeve could recover his gear. They then drove back to the very place they had just escaped. 'We won't be popular,' Maxwell remarked as they entered. The base's exit barrier had been wrecked when Blake's car smashed through it.

'Sorry,' said Blake, with a total absence of contrition.

The exercise had taken place at the Royal Marines base in Hamworthy, Poole. The helicopter Stone had shot – with wax training rounds – waited on the field. Maxwell was referee as well as target. Judging the pilot to be dead, he had ordered him to power down. 'By the way,' he said, 'I've already had a complaint from the CO.'

'What about?' asked Flynn.

'A Marine needed medical treatment. Somebody cut his neck when they "killed" him.' His eyes met Locke's in the mirror.

'A minor wound,' Locke replied without concern. 'I was careful to avoid the arteries.'

'I'm sure he'll appreciate that,' scoffed Parker.

Maxwell was still regarding Locke. 'This was a training mission – and these people are on our side.'

Locke looked away. 'Then I apologise.' Like Blake, there was no hint of sincerity.

An uncomfortable silence followed. 'Still,' Maxwell added, 'at least he'll have a cool scar to show off.' The joke broke the brief tension.

He guided the van to the field. Everyone hurried to the helicopter. Flynn was already inside. Red bursts on her chest showed where the Marine's wax rounds had hit. She gave most of her comrades curt greetings, but Reeve received only an angry glare. He understood why, but felt no need to ask forgiveness.

The mission took priority. Always. That had been drummed into them from the start. Everything else, even their own lives, was secondary.

It was a price Reeve was willing to accept. To become a member of SC9, you *had* to. If Flynn couldn't . . . maybe she wouldn't make the grade.

Reeve put his head back against the seat. It wasn't his call, or his problem. Right now, he was tired. And they still had a long way to go to reach home.

Home was 450 miles away as the crow flew. Their journey was less direct. The chopper took them to the nearby Bournemouth airport. A cramped twin-prop plane then took almost two hours to reach Oban in Scotland. After that came another two hours in a minibus through the dark Highlands.

It was almost 3AM when they finally arrived. 'Okay,' said Maxwell, 'get some sleep. We'll debrief in the morning.'

'Looking forward to *that*,' said Stone sarcastically. 'The whole thing got fucked right into a hat.'

'I disagree,' Maxwell replied. 'You eliminated the target, got the laptop, and nobody was captured.' A pause, then: 'Good work, everyone.'

'Let's hope the boss agrees,' Blake said, as they exited the minibus. It was still raining, even at the other end of the country. Spring had been dismal for the whole of Britain.

Reeve found himself beside Flynn as they reached the house. 'Might not have been captured, but I still got killed,' she complained. She wasn't looking at him, but it was obvious who she was addressing.

'It was just an exercise,' Maxwell reminded her. 'See you all tomorrow. Well, today, I suppose.'

Reeve went to his room. Each team member had their own quarters. None was especially homely, but his was positively spartan. It didn't bother him. No point getting attached to anything. Not when you might have to abandon everything at a moment's notice. He was here to learn, to improve: to push himself. To do the job better than anyone. A faint smile. He had certainly managed *that* tonight.

He washed, cleaned his teeth, then went to bed. Sleep came almost instantly. To his relief, he was too exhausted even to dream.

Grey morning light greeted him when he woke. He checked his watch. After seven. His tired body had taken all the rest it needed. All the same, he was irritated at himself. He normally rose before six.

He dressed in running gear as usual, then went downstairs. Mordencroft Hall housed SC9's instructors – and recruits. Ten months prior there had been eleven of the latter.

Now there were six. Training for SC9 was demanding in the extreme. Fall below the strict standards required, and you were gone.

Reeve had thought his army special forces training was tough. In hindsight, it had been a comparative breeze. How much more he would have to endure, he wasn't sure. He had come this far, though. He couldn't imagine it getting harder.

The smell of food reached him at the bottom of the stairs. Stone, he knew at once. Beyond a certain point in training, the recruits could choose their own meals. The hulking straw-blond Londoner now subsisted on the traditional English fry-up for breakfast. Sausages, eggs, bacon, baked beans, hash browns, tomatoes, all swimming in lard. How he hadn't dropped dead from a coronary, Reeve couldn't imagine.

He entered the large kitchen. Stone was monopolising the hob, two frying pans sizzling and spitting. He barely acknowledged Reeve's arrival. Locke sat at the long wooden table. His breakfast was modest yet refined; French bread and butter, soft cheese, a poached egg. He cut the last with surgical precision. 'Good morning,' he said, fixing Reeve with his piercing gaze.

Blake was also there, about to wash his plate. Grilled kippers and duck eggs Benedict again, from the scraps. 'Ah, our hero arrives,' said the black-haired man. 'Having a lie-in to celebrate, were you?'

'When you need to sleep, you need to sleep,' said Reeve, not taking the bait. He collected two slices of white bread. Blake eyed them with faint contempt, then cleaned his crockery.

The toaster was fully occupied by four slices of Stone's

bread. Reeve puffed out a cheek in mild impatience. Footsteps outside. He could tell from their weight it was Parker. He had a similar lithe build to Reeve himself. 'Morning,' said the crop-haired Liverpudlian cheerfully. 'Hey, guys – I think it's going to be a big day.'

'How so?' asked Locke.

'Most of the staff left at the crack of sparrowfart. They took the minibus. I think,' he lowered his voice, excited and conspiratorial, 'training might be over.'

'About time,' Stone sniffed. 'Finally see some real action. No more fake interrogations and random polygraph tests and practice ambushes.'

'If it is over,' Parker went on, 'd'you think we all passed?'

Locke continued dissecting his egg. 'If anyone hadn't, I doubt they would still be at the Hall.'

'Maybe that's why Flynn's not here,' said Stone, as the toaster popped up. 'She's in a body bag in the back of the minibus.' He laughed at his own joke. Only Blake and Parker seemed amused.

Reeve started to prepare his own breakfast, hearing more footsteps. Too heavy to be Flynn. If Parker was right about the staff leaving, it was most likely Maxwell approaching.

It was. 'Morning, all,' said their instructor.

'Morning, sir,' Reeve replied. The others followed suit.

Reeve tried to judge his mentor's attitude. He was hard to read, a deadpan amiability acting as a mask. You always knew when you had angered or disappointed him, though. Neither was a mood any of the recruits enjoyed. Maxwell, like many former special forces soldiers, appeared almost disarmingly unassuming. That was merely another cover.

Even well past forty, he was a physical match for any of his younger trainees.

This morning he seemed upbeat. 'Something smells good,' he said. 'Hope there are some eggs left.'

'Made sure of it, sir,' Stone told him.

'Good, thanks.' Flynn entered. 'Ah, the gang's all here. Morning, Deirdre.'

'Sorry I'm late, sir,' she replied.

'I only just arrived myself. And besides, there isn't a timetable today.'

'Something going on, sir?' asked Parker, giving the others an *I-told-you-so* smile.

'I'll tell you in a minute. First things first. The debrief.' He gestured for everyone to sit. 'No, no,' he said, as Stone put his plate on the counter. 'You eat, I'll talk. So,' Maxwell began, 'in terms of mission objectives, it was a total success. You eliminated the target – me – and got the laptop. It still works, which I'm glad about.' Quiet laughter from the group.

'Now, specifics.' His eyes swept over them like radar. 'It wasn't exactly a stealthy exit, was it? I had another complaint from the Hamworthy CO, about the wrecked gate. Not that they know who we really are, of course. MI6 are taking the blame. But property damage *and* an injury? They really weren't happy about your knife, Harrison.'

Locke remained impassive under Maxwell's gaze. 'We had to make a high-speed escape,' said Blake. 'It was that or be caught.'

'Yeah, if *someone*,' Stone stared accusingly at Flynn, 'hadn't been spotted, we'd have been fine.'

Flynn reacted with pent-up anger. 'If I'd had some backup,

they wouldn't have got me.' She glared at Reeve. 'You sacrificed me so you could get the kill, you shite. You were supposed to wait for me. If you don't look out for anyone else, nobody'll look out for you.'

Reeve was about to explain that he couldn't have saved her, but Maxwell spoke first. 'Deirdre, I agree. You're all expensively trained assets to the country. When you're working together, you cover each other.'

The auburn-haired woman aimed a triumphant snort at Reeve. 'Yeah. See?'

'However,' Maxwell continued, and her face fell, 'the objective always comes first. *Always*. In this case, Alex acted correctly.' He straightened, addressing the whole group. 'There isn't room for "nobody gets left behind" sentimentality in SC9. If it's a choice between completing the mission or saving another Operative? *You complete the mission.* No exceptions. You all know what you signed up for.'

Flynn broke the silence that followed. 'Sorry, sir,' she said, eyes downcast. 'I made a mistake. It won't happen again.'

'Better not,' said Stone, through a mouthful of bacon. 'We could all have been nailed 'cause you fucked up—'

'That's enough.' Maxwell's tone was sharp enough to make Stone flinch. 'Deirdre, I know it won't. Moving on. Seven tangos down. Quite a high collateral count, but acceptable. Good driving by John to lose the pursuers. Too fast on civilian roads for an exercise, but no harm done. And Craig, nice trick in tracking down my laptop. I wasn't expecting that. Must remember to stay off the Wi-Fi in future.'

Parker smiled. His wide mouth always reminded Reeve of a pit bull's. 'Thanks, sir.'

'And the one casualty on our side was killed, so no inter-rogation risk. Nothing to lead back to SC9. Job done.'

The team shared modest celebrations. 'Now,' Maxwell went on, 'good news. That was your last exercise. Training's over.'

Silence at the sudden revelation, followed by relief. 'So – did we pass?' asked Blake.

'I'll talk to everyone individually. Craig, I'll start with you. Have breakfast first. My office, at nine. Everyone else, take some personal time until I call for you.'

The group finished their morning meals, then dispersed. Reeve returned to his quarters to clean his teeth, then checked the weather. Still raining. Undeterred, he donned a cagoule over his hoodie and headed back down for his run.

Maxwell emerged from the kitchen. 'Going out in this weather, Alex?'

'It's just rain, sir,' he replied. 'It dries off.'

'Brings the bloody bugs out, is what it does. I'll be glad to get back to London.'

'I bet. You'll finally be able to watch Fulham lose in person.'

'Cheeky little bastard.' At six feet, Reeve was actually two inches taller than Maxwell. They both grinned. 'Although, do you remember that exercise in London?'

It had been to track and eliminate a mock double agent. 'Yes?'

'Don't tell anyone, but I timed it so I could watch a match afterwards.'

'Did Fulham win?'

Maxwell held up his hands. 'Well, that's not the point, is

it? Anyway, have your run. I'll see you in a while.' He was about to walk off when his phone rang. 'The boss,' he said before answering. 'Morning, sir. How's the holiday?'

Reeve silently waved goodbye. Maxwell returned the gesture as he listened to his superior. 'Yes, the debrief's done,' he replied. 'Everything's wrapped up.' He listened – then surprise, followed by concern, crossed his face. 'I . . . no, I didn't. Are you sure, sir?' He realised Reeve was still there and turned away. 'I see.' He stalked off down the hall.

Reeve watched him go. Whatever the boss had said, it had rattled his mentor. Some more backlash over events in Poole? Bloody Locke. It was a running joke amongst the others that he was a genuine psychopath. What maniac used a real knife in a training exercise?

It wasn't his problem, though. He zipped up and headed out into the rain.

CHAPTER 6

Reeve ran through the countryside, alone.

Mordencroft Hall was a grim granite block amidst expansive heathland. During the Second World War, it had been commandeered for commando training. Officially, it was still Ministry of Defence property. Signs around the perimeter warned of arrest and prosecution for trespassers. But the remote, bleak landscape drew few visitors.

The isolation suited Reeve. He had raised his shield to others in his early teens, and never lowered it. Well, that wasn't quite true. There had been a few people with whom he felt almost comfortable. Tony Maxwell was one. The others at the training facility, though, were merely colleagues. Once assigned real missions, he probably wouldn't see much more of them.

He was fine with that. Mark Stone, the ex-cop, he actively disliked – as did most of the others, admittedly. John Blake, once a Royal Navy officer, was condescending and smug. Harrison Locke, another former officer – army medical, Reeve suspected – was also patronising, and insane. Reeve was probably closest to Craig Parker, but he could be annoyingly juvenile. And Deirdre Flynn had a chip on her shoulder visible from space.

None of that mattered now. All were professionals. He could work with them if he had to. But if he had to act on his own, it wouldn't be a problem.

He crested a rise at the edge of the grounds. Loch Ailort, a curving finger of water dotted with desolate islands, opened out before him. The occasional 'field trip' aside, he had spent ten months on Scotland's far west coast. Most would have considered it beautiful, but the open moors prompted only dark memories. Right now, the ongoing miserable spring left it grey, sapped of vibrancy. At least the midges hadn't started to hatch yet.

But his desire to run outweighed the irritations. Mordencroft's boundary fences measured six and a half miles. Ten and a half kilometres – almost perfect for a 10K run. Starting beyond the assault course, he could complete the hilly circuit in thirty-four minutes. That was his record, at least. He wasn't pushing today. His watch's timer neared that mark with a kilometre to go. His finishing point was half a kilometre short of the start. He could have simply finished the loop, but who ran 10,500 metres? The irregularity would have bugged him more than any midges.

He followed the fence, turning south-east. The house came back into view. It sat in a shallow natural bowl, hiding it from distant onlookers. Not that there would be any. The main road along the loch was over a mile away, and saw little traffic. Random ramblers would also be spotted long before getting close. Reeve passed a fencepost capped by an unobtrusive black box. It housed a video camera and motion sensor. Others ringed the whole training facility. Anyone approaching would be met by a 'groundskeeper' – an SC9 instructor. They would point out the warning signs . . . with a shotgun hooked over their arm. Nobody ever hung around.

Company ahead, though. Someone was standing at his finishing point.

He increased his pace, covering the last kilometre in just over three minutes. The loch dropped out of sight. He reached the finish. Maxwell, wearing a waterproof overcoat, awaited him. His expression was faintly perturbed, but a smile replaced it as Reeve arrived. 'Alex. Good run?'

'Fair,' Reeve replied. His heart was racing, but would recover by the time he returned to the house. 'What're you doing here?'

'I wanted to meet you. Would have phoned, but, well, trainees aren't allowed them.' A small laugh. 'Although that won't be an issue from now on.'

A flash of excitement. 'I'm in?'

'Let's talk in my office.' Maxwell gestured towards the house.

'After you,' said Reeve.

Maxwell hesitated, then set off. Reeve walked with him. He expected conversation, but his superior seemed pre-occupied. 'You okay, sir?'

'Yeah, yeah,' Maxwell replied, nodding. 'A lot going on this morning. You know,' he added, 'on days like this, I miss being in the field. You get your mission, and crack on with it. Nice and simple.'

'That phone call from the boss wasn't good news?'

'You could say that. But,' he sighed, 'let me worry about it.'

They continued towards the house. On the way they

passed the firing range. Targets were set up at intervals up to two hundred metres. The person practising was not using a rifle, however. 'Wanting some quiet today?' Maxwell asked, as he approached Flynn. She held a compound bow, an arrow nocked but not drawn. A baseball cap kept the rain off her short hair.

'Just keeping my eye in,' she replied, sighting a target fifty metres away. 'I started out with a bow when I was a kid on the farm. My da taught – my dad, I mean, taught me. I was good, killed a rabbit at over two hundred feet once.' In a swift, smooth movement, she drew and released the arrow. It hit the bullseye with a solid *thwack*. 'More range on a rifle. But there's something personal about this way.'

'Good shot,' said Reeve, meaning it.

She shrugged, not looking at him. 'When do you want to see me, sir?'

'Later,' said Maxwell. 'Alex is up next. I'll find you.' The two men carried on, hearing tyres screech. 'I guess John feels he needs to keep his eye in as well.'

An Audi A6 powered around the parking area ahead. It doubled as a training area for tactical driving. Blake was at the wheel. He slalomed through a line of cones, performing looping powerslides at each end.

'Hope he doesn't crash into the other cars,' said Maxwell. 'I don't want to have to walk to the station.'

'The other staff aren't coming back?' Reeve asked.

'Not the instructors. Training's finished. The caretaker's coming on Thursday. We're the only ones here. Got to lock up before we leave.'

'It's not like there's much to steal.'

A chuckle. 'Only a small arsenal and a few thousand rounds of ammo.'

'Oh, *that*,' said Reeve.

Shouts reached them as they neared the assault course north of the house. Reeve spotted Stone amongst the obstacles. He wore a dark blue tracksuit and boxing gloves, and was pounding a hanging punchbag. An obscenity spat from his mouth with each blow. To Reeve's relief, Maxwell didn't strike up conversation.

They reached the house's side entrance. Another resident greeted them. 'Hello, little cat,' said Reeve, stroking the mewing tabby as she stretched up to him. 'Hey, who'll feed her when we go?'

'She'll survive,' Maxwell replied. 'The place has enough mice. It's funny; that cat's probably the best friend you've made here.'

'Except for my instructor.' The admission surprised Reeve, and, it seemed, Maxwell too. 'Well, if you're *allowed* to be friends with your instructor. And boss. And superior officer.'

'None of those things after today,' said Maxwell as he opened the door.

'So . . . I *did* make it in?'

'Like I said, we'll talk in my office.' He went inside.

Reeve followed. The space within had once been a large function room. Now it was a gym, mostly used for combat practice. 'Oh, Harrison,' Maxwell said, seeing Locke. 'We're just passing through, don't mind us.'

'I don't,' Locke replied. He didn't look around. Instead, he regarded a life-sized male dummy standing before him. It had a silicone skin and, Reeve knew, realistic internal organs. It was intended for medical students – but also served well for armed fight training. Several mutilated examples were piled in a corner.

This one's skin was punctured in numerous places: chest, abdomen, neck. Locke's black combat knife was the cause. He stared at the dummy with surgical intensity – then struck, fast as a snake. The blade stabbed deep into its throat.

'Good hit,' Maxwell noted, as he and Reeve passed. 'Did you get Charlie's carotid artery?' The dummies were all nicknamed 'Charlie Crippen' for reasons lost in time.

'Of course,' Locke replied. He withdrew the knife and peeled back the skin. A red rubber tube represented the blood vessel. It had been split cleanly open. 'Without someone applying compression, Charlie would be unconscious in thirty seconds from blood loss. And dead in a minute. Either way, he wouldn't be fighting back.'

'Nice work.' Maxwell and Reeve continued through the gym.

Reeve waited until the blond man was out of earshot before speaking. 'I'm not the only one who thinks he's creepy, am I?'

'Christ, no,' Maxwell whispered back, amused. 'I wouldn't leave him alone with the cat, put it that way. He'll be good at the job, though.'

'So he's in?'

'He will be, after I tell him. But let's talk about you first.'

Reeve began to feel uncomfortable. Maxwell's evasiveness

was causing pangs of self-doubt. Had he failed to qualify? He couldn't see how, but the instructors never revealed what they wrote in their reports. Success wasn't just about circuit times or target accuracy. Attitude also counted. One of the drop-outs had once made cynical comments about the royal family. He was gone two days later. Another had left at the 'point of no return' – when SC9's true function was revealed. An ethical objection, or fear of the potential consequences? Reeve didn't know, but the result was the same: another empty room.

He forced down his concern. He had given it his all. Now, Maxwell would tell him if that was enough . . .

They walked down a hallway. A door was open to one side. Maxwell peered in. 'Starting already, Craig?'

Reeve saw Parker at a computer. Several windows were open on the large monitor. He vaguely recognised the woman's face in one; some young leftie politician? Ten months isolated in Scotland had left him out of touch. 'Background research, Tony,' Parker replied. 'I want to be fully prepared for my first assignment.'

'Keep it up.' An approving nod, then Maxwell moved on.

'He's got an assignment already?' Reeve asked. 'So he's in?'

'He is. You just met SC9's latest member: Operative 65. The boss had a job for him immediately.'

'Fast work.' If Parker had qualified, Reeve thought, *surely* he had as well . . .

They entered Maxwell's office. Reeve was surprised by what he saw. Most of Maxwell's personal items had gone, the desk empty. Even his laptop was absent. Shelves that had held box files were now clear. 'Can't leave anything classified while the place is deserted,' Maxwell explained. 'Most of the stuff went out this morning.' He removed his coat, revealing a casual jacket beneath, and sat behind the desk. Reeve took off his own cagoule, sitting facing him.

The older man gazed at him in silence. Reeve tried to cover his rising unease. 'So,' Maxwell finally said, 'you want to know if you're in.'

Reeve could think of nothing to say. He settled for a small nod.

'Well.' Maxwell looked down for a moment, then back up – with a smile. 'You are.'

A moment to process the news. 'I passed?'

'Welcome to SC9, Operative 66.'

A flood of emotions: exultation, relief, excitement. Reeve let out a long breath. 'You really had me going, sir.'

'Tony,' Maxwell replied. 'You can call me Tony now.'

'Thanks . . . Tony.' Using Maxwell's first name did not feel comfortable. 'So I'm back to being just a number?' For the first few months of training, he had been called only 'Recruit Nine'. His former identity had been left behind at Mordencroft's gate.

Maxwell grinned. 'You get to keep your name this time, don't worry.'

Reeve smiled back. 'Parker's Operative 65? So I'm one better, eh?'

'They're assigned by age within an intake, oldest first. You're the youngest, and he's a year older. Harrison's Operative 61.'

Some rapid mental arithmetic. 'All six of us passed?'

'They did. Bumper crop, actually – the most ever in one go. Usually, it's lucky if four make it through. My intake, only one other guy qualified.'

'You never did say what your number was.'

'Well, now you're a full member of SC9, that's no longer classified. I'm Operative 41.'

'Good to meet you, 41.'

'Likewise, 66.' They both grinned. 'I have to say, I knew you'd make it. You were an exemplary recruit. One of the best all-rounders I've ever trained.'

Reeve felt his cheeks flush at the praise. 'Thank you, sir – Tony,' he corrected. 'I'm looking forward to getting to work.'

Maxwell smiled again, then stood. 'So, a drink to celebrate?'

'I thought booze was banned as well as phones?'

'Only for trainees. And rank hath its privileges. Whisky?'

Reeve didn't feel he could refuse. 'Yeah.'

Maxwell went to a cabinet directly behind him and opened it. 'Like I said, I thought you were exemplary. Fast learner, quick thinker, highly capable . . .'

Something triggered Reeve's warning senses as Maxwell spoke. A faint rustle of clothing, a low creak of the floor as his weight shifted. His voice becoming slightly clearer as he turned back towards him.

The whisper of metal sliding over leather . . .

Maxwell was drawing a gun from a concealed holster. The sneaky old bastard! One last test, one more fake ambush to test his reactions. Reeve rolled from the chair as his mentor pulled the trigger—

The noise of the gunshot a foot from his head jarred his senses. Splinters burst from the desk.

It wasn't a blank. The gun was loaded.

Maxwell had tried to kill him.

CHAPTER 7

Reeve landed in a poised crouch. Shock and disbelief fought for supremacy. This couldn't be happening, something was wrong—

Surprise replaced grimness on Maxwell's face as he realised he had missed. Then his eyes met Reeve's. The gun swept across to follow his gaze.

Reeve threw himself beneath the desk – kicking his chair as he went. It hit Maxwell's legs. The older man staggered as he fired again. The second round punched through the desktop above Reeve's head.

He scrambled back. Maxwell was recovering—

Reeve sprang up – taking the desk with him.

It flipped over as he hurled it. Maxwell was knocked to the floor. The desk landed heavily on top of him.

Reeve hesitated as he looked down at his mentor. He desperately wanted to ask him a question: *why?* But his training overrode the impulse. Maxwell still had his gun. He remained a threat. Options flashed through his mind. Stamp on his head, crush his throat, break his neck. *Kill him*—

He couldn't do it. Instead he ran for the door.

He burst out into the hall – as Parker rushed from the nearby room. He was armed. The gun came up—

Reeve was now in full combat mode, adrenalin surging. He dived and rolled. Flame erupted from Parker's gun, the shot deafening in the narrow hallway. The bullet seared over Reeve's back. A miss, but the other Operative was already tracking him.

A fire extinguisher was mounted on the wall. Reeve grabbed it as he leapt up and swung it like a bat. It hit Parker's arm with a metallic *thunk*. He yelled, reeling. The gun flew from his hand.

He was disarmed, but still a threat. Reeve slammed the extinguisher's base against the other man's head. He went down.

The gun was right outside Maxwell's office. A loud crash from inside as the desk hit the floor. Maxwell was getting up. If Reeve ran to his door, he would be shot.

He sprinted the other way.

The nearest exit was through the gym. Locke was still inside – but he wouldn't know what had happened. He might be able to bluff him.

Reeve rushed in. Locke stood over the fallen dummy. His combat knife was in his hand. 'I heard shots,' he said, concerned. 'What's going on?'

'Parker's gone fucking crazy!' Reeve replied, hurrying for the exterior door. Locke moved to meet him. 'He tried to kill Maxwell.'

Locke reached the door first, gripping the handle – then his cold gaze fixed upon Reeve.

His expression changed. Just the tiniest flicker around his eyes . . . but Reeve knew what it meant. He had seen Reeve's fear and desperation, the look of the hunted – and betrayed. Locke knew he was not fleeing only from Parker.

The knife lanced at Reeve's chest. He jumped back. Locke advanced, the blade held ready. Reeve retreated, eyes not leaving the matt-black weapon. Another strike. He jinked sideways. Locke curved after him, trying to back his opponent into a corner.

Reeve glanced back, moving to avoid the trap – but Locke made a sudden lunge. The knife caught Reeve's right forearm. He gasped. The cut was not deep, but still stung.

Locke took advantage of his momentary distraction and attacked again. This time, Reeve had nowhere to go except backwards. He jumped clear of the thrusting blade—

His foot caught something.

The splayed arm of a lacerated dummy. He stumbled. Only for an instant, quickly recovering – but that was all Locke needed. He charged. The razor-sharp knife rushed at Reeve's abdomen.

Reeve whipped both hands down to catch Locke's wrist. Locke raised his arm in response, trying to drive the knife into his chest. His other hand balled into a fist. He sent a jab at Reeve's unprotected stomach. The younger man grunted, flinching—

Locke brought his trapped arm higher – and jumped at him. Unbalanced, Reeve staggered backwards. Locke's weight forced him over. He landed on the dead mannequins. Locke pounded down on top of him.

Reeve still held his wrist, but the impact sent the knife at his face. He jerked his head sideways. It nicked the side of his jaw. He tried to force Locke off – only to take a punch to the temple.

The blow left him dizzied. The knife jerked back, Locke tearing loose from one of his hands. Reeve clawed at his wrist again, but the older man's free arm deflected him. Locke brought his blade over Reeve's neck. His X-ray gaze locked on, looking through flesh and cartilage for his target—

His pathological need for lethal precision saved Reeve's life. The tiny delay let him send a punch at Locke's jaw. Not as hard as he'd wanted – but enough to jar his opponent. Locke lurched sideways.

The shift of weight freed one of Reeve's legs. He levered himself over. Locke rolled off him – and Reeve kneed him in the groin. The ice-blond man folded.

Reeve pulled out from under him, delivering another punch. This struck with full force. Blood spurted from Locke's nose and lip. Reeve tore the knife from his hand – and stabbed down at his throat.

Even through his pain, Locke saw it coming. He flung his upper body backwards. The carbon-fibre blade missed his neck, punching through skin behind his left clavicle. He screamed as it sank into his trapezius muscle.

Reeve kicked him away and scrambled to his feet. The fight had taken only seconds, but Maxwell or Parker might already be coming. He ran for the exit.

He burst out into the open, the cat rushing away in fright. He had left the house – but still had to escape the grounds.

And there were three trained killers ahead of him.

CHAPTER 8

Reeve ran into the rain. Stone, Blake and Flynn didn't know what had happened. They might not even have heard the shots. If he took a car, he could be at the gate before they responded . . .

That hope vanished as a voice echoed around the bowl. Maxwell, shouting through Mordencroft Hall's infrequently-used Tannoy system. 'Attention! Attention! Alex Reeve is Fox Red! I repeat, Alex Reeve has been declared Fox Red!'

Reeve felt a new chill. 'Fox Red' was SC9 code for an internal threat – a traitor. It was not issued lightly. There was no appeal, no reprieve, only one punishment: death.

The sentence to be carried out immediately.

He looked back. Nobody pursuing, but Maxwell or Parker might emerge at any moment. He swerved into the assault course, using a climbing wall to block line of sight.

Maxwell repeated his warning. Between the obstacles Reeve glimpsed Stone, stopping his punchbag fight to listen. Bewilderment gave way to shock – then anger. The big man tore off his boxing gloves and moved to intercept.

Reeve angled away. He glanced back at the house—

Parker rushed from the gym door.

On his current course, Reeve's back would be exposed to

gunfire. And Parker was a very good shot. He swung back into the assault course. Where was Stone? Behind another wall ahead. Which way past it to dodge him?

Stone had been coming from his left. The ex-cop should emerge from the wall's right side, missing him. Reeve went left—

Huge hands grabbed him.

Stone swung Reeve around, using his own momentum to fling him against the bricks. 'Thought you were being fucking clever, didn't you?' Stone snarled. He clenched his taped fists and advanced.

Reeve knew from past sparring matches that Stone was powerful, and brutal. But he was also *slow*. Not enormously so, but enough to give the smaller man an edge.

If he could avoid being hit.

Stone clearly relished the chance for a bare-knuckle fight. He sent a jab at Reeve's head. Reeve dodged, sweeping his left arm to divert the blow. His wrist struck Stone's bough-like forearm. Even deflected, the strike barely missed.

Before Stone could wind up for another attack, Reeve snapped out one of his own. His right palm rushed at Stone's face. A broken nose would cause severe pain, perhaps even blind him with blood—

Cartilage crunched – but not hard enough. Stone jerked his head back just in time to minimise the impact. 'Fuck!' he barked. 'You little cunt!'

He swept his left fist at Reeve's stomach. Reeve tried to pull clear. Not far enough. Knuckles as hard as his attacker's name pounded his abdomen. He thumped breathlessly against the wall.

Stone's clenched right fist rushed at his face again. This time it struck, knocking his head against the bricks. Pain exploded in Reeve's skull. He tasted blood.

Stone grinned malevolently. His left hand clamped around Reeve's throat. He shoved him hard against the wall, choking him. The big man's right arm drew back, winding up to pulp his opponent's face—

He had left an opening – and Reeve took it. He jabbed his rigid fingers into Stone's larynx. Now it was the Londoner's turn to choke. He stumbled backwards, clutching his throat.

Gasping, Reeve broke loose. He drove his elbow into Stone's sternum as he ran past. Stone grunted in pain, staggering.

Reeve didn't look back. He knew he was the faster runner. He pounded around a scramble net. A glance behind. Parker was in pursuit, Maxwell emerging from the house after him.

Both had guns. But Parker's was raised.

Reeve ducked as a bullet cracked past. Another would surely follow—

Shouts reached him instead. Maxwell, ordering Parker to stop shooting – and a yell of '*Jesus fucking Christ!*' from Stone. He had started to pursue Reeve, unwittingly crossing Parker's line of fire. He dived back into cover.

Reeve ran for the driving track. Blake's Audi slowed as its driver realised something was going on. Reeve headed straight for it, hoping Parker and Maxwell wouldn't risk more friendly fire.

The car stopped. Reeve rushed up as Blake lowered his window. 'What's happening?' he demanded.

'Parker's gone Fox Red!' Reeve panted. Shock on Blake's

face – then Reeve smashed an elbow into it. The older man's head snapped back. Reeve yanked open the door and hit the seatbelt release. Blake started to recover, but was dragged from the car before he could respond.

Reeve took his seat. Blake was taller, his driving position awkward, but there was no time to adjust it. Instead he threw the A6 into gear and stamped on the accelerator. The car leapt forward. He swung around to put metal between himself and his pursuers' guns. The car barrelled over a verge, fishtailing on the wet earth and grass. He caught it, power-sliding on to the house's long drive.

About a mile to the gate. It was closed, and solid enough to wreck the car if he rammed it. The speedometer passed sixty. He had under a minute to think of a way around.

Movement in his peripheral vision, a figure higher on the slope—

The side window behind him exploded. Something slammed into his headrest.

Flynn's arrow transfixed the restraint, centimetres from his head. If it hadn't been deflected by the glass, he would have died like her rabbit. He gasped a curse, then powered on.

A look in the mirror. Blake was sprinting for another car. Parker, Stone and Maxwell followed.

His former colleagues were coming after him.

Blake jumped into a blue BMW 5-Series. He started it, but waited for Parker to arrive. 'What the hell's going on?'

'Reeve's Fox Red,' Parker replied as he took the passenger seat. 'Get after him.'

Blake was about to set off when Maxwell waved for him to stop. He reluctantly held his foot off the accelerator. Stone arrived, the instructor not far behind. 'Wait, wait,' Maxwell called. 'Craig, get out.'

'What?' demanded Parker. 'He's getting away!'

'Harrison needs first aid. Go back to the house and help him. And get to the security station. If Alex gets around the main gate, you open it to let us through.' When Parker didn't immediately respond, he barked: 'That's an order. Move!'

Parker reluctantly exited. Stone was about to take the back seat when Maxwell stopped him. 'No, get to the armoury. Arm up and follow us in one of the other cars. You too,' he added, as Flynn ran up.

'We're using live weapons right on our doorstep?' she asked, surprised. Stone appeared thrilled at the prospect.

'Alex has been declared Fox Red,' Maxwell replied. 'That means we use whatever force is necessary to eliminate him. But avoid collateral casualties. The boss can cover things up with the local police, but only so far.' He took Parker's place in the passenger seat. 'Okay, John, go.'

Blake powered away. Stone, Parker and Flynn all ran in the other direction. 'What's this?' Stone said, indicating her bow. 'Fucking Robin Hood?'

'I almost got him,' she snapped. 'And what the hell's going on? Why is Reeve Fox Red?'

'Fucked if I know.'

'He went in for a meeting with Maxwell,' explained Parker. 'Next thing I knew, there were gunshots.'

'I guess he didn't pass, then,' Flynn said, deadpan.

'I tried to stop him, but the bastard clouted me with a

fire extinguisher. He stabbed Locke with his own knife as well.'

A grunted half-laugh from Stone. 'I told that dickhead it's safer to just shoot people.' They hurried on towards the house.

Wind blasted in through the broken window as Reeve charged along the drive. He had managed to fasten his seatbelt during his pell-mell flight. The heavy security gate came into view. He reluctantly eased off. How to get past the barrier? He could crash through the fence, but the road was flanked by drainage ditches. They might damage his car's suspension, or even rip off a wheel.

He would have to risk it. He accelerated again – and swung off the road.

A fierce jolt as the front wheels hit the ditch. The impact slammed the suspension to its limit – but he was over. Another hideous thump jarred his spine as the car's rear bounded over the obstacle. Dirt showered on to the windscreen, a stone cracking it. He wrestled with the wheel, then jammed his foot down.

The powerful car surged forward – and hit the barbed-wire fence.

Reeve was pitched forward again, the seatbelt yanking hard across his chest. The wooden post to one side ripped from the ground – but the other stayed put. The Audi slewed around. He spun the wheel to counter it. Wires lashed over the bonnet, barbs shrilling as they gouged the metal. Then they finally snapped.

More bone-shaking blows as the car lurched back on

to asphalt. Reeve straightened out, then accelerated. An unpleasant vibration rattled his palms through the steering wheel. A wheel had been knocked out of alignment.

Maintaining control at high speed would be work, but he could handle it. The main thing was that he was out of the grounds. The loch swung into sight below. A road ran along its bank. He would reach it in a few minutes. Turn right, and he would soon be on the A830. The main road linked Mallaig to the north and Fort William to the east – his escape route.

If he could reach it. The others were surely coming after him by now.

And they would be out for blood.

CHAPTER 9

Parker, Flynn and Stone split up as they reached the house. The latter two headed for the main door, the quickest route to the armoury. Parker went back into the gym.

Locke had managed to stand. His right hand was pressed to his shoulder wound, blood soaking his clothing. 'Did you get Reeve?'

'Not yet,' Parker replied, hurrying past. 'Maxwell told me to help you, but you seem to be managing?'

Locke's eyes narrowed. 'I can't close the wound with only one hand.'

'I'll help you – soon as I'm done at the security station. They're trying to catch him at the gate.' He ran on down the hallway. Locke scowled, then followed, lips tight.

The security station was a small room beyond Maxwell's office. CCTV monitors covered the house and grounds. 'Shit,' Parker said, as he checked them.

Locke entered behind him. 'What is it?'

'He got out.' There was no sign of Reeve's car. He pushed a button. On one screen, the main gate began to swing open.

On another, Stone and Flynn collected weapons from the armoury. Stone grabbed an HK416 assault rifle and several magazines. Flynn, on the other hand, chose another AX308 sniper rifle. Her weapon the previous night was chambered for wax simulation rounds. This used live ammunition. Armed, they hurried back out to rejoin the hunt.

'Damn it, he's through,' said Blake, as the BMW approached the opening gate. The wrecked fence beside it marked Reeve's exit.

Maxwell regarded the tracks crossing the ditch. 'That'll have given his suspension a hell of a whack. If we're lucky, he'll be damaged.'

'The luck seems to be entirely on his side, so far.' Blake swept the car through the gate.

Maxwell checked his remaining ammunition. 'Nobody stays lucky for ever.'

Reeve reached the bottom of the hill, braking hard for the junction. The turn was tight, and the road narrow and wet. If he skidded, he could end up in the loch.

But the Audi's tyres maintained their grip. He straightened out and accelerated. The off-kilter wheel's vibration returned. Worse than before. All he could do was hope it held out.

A glance back up the hill. Another car, a BMW, was rapidly descending the winding road. Blake, Reeve was forced to admit, was the better driver. With his own vehicle damaged, his pursuers would eventually catch up.

He had to open up as much ground as possible. Foot down harder, the needle passing seventy. Over the speed limit, way too fast for the road and conditions. But he had to keep going.

A car ahead. Reeve checked the road was clear, then blasted past. He was now doing eighty. Trees and rocks flashed by. He had no room for error – one slip, and he would spin off into them.

How far to the main road? About two miles. The route was familiar from his occasional trips out of Mordencroft Hall. He still had to pass the salmon farm and the tiny hamlet of Lochailort. Several big bends ahead – and he was already dancing on the limit of control.

An island chain came into sight on the loch. A curve would soon follow. He reluctantly eased his right foot, feeling the tyres straining for grip. The car rocked, but held its line through the long bend. A quick look at the rear-view mirror.

Running lights were briefly visible in the distance. It wasn't the car he had overtaken. Blake was already gaining.

A blast of speed on a short straight, then he entered another, longer curve. There was the salmon farm, hatcheries like long barges floating in the loch. He whipped past. Less than a mile to the junction.

He overtook a van, then pulled back in for the final stretch. Lochailort was off to his right. Around the last bend, dipping the brakes to shed speed—

An articulated lorry filled the lane in front of him.

Reeve rammed his foot down hard. The car juddered as the anti-lock system kicked in. Even so, the back end slid out on the wet road. He counter-steered, reapplying power. A lurch as the tyres found grip. Engine howling, he slithered around the bend in a barely-controlled drift. The truck had started to turn right; he cut inside it. He was on the wrong side of the road, wheels going over the white lines.

The Audi's tail slid out again—

Its rear corner struck the crash barrier with a crunch of metal and plastic. Another whirl of the steering wheel. The A6 reeled drunkenly before coming back into line.

Reeve's heart raced, kicked by an adrenalin shot. The truck driver belatedly blasted his horn. The mirrors revealed glass and debris in the road. Nothing too big. The car was still in one piece.

His speed had fallen below thirty. He dropped through the gears and accelerated. The truck rapidly fell away behind.

Past a pub, then through hilly woodland. The A830 was wider than the road he had just left, but not by much. Still only one lane in each direction – and it would be more busy. Even in this miserable weather, it was a major tourist route. The nearby railway line was world-famous as the route to Hogwarts in *Harry Potter*.

Several cars ahead, doing about fifty behind a dawdling camper van. The speed limit here was sixty. Double white lines down the road's centre meant no overtaking. He ignored them. Full power, and he pulled out to pass the unwilling convoy.

A risky manoeuvre. He only just made it back in before reaching a blind crest. A moment later, a car whipped past the other way. He had barely avoided a head-on collision.

Breathing heavily, he powered on. The railway line came into view to his left, parallel with the road. The shuddering worsened. He gripped the wheel more tightly, trying to feel the knife-edge of controllability. Every time he crested a rise, the steering went light, slack. If he lost grip going into a corner, he would plough into the trees. Every instinct warned him to slow. But if he did, Blake would soon be upon him.

More cars ahead. The woods blocked his view of an approaching curve. Dare he risk a blind overtake?

The traffic was moving slowly. He would have to.

Reeve came up behind the last car. He still couldn't see through the trees. A dangerous gamble, but he had to take it.

Into the bend – and he pulled out and accelerated.

Past the first car, second, third. Nothing coming at him. Over a small bridge, the railway flashing past below. A hump ahead, the turn tightening. Ease off, ride the knife—

He topped the rise – and saw an oncoming truck.

A split-second of terror. Then his training kicked in, learned instinct overpowering primal. Brake, *brake*! The speedometer plummeted, sixty, fifty. Still cars to his left—

He swung into a gap. It wasn't big enough. He knew – but had no choice.

His Audi hit a small Vauxhall Viva hatchback, barging it off the road. It scythed down marker poles along the verge as the truck whipped past. He pulled out again—

More cars formed a train behind it. Reeve veered back into the gap. The Viva jolted to a stop in a ditch. Low-speed crash; the driver should be okay.

The other lane was clear. Down into second, and he peeled out. Full power, and he cleared the line of traffic in seconds. A log truck at its head was causing the hold-up. Past it, back in, and he was free again.

He rounded another tight bend, raw granite walls to both sides. Then the landscape opened out, grey water stretching away to his right. Loch Eilt. The road followed its northern shoreline for about three miles. The railway was on the opposite side; he glimpsed a train travelling eastwards along it.

No traffic ahead. The truck had caused a vehicular logjam. Back up past seventy, sweeping through the curves—

Lights in the mirror.

He knew at once it was his pursuers. The other car was moving even faster. He had ridden with Blake before. The black-haired man had the reflexes of a Formula 1 driver.

Reeve pushed as hard as he dared. Any more, and he would lose control through the bends.

It wasn't enough. Blake was gaining.

He glimpsed a second shadow in the BMW. Maxwell or Parker, he couldn't tell. Either way, they would be armed.

Hitting a target from a moving car was extremely hard, whatever the movies claimed. Blake would instead use his own vehicle as the weapon. He would try to knock the A6 into a spin. *Then* his passenger would open fire.

There were counters to Blake's attack. Blake knew them all, of course, but if Reeve picked the right moment—

He had glanced into the mirror to locate his opponents. Just for an instant – but when he looked back ahead a tractor filled his vision—

Too late to brake. Reeve jerked the wheel to swerve around it. The Audi rolled on its suspension – and the rear tyres lost their grip.

The back end broke loose. A shrill screech from the road as he slid sidelong—

If he braked, he would spin for sure. And his pursuers could put bullets straight through the windscreen into his head. Instead he accelerated, turning the wheel even harder to the right. The car wavered – then snapped back around. He caught the spin, straightening out—

Another bend ahead. He was coming in too fast. *Brake!*

The car weaved frenziedly as it shed speed. He tried to sweep it through the corner – but the front wheel went off the road.

Gravel spat up, the suspension juddering. A black-and-white warning pole disappeared under the Audi's nose with a bang. Reeve grimaced, foot still crushing the brake pedal. Trees loomed as he slid into the undergrowth—

He slowed enough to regain control. Wheel hard over, he swung back on to the road—

Blake's car rushed around the bend.

The other Operative hadn't expected him to be so close. The BMW's nose dipped sharply as Blake hit the brakes. Reeve kept his foot down. The gap opened up.

For a moment. Then the 5-Series surged forward again – coming right at him.

Blake had avoided an uncontrolled collision, but now a *controlled* one was his objective. He swept over to the road's right side. Reeve did the same, moving to block him. Blake was trying to perform a Pursuit Intervention Technique: the PIT. Swipe the target's rear corner with his own car's nose to cause a spin. As soon as Reeve slowed, Blake's passenger – Maxwell – would shoot him. His former mentor already had the window open, gun ready.

Reeve hunched lower. Just because the shot was hard didn't mean Maxwell wouldn't take it. He stayed on the right to restrict his firing angle.

Blake veered back to the left, determined. Reeve only just did the same before he could swing into a PIT. The two cars' bumpers scraped, a piece of the Audi's damaged rear shearing off.

Another bump, harder, deliberate. Blake had changed tactics, trying to ram him off the road. Now Reeve was on the defensive again. Full throttle, but the other car was faster. He looked ahead. Another bend followed the lochside to the right, lined by trees.

A flicker of red between them.

The BMW hit him again. He gripped the wheel harder and swung back to the right. Would Blake follow, or try for another PIT?

Blue filled the mirror. Blake was back behind him. Ramming as they entered the bend would knock Reeve into the ditch on its left. The curve rushed at him. Turn—

Reeve did so – darting *left*, not right. He swerved back into the proper lane as a red Ford Mondeo came around the bend.

He had glimpsed the oncoming vehicle through the trees. Blake, focused on the pursuit, hadn't seen it.

He did now, though.

The 5-Series suddenly fell away as Blake slammed on the anchors. The Mondeo whipped past Reeve's Audi, missing by inches.

Blake wasn't so lucky. The other vehicle hit the BMW's rear quarter. Both spun in a spray of shattered glass and plastic. Blake's car went backwards into the ditch. The other whirled to a stop in the middle of the road.

Reeve let out a relieved breath and checked the mirror.

The BMW was off the highway, nose angled upwards. Recoverable, but it would take a few minutes. That was the gap he needed to get away—

New lights flared behind. A silver Mercedes C-Class swept around the red car and powered after him.

Stone and Flynn had caught up.

CHAPTER 10

Reeve raced along the bank of Loch Eilt. His eyes flicked between the road and the mirror. There would be no PIT attempts from his new pursuers. Stone was in the passenger seat – with an assault rifle.

The big man leaned from the window. Reeve swept to the right to limit his angle of fire. Stone merely scrunched his wind-blasted face and edged out higher.

The HK's barrel swung towards the Audi—

Reeve dropped low as the rifle barked. A full-auto burst, six or seven shots. The rear windscreen burst apart, a round thunking against the door pillar beside him. He jerked the wheel, snaking from side to side. Stone fired again. Metal puckered and clanked as more bullets hit the bodywork. A fist-sized hole blew open in the front windscreen.

Oncoming traffic. Reeve waited until the last second to dodge it, hoping Flynn had been unsighted by his car. But she followed – although Stone was caught by surprise, reeling from the window. He yelled an obscenity, then brought his gun back up.

Reeve hunched down again, but Stone was now aiming at the car, not its driver. The clamour of a metal hailstorm filled the cabin as rounds pounded its back end. Then the noise stopped – but Stone was already withdrawing to reload.

A corner ahead. Reeve had no choice but to slow. He was driving heel-and-toe like a racer, right foot on both accelerator and brake. He subtly shifted pressure to the latter as he swept into the turn. The road ahead was clear for the next few seconds. He risked a look at the mirror.

Stone was back in position. Fire blazed from the rifle's muzzle, more bullets slamming into the Audi—

It lurched. The wheel jerked in Reeve's hands. He gripped it tightly to hold course. Had Stone shot out a tyre?

No. If he had, the car would be in the trees. But something was definitely wrong. The A6 suddenly felt *heavy*, as if dragging an overloaded trailer . . .

A hissing noise gave him an answer. One of the rear brakes was jammed, pads rubbing against the disc. He released then reapplied the brake pedal, trying to free it. No luck.

He increased power out of the curve. The hiss grew louder. An acrid smell reached him: the brake pads starting to burn.

And now the vibration grew stronger. His car was dying.

He would soon join it if he didn't escape.

Stone had retreated inside his car as it rounded the bend. Back on the straight, he re-emerged, taking aim. Reeve looked ahead. A small hump was coming up. Foot down, and he sped towards it. He readied himself for the steering to go light.

Over the top, a momentary roller coaster sensation in his stomach, then back down—

He slammed on the brakes.

Flynn briefly lost sight of him beyond the rise. When she saw him again his rear lights were blazing. She braked hard as well—

Too late.

Her Mercedes ploughed into the Audi's rear.

Reeve was braced for the impact. A sharp bang as the airbag inflated. His face struck it, but the blow was not severe.

Stone and Flynn were not so fortunate.

Flynn slammed into her own erupting airbag with the force of a punch. Stone, meanwhile, was desperately dropping back inside when the cars collided. With no seatbelt, he was thrown against the windscreen pillar. His gun spun down the road.

Reeve's wrists and forearms burned from venting gas as the bag deflated. He clenched his jaw to overcome the pain and accelerated again. Debris scattered across the tarmac as the two vehicles ripped apart. The Merc's nose had been smashed by the collision. Bonnet buckled, radiator ruptured, it slewed off the road.

His own vehicle was only marginally better off. The boot was crushed, and he could smell petrol. It wouldn't get him to Fort William. It wouldn't get him much further than the end of Loch Eilt. He looked ahead. The lake narrowed; the road went into a pass at its end. About two miles beyond was a railway station—

The train.

He looked back. The four-coach diesel multiple unit was visible across the loch, some way behind.

A plan formed. It was risky, dangerous – but he had no

alternative. His bullet-riddled car would never reach the station.

He checked the mirror as the road started to climb. The mangled Mercedes was stationary on the verge. Stone was still alive, levering himself back into the cabin. Another car raced along the road in the distance.

Maxwell and Blake were back in pursuit.

He was some way ahead, but that wouldn't last. His car was already straining up the slope. The burning smell grew stronger. Flames and leaking petrol – a great combination. How much longer did he have?

Not much. He gripped the juddering wheel as he guided the Audi into the pass.

'Shit, look,' Maxwell said to Blake. 'That's Deirdre and Mark.'

The silver C-Class had overtaken them while they were extricating their car from the ditch. Now, its crumpled front end told Maxwell it was out of the chase.

No other cars nearby; the only thing it could have hit was Reeve. 'Pull over,' he ordered.

'Reeve's getting away,' Blake reminded him. The subtext was clear, Maxwell's own words returning: *the mission comes first*.

'If their car got that smashed up, his won't be much better off. Stop.'

Blake reluctantly halted behind the wrecked Mercedes. Maxwell hurried to it. Stone and Flynn were inside. 'Are you okay?'

'No, I'm fucking not,' Stone growled, clutching his chest.

'I was hanging out of the car when Flynn crashed into him.'

'Oh, get to fuck,' Flynn snapped as she clambered out. One hand covered a bloody nose. 'Sir, he deliberately braked so we'd hit him. His back end's wrecked. I don't think he'll get far.'

Maxwell looked down the road. No sign of Reeve's A6. 'We'll catch him. Grab your weapons and get in the back.'

Flynn retrieved her sniper rifle. Stone unsteadily got out, face twisted in pain. 'I'm going to fucking kill that bastard.'

'How? You won't be shooting him,' was his companion's caustic comment. Stone swore as he realised his rifle was gone.

Maxwell surveyed the roadside. The stock of Stone's weapon jutted from a patch of heather. 'Over there.'

He returned to the car, Flynn getting into the rear seat. Stone jogged clumsily to retrieve his weapon, returning with an even more pained expression. 'Think I've broken a fucking rib,' he muttered, as he squeezed into the back.

'John, go,' Maxwell ordered. 'Cracked, at most,' he told Stone as Blake pulled out. 'You wouldn't be moving like that if it was broken.' Had it been anyone but Maxwell, Stone would have had an insulting retort. Instead he merely scowled.

'We're leaving a hell of a trail, sir,' said Flynn. 'And like I said, it's all on our doorstep. At least two civilian cars wrecked, and there could be casualties.'

'And like *I* said, the boss will handle it,' Maxwell replied. The confidence in his voice far exceeded that in his head. 'Let's deal with Alex first – *then* worry about the clean-up.'

Blake was by now back at full speed. The BMW hurtled towards the end of the loch.

CHAPTER 11

Reeve emerged from the pass, cloud-shrouded hills opening out around him. The railway line swept in from the right to run close to the road.

His car was almost finished, trailing smoke. He rounded a bend, seeing the road straighten ahead. That would do.

That would *have* to do.

He had rifled through the glove box while traversing the pass. The most solid thing inside was a plastic first-aid box. Not ideal, but it was all he had. He unfastened his seatbelt, then took his foot off the accelerator. The Audi immediately slowed.

A car was coming the other way. He waited for it to pass – he didn't want witnesses. Once it was gone, he angled to the opposite side of the road. The verge rolled past below his window.

Reeve pulled the door handle to unlatch it. It swung open a few inches. Holding it with his elbow, he bent forward and wedged the box against the accelerator.

The engine note rose to a howl. The car picked up speed – but Reeve was already gone.

He threw himself at the verge, tucking himself into a tight ball—

He landed on the centre of his back, exactly as he had been taught. The impact hurt, but was spread out enough to protect him from damage. Eyes closed, arms crossed over his chest, he rolled through the wet grass. One elbow hit a stone, pain shooting down his arm. He cried out, but could do nothing but tumble helplessly on. Over and over, dizzied . . .

And stopping.

He opened his eyes. His head was a hand's width from the base of a metal signpost. Jesus! He had narrowly avoided injury – or death. He moved, testing for pain. His elbow flared, but there was nothing more severe than bruising.

He sat up. His car was still heading uphill, drifting right-wards. It was going to crash too close to him . . .

Reeve willed it back towards the road's centre. He was surprised to get his wish. The A6 slipped on to the verge, clipping marker poles – and veered back into line. It would travel maybe another couple of hundred metres to the next curve.

That was all he needed.

He crawled down an embankment. The sound of another car rose above the over-revving frenzy of his own. He slithered behind a line of trees and waited.

Blake's blue BMW tore past. Its occupants would be watching his vehicle. He rose, then scurried towards the railway line.

He crouched amongst bushes beside the track. A look back. His car was some three hundred metres away, and still going. Not for much longer, though. It had angled towards the road's left side, about to go off—

It bumped over earth and grass – then hit a rock. The

Audi flipped over, bowling back across the road in a shower of glass. It skidded down the embankment on its roof to slam into a ditch. A flicker of orange light inside a rear wheel arch abruptly flared into a blaze.

Blake's car stopped on the road above. He had picked up passengers, Flynn getting out along with Maxwell. Stone followed too, hand to his chest. The foursome hurried towards the wreck.

Not to save the driver. To check if he was dead. And if he wasn't . . . to make him so.

Reeve felt brief satisfaction. With the car on fire, they would take longer to realise he wasn't in it. By then, he would be clear.

If he could catch the train.

He turned – to see it emerge from the pass. Two hundred metres away, doing forty miles per hour. The steel track began to sing as it approached. Reeve readied himself. Maxwell and the others were still heading for the crashed car. He looked back at the train. Fifty metres. He could *feel* it, a rumble coming through the ground. The first carriage was on him, huge and frighteningly close. The juggernaut swept by, painfully loud. Second carriage, third—

Reeve burst into motion.

He sprinted at the train as the final carriage thundered past. A metal step extended below the last passenger door. He leapt – and grabbed it.

The jolt of acceleration strained his shoulder muscles. Feet dangling above the stony ballast, he was swept along by the train.

A handrail was set into the bodywork above. He found

the wet metal with his left hand and pulled himself higher. He was directly over the carriage's rear bogie, the wheels squealing and shrilling.

The train passed his crashed car, a hundred and fifty metres away. His former colleagues reached the inverted wreck. Maxwell crouched to peer into the cabin, the others clustered around him. Reeve made himself as small as possible. He was in plain sight; if someone glanced at the train . . .

But they were focused on their target. The train rolled on, carrying him clear. He looked along the line. Trees in the distance ahead. Once he reached them, he would be out of sight.

The station – Glenfinnan, he remembered – was only minutes away, even at this ambling pace. It was a tourist spot, another *Harry Potter* location. He could jump off there and find another car.

Buoyed, he glanced back again. Everyone was still checking the burning vehicle. His satisfaction returned. He had got away. His pursuers were the best of the best – and he had beaten them.

'He's not in there,' Maxwell announced. The Audi was now fully ablaze. All he saw through the fire were burning seats.

'Then where the fuck is he?' said Stone.

Blake looked back at the road. 'He must have bailed out.'

Everyone followed his gaze. 'It couldn't have been too far away,' said Maxwell. 'After he came out of that bend . . .'

No sign of Reeve on either side of the road. But there were

plenty of trees and bushes to provide cover. He was about to order the others to start searching—

'There!' Flynn cried. She was looking in the other direction. Maxwell spun, seeing the retreating train – and a figure clinging to it.

'He's on the fucking train!' Stone said in disbelief.

'Back to the car,' Maxwell barked, breaking into a run. 'We can beat him to the next station.'

'What if he jumps off before then?' asked Blake. 'We can't search the entire countryside. And we've drawn too much attention already.'

'Doesn't matter,' Stone growled. 'He's gone Fox Red – we've got to nail him. The road goes right alongside the track. If we catch up with the train, we—'

'I can get him,' Flynn cut in. Absolute certainty in her voice.

'At this fucking range?' said Stone.

Maxwell was less doubtful. 'You sure?'

She nodded. 'Yes.'

'Then do it.'

They reached the BMW. Flynn ducked into the back seat, reappearing with her AX308 rifle. She dropped to one knee for stability and raised it.

'He'll be out of sight any second,' Blake cautioned. The train was over half a kilometre away, approaching a stand of trees.

Flynn didn't reply, her expression a stern frown of concentration. She lined up the sights, finding the train. Reeve was hanging on to a handrail above its rear wheels. She tracked him, judging the range, the degree of bullet drop. A tough shot, but the target was moving predictably. She slid the crosshairs slightly above and ahead.

Her finger curled around the trigger. Breathe out, let her heartbeat steady . . .

The train rocked. Reeve swung on his precarious perch— *Pull*.

Reeve's palm slipped down the handrail as the train swayed over bumpy track. He squeezed tighter, catching himself. A glance back as he reached the trees. His pursuers had returned to their car—

Something exploded in his raised arm.

Searing pain overcame his senses. He lost his hold – and fell—

His other hand had clutched the steps for extra support. It saved his life. His left arm flopped limply as he clung on with his right. A heel caught the ballast, kicking up stones. The jolt almost dragged him loose. Panic surged – then his mind caught up. *You've been shot! Pull yourself up!*

Reeve flattened himself against the train's side. He managed to raise his flailing foot. Gripping the steps, he looked at his wounded arm.

The bullet had gone through his biceps. Torn muscle glistened with running blood.

He needed to stop the bleeding, but couldn't let go with his other hand. He strained hard to twist and press his right arm against it. The pain was so intense he almost lost his grip again. Somehow, he held on, refusing to surrender.

He lifted his head. A burst of blood surrounded a bullet hole at the door's foot. Had anyone aboard heard the impact?

If they had, the train wasn't stopping for it. He looked towards the road. It tracked the railway, intermittently visible through trees and undulating terrain. Vehicles swept along it. None were SC9's BMW.

But it would surely be coming after him.

Muscles burning, he hung from the train, struggling not to pass out.

CHAPTER 12

'Did you get him?' Maxwell demanded.

Flynn lowered the rifle. 'I definitely hit him. I saw blood.'

'Did he fall off?'

'I didn't see. He went behind the trees.'

'Then maybe you only scratched him,' said Stone, accusing. She shot him a dirty look.

Blake stared after the train. 'Always confirm the kill. That's my motto.'

Maxwell entered the car. 'Let's get to the station.' Glenfinnan was less than three miles away. They could beat the train.

Reeve peered ahead through pain-clenched eyes as the train rounded a bend. A stone bridge carried the main road over the line. He remembered the landmark; Glenfinnan was not far beyond.

The train began to slow. The deceleration rocked him, his right arm coming away from the wound. He gasped as his blood-soaked sleeve tugged at the torn skin. Eyes streaming, he clung on and waited.

He had never been to the station itself. It was set back from the A830 on a side road. But he remembered there was a hotel before it, close to the line. If he jumped off there, he might find another vehicle before SC9 arrived.

The train rolled under the bridge. Stonework sliced past. Then he was through, passing a cottage and going over another bridge. The station was in sight. Trees rose on both sides of the track. He was out of sight of the road. The train had slowed to twenty miles per hour—

He threw himself clear.

This time, he couldn't cross his arms. He landed hard on his side. A breathless cry as he tumbled helplessly – then he crashed against a bush. Twigs slashed at his face.

The train rolled on, steel screams fading. Reeve struggled to sit up. He could still use his left arm, but every movement was agonising. He staggered to his feet.

The rear of a white building was visible through the trees. The hotel. He pressed his right hand to the wound and stumbled across the track. Into the trees—

Noise from the road, a car's engine roaring. Reeve instinctively dropped low. It powered past. A skirl of stressed rubber as it braked hard. It was going to the station.

He picked his way through the undergrowth to find himself behind the hotel. Nobody in sight. He warily moved down the building's side. The road was just ahead. He stopped at the hotel's corner. No sign of the speeding car.

Across the road was a gravel car park, several vehicles in it. A sign confirmed it belonged to the hotel. He regarded the cars. All were too modern to hot-wire easily. There were ways, but he lacked tools – and time.

One car had a trailer, though . . .

He scurried across the road. Still nobody in sight. Acting

as nonchalantly as a man with a bloodied arm could, he entered the car park. The car with the trailer was a Peugeot estate – with two dogs in the back. They responded to his approach by barking angrily.

Ignoring them, he reached the trailer. A crumpled tarpaulin part-covered sacks of loam and large earthenware plant pots. A look at the hotel. The barking hadn't drawn attention – yet. He clambered into the trailer. It rocked under his weight. The dogs' fury rose as the car jolted. Reeve pulled the tarp over himself. Hand on the wound, he turned on his side to keep it above his heart. That was all he could do to minimise the bleeding.

He waited, hoping the Peugeot's driver would return soon – and not check his cargo.

Blake skidded to a stop at the station. The BMW's occupants piled out. 'Careful,' Maxwell warned, seeing people on the platform. 'Lots of civvies around.' East of Glenfinnan was a viaduct that featured prominently in the *Harry Potter* films. There was a regular steam train service: the Jacobite. Potter fans, trainspotters and connoisseurs of stunning scenery all congregated here.

The arriving train was a mundane diesel Sprinter. Maxwell strode briskly to the platform, hand close to the gun beneath his jacket. Stone and Flynn had, sensibly, left their rifles in the car. Maxwell headed towards the train's rear as it pulled up. Flynn came with him, Stone and Blake covering the station's other end.

Reeve had been on the Sprinter's far side. Maxwell waited for it to stop, then crossed the track. His fingers slipped around his gun's grip. If he was there . . .

He wasn't. But there was a faint splash of rain-washed blood on the carriage's side.

Reeve couldn't have entered the train without anyone knowing. The doors were controlled by the driver, and all the windows were intact. So had he jumped, or fallen? Maxwell looked back along the track. Nobody in sight.

Blake hurried towards him from the platform's far end. 'He's not between the carriages. Or under them.'

Maxwell pursed his lips, then addressed Flynn. 'Where did you hit him?'

'His arm,' she replied.

He regarded the bloodstain again as the door slid shut. A bullet hole was at the heart of the elongated teardrop. The round had gone straight through Reeve's arm. It hadn't hit an artery, though; the splatter wasn't big enough. A flesh wound. Big, painful – but survivable. Unless the initial shock made him fall, Reeve had probably kept his hold.

The train pulled away with a diesel roar. The passengers filed across the track in its wake. Maxwell, Flynn and Blake remained still, Stone joining them. 'So he's not here,' said the Londoner. 'Where is he?'

Maxwell didn't answer. 'Go back to the car,' he ordered instead. 'There's a car park opposite the hotel back along the road. Wait for me there.'

'Where are you going?' Flynn asked.

'To check something. Cover me so the staff don't see.' They crossed back to the end of the main platform. The others took up position to obscure him as he jogged down the track.

He surveyed the line, looking for any signs of a disturbance. Even at low speed, Reeve would have had a hard landing . . .

He had covered a hundred and fifty metres when he saw it. Scattered ballast, on the other side of the track. Something had hit the ground hard enough to knock stones flying. His gaze went to the vegetation beyond. Churned mud, flattened grass – and a broken bush.

It had to be where Reeve had jumped off the train. Where had he gone?

Maxwell examined the ground with a detective's intensity. No footprints in the dirt beyond the bush, so . . .

There! Red spots on a sleeper. The rain hadn't yet washed the blood away. It had been left very recently. Reeve couldn't have got far.

His eyes followed the path from the bush to the blood, and beyond. There was a building through the trees. The hotel. Reeve might have found a car already—

Maxwell ran down the slope. Nobody in the hotel's rear garden. He hurried for the road.

'All right! I'm coming.'

Reeve heard a Scottish man approaching the car. He stayed motionless under the tarp. The dogs kept barking. 'Quiet now,' the man said as he got in. 'Quiet!'

The animals continued their warning, but were ignored as their owner started the car. A lurch, then Reeve was in motion.

The journey was only a few metres. The Peugeot paused at the exit, waiting for traffic to pass. Gravel crunched as another car pulled into the car park – coming in fast. A shot of fear. Had Maxwell and the others found his trail?

The Peugeot pulled out, turning east. Reeve listened, expecting the other car to come after him . . .

It didn't. If it was SC9, they had stopped.

Relief, tempered by pain. Each jolt from the road felt like a kick. But he endured it. He would have to, until his ride ended. Wherever that might be.

But at least he was clear of his last identifiable position – and of his hunters.

Maxwell ran to the car park. The others emerged from the BMW to meet him. 'He was here,' he said. 'Jumped off the train before it reached the station.'

'So where is he now?' Stone demanded.

'Either looking for a car, or holing up to treat his wound.' He was about to say more when he heard a siren. 'We've drawn enough attention. We need to leave.'

'What about Reeve?' said Stone. 'For all we know, he might be in that car.' He pointed after the departed Peugeot. 'We should check.'

Blake's response was scathing. 'What, stop it at gunpoint on a public road with the police on the way?'

Stone scowled at him. 'If we have to. The boss can get us off.'

'The boss *can* get us off,' cut in Maxwell, 'for some things. Breach of Section 19 of the Firearms Act isn't one of them. You should know that. Beyond a certain point, we're on our own. Do you want to be sent down before you even officially make Operative?' The big man's expression was a mix of anger and abashment. 'John, help me with the plates.'

Blake took a pair of number plates from the boot. He clamped one magnetically over the existing rear plate; the registrations were different. Maxwell did the same at the front. SC9's vehicles had been chosen because they were common and anonymous. With the plates changed, the 5-Series would not be identified by the police – in theory.

'That might be a giveaway,' Flynn noted, indicating the dented bodywork.

'The cops have bigger things to worry about,' said Maxwell. They all re-entered the car. 'We need a new plan of action. Organise a search, check with local police and hospitals for anyone with gunshot wounds. And,' he added with a heavy sigh, 'I have to report everything to the boss.'

'Rather you than me,' Blake said. He brought the BMW to the exit, halting as a police car tore past. Everyone tensed, but it didn't stop. If it had a digital plate reader, it had accepted the replacements as real. He pulled out, heading back west.

Stone was first to break the silence. 'So,' he said to Maxwell, 'I passed, then?'

CHAPTER 13

Staying conscious in the trailer was the hardest thing Reeve had ever done. The simplest way to counter his slips towards oblivion was also the worst. He squeezed his wounded arm, pain blasting him awake.

The journey ended after thirty minutes. The Peugeot stopped, its driver opening the boot. Both dogs howled again. 'Shut up, you buggers!' the man complained. He pulled the still-barking animals out and led them away.

Reeve waited until he heard a house door close, then rose. A new surge of pain from his arm. He let it subside, then pulled away the tarp. Where was he?

A drab residential street. From his travel time, either Fort William or neighbouring Inverlochy. The Peugeot had stopped on a drive leading up to a house. Nobody at the windows. He climbed from the trailer, stiff and aching.

Blood was still oozing from his arm. He needed to wash and bandage it at the very least. It really required sterilising and stitches, but that was not an option. At a hospital, the staff would by law have to report the gunshot wound. The police would soon get involved – followed by SC9.

He went to the road, aware of how conspicuous he looked.

Luckily, the street was quiet. The rain was keeping people indoors.

Which way? He turned right at random. Small houses faced him on both sides. A side street led uphill. He was about to pass it when he heard voices.

Two elderly women were chatting at the gate of the second house up. The apparent owner, holding an umbrella, had come out to meet her passing friend. The front door was open.

No car outside. She was probably the only person in. Reeve hesitated, a moment of moral distaste at his plan, then continued on.

He passed the house at the bottom of the street. It was surrounded by a waist-high wooden fence. No one in sight. He climbed over and hurried uphill through the garden. Over another fence, and he was behind the old lady's home.

He went to the back door. It wasn't locked. Another twinge of disgust, then he slipped through.

The kitchen. The inner door was closed. He dimly heard voices; the owner was still outside. He quickly checked the cupboards. Would she keep medicines and first-aid materials here, or in the bathroom? Crockery, food, food—

A clutch of dark bottles and packs of cold remedies. But he was more interested in the translucent Tupperware box beside them. A moment to listen. The women were still talking. He opened the container.

Assorted waterproof plasters, a packet of paracetamol painkillers – and a roll of gauze dressing. He took them all to the sink and ran the hot tap. A gas boiler hissed, steam rising.

Reeve gritted his teeth, then peeled off his hoodie. The

sleeve was stuck to his skin with congealed blood. A choked gasp as it tore free. He dropped the wet garment. The tap was a mixer; he adjusted it to just below scalding.

Then he held the wound beneath it.

The pain was so fierce he almost screamed. He held it in, only a strained groan escaping. Blood sluiced into the sink. He ran more water over his arm. The cloying red mess around the injury slowly dissolved.

He examined it. The bullet had gone through the short head of his biceps. Despite the pain, he knew he had been lucky. It could have been far worse. He turned off the tap, then listened. The conversation outside had stopped. Was the old lady coming back?

Move fast. He wrapped the dressing around his upper arm. More daggers drove into the torn muscle. Holding it in place against his chest, he fumbled with the plasters. Four of them, clumsily applied, stuck the bandage down.

He grabbed his bloodied hoodie and the painkillers, then hurried to the back door. Footsteps; the woman was inside. He darted into the garden and ran to the fence.

A shrill cry from behind as he vaulted it. She had discovered his break-in. He ducked into the cover of the lower house, putting his ruined top back on. His arm burned as the sleeve tugged at the bandage. But at least now the wound was covered.

The police would be here in minutes. He had to get clear. A man in blood-soaked clothing would be an instant target for arrest if sighted. He swallowed two pills, then rapidly departed.

*

Twenty minutes later, Reeve was on the shore of Loch Linnhe.

Following a circuitous route into town, he had spotted a sign for a truck park. That was what he needed. He had to travel not merely incognito, but unseen.

The truck park was near a supermarket. Seven articulated lorries stood in it. Reeve walked by as if heading to the shop. He read the names and logos on the vehicles as he passed. A local haulier was little use to him. Someone returning to a depot beyond the Highlands would be preferable.

Three vehicles were based in Fort William or nearby. That left four. Two had solid locks on their trailer doors. Only two left. One had a driver in the cab, eating a sandwich. About to leave? His truck was based in Glasgow. A drive of roughly three hours. And a city would give Reeve places to hide.

Not drawing attention, he looped back around behind the trucks. His target vehicle's trailer was closed, but not pad-locked. Nobody watching him. He opened it and peered inside. Its cargo had apparently been delivered. All it contained were pallets and lengths of torn plastic wrap.

He clambered in. The trailer couldn't be bolted shut from inside. A flapping door would see the truck stopped in short order. He twisted one of the plastic lengths into a crude rope. A minute's work, and he tied the locking bar outside the door to a pallet. It would hold it shut – while letting him get out in moments.

Reeve sat and waited. Ten worrying minutes – maybe the driver's shift was over? – but then the truck's engine started. A jolt, and the vehicle set off. The door banged, but held closed.

He was on his way. To where, he didn't know – but it was away from his pursuers.

Reeve bunched up more wrapping as padding, then leaned back. Despite his efforts to stay alert, exhaustion claimed him in minutes.

The mood at Mordencroft Hall was grim.

'So, where will Reeve go?' asked Blake. 'What's his background? Who will he run to?'

Maxwell's laptop was open, the instructor accessing Reeve's file from SC9's distant servers. 'No immediate family in the country,' he said. 'His mother's dead, and his father's in prison.'

'He might still try to see him,' suggested Parker.

'I doubt it. Alex's testimony put him there.'

Stone raised his eyebrows. 'He grassed up his own dad? Knew there was a reason I didn't like him.'

Locke's shoulder wound had been bandaged, his arm in a sling. 'It may have been entirely justified,' he said.

Stone snorted. 'You never grass on your own.'

'It doesn't matter,' said Maxwell. 'His nearest relatives are in Australia, so he won't be popping in.'

'What about friends?' asked Flynn. 'I know he was in the forces. Maybe he's got some old army buddy who'd help him.'

'Not according to his record – he was in the Special Reconnaissance Regiment, by the way. He was noted as a loner with no close friends. Everything was about the job. Which was one of the reasons he was approached by SC9, of course.'

'SC9,' Parker said, with a small smile. 'The Billy No-Mates brigade.'

Another snort from Stone. 'You lot, maybe. I had loads of mates.' Expressions of disbelief from the other recruits. 'Fuck off.'

'Let's concentrate on Alex,' Maxwell said impatiently. 'His SRR training means he's adept at escape and evasion in any environment. That was even before everything he learned here.'

'Where is he from originally?' said Locke.

'Manchester. Clayton, specifically – not one of the nicer parts. *Coronation Street* on crack, from what I gather. So he'll feel more at home in that kind of environment. He'll probably head for a major city.'

Maxwell's phone rang. 'The boss. This should be fun.' Maxwell had left a message with his superior on the drive back. He waited for audio confirmation that the line was secure, then spoke. 'Sir.'

'Maxwell.' The voice was upper-class, condescending – and taut with anger. 'So. What the hell happened? Why is Reeve not only still alive, but on the run?'

'We *did* train him to be the best,' Maxwell replied, regretting it as he spoke.

The remark was, as expected, not well received. 'Do you think this is a *joke*?'

'No, sir.'

'Damn right it's not. There's a traitor in our midst, and you let him escape.'

'Sir, I did not *let* him escape,' said Maxwell. 'He was shot and wounded. I've already arranged to be notified if he's admitted to any nearby hospitals.'

The condescension grew thicker. 'I'd suggest you widen the search radius. He could be anywhere.'

'We're already working out where he might go.'

'We?'

'The other recruits. The other Operatives now, I suppose. They did all pass.'

'Fucking *knew* I made it,' muttered Stone with a victorious smile.

Maxwell ignored him. 'Unless you're reconsidering the results, sir?'

'No. They all qualified.' A lengthy silence, enough to become concerning. 'Maxwell,' the voice finally said, 'this . . . *fiasco* reflects very badly upon you. You were on my shortlist to head the agency when I retire. I'm now seriously debating that decision.'

'Sir,' Maxwell protested, 'I was working without full information. I wasn't told *why* Alex was declared Fox Red. If I'd known why he was a security threat — which personally I didn't see—'

'That wasn't your decision to make,' his superior snapped.

'No, sir – but I would have been better prepared. Nothing I'd seen suggested that he was a traitor.'

Cold anger at being challenged. 'The profiles don't lie, Maxwell. And you helped compile them. Reeve was a threat. To SC9, and to the country. I gave you orders to eliminate him – and you failed to carry them out. Maybe I should replace you with someone more capable.'

Maxwell felt a cold weight in his stomach. 'Sir, we can still track him down. Reeve is good, but so are the others. And it's one against six. We'll find him.'

Another unsettling pause. 'Very well. Put me on speaker.' Maxwell did so. 'You've all qualified as SC9 Operatives. This is your first mission. Hunt down and kill the rogue asset – at all costs.' The call ended. The others exchanged looks.

Maxwell took a breath to compose himself. 'Well, those are your orders. To kill the man you've spent nearly a year training with.' He met each of their eyes in turn. 'Can you carry them out?'

'Fuckin' hell, yes,' exclaimed Stone immediately. 'Never trusted that autistic northern cunt.'

Blake nodded. 'He's a traitor. He deserves to die.'

'I can't think of a better way to prove our effectiveness,' said Locke.

Parker's reply was succinct. 'Yes.'

'If he's turned against us,' said Flynn, 'then . . . yeah. We have to.'

'All right.' Maxwell stood. 'Then let's find him.' He began to pace around the room. 'He's running. To where? What's his objective?'

'Fleeing the country,' said Blake. 'He's a traitor, so he's working *for* someone. He'll go to them for sanctuary.'

Nods from the others. 'We should get his picture out to all ports of exit,' said Locke.

Flynn picked up on Maxwell's uncertain frown. 'You don't think he'll try to leave the country, sir?'

'You can call me Tony now, Deirdre,' he replied. 'You all can. You made Operative; we're all equals now. Except,' he continued with a wry smile, 'I'm more equal than others. I'm still your superior. For this mission, at least.' The curl vanished from his mouth. 'Alex's reaction after I tried to shoot him . . . it wasn't someone who'd been caught. He was *confused*. Surprised – *unsuspecting*. Not what I'd expect from someone whose cover was blown.'

'He seemed ready for action when he attacked me,' Parker countered.

Stone gave Maxwell an aggressive, questioning look. 'How come you didn't kill him, then? How could you miss?'

'Because he's one of the best I've ever trained,' Maxwell shot back.

'He's not better than me.' The instructor's lack of a reply only made Stone's scowl deepen.

'Surely you can't think he's innocent?' Locke asked. 'He tried to kill us.' His cold eyes flicked towards his wounded shoulder.

'We have our orders . . . Tony,' added Parker. 'Straight from the boss.'

'I know what our orders are,' Maxwell said. 'And I intend to carry them out. But to kill Alex, we have to *find* Alex. Like I said: what's his objective? Escape, yes – but that's his most immediate priority. What comes *after* that?'

A lengthy, contemplative silence. Flynn was first to speak. 'You said he seemed confused,' she said to Maxwell. 'Do you mean . . . like he wanted to know *why* you'd tried to kill him?'

'Exactly that,' Maxwell told her. 'There was a moment when I thought he was actually going to *ask* me. But then he ran . . .' His brow furrowed. 'I know his objective.'

'What?' Parker asked.

'He *does* want to ask me.'

'I don't share your reasoning,' said Locke. 'He knows

why. Because he was a mole, and he was discovered.'

'Humour me, for now,' said Maxwell. 'I know Alex better than anyone else here. And I think he wants answers – from *me*. I'm the only person who can give them. He can't ask the boss; he doesn't know who he is. You lot don't either, so he won't come after you. He'll try to find me.' He folded his arms. 'We have to be ready for him.'

'How would he find you?' asked Flynn. 'We all got new identities when we were recruited. We haven't given him enough personal info to track us down.' A cutting look at Stone. 'Not even Mister "I was in the Met Police's Territorial Support Group" there.'

Stone was caught off-guard. 'I never fucking told anyone that. And definitely not fucking Reeve.'

'Not directly,' Locke said. 'But you revealed enough over time for it to be a straightforward inference.'

'Yeah? Well, I inferred plenty about you too. Fucking psycho.'

'That's enough,' Maxwell said firmly. 'I know that talking about your background is against regs. But shit happens. Even I've let things slip.' His voice took on a new, meaningful tone. 'What's the one thing you all know about me?'

He let the question hang in the air. Realisation gradually spread around the table. 'That's right,' Maxwell went on. 'You know it; Alex does too.' A confident smile slowly appeared. 'And *that's* how we'll catch him.'

CHAPTER 14

Reeve jerked awake.

A moment of confusion. Where was he? A dark, noisy room, being shaken. Interrogation training—

Memory returned – along with the pain in his arm. The truck.

A glance at his watch. He'd left Fort William just under three hours ago. Enough time to have reached Glasgow.

He peered through the gap between the doors. Slow-moving traffic behind, numerous grey buildings. Definitely in the city. Once the truck reached its destination, he would quickly slip out.

And then what?

Only two options came to him at first. Hide – or run. He could escape the country even without money, or a passport. There were ways through any nation's security checks. He had been taught how to exploit the holes in Britain's own.

But . . . where would he go? Even if he reached mainland Europe, what then? He would still be a priority target for SC9. Fox Red status would never be rescinded. His former colleagues wouldn't end the hunt – until he was dead.

The same would happen if he hid, though. Staying off the grid in Britain for any length of time was nearly impossible.

It was a small, crowded country full of snoops and curtain-twitchers. Without contacts, without money, he would have to use alternative methods to survive. Methods that would draw the attention of the authorities.

And SC9 would quickly follow.

SC9. They had recruited him, trained him – now they were trying to kill him. Why?

He had been declared Fox Red. A designation for threats to the agency itself. He knew he wasn't a traitor, so why did they think he was?

Two possibilities. One, he dismissed out of hand. An error, some misinterpretation of events. Unlikely. From what he understood, SC9's instructors all contributed to a profile of each trainee. Even if one mistakenly thought him a threat, the others would surely have been consulted. This was no accident of circumstance.

It was the other possibility. He had been set up.

The truck slowed and lurched over a gutter. He went back to the doors. Stationary lorries rolled past. Another truck park. Time to bail out.

Reeve waited for his ride to stop, then moved the pallet. He opened the door enough to look outside. No observers. He jumped down. The jolt made his arm hurt. He winced, then closed and bolted the door before moving clear.

The rain hadn't ceased despite his hundred-mile journey. He splashed across the concrete. Of his two options, running seemed the best. It would at least give him time to recover and plan his actions. He regarded the trucks. Several were owned by European hauliers: French, Dutch, Polish.

Thanks to Brexit, police cooperation between the UK

and European Union had drastically reduced. If he drew attention on the continent, it would take time to be relayed home. And he was now fluent in several languages; more intense SC9 training. Enough to pass as a citizen of one EU country while in another. He could stay a step ahead of his pursuers . . .

But something held him back from the Europe-bound trucks. An image of Maxwell flashed through his mind. His instructor's face after firing the first bullet. Maxwell had looked grim, but in a distinct way. It was *reluctance*; the expression of a man obeying an unwelcome order.

Maxwell hadn't wanted to kill him. He had been told to do so by his superior. Why?

It came back to the set-up. Who had framed him? Not Maxwell; his unguarded emotion had seemed genuine. Not his boss, either. SC9's head wouldn't need to fabricate a reason to declare him Fox Red. His word alone would be enough.

It had to be one of the other recruits. But which one? And again: why?

Only Maxwell could provide any answers. But how could he possibly get them? His mentor was now leading the hunt for him. If he got too close, he would be a dead man . . .

No, Reeve told himself. He was thinking of himself as the target, a victim. Reverse it. *Maxwell* is the target. You have to get to him. How?

First step: locate him. Find out where he is – or where he will *be*.

Reeve felt a sudden, unexpected sense of anticipation. He was starting a hunt of his own. It would be a challenge – the toughest he had ever faced. Potentially a deadly one. But he *could* get to Maxwell. And if he did, he could find out who had framed him.

The decision was made. He had to reach London.

He turned away from the European trucks. Several others displayed London phone numbers. He picked the best candidate and sneaked inside. This was half-loaded with pallets of shrink-wrapped cardboard boxes. A shipping label had a London address; the truck was going where he wanted. He shut the door as best he could, then climbed over the boxes. A hidden space behind them. He nestled into it, then waited, enduring the pain.

Nearly thirty minutes passed, then someone came to the door. 'Oh, fuck,' came a rough voice. The driver, realising his trailer was open. Reeve hunched low. Both doors swung wide, the man clambering up. Heavy footsteps. A light came on; his phone's torch. Reeve stayed motionless as it swept over the boxes . . .

And flicked off again. Satisfied his cargo hadn't been stolen, the driver clomped back out. The doors slammed. Metal rattled and scraped, and they were locked.

Reeve raised his head. The trailer's interior was almost totally dark. He cursed. There was no way to reach the locking bars from inside. He was stuck in here until someone opened the doors.

He already felt thirsty, and hunger would inevitably follow. He had to hope the truck wouldn't park up overnight. Resigned, he fumbled for more painkillers, then lay down.

Another few minutes, then the engine started. The truck jolted out of the city, eventually roaring on to a motorway.

Sleep claimed Reeve once more.

This time, exhaustion couldn't hold off nightmares. Maxwell loomed over him again, smoking gun in hand. The other recruits rolled behind him. Parker, Locke, Stone, Blake, Flynn. All were armed and ready, trying to kill him. He was running, but couldn't get away—

Armed and ready. The thought echoed as if spoken. What did it mean? *Armed and ready.* It was important, but he couldn't grasp why. *Armed and ready . . .*

The dream finally dissolved into darkness.

Parker leaned through the door of Maxwell's office. 'Ready?'

'Almost,' Maxwell replied. His decision was made: the group would head for London. He was certain they would find Reeve there. He knew some of the others disagreed, but didn't care. He was still in charge of the hunt for SC9's rogue asset. If he was wrong, it would be on his head.

No helicopters or private flights this time. They had a five-hundred-mile-plus drive ahead. But first, they had to clear and secure the Hall. At least, he thought with dark humour, there was less to store in the armoury. The team were now armed and equipped for any eventuality.

Parker retreated, and Maxwell turned back to his laptop. On screen was the situation update he had written for the boss. One final check before sending it. Both to make sure it was accurate, and presented his actions in the best light. Even in this business, office politics were inevitable. Especially, he mused, glancing at the desk's bullet holes, with his career on the line.

A faint sigh, then he clicked send. He would know what

the boss thought of the report soon enough.

That thought triggered another. Something the boss had said. About his reports. Rather, the reports that had been electronically compiled to form Reeve's profile. The profile that had led to his being declared Fox Red.

Something was tugging at a thread in his mind. Why?

He wasn't sure, but Maxwell had long since learned to trust his instincts completely. They had saved his life more than once. If something *felt* wrong, it almost certainly *was*.

But what?

He stared at the laptop for a moment – then started to search through his files. Even knowing he was about to depart, there was something he had to check.

CHAPTER 15

A clash of metal kicked Reeve from his sleep. He pushed himself upright, remembering too late his wounded arm. He gasped – rather *rasped*, his mouth dry.

Where was he? His watch told him it was past two in the morning. He could have reached London. What had made the noise? He looked towards the doors. The salmon pall of sodium lights leaked around them. He must have reached the truck's depot—

A second scraping bang. The other locking bar being released. Someone was opening the trailer.

Reeve ducked again. Stowaways were not welcome in the haulage trade. He wanted to avoid a confrontation with the driver, and especially the police.

The doors swung open, sickly light flooding in. 'Let's 'ave a look,' someone said. Essex accent, coarse and harsh. 'Where's the paperwork?'

'Here.' The driver. 'You need a hand?'

'Nah, I got the trolley. You goin' straight 'ome?'

'Fucking right I am.' A laugh, then both men walked away.

Reeve raised his head. The truck had reversed to a loading dock. A warehouse, pallets of goods stacked high. The retreating men had their backs to him. He climbed over the boxes, stiff from the long journey. Hunger clenched at his stomach, and he felt clear symptoms of dehydration. His priority was finding water and food.

After he got clear. He crept to the doors. Rain drummed on a corrugated awning above. The two men were still heading away. He slipped out and jumped down to the tarmac—

'Oi!'

A bald, burly man was having a smoke between the loading docks. 'What the fuck are you doing?' He flicked away his cigarette and advanced, calling out: 'We've got a thief here!'

Reeve lifted his empty hands. 'I didn't steal anything,' he said. 'I just needed a ride.'

'Yeah, that's what you all say. Fuckin' gippos.' Behind, Reeve heard the two other men running back towards him.

'I don't want trouble.' He tried to walk on, but the man blocked him. 'Just let me past, and you won't see me again.'

The bald man glowered. 'You're not going anywhere, you thieving bastard.' The other pair reached the loading dock, one jumping down beside the trailer. 'Come here—'

He grabbed Reeve's injured arm.

It felt like a branding iron searing his flesh. Reeve lurched back – then trained instinct took over.

He twisted free of his opponent's grip – and whirled. His right elbow smashed into the man's meaty face like a hammer. A sickening *snap* as he felt a tooth break. The man's head jerked backwards. Before he could even spit out a bloodied scream, Reeve completed his spin. His foot slammed into the bald man's paunchy stomach. He crashed against the neighbouring truck.

Reeve faced the man who had jumped down. His eyes were wide in fear. 'Whoa, *fuck*,' he gasped, hurriedly retreating.

The other man above him looked to be considering avenging his workmate. Reeve stared at him. He backed away. His companion scrambled up on to the loading dock. 'Call the fuckin' cops!' he yelled.

Other voices rose inside the warehouse. Reeve turned, vaulting the moaning man to run out from between the trailers.

He was in a transport company's yard, the open gate thirty metres away. He raced past parked trucks towards it. More shouts from behind. Someone was calling the police. He charged out on to a street.

An industrial estate lay beyond, anonymous buildings behind tall, barbed-wire-topped fences. A few cars and white vans were parked on the potholed road. No landmarks; he could be anywhere. Which way – left or right?

The nearest corner was left. He ran around it. The new street was as nondescript as the other. Most of the businesses were closed and dark, gates chained shut. He hurried past them. With someone attacked and injured, the police would be quick to the scene.

He had to get away before they arrived. If he was arrested, his wound would be recorded in the system. SC9 would be alerted. They would come for him.

They would kill him.

Reeve reached a junction. The road to the left led only to

a darkened building. He continued right. A street sign. The name meant nothing – but after it was written SW19. Southwest London; at least he now had a vague idea of his location.

He ran on, past a cement works, a scrapyard, more industrial units. The road angled left—

Shit.

Dead end. An electricity substation was backed by a railway line. All the walls and fences were topped by spikes or barbs.

No way out.

An elderly Seat Ibiza hatchback was parked nearby. He hurried to it. From the plate, over twenty years old. Not fast, not powerful – but it didn't have an immobiliser or alarm. He could break the steering lock and hotwire it in minutes—

He didn't *have* minutes.

A siren warbled. The police were coming.

He wouldn't be able to start the car before they arrived. If they saw him trying to steal it, they would know he was their suspect. They would be ready for a fight.

But if they weren't *certain* . . .

Reeve left the car, walking – strolling – back the way he had come. In the truck's shadow, the workers wouldn't have got a good look at him. The description they gave to the cops would be vague. White, six foot. Maybe they had noticed he was wearing a hoodie. The police would be suspicious if they saw him – but not *sure*. Their approach would be cautious rather than aggressive.

He hoped. If they were anything like Stone, they might start with batons drawn and escalate . . .

Hood up, he maintained his casual walk. The siren had stopped, but he now heard an approaching car. Strobing blue flashes preceded it around a corner. A Metropolitan Police Vauxhall Astra estate with blue-and-yellow Battenberg markings. No yellow dots on the windows. Not Armed Response, then, but a standard patrol car. No guns.

They would still have weapons, though. Tasers and incapacitant sprays.

The Astra swung towards him with a quick *whoop-whoop* of its siren. Reeve slowed, feigning surprise. The driver's window lowered, a man regarding him warily. 'Excuse me, sir. Can you stop, please?'

Reeve did so. If they were certain they had their suspect, they would have ordered, not asked. 'What's up?'

The car halted. Two officers in rainproof hi-vis jackets got out, leaving the engine running. The equipment on their belts was exposed and in easy reach – including incapacitants. The driver stopped in front of Reeve, the other to his right. He shifted to keep his bloodied left arm in shadow. 'A man was assaulted not far from here,' said the driver. 'The suspect ran in this direction. Have you seen anyone?'

Reeve shrugged. 'No.'

The other officer spoke. 'What are you doing here?'

Another shrug. 'On my way home from a mate's.'

The two men exchanged looks. They knew the road was a dead end. The driver sidestepped, trying to get a better look at Reeve's left sleeve. 'Sir,' he intoned, 'I have reasonable suspicion to believe you were involved in the incident.'

A huff of affronted innocence. 'What? I haven't done anything.'

Both officers stepped closer. 'We have the authority to search you under the Police and Criminal Evidence Act 1984. If you will turn around and show us your clothing—'

Reeve turned – and kept turning.

The second cop was already reaching for him as he spun. Reeve scythed his feet out from under him with a leg sweep. The unprepared man fell heavily to the kerb. Before he even hit the ground, Reeve had spun back at his partner. He slammed the heel of his open palm against the driver's nose. Cartilage crunched. The man staggered back, howling.

Reeve ducked and tore open a pouch on the officer's belt. He snatched out a container of CS spray and squirted it at the driver. The cop screamed, clawing at his eyes. Reeve whipped back around and sprayed his partner too. He had been getting up; he dropped again, wailing and swearing.

Reeve leapt into the car. He reversed at speed, making a fast J-turn and powering away. He couldn't drive it for long. All Met vehicles had trackers, and the downed cops would soon raise the alarm. He just needed to get clear of the industrial estate. Once out, he could lose himself in the capital's streets.

He shot past the haulage yard, onlookers watching in surprise. A couple of turns, and he reached flats and houses. He kept going, registering a direction sign for a hospital. Several more corners, then he pulled over.

Nobody about. Unsurprising, at two-thirty on a miserable night. First job: clean the car of fingerprints. He tugged his right sleeve over his hand and wiped down the steering wheel. Same again on the gear lever and door handles. He had kept his hood up and head down while driving. The interior cameras hopefully hadn't got a clear shot of his face. Hand still covered, he opened the door and got out.

He had no idea where he was, but at least he was no longer penned in. He started walking. Even though he hadn't used his left arm in the fight, it was hurting again. Paracetamol wouldn't cut it. He needed something stronger.

The hospital. Head lowered, he walked on through the rain.

CHAPTER 16

Connie Jones fought to contain a head-splitting yawn as she closed her locker. *Don't go to sleep yet! You still have to drive home.*

She donned her coat over her staff nurse's uniform, then shouldered her handbag. Three in the morning, indeed. Why had she agreed to work such ridiculous shifts? But if she hadn't, someone else would have had to. With the staff stretched to the limit, sharing the worst shifts equally was only fair. Besides, patients didn't stop needing help just because it was dark.

It had been a tough night. One of her patients had died. A gentle old lady called Sandra finally succumbed to a lung infection. The previous evening, they had shared a joke about politics. Now she was gone. Her smile existed only in memory. A wave of sadness at the idea. Sometimes, Connie wondered if she was in the wrong profession. No matter how much help she gave people, in the end . . .

She shook off the maudlin thought. The inevitability of death wasn't what mattered. Helping people live as best they could before it arrived did. She had done all she could to make Sandra comfortable in her last hours. Nobody should die alone and scared and in pain. At least she *had* been able to smile.

A sigh, then she turned to leave. Ten hours, and she would be back. Before Brexit, many of the hospital's nurses had been Spanish or Portuguese. Now most had returned home, those remaining having to cover the gaps. And there were a lot of gaps. But people didn't stop getting sick, whatever belt-tightening cruelties the politicians and accountants imposed.

She said goodbye to friends as she headed out. The last was Martin, the night porter. 'See you tomorrow, Martin.'

'Not if I win the lottery,' he said, looking up from his sudoku.

Connie smiled, then took the lift up through the car park. Another 'perk' of the job; paying for the privilege of parking at her own workplace. At least she got – woo! – a whopping ten per cent staff discount. But she had little choice. Her flat was beyond walking distance, and public transport added forty minutes' travel each way.

Her car was on the top floor, an ageing gold Citroën Saxo. She scurried to it through the rain. Another yawn as she took her seat, then she pulled out.

Down the concrete spiral to the gate. The machine swallowed her ticket, and the barrier rose. She turned on to the road—

'Oh, shit, *shit*! Shit shit *shit*!' Connie slapped a hand on the wheel at her own stupidity.

She had forgotten her phone! It was still in her locker; she couldn't use it while on duty. How could she not have picked it up? Idiot!

The car passed the hospital's pedestrian entrance, but there was nowhere to stop. Every street within half a mile was either double-yellow or permit parking only. And it was entirely possible to get a ticket even in the dead of night. She knew that from experience.

She had to go back. But using the car park again, even for five minutes, meant another few pounds wasted. She objected on principle as much as to the hit to her restricted finances.

Wait – the delivery area. Parking there was strictly *verboten*. But nobody would be coming at this time of night, and Martin surely wouldn't object . . .

She went around the hospital. The loading bay was down an alley. She swung the Saxo in. Multiple warning signs, and the whole area was hatched with red lines. But it wasn't an ambulance bay, so she wouldn't be obstructing anything important. Just to be sure, she backed into a corner out of sight of the road.

Martin was already at the entrance when she got out. 'Hey! You can't park – oh, Connie.'

'Hi, Martin,' she said with her brightest smile. 'I'm sorry, but I left my phone. I'll be two minutes. Please, *please* let me stop here while I get it.'

He sucked air through his teeth. 'I shouldn't, but . . . okay. Be quick.'

'I always knew there were still good guys around,' Connie told him, as she hurried inside.

Reeve looked up at the hospital. It was a mix of shabby Victorian buildings and characterless brick-and-glass blocks.

He hoped more money was being spent on patient care than upkeep.

But he wasn't planning to check himself in. Rather, he needed medical supplies. The Accident and Emergency department was the place to find them. Examination rooms would have stocks of lidocaine local anaesthetic, Steristrips, antiseptic wash, antibiotics and dressings. Stronger pain-killers too.

How to get them? Normally, he would have properly reconnoitred the place, inside and out. But he had heard more sirens. The police were hunting for him. He had taken down two of their own. That would not be allowed to stand.

So it would have to be a lightning raid; smash and grab. Risky – maybe too risky. A dangerous cocktail of pain, tiredness, hunger and thirst was affecting his judgement. That he was aware of it was a good sign. It meant his mind still had some focus. But it wouldn't for much longer. If he didn't deal with it, he would make mistakes.

And then he would be dead.

Reeve made his way around the hospital. That looked promising: an alley between a Victorian wing and one of the newer blocks. A loading bay at the far end. Swing doors, ajar.

He picked out a camera above the entrance as he walked on. With his head down and hood up, it wouldn't catch his face.

Have to chance it. He crossed the road, then doubled back to the alley. A glance around the corner. Still nobody there.

Go for it.

Reeve lowered his head, then ran for the doors.

*

Connie got back into the Saxo. She still couldn't believe she had forgotten her phone. Tiredness was scrambling her brain. At least she wasn't performing neurosurgery. She started the car and moved off—

Really? Headlights! The phone wasn't the only thing she'd forgotten. She glanced down to find the switch.

The lights came on as she rounded the corner—

Someone flashed through them – and tumbled over the bonnet with a bang.

Reeve raced down the alley – and a car swung around a corner and hit him.

He bowled over its nose, rolling off the side. He hit the wet ground hard.

The driver's door opened. He looked up to assess the threat—

'Oh God, oh my God!' Connie cried, as she jumped from the car. The man on the ground looked up at her. 'Are you okay? I'm so sorry!'

He was hurt, and not just by her car. She saw blood on his dirty clothing, a red-stained bandage around his arm. Cuts and bruises on his face. A homeless man who'd been in a fight?

No. She was sure of that, without even fully knowing why. He wore running gear, enough bodily contours discernible to reveal he was in excellent shape. The kind of lithe muscularity that came from testing, determined exercise. Late twenties, she estimated. None of a drug abuser's facial haggardness or the puffiness of an alcoholic. A mugging victim, rushing to the hospital for help? But the bandage seemed to have been on for some time . . .

All those thoughts flashed through her mind in the moment before he responded. 'I'm – I'm okay,' he said, taking in her uniform. 'I'm not hurt.'

'Yes, you are,' Connie protested. 'What happened to your arm? Have you been stabbed?'

'No, no.' He put a hand on the car for support as he stood. A wince as he straightened his legs.

'No, you're really hurt. Let me help.' She moved to aid him. He tried to shrug her off, only to gasp as he moved his left arm. 'I'll get you to A&E.'

'I can't,' he replied. 'It's a bullet wound. If it's logged into the system, there'll be questions.'

Her gaze flicked to his injured arm. 'You were *shot*?'

'Through-and-through penetration of the short head of the biceps. The long head and brachial artery aren't damaged. I've washed the wound.'

Connie blinked at his professional and precise terminology. 'Are you a qualified medic?'

'No, I'm just an interested amateur.'

The remark produced an involuntary laugh. 'Well, I'm a professional,' she said, smiling. 'And you *do* need medical attention.'

He shook his head. 'I can't. I'm sorry.'

'I'm the one who should be apologising. I just hit you with my car!'

'My fault. I should have been paying more attention. I need to go.' He looked back towards the road.

'Wait, wait,' said Connie. 'You said you washed the wound. With what?'

'Just water.'

'No alcohol or antiseptic?'

'No.'

'I'm guessing it hasn't been sutured either.'

'No.'

She waved her hands in pleading exasperation. 'You *can't* go. You've basically still got an open wound. It'll almost certainly be infected. At the very least, it needs to be cleaned properly.'

He indicated the hospital. 'If I go in there with a bullet wound, you'll have to log it. The people who shot me will know I'm here. They'll come to finish the job.'

Her exasperation moved to a professional level. 'You know, we don't generally let criminals access our records.'

'They're not criminals.'

She became uneasy. 'You were shot by the police?'

'No. And before you ask, I'm not a criminal either. Obviously,' he added, 'you only have my word on that. But I'm really not.'

There was an almost innocent sincerity in his voice that made her believe him. Or rather, believe that *he* believed it. 'So who did shoot you? And why?'

He hesitated before answering. 'This morning – well, yesterday morning, now – everything was fine. Then suddenly . . . the people I've worked with for nearly a year tried to kill me. And I don't know why.' Again, he seemed completely honest in his reply.

Connie looked back at his arm, shocked. 'You've had an

untreated bullet wound for almost a whole day?' The pain he must have endured would have incapacitated most people by now. Yet he was still standing – even after being hit by a car. 'Please, you *have* to let me help you.'

'I can't.'

'Then where will you go?'

'I . . . don't have anywhere.' The admission was almost plaintive.

'Come with me. I can help you at home.' She was surprised – shocked – by the offer even as she made it. Where had it come from? *Waifs and strays*: her mother's voice in her mind, with gently mocking amusement. Wounded birds and lost kittens had often been brought home to be cared for.

The man was equally surprised. 'I . . . no, I can't. Sorry.' He turned to leave—

'Connie! Is everything okay?'

A voice from the loading bay. Martin was at the doors, regarding the scene with concern. She glanced back at the injured man. He was about to break and run. 'Everything's fine,' she said quickly. 'He's looking for A&E. I'll take him round.'

Martin gave him a dubious look, but nodded. 'Okay. If you're sure.'

'I'll see you tomorrow, okay?' The porter waved in response, then withdrew.

She looked back at her companion. 'Come on, then.' She gestured at her car.

It was his turn to blink. 'What?'

'Like I said, I can help you at home. I'll clean the wound and stitch it up for you.'

His expression was almost suspicious. 'Why would you do that? You don't even know me.'

'I'm a nurse – it's my job to help people who need help. And, you know, I hit you with my car. It's the least I can do.' There was also, she admitted, a certain intrigue about the situation. 'Come on,' she repeated, entering the Saxo.

He watched her askance, hesitating . . . then got in beside her. 'Thank you,' he said, still uncertain.

'No problem.' She restarted the car. 'By the way, I'm Connie.'

Another hesitation before a clipped reply. 'Alex. Alex Reeve.'

'Connie, Connie Jones. Nice to meet you, Alex. Even if it wasn't exactly the best way of doing it.' She held out her hand.

'Yeah, I can think of nicer ones.' He managed a half-smile, then shook it.

Connie set off. 'We'll be there in about twenty minutes,' she said, as she guided the car down the alley. The man – Alex – nodded.

A voice at the back of her mind yelled in warning. *What the hell are you* doing? *You don't know this guy. He might rob you, rape you, kill you* . . . She couldn't argue. Had she seen another woman in the same situation, she would have been worried too.

But she got no sense of threat from him. Even now, he seemed more likely to jump from the car and run.

If he could stay awake, that was. Within minutes, she saw him flinch as he caught himself dropping off. 'Don't worry,' she said. 'We'll be there soon.'

'Thanks,' came the tired reply.

She drove on. Another few minutes, and she glanced sidelong – to see her mysterious passenger was asleep.

CHAPTER 17

Reeve struggled through a dark fog. The ground was glutinous, sucking down each footstep. But someone was chasing him, treading as lightly as a ghost.

Right behind him, a gun coming up—

'We're here.'

He jerked awake. 'What?'

'We're here,' a woman repeated. 'At my flat.'

The nurse from the hospital. Connie. She had offered to help him. Why? Was it a trap? Was Maxwell lurking behind her front door—

Don't be ridiculous. He had reached the hospital at random, met her by fluke. 'Oh, okay,' he said. 'Thanks.'

They got out into the rain. Reeve surveyed his surroundings. A terraced street lined with cars, few of them new. Some shops nearby, graffiti-covered shutters over the windows. Even past three in the morning, he heard music thudding from an open window.

It was alien in the details, yet familiar. He had grown up on a similar street, half the country away. The kind of place nobody *chose* to live, merely *had* to.

'Sorry I had to park a bit away from the flat,' Connie said. 'It's always hard to find a space. Can you walk?'

'Yeah, I'm fine.' In truth he wasn't, his legs bruised and his arm pulsing with leaden fire. But complaining would change nothing. He went with her down the street.

It took about five minutes. Reeve tensed as a car approached, but it cruised past without slowing. Connie brought him across a side road to an end terrace. 'This is it.'

He took in the unattractive brick house. A narrow yard separated it from the street. It was on a slope, the road beside it leading downhill. Two floors at the front, three at the back. There looked to be a garden at the rear through a tall wooden gate.

Connie went to the front door. Three wheelie bins in the little yard. When built, the house would have been home to a single family. Now, it had been chopped into separate flats. The other nearby houses were the same, or worse. No wonder parking was so hard. She unlocked the door. 'Come in.'

He followed her into a cramped hall. Narrow stairs led up and down. Junk mail sat piled on a windowsill over a small rusting radiator. A trio of electricity meters were crammed high and crooked in a corner. Skeins of wiring disappeared through ragged holes in the wall and ceiling. Whoever converted the house into flats hadn't cared about doing quality work.

Connie went past the stairs to a door. 'Here.' She ushered him through.

She had done her best to make the flat cosy. A cheerful yellow sofa was covered in plush, colourful cushions. Pictures of faraway landscapes hung on the thinly-painted walls. Italian countrysides dominated, with some more exotic vistas amongst them. A counter with a laptop on it divided off a kitchen area. Two doors presumably led to the bathroom and bedroom.

Connie took off her coat. 'Let me get you a towel,' she said. Reeve removed his wet shoes at the entrance, then peeled off his soaked hoodie. The movement tugged at his bloodied bandage. He drew in a breath. She caught it. 'You okay?'

'I think you're right about the infection.' More carefully, he worked the ruined garment clear of the wound.

'I've got some antibiotics,' she said, entering the bathroom. 'I caught a throat infection last year. Hazard of the job.' She returned with a fluffy white towel. 'I should have chucked them out, but forgot. Some nurse, hey?'

'I won't tell anyone.'

Connie gave him the towel. He quickly dried his hair and arms as she went through cupboards. She collected a large first-aid kit and assorted medical supplies. 'Sit down,' she said, indicating the sofa. He re-folded the towel to act as a damp-absorbing cushion, then sat. 'Let me see.'

A check of the bandage, with a disapproving bite of her lower lip. 'It's a mess. You *sure* you don't want to go to A&E?' He gave her a wordless stare. 'Okay, right. I'll see what I can do . . .'

She carefully used scissors to snip open the dressing. Reeve sat stoically, then looked around at the sound of a crying baby. 'Upstairs,' said Connie. 'Poor thing. Poor both of them, actually. Her mum's on her own. Well, the dad occasionally comes around, but usually to argue.'

She gently lifted the wet bandage. Reeve inhaled sharply as it came clear. Connie winced. 'Ooh, not nice. I'll clean it, but it definitely looks infected.' The wound's edges were inflamed. 'Hopefully we'll catch it before it gets too serious.'

'Yeah,' was all Reeve could manage in reply.

She donned a pair of latex gloves. He assessed her as she worked. About thirty, long dark hair with golden streaks. A hint of Mediterranean olive in her skin tone. Tiredness around her friendly brown eyes. Unsurprising, if she regularly worked nightshifts.

It took several minutes of intense pain for her to clean and sterilise the injury. Reeve regarded the wound, giving a moment of dark thanks for the discomfort. A fraction deeper, and the bullet would have blown his arm open. He wouldn't be feeling *anything* right now – because he would be dead. Either after falling from the train, or passing out . . . and bleeding out. 'Can you close it up?' he asked.

'I can,' she said, before giving him a quizzical look. 'And . . . I suspect you could too, if you weren't the one who'd been shot.'

He stayed silent, letting her draw her own conclusions. She narrowed her eyes – in amusement, not annoyance – then resumed her work. 'Afraid I don't have any anaesthetic.'

'I doubt it could hurt any worse,' he said, through his teeth.

'I wouldn't bet on it. Let me give you a painkiller.' She brought a glass of water from the kitchen, then checked the first-aid kit. 'Here. Tramadol.'

He took the little plastic bottle. 'Not exactly over-the-counter.'

A flash of guilt. 'They were going to be thrown away at work. And no, I'm not addicted to them or anything like that,' she hurriedly clarified. 'They're just a lot stronger than anything you can buy at the chemist. Be a nurse for long enough, you realise you never know when you'll need something. And I'd say this qualifies.' She gave him the water. 'Anyway, take two. They're fast-acting.'

He gulped them down, emptying the glass. 'You couldn't have given them to me *before* cleaning the wound?'

'Sorry,' she replied, with an abashed smile. 'Were you thirsty?' He nodded. She refilled the glass for him. He thankfully drained it. 'Okay. Let me put on some new gloves, and I'll get started.'

Tramadol, Reeve quickly discovered, didn't fully eliminate pain at this dosage. He barely contained a cry at one especially agonising tug of the needle. Connie cringed and apologised, but kept working. The wound gradually closed. 'There,' she said at last, relieved.

He examined it. 'Neat work.' The sutures were small and precise.

She smiled. 'I was always good at needlework as a kid. I'll get some more dressings to cover it.'

Reeve leaned back as she searched her supplies. The baby had finally returned to sleep, to his – and no doubt the mother's – relief. But he now heard other voices, from below. Both male. One aggressive and badgering, the other timid and hesitant.

Connie heard them too. 'Poor guy,' she said.

'What is it?'

'He's stuck in a bad situation.'

'Abusive relationship?'

'No, no.' She didn't want to talk about it. 'Anyway, let's

get this bandaged.' She gave him a pill. 'Antibiotics.' He took the medication as she began to cover the wound.

The job was done quickly and professionally. 'There,' she said, securing the dressing. 'All done.'

'Thanks.' The painkillers had reduced the burning in his arm to a dull throb. He started to stand. 'I'd better get moving.'

'What? Don't be ridiculous,' She put a hand on his shoulder to stop him. He was weak and tired enough that she succeeded. 'You've just undergone surgery. Look, I'll get a duvet. You can stay on the sofa.'

'Really, you don't have—'

'I insist. As your medical professional.' They shared smiles. 'Besides,' she added, 'even if you actually *are* a criminal or a murderer or something? Right now, I think I could take you.'

Reeve wasn't sure how to respond, until he realised she was joking. 'Thanks,' he said again.

'Just for tonight, though,' Connie told him as she got up. 'You'll have to leave in the morning.'

'That's fine. I . . . can't thank you enough.'

She returned with a duvet, sunflowers on its cover. 'Here.' A door banged downstairs; the louder of the two men was leaving. Brief relief on her face. 'If you need anything, just call for me,' she went on. 'Otherwise, I hope you sleep well.' She headed for the bathroom. 'I'll see you tomorrow.'

'Thank you,' he said. She smiled, then closed the door.

Reeve was asleep before she emerged. It was, again, anything but restful. The hunt continued, his pursuers drawing ever closer. One by one, every escape route was cut off. He was surrounded, helpless . . .

Exhaustion finally dissolved the dream. One last thing remained before it too faded. The same thought as before, urgent yet inexplicable.

Armed and ready . . .

CHAPTER 18

Hunger finally forced Reeve awake.

He blearily opened his eyes. Grey daylight seeped around the curtains of an unfamiliar room. No, wait. he knew where he was. Connie's home.

That he was here told him how much his judgement had been impaired. If he'd been thinking straight, he would have kept running. But pain and exhaustion had made him accept help. That decision could have got him killed . . .

Except it hadn't. If Connie meant to turn him in, he would have been caught already. He'd been lucky.

He checked his watch. To his shock, it was afternoon. He had been out for close to twelve hours. His left arm ached, but not badly. He checked the bandage. No new bloodstains.

'Hello?' he said. No answer. Connie's coat and shoes were gone.

A note on the table. He picked it up. Her handwriting was flowing and loopy, cheerful.

Alex,

You were still asleep when I had to go to work. Eat whatever you want. If you need more painkillers, they're on the counter. Same with antibiotics. (Only one every 12 hours, please.) Your hoodie is ruined, so there's an old jumper you can have. I won't be back until late, so afraid I won't see you. Good luck, and stay safe.

Connie

Reeve smiled. It was a nice way of saying *don't outstay your welcome*. He didn't intend to hang around. He had to find Maxwell.

The jumper was on the countertop. It was a neutral colour-flecked grey. The style was also neutral, slightly tending towards feminine. He tried it. On her it would have been baggy; on him, somewhat tight. But she was right; his blood-stained hoodie was fit only for the bin. Beggars couldn't be choosers.

A train's low rumble told him the flat was near a railway line. He looked for food. The fridge's contents revealed she was vegetarian. He didn't disapprove, but needed more than salad right now. The search continued. Bread, eggs, cheese, cereal. They would do. Protein so his body could repair itself, carbs and fat for energy.

He noticed as he found a frying pan that Connie's laptop had gone. Any other valuables had also disappeared. He didn't blame her. Under where the laptop had been was a newspaper; the *Guardian*.

He checked it. Was there anything about his encounter with the police? But it was a couple of days old, the main picture a young woman. He recognised her from Parker's computer at Mordencroft. Elektra Curtis, that was her name; the up-and-coming politician. The hashtag *#MakeThemPay* was emblazoned on a banner behind her. He imagined she meant the rich and taxes rather than criminals and justice.

Food was more important right now than politics. Reeve cooked a large late breakfast. Toast, a mound of scrambled eggs with cheese, grilled tomatoes. He started to eat, thinking. How would he track down Maxwell? His former mentor lived in London. So did nine million others. There was only one other fact about him that he knew for sure. Could he use that to find him? It was a long shot – but there was nothing else. So he needed information. Dates, times, addresses . . .

Noises cut through his thoughts. Heavy footsteps in the flat above, pacing back and forth. The baby was crying again. He also heard argumentative voices; a man and a woman. The former was getting increasingly aggressive, the latter defensive.

More than that. Fearful. Scared for her own safety, or her baby's. Reeve felt an involuntary anger rise. Unlike whatever went on in the flat below, this was definitely an abusive relationship. He knew the tone even without being able to discern the words. A thud as a foot came down hard, and the man shouted. Now Reeve could picture his actions. One fist clenched, the other's forefinger jabbing with each word. The chance of the jabs turning into a strike was growing. He should do something—

No. He suppressed the urge. He couldn't draw attention to himself. A deep breath, then he resumed his meal.

But he could no longer focus. The voices grew louder, as did the baby's cries. He could hear the man through the ceiling. 'This is your fucking fault. You could have had a fucking abortion! But no, you wanted to make me pay for everything.'

Reeve's hands tightened around his cutlery. He knew what was coming. But he couldn't intervene.

Shouldn't intervene. The rational part of his mind was acting purely on self-interest. But his surroundings reminded him that someone had selflessly – irrationally, perhaps – helped *him*. If Connie hadn't gone against *her* rational instincts, where would he be now? Wandering the wet streets with an infected wound, hunted by the cops . . .

'How can you even *say* that?' the woman wailed. 'You're talking about our *child*. You didn't want a baby? Maybe you shouldn't have been too cheap to buy a condom!'

A pause – then the moment Reeve had expected arrived. The floorboards creaked as the man's weight shifted—

Then the *smack* of impact. A shriek, a thump as she fell. The baby screamed—

Reeve was already moving.

Out of the flat, up the stairs to the door above. He pushed the handle. It opened. He swept through. The apartment was smaller than Connie's, furniture old and tatty. The howling baby, maybe six months old, was in a cot. A terrified young black woman had fallen beside it, a hand to her face.

Standing over her was a white man. Short dark hair, sallow skin, gold glinting around his wrist and fingers and neck. He looked around at Reeve in surprise, then anger. 'Who the fuck are you? Fuck off out, or I'll fucking make you.'

Reeve assessed him. Early twenties. About the same height. His challenger was both thinner and fatter: less muscle, more weight around the gut. He wasn't afraid of the intruder. That suggested he was used to fighting – and winning. He didn't have the build of someone who trained regularly, though. So he took on softer targets. A bully.

'Liam, no!' the woman cried.

The man ignored her. 'All fucking right,' he growled. He advanced, raising his fists. Reeve retreated. Not out of fear, but to get clear of the woman and her baby.

His opponent mistook his withdrawal for cowardice. Confidence on his face – then he lunged, arm swinging to punch him.

To Reeve, the motion was as predictable as the arc of a thrown ball. He dodged, twisting aside – and caught Liam's fist in his right hand.

The other man was startled by the interception. He tried to pull free, but Reeve kept hold. Another twist – and he jabbed him in the stomach with his right elbow. Liam barked in pain. He jerked backwards, breaking from Reeve's grip. A moment to recover, then another swing, an angry haymaker.

Reeve easily deflected it. Liam staggered as his balance shifted. Before he could recover, the heel of Reeve's open palm slammed up under his jaw.

His teeth clacked together, hard. He stumbled back. Reeve waited for his response. If he was a good or smart fighter, he would change his approach now . . .

He was neither. Liam's rat-like face flared with anger. With a roar, he dropped his head and charged.

Reeve easily swung aside. Before Liam could come about, he delivered a rapid jab to his cheek. The other man staggered – then lashed out with one leg. It caught Reeve's left shin where Connie's car had hit him. Resurgent pain knocked him back with a grunt.

Liam realised he had scored a point and kicked again. Reeve barely jumped clear. A surge of anger. Time to end this. He waited for Liam to straighten – then ploughed a punch into his stomach.

The other man saw it coming just in time to flinch back. Even so, the blow still hit. He let out a hoarse whoop of expelled air.

Reeve watched him. Would he accept he was outmatched, or—

Liam's face contorted into a furious, mindless snarl – and he charged again.

This time, Reeve didn't have enough space to dodge. A table's corner jarred his hip. He stumbled clear, but now the other man was on him—

Another haymaker. Reeve tried to duck away – but it clipped his left arm. Even though it didn't hit the wound directly, the impact was still agonising. He cried out.

Leering glee as Liam realised what had happened. Reeve knew every attack would be now aimed at his bandaged arm.

That wasn't going to happen.

Liam took another swipe. Reeve dodged it by spinning into a half-turn – and hurling himself backwards. He slammed against the other man. Right elbow hard into his sternum. He whirled back around. Liam's eyes were wide in shocked pain from a skipped heartbeat. A chop to his throat. Liam fell. Reeve stood over him, about to slam a heel into his chest—

The baby's frightened cry stopped him. The woman stared at him in fear and astonishment. Was she going to side with her ex against him, or call the police?

He stepped away. Liam, gasping, looked up at him. Reeve

gazed impassively back. *Take the hint. The fight's over. Don't make me finish it* . . .

The younger man forced himself to his knees, then stood. Reeve glanced at the door. A poisonous look, then Liam shambled towards it.

He was about to exit – then shot the woman a pointed glare.

Reeve had been going to let him leave. Now, he couldn't. He knew that look too well. *I'm coming back as soon as you're alone.*

Not this time.

Liam walked out – only for Reeve to catch him on the landing. He didn't want the woman or her baby to see. Another brutal chop to the side of Liam's neck. He staggered, momentarily stunned by the karate blow. Reeve drove another punch into his kidneys. As Liam reeled, he hauled him down the stairs. By the time he reached the bottom, the other man was recovering.

He waited for the inevitable enraged punch – then delivered a precise one of his own. His knuckles smashed into the nerve cluster under Liam's right shoulder. Liam squealed as his whole arm fell limp.

Reeve shoved him against the wall, then rapidly turned out his pockets. He let the squirming man collapse as he found his driving licence. 'Liam James Northwood,' he said, reading it. Liam looked at him through tear-filled eyes. 'I know where you live.' He tapped Liam's address on the plastic card. 'If you hurt the lady upstairs again, I *will* come and find you. And next time, I'll use both arms. You understand?'

'Yes . . .' was the weak reply.

'If you're going to be a father, be a good one.' He bent lower to look Liam in the eyes. 'Because I'll be watching.' He handed the other man's belongings back to him, then straightened. Bewildered, Liam scrambled to the front door. Reeve didn't follow. A last fearful glance, then Liam was gone.

Reeve turned at a noise. A middle-aged man peered anxiously at him from the downstairs flat. 'It's okay, there's no trouble,' Reeve told him. The ginger-haired neighbour sucked nervously on his lower lip, then retreated.

The woman, holding her baby, came on to the upper landing. 'What – what happened to Liam?' she asked in a strong south London accent.

There was a fresh bruise on her cheek. 'He won't hurt you again,' Reeve told her. 'Are you okay?'

'Yeah, yeah.' Her hand went unconsciously to the mark on her face. 'Is he . . . all right?'

'He'll recover.'

'Oh.' She sounded disappointed. Then: 'Not that I'm wishing he'd been badly hurt or anything,' she hurriedly clarified. 'I mean, he's my baby's dad. It's just, he's, well . . . '

Reeve nodded. 'I totally understand.'

'Wow.' A giggle of nervous relief. 'Thank you.'

'No problem.'

'I mean, really, thank you.' A broad grin, followed by another nervous giggle. 'Jaz. I'm Jaz. Short for Jasmine. And this is Hallie.' She nodded at the baby, who while still unhappy was no longer crying.

'Hi, Jaz. And hi, Hallie. I'm Alex.'

She smiled again, then glanced towards Connie's open door. 'Are you with Connie? She didn't say she had a boyfriend.'

'I'm not. I'm just visiting.'

'Oh, right. Right.' She nodded, a little too vigorously. 'Well, ah, I'll let you get on. Thank you again. Alex. Nice to meet you. Well, maybe not "nice"? But I'm very glad you were here. Thank you. Thanks.' She backed into her flat a little further with each word, finally waving. 'Bye.'

'Bye,' he replied. She beamed again, then closed the door.

Reeve returned to Connie's flat. He finished his breakfast and washed up, still considering his options. Finding Maxwell would be dangerous. SC9 would likely anticipate his actions. He had to outthink them—

A knock at the door.

Reeve whipped around, instantly on alert. It couldn't be Connie; she wouldn't knock. The police, making door-to-door enquiries? Unlikely: he was miles from last night's incident. Unless someone had seen Connie with him. The hospital porter – had the cops spoken to him? He stood, fight-or-flight reflexes kicking in—

'Hi?'

Jaz. He relaxed, slightly.

Still cautious, he opened the door, one foot positioned to wedge it if needed. But she was alone. No baby. 'Hi.'

'Hi. Again.' A nervous little wave. 'Er . . . can I come in?'

Reeve hesitated – it wasn't his flat – but it seemed rude to leave her standing outside. 'Okay.' Jaz entered. He stepped back, blocking access to the rest of the room.

If she was offended, it didn't show. Her broad smile

returned. 'I just wanted to say – well, thank you again. But also, *wow*.'

'I was just stopping him from hurting you,' he said, slightly awkwardly.

'No, no, I mean – it was like a martial arts movie. He hardly even touched you.'

Reeve's left arm was still sore. 'I wish that was true.'

'Nobody's ever stood up for me like that before. Never. And you don't even know me.'

'I . . . just have a thing about bad dads,' he said, discomfort increasing. He wasn't used to this level of attention, or praise.

'Me too. Except I was still stupid enough to get involved with one. I got Hallie out of it, and she's wonderful, but . . . ' Jaz glanced down, embarrassed, then gazed back up at him. 'Alex . . . can I ask you something?'

Was she coming on to him? His reply was hesitant. 'Yeah?'

Connie bustled into the hall, checking the windowsill for post before going to her door. Normally she would have spent her shift break at the hospital. Today, though, she returned home. She didn't *think* Alex Reeve would have robbed her, but had to be sure . . .

She walked in – and stopped in surprise.

Not only was he still there, but he was holding a baby.

'Okay . . .' she said. 'How long was I gone?'

CHAPTER 19

'I'm *so* sorry if this was any trouble,' said Jaz with an apologetic smile. Hallie was cradled in her arms. 'It's just – after what happened with Liam, I kind of . . . crashed? I needed to sleep, but I couldn't leave Hallie alone . . .'

'That's okay,' Connie replied. 'You had a nasty experience. Your adrenalin spiked, and then it has to go somewhere.'

The young woman nodded. 'Normally I would have forced myself to stay awake. And I would *never* normally have given my baby to someone I'd just met. But I knew that if you trusted him, I could too.'

'I guess you can.' She glanced at Reeve, who shrugged sheepishly.

'But,' Jaz went on, 'I had two hours' sleep. And I feel *so* much better for it.' She addressed Reeve. 'Hallie wasn't any trouble, was she?'

'None at all,' he said.

Connie peered at Jaz's bruised cheek. 'Are *you* okay? If you want to get the police or social services involved—'

'No, no,' Jaz quickly cut in. 'I don't want to make things worse with Liam.'

'That's what a lot of abused women say,' she said gently. 'It usually doesn't help.'

Jaz looked at Reeve. 'Alex put the fear of God into Liam. I don't think he'll try to hurt me again.'

Connie followed her gaze. 'Really?'

The remark was meant for Reeve – what had he done? – but Jaz answered it. 'Yeah. He was . . . amazing. A real hero.'

'I'm no hero,' said Reeve. He seemed uncomfortable with the praise. 'I just helped someone who needed it.'

'Isn't that what a hero does?' She beamed at him. 'Again, Alex, thank you so much.'

Connie showed her out, then closed the door. 'So,' she said, not facing Reeve. 'This was unexpected.'

'I know,' he replied. 'I'm sorry. I would have gone by now, except . . . well.'

She turned, face hard. 'What did you do? Go upstairs and beat up Jaz's ex?'

'I stopped him from hurting her, and didn't let him hurt me. Then I warned him not to do it again, or I'd find him.'

Connie frowned. 'Are you trying to show off how tough you are?' Had she misjudged him? If he was just some macho idiot—

'No, not at all.' He was taken aback by the accusation. His remark had been a statement of fact.

She saw something on his left sleeve. 'Oh – but I think he *did* hurt you.'

'What?' He looked at his arm. A small oval of blood marred the tight material. 'Damn. I hadn't even realised.'

'You didn't feel it hurting?'

'Oh, I felt it hurting. I just didn't know it was bleeding.'

'Let me look.' She ushered him to the sofa. 'Take that off.'

He struggled to remove the tight garment. 'Sorry about your jumper.'

'Never mind that.' The bandage had a larger stain. 'Let me get my stuff. I'll have to take off the dressing.'

It didn't take long for her to cut it away. 'You've torn a stitch. God, that must hurt. Have you taken any more painkillers?'

'No.'

'Really? Are you *sure* this isn't some macho thing?'

A faint laugh. 'Who would I have been trying to impress? The baby? I wanted to save the pills for if I really needed them.'

She gestured at the broken suture. 'And that doesn't count?'

'Well, in hindsight . . .'

Connie shook her head. 'God. Men. Okay, I'll fix it up *again* . . .'

The inflammation had reduced slightly. The antibiotics were working. She made him take more Tramadol, then snipped out the broken suture. Once done, she cleaned the injury, then re-stitched it. 'Some medical advice? After having stitches, avoid getting into fights.'

A very faint smile. 'I'll try to remember that.'

'I'm not sure what I can't believe most,' she said, sighing. 'That you *did* get into a fight with this wound – or that you won.'

'I've had training. He hadn't. But he won't give her any more trouble.'

From past experience with victims, she was unconvinced. But he wasn't evincing any doubt. 'Would you really go and find him if he did?'

'I don't think I'll need to.'

She eyed him. 'That's not what I asked.'

Reeve grimaced as the suture pulled tight. 'I don't like bad fathers. Or abusive partners. He was both.'

There was hurt in his tone beyond physical pain. 'Does that come from personal experience?'

No answer. Realising none would be forthcoming, she continued her work. Before long, the injury was bandaged once more. 'There,' she said. 'How does it feel?'

Reeve carefully moved his arm. Even with the painkiller, he let out a grunt. 'Not great.'

'I'm not surprised.' She cleared up her supplies, then sat beside him. 'I know you want to get moving, but I *really* think you should stay here. At least until tomorrow. Otherwise your body won't have any chance to recover. You need rest.'

'I can't argue with you,' he said wearily.

She smiled. 'The antibiotics seem to be working, so keep taking them. The painkillers in a few hours, as well. Now, I need to get back to work. Please, still be here when I get home?'

'Don't worry, I'm not going anywhere.' He settled back on the sofa.

'Okay. I'll see you later. I should be back around midnight – shorter shift.' She waved, then departed, leaving the exhausted Reeve alone.

*

'Welcome to our temporary home,' said Tony Maxwell. The house was a modest brick terrace in a quiet part of north London.

Harrison Locke gave their surroundings a supercilious look. 'Hardly the pinnacle of desirability. Who owns it?'

Maxwell unlocked the door. 'MI5. One of their safehouses. The boss procured it for us. We need a base to track down Alex, so this is it.'

The group filed in, dispersing to lay claim to sleeping areas. Mark Stone opened a connecting door into Deirdre Flynn's room. 'We're neighbours,' he said with a lecherous smirk. 'That why you picked this room?'

'It'll be locked tight, don't you worry,' she replied.

The smile became nastier. 'Good. Wouldn't want to walk in on you frigging yourself.' He darted his tongue from his mouth with a *slop*, then slammed the door. Flynn made a disgusted sound.

'Mark? Enough of that,' snapped Maxwell from the landing. 'We'll use the dining room as an op centre. I want everyone down there in five for an update.'

'We've got intel on Reeve?' John Blake asked, emerging from another bedroom.

'I'll tell you downstairs.'

Everyone was assembled well before the five minutes were up. Maxwell tacked a large map of London to one wall. 'Okay. I thought Alex would head for London, and I was right. A truck arrived from Glasgow at a depot in Wandsworth early this morning.' He put a marker on the map. 'A man whose general description matched Alex's got out of the trailer. He had a fight with the truckers; put one in hospital. Not long after, two police officers were also taken down.'

'Lethally?' asked Stone.

'No. He sprayed them with their own CS.'

The ex-cop was affronted. 'Bastard.'

'Their description was more clear. It was almost certainly Alex. He had a wounded left arm. A fair bit of blood on his sleeve, apparently.'

'I *knew* I got him,' Flynn said.

'So where did he go from there?' wondered Blake, gazing at the map.

'No idea,' said Maxwell. 'If he'd been admitted to any hospital in Greater London, I would have been informed. He hasn't been arrested either.'

'Maybe we got lucky and he's died,' Craig Parker suggested.

'Already checked; no bodies found either. So our job is still the same: find him, and eliminate him. Ideas?'

Various options were mooted, none met – or even proposed – with particular optimism. 'He definitely has no personal contacts here?' asked Locke.

'None we're aware of,' Maxwell replied. 'The boss had Five and GCHQ check back through all his old logs. Phone and internet, bank records, whatever they had. Which I assume was a lot, since they never *really* delete anything. Whatever the law says. But they didn't find anyone of consequence connected to him in London.'

'Then he may indeed be coming after you.'

'It's a strong possibility. Which gives us three days before he'll have the opportunity.'

'I'm not going to sit around on my arse waiting for him to pop up,' said Stone.

Maxwell raised an eyebrow. 'You've got another idea?'

'Yeah. If I call my old mates in the Met—'

'You know you can't do that,' snapped Blake.

Locke's response dripped with acidic sarcasm. 'It does rather defeat the point of adopting a brand-new identity.'

'They don't know I'm someone else now, do they?' Stone shot back. 'Far as they know, I just got a new job.'

'I doubt that's the official story,' said Locke. 'It certainly wasn't for me.'

Maxwell nodded. 'Officially, we all left service under a cloud. That way, the country's protected if anyone connects you to your past. You can be written off as "disgruntled", "embittered", or whatever.'

'Yeah, I know that,' Stone complained, scowling. 'But I haven't been caught by the fucking FSB or FBI. I'm just calling in a favour. And it might get us something that official reports don't.'

'If you say the wrong thing, you could expose SC9,' protested Flynn. 'And there's a good chance of that, 'cause you're a fucking gobshite.'

Maxwell waved her to silence. 'No, Mark might have a point.'

'Reeve's more likely to expose SC9 than Stone,' Parker noted. 'What if he goes to the media with his story?'

'Another very good point.' Maxwell didn't like Stone's proposal, but Parker was right. If Reeve went public in a bid to get protection . . . 'Okay, Mark, do it. But . . . be subtle.' He tossed Stone his phone.

The big man caught it, smiling smugly. 'You know me, guv.' He dialled a number from memory. 'Richy!' he cried when someone answered. 'It's me, Caggy! Nigel Cagg. How're you doing, mate? Long time-o, no speak-o.'

'Jesus Christ,' Flynn muttered. 'I preferred him as a miserable arsehole.'

Stone finally got down to business. 'Yeah, I'm in private security now. Trying to track someone down. Nasty little fucker. Can you do me a favour and keep an ear out? Yeah?' He gave his observers a triumphant smile. 'Fuckin' fantastic, mate. You got a pen handy? Okay, his name's Alex Reeve.' He gave a description. 'Now, he's had a gunshot wound to the left arm. No, I didn't shoot him,' he added with a laugh. 'If I had, he wouldn't still be fucking running around. Thing is, he's not going to check into any hospital. He knows the police'd get involved. So I'm thinking he'll go underground. He'll need a pro who can patch him up. Now, people like that aren't exactly ten a penny. I'm sure you know some prospects. If you can put the word around, see if anyone's helped Reeve out? Nice one. I'm getting a new phone, so I'll text you the number soon as I can. I owe you, mate. Yeah, we'll have to catch up.' He disconnected. 'See? A word with the right people does wonders.'

'Just don't make a habit of it,' Maxwell cautioned.

'And nice work telling us all your real name,' added Flynn. '*Nigel*.'

'The replacement is a considerable improvement,' said Locke. Stone irritably mouthed *fuck off* at them.

Maxwell returned to the map. 'That's one avenue of

investigation, then. But we can't rely on it. We've got to keep looking ourselves.'

'You think we'll find him?' asked Parker.

Maxwell fixed him with a gaze of steel. 'We're SC9. We'll find him.'

CHAPTER 20

Reeve kept his word, resting in Connie's flat for the remainder of the day. Eventually he fell asleep. She returned after midnight; he snapped awake. A moment of alarm, then he relaxed. He returned to sleep within minutes.

He woke the following morning to find her already in the kitchen. 'Morning,' she said brightly.

After ten, according to his watch. Mild annoyance at himself. Even if he was recovering from an injury, he still felt himself to be slacking. 'Morning,' he replied, standing and stretching. His arm felt better than the previous day. It was still far from healed, though.

'I got you some clothes,' she said, gesturing at a bag. 'No Armani, just Primark, I'm afraid. But that jumper didn't suit you. Even without the bloodstain.'

'Thanks,' he said, surprised. A quick look revealed cheap but serviceable outfits. 'For everything. I'll leave today.'

She shook her head. 'You're still not recovered. Look, stay until I'm sure the infection's cleared up, okay? Please? At least that way I won't worry about you keeling over.'

'Okay,' he said, with reluctance. 'I'll get changed, then.' He picked up the bag. 'Oh, and . . . is it okay if I have a shower?'

'Of course it's okay. Try not to get the bandage wet.'

'I'll do my best.' He went to the bathroom.

He cleaned himself with military quickness, careful to keep the bandage dry. Once finished, he donned the new clothes. They fitted well enough, even if he would get no points for style. Still, that had never been a concern of his. He bundled his old clothes and emerged. Connie was near the front door, putting money on a small shelf.

'The rent,' she explained. 'I don't like the guy who collects it. I make sure the money's right here when he arrives. The faster I can get rid of him, the better.'

'He's trouble?'

'Just a creep.' She looked him up and down. 'Well, everything fits. That's a relief. I had to guess your sizes.'

'Thanks,' Reeve said again. He went to put his dirty clothes in the kitchen bin.

Someone knocked at the door. Connie opened it just wide enough to look through. The sudden tension in her shoulders told Reeve the caller was who she had expected. 'Oh. Hi.'

'Hi, Connie,' came the reply. 'I've come for the rent.' Male voice, London accent. Reeve could tell from his tone the man was giving Connie a lascivious smile.

He could also tell she wasn't returning it. 'Yeah, here,' she said, collecting the money. 'And I'd like a receipt as usual, please.'

'Sure, sure.' A hand came through the gap to take the money. Reeve frowned as the fingers deliberately closed on Connie's. 'Let me get my book. Oh,' the unseen smirk widened, 'I forgot my pen. You got one?'

Connie looked back at Reeve in exasperation. 'Yes. Wait there.'

She went to a chest of drawers. The door swung wider as the man nudged it with his foot. He leered at Connie's backside as she bent forward.

Reeve stepped into his sightline. 'Morning,' he said. He took in the rent collector. Caucasian, mid-twenties, black hair, shaved sides below a longer styled sweep. Carefully trimmed beard. Heavy eyelids gave him a look of lazy arrogance. Expensive watch. He fancied himself – both as a womaniser and a tough guy. Reeve knew the type. He already disliked him.

The man reacted with surprise, then annoyance, that she wasn't alone. 'Huh. Got company?'

'Yes,' Connie replied pointedly.

'Better not be having any wild parties. It'd violate the lease.' A mocking smile as she returned with a pen.

'Highly unlikely,' she told him.

'Maybe you should come to my place. I have 'em all the time.' She held out the pen at arm's length. He stepped closer to take it.

'No, thanks. I work nights.'

'I'm flexible.' Another leering smile. She remained stone-faced. He scribbled in a notebook. 'There's your receipt.'

'Thanks. My pen?' He returned it. 'Bye.'

His lips curled, but the smile lacked any humour. 'See you next Thursday.' Connie closed the door on him. She didn't seem to realise he had just insulted her. *See* – C. *You* – U. *Next* – N. *Thursday* – T. Reeve decided she would be happier not knowing.

She returned the pen to the drawer. 'Ugh,' she said, shuddering. 'Horrible guy.'

Reeve glanced towards the door. Footsteps outside; he was going to the flat below. 'He like that all the time?'

'Worse, usually. You put him off. His name's Jammer. Well, that's what he calls himself. Don't know his real name, and don't want to either. It's why I started demanding receipts. He's tried to sleaze sex out of me in exchange for rent. I'm certain he's tried it with Jaz as well.'

'You should complain to the landlord.'

A resigned shrug. 'I *have* done. The house is owned by some company. They don't care – even though I'm sure he's also dealing drugs here.'

Reeve's dislike of Jammer grew still further. 'How?'

'The flat downstairs. A man called Mr Brownlow lives there.'

'I saw him yesterday.'

'Poor guy. He seems like a nice, harmless man – who's been forced into some bad things. He's been "cuckooed" – his flat's being used by drug dealers to do their business.' Reeve knew what 'cuckooing' was, but let her continue. 'People come and go all the time, but Jammer's a regular. I think he's forcing Mr Brownlow to do it. He's probably too scared to ask for help.'

'If he won't report him, maybe someone else should.'

'Like me? Believe me, I would *love* to see that horrible creep be arrested. But,' resignation entered her voice, 'I work at a hospital. I've seen too many people who tried to stand up to the local dealers. They end up being stabbed – or worse. And Jammer,' she said with a sigh, 'knows exactly where I live.

'Scum,' said Reeve, with a vehemence that surprised her. 'I really hate dealers.'

'That . . . sounds personal.'

'I grew up somewhere with lots of drugs going around.'

Before she could respond, they heard a crash from below. The sound was followed by a plaintive cry. A man – Brownlow, Reeve assumed – protested fearfully. Someone else laughed mockingly. He recognised the voice: Jammer. More from the younger man he couldn't make out – then crockery smashed. Brownlow cried out again in dismay. Whatever had just broken had more meaning than mere plates and bowls.

'This needs to stop.' Reeve strode towards the door.

'Wait, wait,' Connie said, following. 'You got into one fight yesterday, and now you want *another*?'

'I just want to talk to him. If he knows there's a witness, he'll leave Mr Brownlow alone.'

The lower flat's door was ajar. The voices became clearer as he descended the stairs. 'I really don't give a fuck,' said Jammer, condescendingly. 'My customers are more important to me than you. You don't get to choose when they call, okay?'

'But – it was the middle of the night,' Brownlow objected. He sounded on the verge of tears. 'We had an agreement. You can't—'

Something else burst apart on the floor. 'You do what I fucking tell you!' growled Jammer. '*That's* the agreement.'

Reeve pushed the door wider. 'Do you need any help, Mr Brownlow?'

The two men inside turned in surprise. Brownlow was afraid of the newcomer – or possibly *for* him, glancing in fear at Jammer. Jammer himself, though, immediately became aggressive. 'No, he doesn't. This is private property. So if you don't mind – fuck off.'

Reeve looked past Jammer. A portable television lay broken near a door to the rear garden. Closer by were the smashed remains of crockery. The pieces of a large plate appeared to form a picture; crude, colourful, childlike. He guessed that was what Brownlow was upset about – something personal.

He locked his eyes upon Jammer, hiding his loathing. The dealer was just like any other, callously destroying things precious to others for greed. 'I don't want trouble,' he said, tone calm. 'I just don't want anyone to get hurt.'

One of Jammer's hands clenched tighter. There was something in it. A key, Reeve realised, the blade jutting out between his first and second fingers. An improvised knife. It could slash his face, even blind him.

Jammer's intentions were clear. He masked his own, waiting to see how the situation developed.

Connie came down the stairs behind him. 'Yes, yeah,' she added on seeing the tableau. 'We just want to make sure everyone's okay.'

'Everything's fine,' Jammer scoffed. He started towards Reeve. 'Just a disagreement with a tenant. There won't be any problems. Will there, Mr Brownlow?'

The older man retreated towards the garden door, cowering. 'No, no.'

'Good.' Jammer was almost within arm's reach of Reeve. 'See? So now you can just—'

The metal spike in his clenched fist lanced at Reeve's face.

CHAPTER 21

Reeve was ready for it.

He swept sideways and whipped up his right arm to deflect the blow. Forearm under Jammer's elbow, he clamped his hand around his wrist. Lean forward, rotate arm – and his opponent howled as his elbow bent the wrong way.

He kept hold, twisting to force Jammer to the floor. The other man lashed out with his free hand. Reeve instinctively blocked it with his left arm. His wounded biceps burned as if he had been branded. A flare of anger, and he sent his fist at Jammer's face—

He arrested the blow just before impact, remembering his words to Connie. Instead he opened his hand. A loud *clap* echoed through the room as he slapped Jammer's cheek. The younger man flinched at the stinging pain. Reeve held him down. Jammer's eyes widened in fury at the humiliating strike.

The entire exchange took barely two seconds. Connie stared in shock.

'I think you should leave,' Reeve told Jammer. 'Like I said, I don't want anyone to get hurt.'

'Fuck you!' Jammer roared. 'I'll fucking kill you!' He tried to move, but was still pinned.

Reeve slapped him again, then emptied the downed man's pockets. A top-end smartphone in a waterproof case. Keyring, the electronic key fob for a Mercedes attached. Another set of car keys, unmarked. A roll of twenty-pound notes—

Wallet. He quickly searched it. More money, several hundred pounds in mixed denominations. Credit cards in the name *Jahmir Haxhi*. That explained where 'Jammer' came from. The surname; Albanian?

Driving licence. A beardless, monochrome Jahmir Haxhi stared insouciantly from it. Reeve memorised the address. *This is becoming a habit*. He stood. 'Jahmir Huxhi?' The dealer glared up at him. 'I know where you live – so I know how to find you.' He dropped the licence on his chest and withdrew. 'Get a new job. Something honest. I'm giving you a chance to walk away, so don't come back.'

Jammer was about to snarl a reply, but thought better of it. Warily watching Reeve, he struggled upright. He put a hand to his reddened cheek. 'You fucking piece of shit. I'll—'

Reeve stepped closer. Jammer flinched away. 'Leave. Now.'

The dealer retrieved his things, then went to the rear door. He gave Brownlow a poisonous look as he passed, then back at Reeve. 'You're a fucking dead man,' he growled. Reeve took another step. Jammer hurried out into the garden.

Reeve went to the door to make sure he had gone, then turned. Brownlow regarded him owlishly. 'Are you okay?' Reeve asked.

'Uh – yes, I'm fine.' Reeve got his first proper look at Connie's downstairs neighbour. In his forties, he guessed, but stress had aged his face. The meek, hangdog appearance of someone dealt a bad hand by life.

'Are you sure?' Connie asked.

'Yes, yes,' said Brownlow. 'Thank you. Thank you both.'

She regarded the debris. 'Oh, my gosh. Let me help you clean this up.'

Reeve joined in, picking up the television. 'Afraid this is broken.'

'I . . . didn't watch it much anyway,' Brownlow replied, with a resigned sigh. He crouched to assist Connie, looking sadly at the broken crockery. The picture on the jagged jigsaw was a house, childish stick figures outside.

'Was it something special?' she asked quietly.

'My son made it.' A glance at several framed pictures on one wall. A happier Brownlow with a boy, growing from a baby to about ten. They were well travelled; backgrounds included Paris, San Francisco and snowy mountains. Another sigh, then he started to collect the pieces. Connie and Reeve helped.

'I didn't know you had a son,' she said.

'He stayed with my wife – my ex-wife.'

'I'm sorry.'

He gave them a glum look – then turned at a knock. Jaz, carrying her baby, was at the door. 'Is everyone okay?'

'We're all fine,' Connie assured her.

'I heard all the noise.' She took in the room. 'Oh, my God. What a mess.'

'Not as big a mess as Jammer,' said Brownlow. There was a hint of glee behind his gloom. He turned back to Reeve. 'You – you really sorted him out. Thanks. Thank you so much. By the way, I'm Philip. Philip Brownlow.'

'Alex Reeve.' They shook hands.

'We'll help you tidy up,' said Connie.

Between them, the task did not take long. 'Why did Jammer smash your place up?' Jaz asked.

Brownlow drew in a deep, unhappy breath. 'I didn't want to be his mug any more.'

'How do you mean?'

'After the divorce, I had to find a new place to live. This was all I could manage. And then,' another sigh, 'I lost my job. No job, no rent money. I didn't know what to do. But then Jammer told me he had a deal with the previous tenant. I could continue it.'

'Dealing drugs,' Reeve said, not hiding his disapproval.

'I was desperate,' Brownlow protested miserably. 'He said he'd help with the rent in return for using the flat. It was only meant to be an occasional thing. Once a week, maybe – he'd come in, meet someone, do the deal, then go. I just got out of the way. He could do it in private, and the police couldn't come in without a warrant.'

Reeve's expression was cold. 'I know how they work.'

'But then,' Brownlow continued, agitated, 'he started coming around more and more. Sometimes two or three times a day. And the people meeting him . . . They weren't just users any more. They were other dealers, scary people.'

'Sounds like Jammer was going up the ranks,' said Connie.

'I know. The deals were getting bigger. And they were being done in my home!' he cried. 'I – I wanted to stop it, I really did. But Jammer wouldn't let me. I tried to stand up to him today, but . . .' A tear rolled down his cheek.

'I don't think he'll be coming back,' Connie offered in sympathy.

'I hope not. God, I hope not.'

'Does he keep any of the drugs here?' Reeve asked.

'Not usually. There's nothing here now.'

He thought back to the contents of Jammer's pockets. Two sets of car keys. Maybe the second car was parked nearby and used as a drop-off. Jammer would collect the drugs from it before coming to Brownlow's flat for the sale. He would only have the merchandise on him for a brief time. 'Then there's nothing for him to come back for,' he said. 'Hopefully he'll leave you alone.'

'We'll watch out for you,' Connie assured Brownlow. 'If you need any help, just ask.'

He managed a feeble smile. 'Thank you.'

The flat tidied, the visitors left. Reeve and Connie returned to her flat. 'Okay,' she said, after closing the door, 'I saw you fighting Jammer.'

'I didn't want to,' Reeve replied defensively, expecting criticism. 'I gave him every chance to walk away.'

'I know. You got rid of him without hurting him. What I meant was . . . I've never seen anything like that before. You were . . .' She was briefly lost for words. '*Fast*. Are you in the SAS, or something?' There was a cat-like intrigue in her eyes.

'Something,' he admitted, sitting. 'I used to be, anyway.'

Connie sat beside him. 'You left?'

'Yeah.' He knew he shouldn't tell her anything more. But he felt obliged to give her *some* details. 'I was in the Special Reconnaissance Regiment. It's the army's undercover special forces unit,' he added, seeing she'd never heard of it.

'Undercover? What, like the police?'

'Kind of. It's a cross between being a soldier, a detective and a spy.'

'Was it dangerous?'

'You're gathering intel on Britain's enemies. People who'd kill you in a second if they knew who you really were.'

'I thought that was the job of whoever James Bond works for?'

'SIS? MI6, I mean – that's what most people call them. They do, but the army doesn't want to depend on someone else's intel. Sometimes, you want your own men – or women – on the ground. That was what I did.'

Connie nodded. 'How did you get into it?'

'I joined the army straight out of school,' he said. 'To get away from where I was, more than anything. My childhood wasn't great.' A brief, unwelcome memory: cold, grey moorland, a dark ditch before him . . . 'Turned out I was good at being a soldier. And I wanted to be the *best* at it. So I worked, and worked, until one day my CO called me in. He told me the SRR was looking for volunteers.'

'So that's how you joined,' she said. 'And you liked it?'

'Yeah.'

'Then why did you leave?'

He should have expected the question. 'There was, ah, another opportunity.'

Connie immediately recognised that he was prevaricating. 'Something to do with the people who shot you?'

Reeve realised he had made a mistake. Now, Connie wouldn't be satisfied until he told her more . . .

She would have to stay unsatisfied. 'I'm sorry. I can't say anything else.'

Surprise on her face, then almost offended disbelief. 'What? Oh, come on! Don't you trust me?'

'It's not about trusting you,' he protested. 'It's about protecting you. And the country. What I was doing is classified. I already said more than I should have.'

'Whoever they are, they tried to kill you.' She pointed at his bandaged arm. 'I don't think you owe them your loyalty any more.'

'That's for me to decide.' He said it more sharply than he'd intended. Connie drew back, hurt. 'Look,' he went on, trying to mollify her. 'I can tell you this much. I came here to find out *why* they tried to kill me. The only person who can tell me is my main instructor. He lives in London.'

A small, teasing smile. 'That doesn't really narrow it down.'

'I wasn't planning to go door-to-door. I don't know whereabouts he lives. But the one thing I *do* know is . . . that he's an absolutely insane Fulham fan.'

'The football team?'

'He never misses a game if he can help it. So the next time Fulham play at home, I'll be looking for him.'

Connie was sceptical. 'And what if you can't find him?'

'I *have* to find him. If I can't, then . . . all I can do is run. Until they find me. And they're *trained* to find me.'

'And kill you,' she said quietly.

A grim nod. 'Yeah.'

They sat in silence. Connie broke it. 'So . . . what can I do to help?'

'You've already helped me more than I would ever have asked,' Reeve replied.

She blushed. 'Helping people is what I do. But I think you

need more than bandages and painkillers now.'

'Afraid so.' He sat upright. 'The main thing I need is information. I have to reconnoitre the area around the football ground. All the ways in, all the ways out.'

'For him, or you?'

'Both. And,' he added with faint humour, 'the next home match's date would probably help.'

'Easy enough to find out.' She got her laptop and ran a search. 'You're in luck – it's this Saturday. Kick-off's at three o'clock.'

He pursed his lips. 'That might not be so lucky. It only gives me tomorrow and Saturday morning to check the place out.'

Connie started to speak, hesitated, then continued. 'I can help you. I've got Friday off.'

'Thanks, but it'd be better if you didn't.'

'Why?'

'They might expect me to go there to look for Tony.'

'Tony?'

'My instructor.'

'Oh, it's good that you're on first-name terms with the man trying to kill you.'

That brought a genuine laugh from him. 'But if they're there,' he went on, 'it won't be safe for you. I've got to do this on my own.'

She was not convinced. 'Can I just say two things?'

Reeve smiled again. 'It's your flat. I can't stop you.'

'Okay, first thing is: I've lived in London all my life. I know pretty much everywhere. You don't. You've got a little bit of a northern accent, so . . . Liverpool?'

'Manchester,' he corrected.

'But not London.'

He shook his head. 'I've spent maybe two weeks total here in my whole life.'

'So I can help you find your way around. Second thing: they're looking for you, yes? *Just* you?'

'That's right,' Reeve said, unsure where she was leading.

'But not a couple.'

'No, they—' *Now* he realised. 'No, it's too dangerous. If they recognise me—'

'Then,' Connie cut in, 'we'll have to make sure they *don't* recognise you.'

CHAPTER 22

'So,' Connie asked, 'do you like the new outfit?'

'It's not what I would have picked,' Reeve replied.

That morning, Connie had made another shopping trip. Reeve now wore a baseball hat, an oversized coat and ripped jeans. If he'd been ten years younger, he might have considered his outfit trendy. Now, it felt faintly ridiculous.

She smiled from under her umbrella. 'I bet. But to be honest, you almost didn't need my help. I can't believe how different you look.'

Even without new clothing, Reeve's appearance had changed. He had exaggerated his three-day stubble using items from her makeup. At a casual glance, it now looked like two weeks' growth. More makeup had added fake light and shade to his nose. The effect was to reshape it, appearing thinner and shorter. Again, at close range the trick was obvious. But he hoped nobody would *get* that close.

'Disguise techniques,' he said. 'Something they taught us. A bit more kit, and I could probably pass myself off as Mr Brownlow. Or Jammer.'

'But not Jaz?' Connie asked with a grin.

'That'd be a stretch, yeah.'

They made their way towards the Thames through streets

of red-brick terraced houses. Floodlights rose ahead. 'That's it,' said Connie. 'Craven Cottage.'

'You've been here before?'

'I went to a match with an ex-boyfriend once. Not my cup of tea. But I know the area.'

Reeve slowed as they neared the street's end. The football ground stood beyond it. More red-brick buildings, *The Fulham Football Club* painted on one. He lowered his head, shoulders slumping. The shift effectively shaved two inches from his height. 'What're you doing?' Connie asked.

'Blocking facial recognition on the CCTV cameras,' he said, adjusting the hat. 'They might be running gait recognition as well.'

'*Gait* recognition? What, they know how you walk?'

'London has the highest concentration of CCTV in the West. The intelligence services have real-time access to most public cameras. They can run facial and gait recognition on them.'

'You sound like you know what you're talking about.'

'I do.' A quick smile of reassurance. 'Okay, this is it.'

They turned on to Stevenage Road. Craven Cottage was across the street. It backed on to the Thames, Reeve knew from his online research. There were no rear entrances; all visitors had to come along the same road. 'Away supporters go in at this end,' he said, indicating the nearby turnstile gates. 'Problem is, home fans can use either end. I don't know where Tony will be. I'll need to cover them both.'

'How will you do that?'

'I don't know, yet. But running back and forth between each end might be a bit conspicuous.' He had already spotted a tall pole supporting several CCTV cameras. There would be others.

There was also the human element to consider. He paused, pretending to adjust a sock as he surveyed the street. Several people were walking along it. Some would be tourists. Anyone following the Thames Path had to come inland to go around Craven Cottage. But that would also be good cover for his former colleagues . . .

Unless they had really gone to town with their disguises, though, none were here. He turned his attention to the road. The parking bays required either a resident's permit or payment. Only a few vehicles were in them. Surveillance teams would use common, inconspicuous cars and vans.

No vans. That made spotting any observers a little easier. 'Stay close to me,' he said, setting off again. To Connie's surprise, he put his arm around her. 'Pretend we're talking about something really fun.'

'What could be more fun than seeing if anyone's waiting to kill you?' she said. He grinned.

Connie joined in with the ruse, holding him. She began an enthusiastic, if one-sided, discussion of some reality TV show. Reeve pretended to respond, checking each vehicle they approached. All were empty – so far.

They neared the ground's north end. A path beyond it led to the Thames. A car was parked opposite, facing away from them. A Ford Focus, silver, less than two years old. The kind of vehicle filling the car pools of the intelligence services. Its weight distribution was off, the driver's side canted downwards. Someone was inside.

They drew closer. Reeve saw a figure in the driver's seat.

But the wing mirrors had now drawn his attention. They were out of alignment. Not by much, but enough to raise his suspicions. The driver had given himself a wide view of both sides of the street behind.

Exactly as Reeve would have done on a surveillance mission.

'So, yeah,' he suddenly said, again surprising Connie. 'I couldn't believe he did that!' His accent had completely changed, becoming pure Estuary. 'I mean, fackin' 'ell. What was he doin'?'

She played along, responding as they reached the car. Reeve kept his head moving to deny the man inside a clear view. He got a good look at the face in the mirror, though.

John Blake.

A sudden chill. Fear. His hunters had found him—

Reason overcame instinct. If they knew he was here, there would be more than one Operative. And Blake wouldn't have an expression of utter boredom. SC9 only *suspected*, not expected, that he might come.

They passed the door. Reeve gesticulated as he spoke – his hand just happening to obscure his face from Blake. 'Carry on like that in public, you'll get fackin' nicked, woncha? He can't take his booze, never could. Fackin' idiot.'

Then they were past. Still blathering, Reeve tensed, listening. If the door opened, or the window came down—

Neither happened. Blake hadn't recognised him.

He felt Connie shift. 'Don't look back,' he whispered, London accent vanishing. 'Keep going.'

She resisted the urge to turn her head. 'Was he one of them?'

'Yeah.'

'Do you think he saw you?' Worry in her voice. The danger of the situation had hit home.

'If he had, I'd be dead. He would have shot me in the back.'

'What, in broad daylight?'

'Yes.'

'But there are cameras everywhere.'

'Any footage of him would be scrubbed within the hour. The car would be crushed. Any witnesses would have their statements taken, then "accidentally" lost. News coverage would either be suppressed or claim the shooting was drug-related.'

Connie looked at him, eyes wide. 'Only the government could do all that.' He didn't reply, letting her draw her own conclusions. 'You're a spy or something?'

'Something,' was all he would give her. None of the other cars ahead were occupied. His tension eased, slightly, but he was anything but relaxed. As long as Blake was behind him, he was still in danger. 'Okay, when we get to the next junction, go right.'

They soon reached it. Reeve risked a brief glance back as he rounded the corner. Blake had not left the car. An involuntary exhalation. Connie caught it. 'Are we clear?' she asked.

'Yes.'

'Oh, my God.' Her own relieved breath was much louder. 'Well, now what are you going to do? You can't come to the match tomorrow – they'll be watching for you.'

'They didn't see me today. I can do it again.'

'What if there are twenty of them looking?'

'There won't be. I know who they all are.' Reeve knew that was not strictly true. He knew everyone he had *trained* with. If Maxwell called in other Operatives he had never met . . .

He pushed the thought aside. He *had* to get to Maxwell. It was the only way to discover the truth.

'I've recce'd the football ground,' he continued. 'Next thing I need to do is check all the nearby Tube stations. Do you want to come with me?'

'There's nothing more exciting than looking at Tube stations.' The sarcasm was cover for Connie's concern. 'But . . . yes. I'll come with you.'

He nodded, appreciative. 'Thanks.'

'I'll have to,' she went on with a smile. 'You don't have a card, or any money. You need me to buy your ticket.'

'Something else I'll have to owe you,' he said ruefully. 'I don't know how I'm going to pay you back.'

'I'll think of something.' She grinned, then took his hand, resuming their cover. Reeve was surprised, but said nothing.

'He's not coming,' Blake told Maxwell. His boredom and exasperation were clear even over the phone. 'This is a waste of time.'

'Humour me,' Maxwell replied. His own tone made it plainly an order. 'Craig will take over at three.'

Parker looked up from his laptop. 'I really need to keep working on this research.'

Maxwell frowned. 'Okay, Harrison will take over instead.' He ended the call.

It was Locke's turn to object. 'I shouldn't need to remind you, but I can't drive.' He indicated his left arm, still in a sling.

'Craig will drive you there.'

'Ah, so I stand in the rain for six hours. Marvellous.'

'Craig takes you, then John drives him back in his car. Jesus *Christ*.' The testy exclamation was not loud, but may as well have been shouted. Silence followed, Locke staring unreadably at him. 'Sorry,' Maxwell said at last. 'Cabin fever.' The apology didn't change Locke's expression.

'Maybe he isn't looking for you after all,' Flynn suggested.

'Like I told John, humour me,' Maxwell replied. 'I just have a feeling he'll show tomorrow. If he doesn't, then I'm wrong and we need another plan. I'm open to suggestions.' He indicated the map. No new markers had been added. No proposals came either.

Stone came into the room. 'Just got off the phone with my mate,' he announced. 'He's asked around on the scumbag grapevine. Nobody's seen Reeve or treated him for a gunshot wound.'

Maxwell nodded. 'I widened the search net for hospitals. No one matching his description has been treated in the whole country. He hasn't been picked up by any police force either.'

'So where is he?' asked Flynn.

'He could have found someone with medical expertise to help him off-book,' Locke mused.

'Or he could be dead,' chirped Parker.

'Can but hope,' said Stone, 'but the fucker won't make our lives that easy. Although . . . ' His expression suddenly changed as an idea came. 'Hold on a minute.'

165

He made another call. 'Richy, it's me again. I just thought of something. No, it didn't hurt, you cheeky cunt. Listen: the guy I'm after, he's a proper hard-case. Ask around and see if anyone's been beaten up by a professional. He did over two of our boys and a truck driver in Wandsworth early Wednesday. He might have done the same to someone else. Yeah, check hospitals too. Thanks a lot, mate.'

Maxwell gave him an approving nod. 'Good call.'

'If Reeve's gone underground, he might have trouble with the shit you find down there. He'll need stuff, and since he won't have money, he'll have to take it.'

'Eloquently put, as always,' said Locke.

'But true,' Maxwell added. 'All right, we'll see what comes of it. In the meantime, we keep up the search.'

CHAPTER 23

'A tour of District Line Tube stations,' said Connie, as they entered the flat. 'You know how to show a girl a good time.'

Reeve smiled. 'Thanks for helping me.'

'You think it'll be useful?'

'All intel is useful.'

'There's the spy talk again. But you still won't tell me anything about what you do?'

'It's safer that way.'

She filled the kettle. 'You know, there have been chancers who've pretended to be secret agents to con women . . .'

'They don't generally shoot themselves to look convincing,' Reeve pointed out.

'There is that. How *is* the arm, by the way?'

'Better.' The pain in his torn biceps had diminished. Making more than the easiest movement still hurt, but he *could* use his arm. He slowly extended it. 'You've done a good job fixing it.'

'Thanks. Coffee?'

'Yes, please.' Still testing his arm, he examined a landscape in detail for the first time. He had assumed it was a painting, but it was actually a photograph. His mistake had been because it looked almost too beautiful to be real. 'Is this Italy?'

'Hmm? Oh, yes,' Connie said. 'Tuscany. My mum was from there.'

'You're Italian?'

'Half Italian. My dad's from Bermondsey. Not quite as exotic.'

'Do you speak Italian?'

'*Un po,*' she said with a giggle. 'A bit. I should practise more.'

He took in the other pictures. 'Are these places you've been?'

'Oh, I wish. I'd *love* to go and live in Italy. Technically I could. I'm entitled to an Italian passport because of my mum. I just never applied because of the expense – and the hassle. I've heard Italian bureaucracy can be . . . slow.'

Reeve gave her a knowing smile. 'You can get a passport overnight if you know who to ask. And have the money.'

'Ah, money,' she sighed. 'Where would I be without it? Oh, right here.' She waved a hand across her flat.

'It could be worse.'

'Well, yes. I could be sharing with sixteen other people. But over half my wage goes on rent. And for that, I get . . . this.' Another dismissive gesture. 'My three-room world.'

'I see why you have all the pictures. Makes it seem bigger.'

'Yeah. I would absolutely love to travel. Not just to Italy – everywhere.' She gave the more exotic photographs a longing look. 'But I can't.'

'Why not? What's stopping you?'

She brought two cups of coffee to the sofa. Reeve sat beside her. 'Well, money, for one. I've never had it, and in my job, I never will. But the main reason *is* my job. I love what I do. I'm helping people – helping them stay alive, a lot of the time.'

'And I'm very grateful.'

She smiled. 'I know I'm making a difference. But . . .' The smile faded. 'The work's getting harder. Nurses leave, and way too often they don't get replaced. Everyone has to cover for each other. And things get privatised, bit by bit – but there never seems to be more money. Not for patients or the nursing staff, anyway.' She sipped her coffee. 'I never used to drink this stuff. I always drank tea. But I need it to stay awake through a shift now.'

'You're still there, though,' Reeve said. 'You're sticking it out.'

'That suggests it'll get better in the long run.' Another sigh, and she gazed into the distance. 'I don't think it will. Not just in the NHS; everywhere. The whole country seems to be falling apart . . .'

'If it is, it's because people aren't trying to fix it.' The firmness in his voice brought her gaze back to him in surprise. 'You can't just sit back and hope someone else handles things. If you want to protect the country, you have to work at it.'

'That was your job?' she asked. 'Protecting the country?'

'Yes.'

'But now the people you were working for are trying to kill you?'

It was a contradiction for which he didn't have an answer. 'If I can talk to Tony tomorrow, I can find out why,' he eventually said. 'Whatever's gone wrong, we can fix it.'

Connie cocked her head. 'You know, if my boss tried to kill me? I'd take that as a sign I was in the wrong job.'

Reeve drank his coffee to avoid saying more. The thought had indeed occurred to him. It had been unwelcome.

Connie picked up on his discomfort. 'So,' she said, turning towards him. 'You know about me. What about you?'

'What do you mean?'

'I mean, who *are* you, Alex Reeve? You literally fell into my life – over my car's bonnet. All I know about you is that you're from Manchester. You *really* don't like drug dealers or bad fathers. You used to be some kind of undercover soldier. You were training to be something even more secret. Oh, and the obvious: someone shot you. Apart from that, I don't know anything about you.'

'Maybe there *isn't* anything more,' he said.

'Uh-huh,' she said, mocking. 'Come on. You're from Manchester – nice bit? Nasty bit?'

'Nasty bit,' he reluctantly admitted. 'Clayton.'

'I don't know it.'

'It's not exactly on the tourist trail. Rough part of town. People who live there generally want to get out. Problem is, they don't have the money.' His expression darkened. 'One way to get it is by dealing drugs.'

'And that's why you don't like dealers, yes?'

'Yeah. I saw a lot of people suffer from what they were selling. Some of them died. Some of them were my friends.'

'I'm sorry.'

'Not your fault.' An uncomfortable silence, then: 'Mine in a way, though.'

She was surprised. 'How?'

'I should have *done* something. But . . . I was a kid. What *could* I do? These people have knives, even guns. And they control the streets. You're scared, all the time.'

'Even at home?'

He gave her a grim look. 'My dad was one of them.'

'He was a drug dealer?'

'Not one of the big guys. Although he *was* a big guy, physically. He did it sometimes for extra money. He was . . .' Reeve paused. His father was a subject he had always avoided discussing. 'More like a debt collector for the big dealers. He made sure people paid what they owed. By beating them up.'

'Jesus.'

'That was the nearest thing he had to a full-time job. Debt collecting. He'd make me come with him sometimes, to watch the car. He'd come back with the money. And other things, if he saw something he wanted. He'd just take it. He'd get into the car, and . . . there'd be blood on his hands.'

'How old were you?' Connie asked, appalled.

'Nine, ten. Something like that.'

'No offence, but . . . your dad doesn't sound like a very nice man.'

He forced out a laugh. 'That's the polite way of putting it.'

'Is that why you joined the army? To get away from him?'

'I haven't seen him since I was thirteen. If I never see him again, that'll suit me. But anyway, now you know about me. That's all the past. I'm more bothered about the future right now. Got to plan for tomorrow.'

She still clearly had questions, but shelved them. For now. 'Is there anything you'll need?'

'More clothes, for a start. I'll find a way to pay you back, I promise,' he added.

'It's not a problem,' Connie insisted.

He knew that wasn't true. His presence was stretching her limited finances. But he needed her help. 'Hair dye or bleach might be useful as well. The more ways I can change my appearance, the bet—'

The door burst open.

Connie shrieked. Reeve jumped up as someone rushed in. Jammer.

He was not alone. Two more men entered behind him.

And he was holding a gun.

CHAPTER 24

'Don't fucking move,' Jammer snarled, thrusting the gun at Reeve and Connie. It was a Walther PPK automatic, worn and scuffed. James Bond's gun. But Reeve knew Jammer had chosen it for a more pragmatic reason. There would be newer, more reliable, more deadly guns circling the underworld.

But this one could take a silencer.

A matt-black tube extended six inches from the Walther's muzzle. It swung up at Reeve's face. 'Go and get the others,' Jammer ordered. His companions went back out.

Connie stared in terror at the gun. 'Oh my God! What do you want?'

'What do you fucking think?' No sleazy flirtatiousness today. 'I'm going to give this fucking cunt what he deserves.' He glared at Reeve. 'Not so fucking tough with a gun in your face, are you?'

Reeve said nothing. He assessed the threat. High: Jammer's finger was tight on the trigger. He was untrained, but that actually made things more dangerous. One accidental flinch, and he could blow his target's head off . . .

And untrained or not, he was smart enough not to move within Reeve's reach. Six inches closer, and Reeve could

173

disarm him in under a second. But he was just far enough away to make an attempt too risky.

Cries of fear outside. Jaz and Brownlow were being rousted from their flats. The baby screamed as her mother was dragged away. 'Hallie!' Jaz wailed.

'Into the hall,' Jammer barked. At gunpoint, Reeve and Connie reluctantly left the flat. The two other men returned. One shoved Brownlow up from below. The other pulled Jaz downstairs by her wrist.

'What are you doing?' Connie cried. 'You've left her baby alone!'

'I don't give a shit about her baby,' Jammer sneered. 'I want you all to see what happens if you fuck with me. I know the landlord. You *think* about going to the police, you'll be out on the street. Locks changed, all your shit dumped on the railway.' He jerked his head to indicate the cutting beyond the rear garden. 'And then you'll get the same.'

'The same as what?' said the terrified Jaz.

'As what he's going to get.' Jammer stepped back, gesturing to his friends. Both were large, beefy, hair and clothes styled to look tough. They released their prisoners and advanced on Reeve, fists raised—

Crossing in front of Jammer.

The instant his line of fire was blocked, Reeve moved.

His right hand lanced out in a lightning-fast strike at the nearest man's face. His nose flattened with a ghastly crunch. Blood exploded from both nostrils. The man reeled back with a gurgling squeal.

His companion froze in shock. Reeve swept at him before he could recover. He grabbed his right arm and drove it up behind his back. A gruesome wet *pop* from his shoulder as the joint was dislocated. The man screamed, other arm flailing. Reeve swung his victim towards Jammer. The gun was still raised. 'No, *no!*' the man shrieked. 'Don't shoot!'

Reeve shoved him forward. Jammer's gun was relatively low-powered, and the suppressor would sap it further. If he fired, his human shield would take all the damage—

The shot didn't come. Jammer was afraid of hitting his friend. Reeve took full advantage of his hesitation. He kicked the squirming man at him. They crashed together. The thug was bigger and heavier, knocking Jammer backwards. He stumbled at the top of the stairs – and fell down them.

Reeve grabbed the thug's hair and smashed his face against the banister ball. He fell, senseless. A pained yell from below as Jammer hit the floor. Reeve ran after him.

Jammer's gun had been jarred from his hand. It skidded into Brownlow's flat. He scrambled to retrieve it as Reeve jumped down behind him.

Jammer clawed frantically for the pistol. Reeve charged through the doorway. The gun came up—

He dropped and darted sideways. A flat, metallic *ptchak* as Jammer fired. Wood and plaster splintered beside the door. The shot would have missed even if Reeve hadn't dodged. The younger man was too panicked to aim.

But Jammer had already realised his mistake, swinging the gun—

Several hardbacks were piled on a small bookcase. Reeve snatched one up and threw it. The book hit Jammer's head. Another shot, but this went even wider as he lurched back.

Reeve rushed at him. He slammed his right wrist against

Jammer's, knocking the muzzle away from him. Before his opponent could react, his left hand wrenched the gun from his grip. He released Jammer, flipping the Walther around. Reeve thrust it into his face.

Jammer's expression became one of pure fear. Reeve kept the silenced weapon locked motionlessly upon him. 'Leave,' he said, voice as cold as a grave. 'Now. And don't come back. Ever.'

Jammer stared at him, mouth open. He backed away. Reeve tracked him with the gun. Eyes fixed on it, Jammer reached the garden door. He fumbled with the handle and backed out.

Reeve watched him go. *Just leave, you idiot. Don't let your pride make things worse . . .*

'You – you're fucking dead!' Jammer yelled. He was practically peering around the doorway, ready to break and run. 'And your fucking friends'll get it too! Those two bitches are gonna get fucked up, right in front of the baby! You don't know who you're—'

Reeve cocked his head – then tossed the gun on the sofa and ran after him.

Jammer's bellowed threats suddenly became a yelp of fear. He rushed for the gate.

Reeve barrelled out of the house. Jammer flung the gate open and charged on to the side street. He ran for a Mercedes SUV parked on yellow lines a short way downhill. Reeve followed, seeing him fumble in a pocket.

Jammer reached his car, but hadn't yet unlocked the doors. 'Fuck, *shit*!' he cried, clawing at his key fob. He couldn't get into the Merc before Reeve caught up. Instead he ran on towards a bridge over the railway.

Reeve caught up before he reached it. He launched himself into a diving tackle. Both men hit the wet pavement hard.

Jammer flailed an arm. By sheer luck his elbow caught Reeve's jaw. Reeve was knocked against the wall. Jammer scrambled up and launched a desperate kick. It hit Reeve's left arm, hard. He yelled in pain.

Jammer grinned like a wolf. His foot drew back again, swung—

Reeve whipped up his right arm to intercept the kick.

Leather thudded against muscle and bone. It hurt, but he could take it. Before Jammer could withdraw, he hooked his arm around his ankle and rolled. The other man staggered. His leg popped free of Reeve's hold as he thumped against the bridge's parapet.

Arm burning, Reeve jumped up. He was done with restraint. Jammer saw him coming, raising his fists—

Reeve's right foot struck like a piledriver. A horrific crack of bone – and Jammer's ankle snapped. His foot bent gruesomely to one side. He screamed.

Reeve punched him, knocking him to the ground. 'I gave you a chance to walk away. Should've taken it.'

He emptied the whimpering Jammer's pockets. All the items he had seen before – and a wrap of what he guessed was heroin. He tossed it over the bridge. Then he collected Jammer's phone. 'Unlock it,' he ordered.

The younger man stared up at him through streaming eyes. 'What?'

'Unlock your phone.'

'Fuck you!'

Reeve regarded him impassively. Then he reached down and, before Jammer could react, snapped his left little finger. Jammer shrieked. 'Unlock your phone,' Reeve repeated. 'Or I'll break the rest.' He took hold of his ring finger and applied pressure.

'Jesus Christ, okay, okay!' Jammer squealed. He pushed his thumb to the screen. The phone unlocked, the grid of apps appearing.

Reeve opened the settings. 'Now unlock it permanently.' Disabling the screen lock required Jammer to confirm his identity. 'Put in your PIN.'

'What? No! I'm not fucking—'

Growing impatient, Reeve rested one foot on his broken ankle. 'Do it. Now.'

Jammer surrendered and shakily tapped in the six-digit number. Reeve watched, memorising it. The phone asked if he was sure he wanted to disable the lock. Reeve took it back and tapped *OK*. He then pocketed the downed man's belongings and looked around. The street was quiet. If anyone had heard the commotion, they were not coming to investigate.

He brought up the phone's keypad and dialled 999. A request for an ambulance, then he spoke to the operator. 'I just found a man who's been mugged. I think his leg's broken.' He gave the address, then disconnected. 'Right,' he told Jammer. 'Remember that I know where you live. If you talk to the police, I will kill you. If I ever even see you again, I will kill you. If anything happens to the people in that house, I will kill you. And it will look like a suicide. You understand?'

Despite the broken bones, Jammer still would not accept submission. His mouth curled into a snarl. 'You have *no idea* who you're fucking with.'

'Nor do you,' Reeve rumbled. He was filled with a sudden, visceral loathing of the man before him. Jammer was scum, pure and simple. He could kill him. He *should* kill him. A net benefit to the nation. It would take only seconds . . .

He fought back the urge. Doing so would draw unwanted attention – the police, even SC9. And he knew Connie would be horrified. Instead he leaned down. Jammer shrank back, eyes wide in fear. Reeve let him feel it for a moment – then his right arm lashed out. An axe-chop struck Jammer's neck. The drug dealer slumped unconscious.

Reeve ran back to the house, going through the rear gate. Brownlow had shut his door; he knocked. The older man nervously opened it. Reeve entered. 'Is everyone okay?'

'Yes, we're all fine,' Brownlow replied. 'What happened to Jammer?'

'He won't bother you again. He won't bother *anyone* for a while.'

'Alex!' Connie, from the main hall. He pocketed the gun and hurried to her. Bloodstains marred the shabby decor, but the men who had left them were gone. 'Oh, my God,' she cried. 'Are you okay?'

'Yeah,' Reeve lied. His wounded arm felt as if molten lead were being dripped on to it. 'Where did the other guys go?'

'They ran off. Where's Jammer?'

'On the street. I called an ambulance for him.'

Her eyebrows rose in surprise. 'Generous of you.'

'It was better than a hearse. Look, I have to get out of

here. The police are bound to come and ask questions. Just tell them you didn't see anything – Jaz and Philip too. Oh, and you'd better clean that up.' He indicated the bloody marks. 'Don't let them into any of your flats, and you'll be fine. Okay, I've got to go.' He ducked through her door and grabbed his coat, then went to the exit.

'Wait, wait!' Connie cried. 'Are you coming back?'

'I'll call you later. What's your phone number?'

She recited it, then frowned. 'But you don't have a phone.'

'I do now. See you later.' With that, he left.

'Bye,' the bewildered Connie called as he went.

Reeve quickly rounded the house to the side street. A look towards the bridge. Jammer was still unconscious, but had been found. A man and woman crouched beside him. He used the key fob to unlock Jammer's Mercedes GLE Coupé and got in.

The man made a phone call. Reeve started the SUV and unhurriedly pulled away. He didn't want the couple to take any notice of him as he drove past. Neither did.

Where to now?

There was one place he felt reasonably sure he wouldn't be disturbed. He stopped a few streets away. Recalling an address from memory, he entered it into the satnav. The route appeared on the screen. He set off again, heading for Jammer's home.

CHAPTER 25

Jahmir Haxhi had done well from his trade, Reeve saw. The satnav led him to a new and stylish apartment block in Nine Elms. He wasn't an expert in London property values, but Jammer's place didn't look cheap. The rewards of vice.

Unsure how to get in, he drove to the garage access. It opened as he approached. Either a plate reader at the entrance, or a radio tag in the car. He entered, looking for Jammer's flat number.

The matching space was empty. Reeve parked, then checked Jammer's key ring. Three keys: two brass, the other shiny steel. He imagined the steel was for the flat, the brass pair for the building's exterior doors. He hoped, at least. If there was a keypad entry lock, he didn't know the code . . .

He got out. *Move as if you own the place*. He marched to a flight of concrete stairs and jogged up them. The suppressed gun was awkward inside his coat. A security door blocked the top. No keypad. He tried one of the brass keys. It didn't turn – but to his relief the second did.

Reeve went through into a marble-floored lobby. More relief. The place was not so high-end as to have a concierge. He wouldn't have to explain his presence. There were security cameras, though; he kept his head low as he went to a lift.

Sixth floor. Flat 608. He tried the steel key. The door opened. He slipped through.

The flat was expensively appointed, but not large. The main room was a wedge, one side with full-length windows to a balcony. The Thames was visible between more towers beyond. A kitchenette, barely bigger than Connie's. Reeve stood still, listening. No warning chirps from an alarm demanding a code.

More importantly, no sounds of other occupants. Jammer didn't seem likely to be in a relationship, but there was no accounting for taste. Reeve's instinct was correct, though. He was alone.

He checked the two other doors. Bathroom and bedroom. The latter was decorated with near-pornographic mono-chrome posters of women. Back into the living room. A large leather sofa faced both the windows and a giant television. A clutter of set-top boxes and game consoles sat beneath the latter.

Something was missing; he hadn't seen a computer. He couldn't imagine Jammer only using his phone. Was there a safe?

He searched the flat. At the back of a kitchen cabinet, he found it. The safe was a dull-grey block, bolted to the rear wall. It was not big enough to contain a laptop. What did Jammer keep inside?

It had a keypad lock. He tried the phone's lock code. It didn't work. There were other ways to get in, though. The safe was consumer-level, enough to foil an opportunistic burglar.

But far from impenetrable.

Reeve had trained to crack numerous safes, including some of government-level security. This was a toy in comparison. He found a knife in the cutlery drawer. Another cupboard had contained a toolbox. He took out a screwdriver, then returned to the safe.

The knife slipped down the door's side until it met the main lock. He jiggled it until it caught on the mechanism. Holding it in place, he jabbed the screwdriver into the narrow gap above the door. He forced it upwards. The tip scraped over metal, then dug in. He pushed harder to lever the door outwards. A faint creak as it shifted and the mechanism moved. The knife twitched in his hand. He eased his hold a little. It held in place.

He released the screwdriver. The door did not return to its original position. Reeve clenched his right fist – then pounded it on the safe's top. Metal clunked inside it.

He turned the handle – and the door popped open.

A faint smile. With security, you got what you paid for, and Jammer had cheaped out. He emptied the contents.

A box of bullets. Several plastic bags containing not drugs, as he first thought, but banknotes. Pounds, euros, dollars – and some he needed a moment to identify. Albanian leks. Added together, about sixty thousand pounds.

An iPad. He pushed the home button. The screen lit up with a wallpaper of hundred-dollar bills, demanding a passcode.

Nothing to lose. He tried the one from Jammer's phone.
It worked.
Unlike the phone, the tablet was sparsely populated with apps. He brought up the most recently used. Some kind of

accounting program; he wasn't familiar with it.

He could guess what it was used for, though. Jammer had been tracking his drug deals. Reeve scrolled through the pages. A lot of money was involved. If he was reading it right, Jammer brought in over sixteen thousand pounds a *week*. He kept about a quarter. The rest went to someone named only as 'VB'; presumably his supplier.

There were other names. And addresses, phone numbers, Jammer's whole network popping up at the tap of a finger. Brownlow was not the only person he had cuckooed. At least twelve other properties had been co-opted. The police would probably be very interested in the file . . .

He put down the tablet. Maybe when he was done in London. Right now, he had other priorities.

The safe's remaining contents were of little interest. Some gold jewellery, a passport, bank paperwork. The money would certainly be useful. He would secure some in a storage locker or similar as soon as possible. The other items were less important. At least now he was armed. If he met SC9 again, he wouldn't be defenceless.

Reeve sat on the sofa, gazing across London, then took out the phone. Several missed calls: probably Jammer's battered companions wondering where he was. He ignored the alerts, instead phoning Connie. She answered, wary at being rung from an unfamiliar number. 'Hello?'

'It's me,' he replied.

'Alex!' Relief filled her voice. 'Are you okay? Where are you?'

'Jammer's flat. He won't need it for a while.'

'What did you do to him?'

'I broke his ankle.'

She drew in a sharp breath. 'Ow. Yes, that'll hospitalise him for a couple of days, at least. But what about you? How's your arm?'

'Sore.'

'I'm not surprised. It should be in a sling.'

'Not an option, I'm afraid.'

'Are you coming back here? The police haven't called.'

'They will. An incident like that, they usually canvas the area the following day. I don't think Jammer will say anything, but someone might have seen me. It's better that I'm not at your place. If I'm arrested, the people looking for me *will* find me.'

She was silent for a long moment. 'So where's Jammer's flat?'

'Nine Elms.'

Another pause. 'I want to come over.'

His reply was immediate. 'No. It's not safe.'

'And *here* is? There are bullet holes in Philip's walls, for God's sake. And I'm not exactly used to lying to the police. What if they realise I'm hiding something?'

'They're not going to interrogate you. You just say you don't know anything, and that's the end of it.'

'I have a horrible feeling "the end of it" is a long way off. What if Jammer's friends come back?'

'They won't.'

'And you're sure of that how, exactly?'

She was right; he couldn't ensure the dealer's associates wouldn't seek revenge. 'Okay,' he said, with reluctance. 'Come over.' He gave her the address.

Fifty minutes later, the doorbell buzzed. Reeve went to the intercom. 'Yeah?' he said, trying to sound like Jammer in case it wasn't Connie.

'I'm here.' It was her. He buzzed her in. She soon arrived, looking around in surprise. 'Wow. He's a scumbag, but he's got a nice flat.'

Reeve noticed she had brought a small suitcase. 'What's in there?'

'Your clothes. And some of mine. I brought some other things you might need, too.'

'Such as?'

'You said about needing disguises, so I found anything that could be useful. More makeup, old glasses, that kind of thing. Oh, and,' she went on, 'my first-aid stuff. And the painkillers and antibiotics. Something else I thought you might need.'

A faint laugh in response. 'Yeah. I might.'

She put down the case. 'Let me look at your arm.'

They sat on the sofa so Connie could remove the dressing. 'Well, that's not as bad as I was afraid of,' she said, relieved. 'The stitches are all intact. Looks like the antibiotics are doing their job as well. You really, *really* need to take it easy, though. Like . . . by not getting into any more fights? I mean, you've had three in as many days.'

'I know. Not what I'd hoped for.' He puffed out a breath, dispirited. 'None of this is what I'd hoped for.'

Connie gave him a sympathetic look. 'Do you really think you'll be able to find this guy tomorrow?'

'I *have* to,' Reeve said firmly. 'Otherwise . . . I honestly have no idea what I'll do.'

'We'll work it out.' He gave her a quizzical look. 'I want to help you,' she said. 'You helped me – you've helped everyone in the house. Also . . . it's my job. And right now,' she cleaned his wound, 'you *need* my help.'

He twitched even at her gentle touch. The injury was still tender. 'I do. Thanks.'

A smile, then she looked around the flat again. 'I like it. It's hardly any bigger than mine, but the view's better.'

'Still only one bedroom, though,' he pointed out. 'I'll take the sofa.'

'I hope there are clean sheets. I don't want to sleep on Jammer's bedclothes.'

He grinned. 'There are some sheets in a cupboard.'

'For squatters, we're quite tidy, aren't we?' Her amusement was replaced by pensiveness. 'We *are* breaking the law by being here, aren't we? What if the police come round?'

'It's in Jammer's best interest not to tell them anything. If he's smart, he'll say he got hit from behind and didn't see anybody.'

'*If* he's smart,' she said. 'Which I don't think he is.'

'Maybe not, but he's got all this,' a wave at their surroundings, 'without drawing attention. He's streetwise, at least.'

'A certain rat-like cunning, hmm?'

'That's one way of putting it.'

She re-bandaged his wound. 'Okay, that's done. Does it feel all right?'

Reeve flexed his arm. It hurt more than it had earlier. That wasn't surprising. Connie was right. One day without a fight would be great . . .

He couldn't guarantee that. Not knowing what he faced. 'Yeah, it's good,' he told her.

She didn't seem convinced, but said nothing. Instead, she stood. 'I'd better sort out the bedroom, then. Big day tomorrow.'

'Yeah,' Reeve said. 'Big day.'

CHAPTER 26

Maxwell strolled through the rain along the Thames Path, heading northwards for the football ground. His pace was languid; his mind anything but. If he was right, Reeve would try to intercept him here. But when? And what would he do when he found him?

His team were fully justified in having doubts. His plan was based entirely on his interpretation of Reeve's reactions at Mordencroft Hall. If he had misread them, his former protégé might not come at all.

Or he *would* come, but not to question him. To kill him.

Other fans around him walked through Bishops Park towards Craven Cottage. Was Reeve amongst them? Disguise was one of his specialities . . .

Most of those nearby he could immediately discount. Too old, too young, too short, too large. Disguise had its limits, even to experts. He doubted Reeve had found the resources to make facial prosthetics. Those who fit the bill physically earned closer scrutiny. Their faces flashed through his mental database. Jaw too narrow, eyes too close together, not him, not him, no.

Reeve was not in his immediate vicinity.

Locke was, though. He trailed fifteen metres behind, on a

parallel path beyond some bushes. Operative 61 stood out, and not just because one arm was in a sling. His stiff distaste at the people surrounding him was clear. 'Harrison,' Maxwell whispered, voice picked up by the little microphone concealed in his collar. 'You look like someone just served you a dog turd on toast. Try to blend in.'

'This is hardly my usual milieu,' came the reply through a tiny earpiece receiver.

'Handy undercover tip: when you're going to a footie match, don't use words like "milieu",' Maxwell told him. Another voice in the earpiece; Stone's mocking laugh. 'Okay, I'm heading for Stevenage Road.'

He turned from the river, following the path along the ground's end wall. The throng grew thicker as fans coming through the park converged. Black and white predominated, hats and scarves and shirts in Fulham's home colours. A much smaller number wore blue and white: the visiting Huddersfield fans. Dotted amongst both were spots of hi-vis yellow; stewards and police officers. Trouble at football matches was quickly stepped on.

He scanned the crowd again. Nobody triggered his warning radar. Everyone slowed to go through the park gate. They joined still more fans beyond. Stevenage Road was closed to traffic on match day, people milling along the street. There were more police here, an officer clopping past on horseback.

'I see you, Tony.' Blake's voice in his ear. Operative 62 was on the road's far side, pretending to make a phone call. Maxwell nodded to him, then continued towards the ground.

Barriers channelled the away supporters to one set of

gates. He went past; his ticket was for turnstile forty-nine, at the north end. The crowd swelled around him. A typical match would see about eighteen thousand fans in attendance. This looked above average. More people would make it harder for them to spot Reeve.

And harder for Reeve to spot *him*.

He continued northwards. There was a hum of excitement in the air, spontaneous chants breaking out. Normally he would have been caught up in it; he had supported Fulham since childhood. He had been looking forward to catching a live match before the season ended. Today, though, tension overrode anticipation. The crowd obscured faces as he neared the turnstiles. Reeve might be only yards away . . .

Sudden paranoia made Maxwell alter course through the throng. A glance back. Nobody was paying him any attention. His wariness eased, just a little. Reeve wasn't nearby—

A distorted crackle in his earpiece. Stone, too loud in his excitement. 'I see him!'

Reeve walked with the fans heading southwards on Stevenage Road. This was his third time traversing the route. He had started his patrol before the turnstiles opened. One end of the ground to the other, and slightly beyond, watching for his quarry. So far he hadn't seen Maxwell – or his former teammates.

The crowd grew thicker as kick-off time neared. He blended in – he hoped. A Fulham hat hid his hair, and he wore a jacket 'borrowed' from Jammer. The frames of Connie's old glasses were unisex enough not to stand out. He had removed the lenses, the black surrounds breaking up his features. Again, he had used makeup to distort his facial contours.

He had other tricks, but would save them for if they were needed.

Or when.

Cold fear as he spotted Stone. The big man was hard to miss, head like a periscope above the tide. He was at the first corner north of the ground, watching everyone pass. Stationary at first – but now moving.

Towards him.

Reeve sidestepped behind a taller man. In the moment when he was blocked from Stone's sight, he made his first change. The hat came off, revealing black hair beneath. A wig, bought from a fancy dress shop that morning. Cheap, not convincing under scrutiny – but it would give him the necessary seconds to disappear.

He stayed low, and slowed. The crowd flowed past him. He resurfaced. Where was the Operative? He had lost track of him . . .

There.

Less than four metres away.

Still advancing with determination, predatory anticipation in his eyes—

Then past.

Stone pushed onwards. Reeve glanced sideways. A man was shuffling along the pavement. Dirty, hair dishevelled, a grubby baseball hat shadowing his face. Drunk or on drugs, almost certainly homeless.

A perfect disguise – or so Stone thought.

Reeve kept moving as Stone slammed the homeless man

against the fence. People nearby retreated from the sudden violence. Stone snatched away the hat, glaring at his victim – then swore. He mouthed something, more quietly. He was talking into a hidden mic. Reporting his mistake.

To Maxwell.

Reeve discounted the possibility that his mentor wouldn't show himself. Maxwell would insist on being live bait. He wanted to draw out his target, maybe even kill him himself. So where was he – and where were his other minders?

The fracas had drawn the stewards' attention. That might get the police involved, taking one of his pursuers out of the game . . .

No such luck. Stone produced something from a pocket. From the stewards' reactions, Reeve guessed what it was. A Metropolitan Police warrant card. On British soil, Operatives could call upon all kinds of useful forged credentials. And if challenged, Stone's police background would easily help him bluff his way out.

But Reeve was now past him. A brief look back. Stone was still browbeating the stewards. One threat passed.

But not eliminated. And there would be others. Reeve surveyed the crowd ahead as he approached the north turnstiles. He couldn't see Maxwell. Or Flynn, or Locke, Parker or Blake. But if Stone was here, they would be too.

The fans slowed to join the queues. More came from the south. Reeve twisted through the crush. Too many people. If he missed Maxwell—

The thought was blown away as he saw another familiar face. Flynn, against the high wall opposite the ground. She was looking away from him. Reeve tried to follow her gaze.

Was she watching Maxwell?

She said something under her breath – then turned.

Reeve hunched lower. For one chilling moment it seemed her eyes had met his. But then she looked in Stone's direction. Reeve angled away from her, head down as he squeezed through the crowd.

'Stone's bullshitted the stewards,' Flynn said, in Maxwell's earpiece. 'They're moving off.'

Stone himself spoke a moment later. 'It was just some fucking homeless skank,' he growled. 'Fuck's sake.'

'Don't take any action until you have a positive ID,' Maxwell chided quietly. 'Okay, I'm almost at the gate.' He followed other fans towards his turnstile.

Neither he nor Reeve realised, but they had passed just six feet from each other.

Reeve continued with the crowd to the ground's southern end.

Still no sign of Maxwell. Nor any of the other Operatives – but they *had* to be there. Stone and Flynn were covering one end, so someone would be watching the other.

He reached the turnstiles. Concern rose. Three passes, up and down, and he still hadn't seen his target. The odds that *he* would be spotted would only keep increasing. Kick-off was thirty minutes away. The crowd was probably at its peak. From here, it would start to thin out as everyone found their seats.

He risked rising to his full height. Was Maxwell in sight? No – but Locke was. About thirty metres away, near the park entrance. The blond man was wearing a sling; he'd survived being stabbed, then. Reeve dropped back down. Parker and Blake could be nearby as well.

Shit. He had gambled, and – for now – lost. Even if Maxwell wasn't already inside, staying on the street was becoming too risky. He would soon lose his cover. He put the hat back on, then turned. Merging into the northwards flow, he headed back up the street.

Flynn had moved, but not far. He stayed in the middle of the crowd until he passed her. Now things would get more difficult; he was past the turnstiles. Moving against the tide would make him stand out. And Stone was here, somewhere.

The Thames Path resumed some ten metres beyond the last turnstile. It was his first available escape route – and the most obvious place to watch. A confined space, no way out if he became trapped. Too risky. He would have to continue along the road.

Only a few people were going north. He followed them. The turn to the Thames Path was just ahead. Reeve glanced down it as he passed.

Stone was there.

The ex-cop lurked around the corner, watching everyone pass. His eyes flicked to the man going against the flow—

Recognition.

Reeve veered deeper into the oncoming fans, but Stone was already moving. He ducked, removing the hat, and this time the glasses. A rapid half-turn and he straightened again. His change of direction would confuse Stone – briefly. But he would already be warning his comrades—

'Police! Out of the fucking way!' Stone bellowed, barging

through the crowd. He was now behind Reeve, heading for where he expected him to be. It would take him only seconds to realise his prey wasn't there.

Reeve made full use of the brief moment. Another turn, and he ducked into the Thames Path's entrance. A huge risk – if Stone had a partner there, he was screwed . . .

But everyone ahead was heading for the match. He slipped between them until he reached the Thames, following the path northwards. His heart thumped, adrenalin flooding his system. No sign of pursuit, but he had taken the obvious escape route. He had to get clear.

Reeve continued past a complex of tower blocks. A wall linked it and a cluster of smaller buildings. He quickly scaled the obstacle and jumped over. A woman shouted 'Hey!' behind him, but he was gone.

A small garden. He hurried through, squeezing around a bush. Below was a ramp leading to an underground car park. He dropped down and hurried between the buildings. Ahead, more fans streamed towards Craven Cottage. He rejoined Stevenage Road and headed north.

The adrenalin shot subsided as he realised he had evaded his pursuers. But it had been close. And he had lost his first chance to find Maxwell. There would only be one more: when the game ended.

But now SC9 had seen him. They would be ready.

CHAPTER 27

The final whistle blew. Maxwell rose as the black-and-white mass around him jumped up in celebration. A song began: 'One-nil, one-niiiil!' Not the most exciting match ever, but a win was a win. He allowed himself a moment to punch the air in victory.

But he hadn't been able to concentrate on the game. Stone had been certain – again – that he'd seen Reeve. This time, Maxwell believed him. That he *hadn't* grabbed a suspect was, perversely, confirmation. If it had been mistaken identity, the unlucky lookalike wouldn't have disappeared.

So what would Reeve do, knowing SC9 were on to him? Abandon his mission? Or continue despite the increased danger?

Continue. Maxwell was certain. Reeve's mere presence proved he had been right. His former trainee wanted answers. Top marks for determination, then. Maxwell would have given him a lower score for good sense, except . . .

Well, Reeve wasn't dead yet. He couldn't fault his survival skills.

'I'm on my way out,' he said into his mic. 'Is everyone in position?' All replies were in the affirmative.

He joined the herd heading for the exits. It took a few

minutes to reach the street. It had been dry under the stand, but now the rain caught him again. Flynn and Blake were across the street. They would take up positions a short way ahead. The others would shadow him at a greater distance from behind.

No sign of Reeve. He wasn't surprised. He was probably some way off – watching the watchers. When they moved, he would know their boss was moving too. He would also know that they knew that he knew (that they knew that he) . . .

Maxwell smiled as the cycle repeatedly endlessly in his mind. In intelligence work, it was too easy to overthink things. To assume an opponent had anticipated your every move. On this occasion, he was playing it straight. Reeve wanted to find him; he wanted to draw Reeve to him. A pure battle of wits. In theory, Maxwell had the advantage – simply of numbers. In practice, Reeve had already beaten worse odds.

It would be an interesting challenge. Okay, "interesting" in the sense of the Chinese curse. His life was at risk. He could have misjudged Reeve; he might just be out for revenge . . .

Time to find out. 'Heading for the station,' he reported. He turned south towards Bishops Park.

His shadows followed.

Reeve took a calculated gamble when he returned to Craven Cottage. His efforts before the match had concentrated on the stadium's north end. He hadn't seen Maxwell there – so he moved to the south.

He followed a circuitous route to Bishops Park. His hope

that Maxwell's watchers had stayed near the grounds paid off. Locke was opposite the closest entrance, looking thoroughly pissed off. If any more Operatives were in the park, they were well hidden. That didn't seem likely. So far, they had been in the open.

He took up position amongst trees fifty metres from the gate and waited. The white triangle of Locke's sling was visible beyond the fence. Eventually a great roar came from the football ground. The final whistle; he guessed the home team had won. Supporters were already leaving, wanting to dodge the crush. Sure enough, less than a minute later the trickle of fans became a tsunami.

Reeve risked clambering on to a small brick plinth to keep line of sight on Locke. Before long, the blond man moved. Heading south down Stevenage Road – no, into the park. Reeve started to climb down. He couldn't risk being spotted—

Wait; Locke had stopped inside the gate. Reeve paused, watching. The striped masses flowed past Locke; blue-and-white miserable, black-and-white celebrating. Was he waiting for . . .

Maxwell.

Reeve recognised his mentor instantly. His baseball cap and glasses would hopefully prevent the reverse. He had swapped the Fulham hat for the former; Stone had seen him in it.

No sign of Stone – but he did see Blake and Flynn. They entered the park ahead of Maxwell. Blake took the path towards the river, Flynn the one that would pass Reeve's position.

He dropped down, crouching behind the plinth. Flynn

came towards him, Maxwell about twenty metres behind. A glance through the trees across the park. Blake was still heading for the Thames Path. Reeve was in cover; he wouldn't be seen.

Nevertheless, he slipped his right hand into the coat. Jammer's suppressed gun was inside. Practice while Connie slept had assured him he could draw it in under a second.

But eliminating his enemies was, in this case, a losing outcome. If he killed anyone, even in self-defence, he would have to flee. Too many witnesses and cops nearby. He would lose his one chance to reach Maxwell.

He waited. Fans marched past—

There went Flynn. Another fifteen, twenty seconds and he should see Maxwell . . .

Twenty seconds, almost on the dot. Maxwell was in no hurry. Now he had to wait for Locke – and watch for Stone and Parker. Another check across the park. Blake was walking along the riverside.

Their most likely destination was Putney Bridge station, about half a mile away. Reeve had reconnoitred it the day before. He knew the route – and the choke points. There were places where he would be at risk of being trapped. That was probably why his target was going that way.

But he had also found ways to avoid them.

Locke's turn to go past. Reeve waited until he was ten metres clear, then peered out. No sign of the other Operatives. He moved up the shallow slope to join the crowded path.

Maxwell and his protectors continued through the park. Reeve followed, regularly checking behind. He finally saw Stone on Stevenage Road, beyond the fence. Standard surveillance technique: cover the routes on each side of the target. Stone was some thirty metres back. Parker was presumably the rearguard, but the crowd obscured him.

Reeve looked ahead again, keeping pace with Locke. Locke in turn maintained his distance behind Maxwell. Impatient fans flowed past Reeve, wanting to beat the rush at the station. Concern; by matching Maxwell's speed, he was moving slower than most. It would make him stand out. Another check to the rear. Still nobody in sight. To the side—

Stone had closed, just fifteen metres away. He was looking over the fence at the people inside the park. Reeve turned away. If Stone drew level, there was little he could do to disguise his profile. He had to stay ahead of him. But if he went faster, he would be too close to Maxwell . . .

Stevenage Road angled eastwards, most of the fans filing through a gate into the park. Reeve moved to the edge of the new crush, away from Stone. Operative 63 entered the park – now only ten metres behind him. Looking in Reeve's direction. Suspicion rather than certainty on his face . . . but he *was* suspicious.

The big man weaved through the throng towards him. Reeve moved faster, rounding a group of chanting men. He hunched down. Off with the baseball cap, back on with the Fulham hat. Staying low, he sidestepped, then rose again. A glance back. Stone was only five metres behind, searching for the cap. Reeve walked more quickly still. He would have to risk closing the distance to Maxwell. He matched the pace of the fans around him, joining the celebrations.

Stone fell back slightly with evident frustration. Reeve saw his lips move. He was reporting his suspicions to

Maxwell. A look ahead. Locke was fifteen metres away. Reeve was gaining. He would soon end up sandwiched between Locke and Stone. The park was also narrowing. Somewhere to the right, by the river, was Blake. He was running out of manoeuvring room . . .

And a major choke point lay ahead. The road on to Putney Bridge, crossing the Thames, was elevated. A pedestrian tunnel ran beneath it. It was the most direct route to the Tube station.

It was also a death trap.

Stone's alert would see Flynn or Blake, even both, wait at its far end. There was no way Reeve could avoid being seen as he emerged. If he followed Maxwell through, he would be killed.

But if he didn't, he might lose him.

Decision point. Maxwell approached the tunnel, Locke not far behind. Another glance at Stone. He was gaining again.

Maxwell vanished into shadow. Locke neared the tunnel entrance. To its left, brick stairs led up to street level. People ascended; there were bus stops above. Stone was five metres away. Reeve hunched lower, one striped hat lost amongst many. But this close, he couldn't stay hidden for much longer—

Locke entered the tunnel – and Reeve broke from the crowd.

He didn't run. That would have drawn instant attention. But he matched pace with a couple of men obviously worried about missing their bus. They started up the stairs. He followed closely. Two Fulham fans became three, all moving together.

He didn't dare look back. Stone would be watching the stairs as well as the tunnel. Would he pick out the cheap wig, remember the coat? Reeve's hand found the Walther . . .

Nothing happened. He kept climbing. Street level. *Now* he turned his head, gripping the gun—

Stone wasn't there.

No time for relief. He had to move.

The bridge was a major artery linking north and south London. The four-lane road was packed with cars and buses. The nearest pedestrian crossing was fifty metres away. Reeve didn't have time to wait for the lights. He found a gap in the traffic and ran into it. A driver braked hard and blasted his horn as Reeve dodged his car. One last lane, and he was across.

He broke into a full sprint. Down a side road, through a crossroads, and into a narrow, bus-only street. The elevated Tube line was ahead. Maxwell and the others would come from a road to the south. He had to reach the station before they did. The thought that it might have been staked out – where was Parker? – crossed his mind. Nothing he could do except react to whatever came at him . . .

He rounded a corner and ran to the station entrance. Fans squeezed slowly inside; he joined them. Maxwell and his bodyguards hadn't arrived yet. They would be here soon, though. He needed to get inside before they appeared so he could keep watch—

Reeve passed through the threshold – and realised he had made a mistake.

The day before, with Connie, he had explored the station. There had been only one route to the platforms. To his dismay, he now saw fans streaming up stairs that had previously been closed. The extra foot traffic on match day would otherwise cause massive logjams. Which way would Maxwell go? Reeve didn't even know if he would take a northbound or southbound train.

He used a travelcard to enter a gate, then went to the nearest stairs. Halfway up, he stopped and looked back. People pushed past him. The metallic rumble of a departing train came from above. He waited, watching . . .

Blake entered the ticket hall.

Reeve backed higher, tracking the Operative's pricey coat to avoid eye contact. The crowd shuffled through the gates. Blake tapped a card to enter. Which way was he going? The northbound platform, or south?

Northbound.

Reeve hurried up to the platform's north end. One train had gone, but a new crowd was already swelling. He found a position where he could observe the other stairs. A display board informed him the next train was three minutes away.

Blake appeared from the main stairs. The dark-haired man moved away from Reeve. That meant Flynn would come towards him. Maxwell would then emerge between them, Locke guarding his rear. The others were wildcards; they could come from anywhere . . .

Two minutes. Flynn was next to show herself. He only glimpsed her for a moment before she was lost amongst taller passengers. He would have to watch out for her in case she got too close—

Thoughts of Flynn vanished as he saw his target. Maxwell reached the platform. He moved clear of the stairs. Locke appeared behind, lurking at the stairwell's top. One minute. Where were the others?

He looked back – and saw Stone.

The Londoner had used the same staircase as him. He moved along the platform, eyes sweeping over everyone.

He would reach Reeve before the train arrived.

CHAPTER 28

Reeve's first thought was to move away from Stone. But that would bring him towards Flynn, even right to her.

A group of Huddersfield fans stood close by. Dejected by defeat, annoyed by the home fans' jubilation. Reeve moved closer. Stone neared from the other direction.

Movement at the crowd's front; the train was in sight. Thirty seconds until it arrived—

Reeve spoke. 'Stone.'

The sound of his name instantly caught Stone's attention. Reeve slipped behind the Huddersfield fans. Stone pushed towards them . . .

Reeve shoved one of the men shielding him. 'Oi! Don't push, you fucking losers!'

The group turned. 'Fuck off, we weren't pushing!' one man replied.

'You fuck off!' Reeve thrust a hand against his chest, knocking him back. At the same moment, he elbowed a Fulham fan hard in the side.

The result was predictable.

The Fulham supporters rounded on their rivals – and a scuffle broke out. Stone was caught on the periphery, a man stumbling into him.

The train swept past, brakes shrilling. Reeve had already retreated behind the angered Fulham fans. Bystanders scrambled clear of the fight. People yelled in warning, afraid of being knocked against the train.

Stone angrily shoved aside the man who had collided with him. That started a new chain reaction of impacting bodies. He barged after Reeve – only for an equally large man to grab him. 'You'll get someone killed, you fucking idiot!' his interceptor roared.

'Fuck off!' was Stone's reply – followed by a punch to the other man's stomach.

The train stopped, doors hissing open. Reeve quickly moved to the nearest entrance. A glance down the train's length. Maxwell was about to enter, looking in his direction. He would have heard Stone's encounter through his earpiece. Flynn and Locke weren't in sight. He looked left. Stone pulled clear of the brawl—

A flare of hi-vis yellow through the crowd. A police officer pushed towards Stone. 'You! Stop there!'

Reeve didn't have time to see Stone's response. He boarded. Standing room only, supporters flooding in with him. It was a modern train, the interconnected carriages open at each end. He could see all the way to the front and the rear.

He peered forward as everyone jostled for space. If Stone had boarded, he couldn't see him. More people squeezed in. Shouldn't the doors have closed by now? Shit. Had the fight delayed the train? He waited, anxiety growing . . .

A warning trill – and the doors slid shut.

The train set off. Reeve looked through the window. A

fleeting glimpse of Stone arguing with the policeman. Then the station became a blur.

One threat removed – but he still had to deal with the others.

Maxwell listened impatiently to the voices in his earpiece. Stone was angrily telling the cop he was a Metropolitan Police detective. He had the credentials to 'prove' it – as long as they weren't challenged. If the officer called in to check, Stone was in deep shit. Not just from the Met, either. Maxwell had always considered the ex-copper a borderline asset for SC9. Sometimes a truly blunt instrument was the right tool for the job, but here . . .

Luck was on Stone's side, though. 'Sorry, sir,' said the officer. 'Didn't realise.'

'Yeah, and now I've lost my suspect,' Stone snapped. 'Nice one. Thanks.' He added something, but the words were lost behind distortion. The team's radios had only limited range, and the train had carried Maxwell past it.

He soon got a phone call. 'I fucking lost him,' Stone growled.

Maxwell looked towards the train's front. If Reeve was there, he was keeping out of sight. 'Did you see him?'

'No, but I *heard* him. I'm certain of it. The next train's in five minutes – I'll catch up.'

'Okay. We'll stay on the planned route.' He disconnected. 'Everyone hear that?' he muttered into his mic.

'Should we search the train?' Locke asked.

'Not enough time,' Maxwell replied. 'We'll be at Earl's Court in seven minutes. If Alex wants to follow me, he'll *have* to use the escalators. We'll spot him there.'

He stared along the train again. Hundreds of swaying people filled it. Somewhere amongst them was Reeve.

Closer to him. The game was becoming more tense.

Reeve moved gradually rearwards at each stop. He halted when he finally glimpsed Locke. The blond man was using his injury to lay claim to a disabled seat.

With Stone removed, Reeve now technically led the chase. He was farthest forward in the train; then Locke, Flynn, Maxwell, and Blake. Parker, he still hadn't seen. That was a factor he didn't like.

Nothing he could do about it. A recorded announcement said the next stop was Earl's Court. Locke shifted, about to get up. Earl's Court was an interchange; was Maxwell changing trains?

Other passengers also prepared to disembark. Reeve moved forward, away from Locke. The station swept into view. The District Line platforms were above ground. If Maxwell was changing trains, he would go underground to the Piccadilly Line.

If he wasn't, he was heading out of the station. Potentially to anywhere in London. He would become much harder for one man to track . . .

And that one man would become easier for his quarry's guardians to find.

The train squealed to a standstill. The doors slid open. Reeve went to them – but didn't exit, instead peering out down the train's length. People jostled him as they squeezed past, but he held his place. Earl's Court was another station he had checked out with Connie. Which way was Maxwell going? If he came towards him, the main ticket hall – and the street exits. Away from him meant descending via an underground concourse to the Piccadilly Line.

He glimpsed Flynn, two carriages behind. Then she was lost in the crowd. Which way had she turned? He couldn't tell—

Locke appeared, much closer. But he didn't step out. He was doing the same as Reeve, watching the platform from inside the doors. Reeve withdrew, looking down the train's interior. He glimpsed the sling between the departing passengers. Then Locke pulled back himself. Reeve glanced out again.

There was Maxwell – turning *away* from him.

He was going to the lower platforms. Flynn shadowed him – as did Blake.

Locke reappeared at the door. Reeve immediately retreated into the carriage – and marched back through it.

Most of those leaving the train were now out. He swept through the stragglers towards Locke. The door alarm sounded. Locke straightened. Satisfied Reeve hadn't left the train ahead of him, he started to step out—

Reeve came up behind him and tore his mic from his collar with one hand. His other thumb drove deep into Locke's shoulder wound.

Locke convulsed, jerking backwards with a strained cry. Reeve clawed harder, twisting his hand. Even through Locke's shirt he felt flesh tear, stitches pop. The doors started to close. He jumped through as they slammed behind him. Locke staggered, then recovered—

The train moved off. He locked eyes with Reeve for a brief, livid moment before being whisked away.

Reeve wiped blood from his thumb, then searched for the other Operatives. He saw Maxwell, back to him as he headed for the concourse stairs. He knew from his recce it would be too dangerous to follow. The Piccadilly Line was reached by escalator. He would be exposed on the descent.

But there was another way down.

He hurried to the stairs leading up at the platform's eastern end. There were lifts to the Piccadilly Line in the ticket hall above. Using them was too much of a risk, though. He might have to wait too long and miss Maxwell's train. But there was an alternative route.

Rather than ascend, he continued along the platform. A barrier warned that he was entering a restricted area, but he squeezed around it. Beneath the stairs was a metal concertina gate. The entrance to an emergency stairwell. He had seen it the previous day, noting it was padlocked.

No problem.

That morning he had bought a box of paper clips. Only a couple were needed. He straightened one and snapped it into two halves. He raised the padlock and slipped one wire into the keyhole. That was his torsion wrench. He pushed it in as far as it would go, then bent it back. It would hold the padlock's barrel in place while he worked.

Next came the other half; the pick itself. He had undergone many, many hours of training at Mordencroft. He found the locking pins by feel. A gentle jiggle until they clicked – then a twist.

The padlock popped open.

Reeve quickly removed it. He would already have been seen rounding the barrier on CCTV. Station staff would be here in a minute, less. He opened the gate and darted through.

He clattered down a tight spiral staircase. Another gate at the bottom, also locked. Opening the padlock from the other side of the bars was more tricky. His forearms wedged between the metal slats; he could only just reach. Hold up the padlock, makeshift torsion wrench in place. Now get the pick into position . . .

The paperclip rasped against the pins. Barely any feel from this angle. He heard people walking past each end of the short access passage. Staff could arrive at any moment. Work the pins, come on, come *on*—

Click.

Relief as the barrel turned. He wrestled the padlock clear and opened the gate. Two platforms: eastbound to his right, westbound the left. Which would Maxwell take?

He went right out of pure instinct. The platform was crowded, a train due shortly. He had to see if Maxwell and his shadows were here – or not. But another task took priority. A CCTV camera covered the emergency exit. He kept his head down to mask his face as much as possible. The Fulham hat was easy to spot, though.

So he discarded it – along with the wig beneath.

Reeve ducked low into the crowd and snatched off both items. The hair revealed under them was now bleached blond. He weaved between passengers, then resurfaced. The CCTV would – he hoped – have lost track of him.

That hope was about to be tested. A man in Transport for London uniform and hi-vis vest pushed closer. 'Excuse me, excuse me sir,' he said as he reached Reeve—

And passed.

Reeve quickly moved down the platform. The underground tunnel was hot and cramped. It was hard to see through the crush. A board told him the train would arrive in one minute.

He wouldn't have time to check the whole platform.

If Maxwell was here, he would come from the far end where the escalators descended. Reeve pushed through the crowd, peering over and around people's heads. Flynn was short enough to be obscured, but he should spot the others—

Blake's smooth, dark hairstyle rose above the impatient mass. Was Maxwell with him? A rising wind as the train approached, wheels clamouring. The clock was running down.

Blake looked back towards the escalator, concerned. He had realised Locke had lost contact. Two watchers down. Would Maxwell bail out? If he did, that ended Reeve's chances of getting answers—

There. Maxwell hadn't run – yet. He was on the platform, like Blake looking towards the entrance. Waiting for a shadow who wouldn't appear.

The train roared into the station. Older stock than the District Line; individual carriages, not interlinked. Reeve kept his eyes on Maxwell. Would he board – or turn back?

'Harrison, are you there?' said Maxwell. He was no longer concerned if anyone noticed he was talking to himself. 'Locke!' No reply. Either Locke was down, or his radio was offline. Neither would have happened by accident.

The train swept noisily past. 'What do we do?' Flynn said in his earpiece. 'On or off?'

Maxwell thought for a moment. Then: 'On. Stay with the plan.'

'Are you sure?' Blake asked. 'Two men are down already. If he gets to you—'

'If I abort, he'll run. We'll lose him. This is our only chance to bring him in close.' The train stopped, the crowd sweeping towards the doors.

'He might get a bit *too* close,' Flynn commented acerbically.

'I'll take it as it comes.' The doors opened, disgorging passengers. Those on the platform replaced them. He followed the flow through a carriage's single rear door. 'Deirdre, soon as you have a connection, phone Harrison and Mark. Tell them to follow the planned route. We'll dawdle at the next change to let them catch up.'

A warbling alarm, then the doors slammed. Maxwell took hold of an overhead rail as the train set off. He surveyed his fellow passengers. Reeve wasn't amongst them – at least, not within sight. Blake was at his carriage's forward end. Flynn would be in the coach behind. A look back, but he couldn't see her through the connecting doors.

A flash of worry. She *should* be in the carriage behind . . .

'Deirdre?'

'Yes?'

'Just checking.' Brief amusement, which quickly faded. *Where* are *you, Alex?*

Reeve was one carriage ahead, watching through the connecting door. He could see Blake, back to him at the first set of double sliding doors. Maxwell had boarded the same carriage, but so far Reeve hadn't spotted him. Anyone else with him was also out of sight.

The train slowed for the next station. Reeve glanced at the map above the exit. Gloucester Road. Blake didn't seem about to leave. Where was Maxwell going? South Kensington and Knightsbridge were the upcoming stops. Reeve doubted either was his destination. SC9 provided Operatives with cover-appropriate homes, but not in the million-plus range. So Maxwell would stay aboard for a few more minutes, at least . . .

The train stopped – and Reeve got off.

He moved to the back of the platform, hiding behind the crowd. Then he went down the train's length. Head lowered, past the entrance where Blake was waiting. Merge into the boarding passengers, and back aboard via the second double doors.

Had Blake seen him pass? No; he was still in the same place.

So where was Maxwell?

Reeve slowly turned. He could see the carriage's end bulkhead, so he couldn't be far . . .

A chill as he saw Maxwell three metres away.

The last time they were this close, his mentor had tried to kill him. He instinctively shrank into the crowd's cover. Maxwell held a ceiling rail, seemingly staring blankly at the route map. Reeve knew that was not the case. Even at his most apparently placid, Tony Maxwell's mind was always working. He could guess what he was thinking. *Where is Reeve? How do I get to him before he gets to me?*

Reeve's own thoughts were a perfect mirror. His target was right in front of him. But how to catch him? He risked rising higher for a better look. Something was visible inside Maxwell's collar. A small mic, just like Locke's. He was in constant two-way contact with his minders. A word, a sound, an innocuous code phrase, and they would be alerted. Would the Operatives risk shooting him on a crowded Tube train?

Yes.

Get in close, wait for the moment of maximum confusion and cover. A silenced round into the back of the heart as passengers move for the doors. Sidestep as the body falls, gun away, keep moving as the screams start. Five seconds to get off the train, then as panic spreads go with the flow. Out of the station by the time the police arrive.

That was what he would do. So the others would do it too. He had to separate them from Maxwell.

But how?

Through more stations. He was well beyond the area he had reconnoitred with Connie. The only names he knew now were from a Monopoly board. If he followed Maxwell off the train, every action would be reactive, improvised. High risk.

So he would have to *keep* Maxwell on the train.

Holborn. Russell Square. King's Cross next—

Maxwell straightened. He was about to get off. Reeve slid into cover as the older man quietly spoke into the mic. He glanced back. Blake was also getting ready to leave.

Reeve's gaze returned to Maxwell. He had one chance. Fail, and he would either never get any answers – or be killed.

One hand on the gun, he pushed towards the doors.

Maxwell hadn't yet moved, letting the knot of people ahead of him leave first. Ignored annoyed tuts from other passengers, Reeve squirmed to the exit. Both Maxwell and Blake were now blocked from his sight. The train slowed, everyone swaying.

Station lights flashed past outside, blurs resolving into individuals. The train stopped. A moment, then the doors opened—

Reeve was first out. He immediately turned and hurried along the platform. People squeezed from the smaller doorway ahead. He shoved into the waiting crowd. No time for politeness. His index finger found the Walther's trigger guard and poised over it. A glimpse of Maxwell through the windows. He pushed forward, drawing the gun as the other man reached the exit—

The suppressor's muzzle jabbed into Maxwell's stomach. 'Back,' Reeve said quietly.

Maxwell froze. Reeve watched his eyes. He could see his mind working frenziedly behind them. Assessing the situation, calculating odds, deciding on a response . . .

A split-second – and the choice was made.

CHAPTER 29

Maxwell retreated.

Reeve moved with him, his coat shielding the weapon from the passengers. He directed Maxwell against the connecting door. Reeve's eyes never broke contact with Maxwell's. The slightest hint of impending action, and he would fire.

Maxwell knew it. He waited until the sliding doors closed before glancing away. A flick of Reeve's own gaze. Blake was outside, on the platform. Alarm crossed his face as he realised Maxwell wasn't with him. The train started to move. Blake looked through the windows – to see both men still inside.

Then he was gone.

Reeve grabbed the older man's right wrist with his left hand. Maxwell was right-handed, his gun – he surely had one – holstered on the left. Reaching it with his free hand would now be awkward. He would be dead before his fingers touched it.

Maxwell's expression told Reeve he wasn't going to try. Rather than speak, Reeve's eyes flicked towards the little microphone. Maxwell understood his meaning. He warily reached up with his left hand and pulled it until it popped loose.

The moment it was disconnected, he spoke. 'So you're not going to kill me.'

Reeve kept the gun pressed against his stomach. 'What makes you think that?'

'If you were, I'd be dead already.'

'The day's not over.'

Maxwell shook his head with sardonic humour. 'You've got three minutes before the next station. What do you want, Alex?'

'What do I want?' Reeve leaned closer, voice dropping to a growling whisper. 'I want to know why you tried to kill me.'

Maxwell nodded, almost imperceptibly, as if a belief had just been confirmed. 'It wasn't my decision.'

'Whose was it?'

'The boss's, of course.'

'Why?'

'Your profile said you were a security threat.'

Reeve was briefly silent, unable to believe his ears. 'Bullshit!'

'Pretty much my initial reaction. But I had my orders.'

Reeve struggled to process the revelation. He'd been declared a security threat? But he hadn't done anything wrong . . . 'Why was I declared Fox Red?'

'I don't know,' Maxwell replied. He seemed almost apologetic. 'It wasn't because of anything I wrote, though. I wasn't lying when I said you were an exemplary recruit.'

'Thank you,' was Reeve's sarcastic reply.

'I'm serious. Serious enough that after you escaped – I was genuinely impressed, by the way—'

More sarcasm. 'Again, thanks.'

'—I checked back over your file. I wanted to see why you'd been flagged.'

'And what did you find?'

'Long story short, there wasn't one thing. More like lots of little things.'

Reeve became impatient. They would soon reach the next station. 'Such as?'

Maxwell's dark eyes revealed a flicker almost of *amusement*. 'Well, that's the interesting part. Do you remember when we talked about your deep loathing of the British class system?'

Reeve's brow creased in confusion. 'No.'

'Nor do I. But it's flagged in the profile as a point against you. I didn't write it, but . . . it's there.'

'So someone doctored my profile to make me look like a traitor?'

A small shrug. 'I don't know. I don't have access to the whole thing. Only the parts I was responsible for.'

'Who does?'

'Nobody at Mordencroft. The only person with access to all SC9's files is the boss.' He hesitated, then: 'Sir Simon Scott.'

It was the first time Reeve had heard his name. The head of SC9 was a figure shrouded in mystery, and menace.

What to do with that knowledge? He wasn't sure. But the three minutes were more than halfway gone . . .

'I need to see him.' The words came out almost before the idea had fully crystallised.

Surprise on Maxwell's face. 'You want to see the boss?'

'I am *not* a traitor,' Reeve insisted. 'I need to know *why* he declared me Fox Red.'

The older man seemed conflicted. 'He's out of the country,' he finally said.

'Where?'

'France. He has a villa in Provence. Spends a lot of time there.'

'Nice work if you can get it.'

'Yeah. It's all right for some.' Another moment of contemplation, then: 'Villa Mielena, about three kilometres north-west of Montsalier.'

It was Reeve's turn to be surprised, even as he memorised the location. 'You're helping me?'

'I don't believe you're a traitor,' was the reply. 'Something's going on – and I think you're the patsy. I can't investigate it any further than I have. Not without drawing attention. But you can.'

'As long as SC9 don't kill me.'

A wry smile. 'You've managed all right so far. So keep doing what you do. Just don't tell Scott I told you how to find him. I don't want to be declared Fox Red either.'

The train started to slow. 'What about Scott?' Reeve hurriedly asked. 'Is he with his family?'

'No. He does have dogs, though. Oh, and he'll have minders.'

'Great.' Nearby passengers prepared to disembark. Reeve hesitated, then released Maxwell's wrist.

Maxwell stayed still. 'I won't stop you,' he assured him.

Despite everything, Reeve believed him. He drew the gun back. 'Thanks.'

'I'll deny this talk happened, obviously.' They both managed to smile. The train came into the station. 'Alex,' Maxwell said, serious once more, 'we won't stop hunting you. Why don't you just get out of the country and run? You know how to disappear.'

'I want answers,' said Reeve. 'And I want to prove that I'm innocent.' The train halted.

'And you think you'll be allowed back into SC9 as if nothing's happened?'

He had no reply to that. But then the doors opened. He backed away from Maxwell. The other man didn't move. Reeve left the carriage, slipping the PPK back into his coat. Where was he? Caledonian Road, according to the signs. The name meant nothing. He followed the passengers towards the exit as the train set off again. One last look back, momentarily catching Maxwell's eye, then his mentor was gone.

Maxwell watched Reeve until the train entered the tunnel. A long exhalation, then he took out his phone, waiting to regain reception. When he got a signal at the next stop, he disembarked and called Blake. 'I'm at Holloway Road. Tell everyone to catch up.' He disconnected before the other man could reply.

It took ten minutes before everyone reached him. Locke's face was ashen, his expression a mix of pain and fury. 'You okay?' Maxwell asked.

'Beyond the newly reopened stab wound? Yes,' came the reply through clenched teeth.

Stone's anger was much closer to the surface. 'What the *fuck* happened? How did that piece of shit get past us?'

'We underestimated him,' was Maxwell's simple reply.

'He got to you – and you're still alive,' said Blake.

Maxwell gave him a sardonic look. 'You sound disappointed.'

'More surprised. That he's still alive, as well. What did he want?'

'He wanted what I thought he wanted. To know why he was declared Fox Red.'

'What, he really doesn't know?' Flynn exclaimed.

'So he says.'

'And what did you tell him?' asked Blake.

'Nothing, because there's nothing to tell. I don't know why he was declared Fox Red either. He wasn't happy, but there was nothing he could do about it. He kept me at gunpoint until he got off at Caledonian Road, then ran.'

Stone shook his head. 'Jesus. Complete fucking clusterfuck. And you didn't shoot him soon as his gun was off you?'

Maxwell gave him a cold glare. 'I generally try not to risk mowing down British civilians, Mark. SC9 can cover up a lot of things on our home turf. That is *not* one of them.'

'So now what?' said Flynn. 'Reeve got away. We fucked up. The boss won't be happy.'

'*I* fucked up,' Maxwell corrected. 'Yes, there's plenty of culpability to go around. But ultimately, this was my plan, and it didn't work. Let me take care of the reports. I'll take the hit from the boss. For now, get back to the safehouse. Go separately, and make sure you're not followed. Just in case.'

'You think Reeve might try to track us?' Blake said.

'I'm not discounting any possibility right now.'

The group dispersed. Maxwell waited until they were

gone, then took out his phone. He scrolled through his contacts to one listed simply as 'Scott'.

He called the secure line. 'Maxwell, sir,' he said, on getting a reply. 'I'm afraid the plan didn't work.' A pause, then: 'Reeve never showed up.'

CHAPTER 30

'You're okay?' Connie said, relieved.

'Yeah,' Reeve replied, as he entered her car. Baseball cap back on, he had made a circuitous tour of London before phoning her.

She pulled away. 'What happened? Did you find him?'

'Yes.'

'And?'

'I need to go to the south of France.'

'Don't we all?' They exchanged looks, the tension broken by laughter. 'What did he say?'

'He told me how to find the man who gave the order to kill me.'

'So . . . he's on your side?'

'I don't know.' Reeve had given Maxwell's motives a great deal of thought. Could he believe him? His former teacher was taking a great risk by letting him go. If the boss – Sir Simon Scott – found out, he would also be declared Fox Red. But . . . something didn't feel right. Was giving him Scott's location a way to draw him into a trap?

He had used Jammer's phone to learn more about Scott himself. What little he could, anyway. Sir Simon Scott, GBE, had been knighted in 2010 for 'services to Her Majesty's

Government'. What those services actually *were* remained mysterious. He was a Cambridge graduate, a civil servant, and sixty-three years old. Anything else was beyond the knowledge of the world's search engines. There wasn't even a photo of him online.

The absence of information, ironically, let Reeve infer plenty. Scott had almost certainly followed a career in British Intelligence. Before heading SC9, he would have been high up in MI5 or MI6. Such people made it a point to avoid featuring in the news.

The spider at the centre of the web. Scott had been the only one to see every report on his potential new recruits. And for some reason, he had decided Reeve was a traitor. Fox Red. Why?

Reeve was going to find out.

'But his boss is in France,' he went on. 'Provence. That's why I need to go.'

'You want to meet him?' said Connie. 'Won't that be dangerous?'

'Probably. But no more than staying in London.'

She eyed him. 'You didn't get into *another* fight, did you?'

'No,' he only slightly lied. 'Some close calls, though. I got lucky. But,' he admitted ruefully, 'I doubt I will again. Not against the same people.'

They stopped at traffic lights. 'So where do you want to go now?' Connie asked. 'Back to Jammer's flat?'

'Yeah. But I need to go back to your place too. I want to ask Mr Brownlow a favour.'

'What kind?'

'I'm hoping he'll lend me his passport.'

'Why do you want to borrow his passport?' she asked. The answer came almost before she finished speaking. 'What? You want to disguise yourself as *Philip*?'

'It's him or Jammer, and Jammer's a drug dealer. If he's been flagged for anything, I'll be stopped. I can't risk that.'

The lights changed, and Connie set off again. 'He's twenty years older than you.'

'I can do it. You'll be surprised.'

'I'll be *very* surprised.' She turned, heading for Jammer's flat.

They stopped in the visitors' car park. Reeve went in alone. He checked the entrance of Jammer's apartment before entering. A hair he had stuck between the door and frame was still there. A very old trick, but one that still worked. The drug dealer hadn't been home. If Connie was right, he would be in hospital for at least another day.

He entered. As per his plan, he had stashed most of Jammer's drug money in a locker. He took a wad of the remaining cash from the safe. A moment of thought, then he also collected the iPad. He returned to the car. Connie eyed the tablet. 'What's that?'

'A way to make sure Jammer doesn't cause you any more trouble. Oh, and when we come back, can you bring your laptop?'

'Can't you use that?'

'It'll be easier to work on a proper computer. Besides, I want to keep this somewhere safe. Jammer'll come back home eventually.'

They drove to Connie's. Reeve got her to patrol the neighbouring streets before stopping. Nothing triggered any mental alarm bells. 'I think it's clear,' he finally said. 'But let's be quick.'

They entered the house. Connie checked the mail, then unlocked her flat. 'I'll get my laptop,' she said.

He looked around the hall while he waited. Leaving the iPad at Connie's was too obvious a hiding place. The same for the other flats . . .

The radiator. He peered behind it, seeing a gap large enough to conceal the tablet. Despite the miserable weather, it was nearly summer; the heating wouldn't be turned on. He slipped the machine into the hiding place and stood back. It was out of sight.

Connie returned with her laptop and locked up. 'Okay, got it,' she said. 'Let's see Philip.'

Brownlow was in. He responded to Reeve's request with surprise, but accepted. 'After what you did for me, I'm more than happy to help.' He rooted through a drawer.

Reeve took out the money. 'This is to pay for it.'

Brownlow did a double-take at the thick bunch of notes. 'But – that must be over a thousand pounds.'

'About two thousand. Consider it a refund from Jammer. You could use it to find a better flat. Somewhere you won't be hassled by drug dealers.'

'I – I can't take that,' said Brownlow.

Reeve put the money on the table. 'I'll leave it there.'

The older man looked torn. 'I'll . . . think about it.' He turned back to the drawer, though kept glancing at the cash. 'Here it is.'

He handed over his passport. Reeve flicked through it. It had been issued eight years prior, still valid for two. Brownlow looked far younger and more vibrant in the photo. Stress had aged and drained him. 'This is great, thanks,' he said. 'I'll get it back as soon as I can.'

'What do you need it for?' said Brownlow. 'Or shouldn't I ask?' Reeve gave him a look. 'I won't ask.'

Reeve and Connie said goodbye, then left. They returned to Jammer's, taking a roundabout route. No one followed them. 'So what now?' Connie asked after they entered the flat.

'Book a trip through the Channel Tunnel on Le Shuttle,' he said. 'I'll use Jammer's credit card.'

'The train?'

He nodded. 'It's the weakest part of UK border security. Hundreds of vehicles board each train within a very short window. The Border Force officers don't have time for detailed identity checks. They count the people in each car, and check the passport photos. As long as things look right, they let the car through. If you're not on a watch list, you're unlikely to be stopped.'

'You sound very confident about that.'

'I've gone through before in disguise on a fake ID. For an exercise,' he clarified. 'I should be able to look enough like Brownlow to fool them.'

Connie remained dubious. 'You know what would make it easier?'

'What?'

'If you weren't driving. If you're in the passenger seat, you're further away, and in shadow. It'll be harder for them to see your face.'

Reeve knew immediately where she was leading. 'You can't come with me.'

'Why not?'

'It's too dangerous for you.'

'No, it'll be *safer*. I still don't want to go home in case Jammer's friends come back. Or the people looking for you, for that matter. And I can't stay at his place; like you said, he'll come home eventually.' Her tone shifted from concern for herself to him. 'It'll be safer for you too. Remember when we checked out the football ground together? The guy there didn't spot you – because you were with me. They're looking for one man, not a couple. And you were planning to take Jammer's car, yes?' He nodded. 'What if he's reported it stolen? Or he's got twenty bags of heroin hidden in the doors?'

She had a point. 'So you're suggesting I take – we take – your car?'

'Yes. I'll call in sick. I wouldn't normally leave the other nurses in the lurch, but this is important.'

'It's important to me, not to you.'

'*You're* important to me.' The statement caught him off-guard, leaving him unsure how to respond. She blushed a little, as if also surprised by her words. 'You're my patient, remember? I just fixed you. I don't want you to get messed up again.'

He felt his own cheeks warming. 'Thanks,' he said. 'But . . . it really will be dangerous. The man I need to talk to will have security.'

'Are they as good as you?'

'They'll have had the same training.'

'But you just *beat* people with the same training,' she pointed out. 'Besides, I wasn't planning to break into this guy's secret lair. I'm a nurse, not a spy.'

'I'm not a spy either,' he replied.

Connie arched an amused eyebrow. 'That's actually the most you've told me about what you do. Even if it's what you *don't* do.'

'Well, you know the saying. If I told you what I do . . . '

' . . . you'd have to kill me?' she finished. 'There's gratitude for you.'

Reeve grinned. 'Don't worry. I wouldn't hurt you. And I'll make sure you *don't* get hurt.'

'So you want me to come?'

'You can come, yeah.'

'That's not *quite* the question I asked, is it?' But she was still happy with his reply. 'Okay, what happens next?'

He indicated her laptop. 'I'll book us both on to Le Shuttle. I already looked up where we're going. Montsalier, in Provence – it's about a nine-hour drive from Calais. If we take the first train, we should get there by late afternoon. Hopefully we'll be able to find a hotel. Oh,' he added, 'I'll need your passport number to make the booking. You'll have to go back home for it.'

Her sly smile told him she had thought ahead. 'No, I won't,' she said, producing the little book. 'I'd already decided I was going with you.'

Reeve took it. 'You're in the wrong line of work.'

Night fell. Connie went to bed, Reeve lying on the sofa. The first train left Folkstone at 6AM; they would have to leave before dawn.

Booking the journey had been no trouble. Using Jammer's credit card had raised no apparent flags. People making reservations for other holidaymakers was common enough.

It was their arrival at the terminal that concerned him. Would a booking at such short notice draw extra attention? And if it did, how far would any disguise get him? If the Border Force realised who he really was, SC9 would come for him . . .

He felt optimistic, though. Even if Maxwell *had* set him up, he couldn't have anticipated that he wasn't alone. The authorities would be looking for a man travelling solo – as Connie had noted.

He could get to Scott. He was sure of it. When he did . . . he would find out *why* Scott had ordered his death.

And then discover who had framed him.

CHAPTER 31

The alarm on Connie's phone warbled in the bedroom. Reeve glanced at Jammer's phone. Three in the morning. He had already been up for an hour.

She reluctantly emerged ten minutes later, finding him in the bathroom. 'Morning,' she said sleepily – before jolting awake. 'Jesus!' She took a closer look at him. 'Oh, my God. I hardly recognised you.'

Brownlow's passport was open beside the mirror. Reeve had transformed himself into the face in its photograph. All he had used were simple stage makeup tricks – but they worked. Small dabs of liquid latex glue crinkled his skin into crow's feet and creases. Connie's makeup kit had also played its part. Powdered light and shade added eye bags, jowls, wrinkles. Cotton wool in his mouth puffed out the cheeks. His bleached hair had changed colour again, to ginger. He had swept it back to raise his hairline. Not only did he look two decades older, but he indeed resembled Brownlow.

As with his earlier disguises, close inspection would reveal the truth. But in a car, from three metres away, he would pass.

He hoped.

Connie was still boggling at the change. 'Wow. Are you wearing one of those *Mission: Impossible* masks?'

'They'd make life a lot easier,' Reeve replied. His voice was slightly muffled by the cotton. He pulled the damp pieces out. 'Are you ready? We'll need to go in thirty minutes.'

She was wearing an oversized T-shirt with a picture of a cartoon unicorn, hair messy. 'Do I *look* ready?'

A joking grimace. 'I'll get out of the way.'

Reeve collected his transformation tools and retreated into the lounge. He packed them; they would be needed for the return journey. 'Where are your car keys?'

'In my handbag, by the bed. Why?'

'I want to start loading up.' He found the keys, then collected the gun and spare ammo. Slipping it under his jacket, he left the flat.

When he returned ten minutes later, Connie was dressed and brushing her hair. 'I made you some coffee,' she said.

'Thanks. You look nice.' The compliment slipped out.

She beamed. 'Thank you. But you should see me when I make an effort.' She glanced at his bag, still on the table. 'I thought you were loading the car?'

'Preparing it, really. Want some toast?'

'Yes, please.' Another smile. 'This is all very domestic, isn't it? Even as we're about to go to France on a spy mission.'

'Life's full of surprises.' Jammer had a large chromed toaster. He put in four slices of bread and pushed them down.

Twenty minutes later, they had eaten and collected their belongings. 'Ready?' Reeve asked.

Connie nodded. She was more pensive now. 'I hope this works.'

'So do I. But if anything goes wrong, just tell them I kidnapped you.'

'Not funny.' They headed for the car.

Early on a Sunday, even London's traffic was minimal. They cleared the capital and were on the M2 motorway in an hour. Connie stayed at the speed limit, not wanting to draw attention. On to the M20, heading south-east towards the coast. They reached the Eurotunnel terminal after an hour and forty minutes. An automated check-in at a barrier printed out their ticket. Jammer's credit card had been accepted, as had Connie's registration. One hurdle overcome. The next few would be bigger, though . . .

They stopped at the terminal building. 'You okay?' Reeve asked. Connie had become increasingly taciturn as the journey progressed.

'Yeah, yeah, fine,' she said, a little too quickly. 'I'm just . . . nervous.'

'It'll work. You know what to say.' They had rehearsed responses to potential questions during the drive. 'Just sound friendly, and don't talk too much.'

Reeve put more cotton in his cheeks, then they entered the terminal. Despite his assurances to Connie, he felt tense himself. The building was dotted with CCTV cameras. There were also numerous security guards. If his disguise triggered anyone's curiosity, he would very quickly be exposed.

But no one paid him any notice. He used the toilet and waited for Connie. Departure boards told him their train would leave in forty minutes. Boarding would start in fifteen; they had time.

As long as they cleared customs.

Reeve's tension rose further as they drove to border control. There were two checks a hundred metres apart; British and French. The former concerned him more. If SC9 had issued an alert, his picture would be there. There was also another worry. 'See those yellow boxes?' he said.

Connie looked ahead. Between each lane were tall, thin metal cabinets. The road alongside each was marked with yellow hatchings: *no stopping*. 'What are they?'

'Millimetre-wave scanners. Like X-ray machines.'

She blinked in alarm. 'They X-ray every car? What, without even warning anyone? But that's really dangerous. The radiation exposure—'

'They're more like radar. But they can see inside the car. They use them to look for contraband. Right now, I'm hoping they won't spot Jammer's gun.'

'*What?* You brought a *gun*?'

'It's spread through the car. I completely dismantled it. I don't *think* they'll recognise all the bits.'

'But – but what if they do?'

'You tell them I kidnapped you.'

She huffed. '*Still* not funny.'

The cars ahead cleared the first customs post. Connie gave Reeve an unhappy glare, then drove past the scanner. They soon reached the checkpoint. A uniformed woman gestured for Connie to lower her window. She did so. 'Can I see your passports and travel documents, please,' the officer drawled. Connie handed them over. The woman checked them, then passed them to someone behind. 'Going on holiday?'

'Afraid not,' Connie replied. Reeve could hear her nervousness; could the officer? 'We've got a sick relative. Going to see her.'

'I'm sorry to hear that,' was the rote reply. The officer peered into the Saxo. 'Just the two of you?'

'Yes, yeah,' said Connie, nodding. Reeve masked his concern. The woman was paying him more attention than he'd expected . . .

The person behind her spoke. She turned; an exchange followed. Reeve forced himself not to clench his fists. The car was trapped. Another vehicle blocked the way behind, and the barrier was reinforced. If he had to flee, it would be on foot. And there were dozens of armed Border Force personnel nearby—

The officer turned back to them. She looked at Reeve, at the passport, at him . . .

Then returned the documents. 'Have a safe trip.'

'Thank you,' Connie replied. The barrier rose. She drove through. 'Oh, Jesus,' she gasped, once they were clear. 'I thought she'd realised you weren't Philip.'

'She might have done if I'd been driving,' he said. 'So you were right. It's a good job you came.'

'Yes, good job,' she echoed sarcastically. 'It's only going to give me a heart attack.'

The French border check was no less tense. Since Brexit, the attention given to UK travellers' documents had increased considerably. But again, Reeve's disguise worked. Eight years was enough time for a person's appearance to change from their passport photo. The male officer looked between Reeve and his picture, then shrugged. The gate opened.

They were through.

'Jesus,' Connie muttered again as they headed for the train.

'Are you okay?' Reeve asked.

'Yeah, yeah. Just . . .' She gave him a worried look. 'It just sunk in that we were committing a crime.'

'But we made it through,' he said. 'We did it once, we can do it again.'

She turned away, unconsciously biting her lip. 'I'm not planning on making a habit of it.'

Reeve realised that, for now, nothing he said would help. He sat back as they joined the cars waiting to board the shuttle. The surroundings were joylessly functional, wet concrete and steel shrouded in particulate grime. Even the train was grey. He used Jammer's phone to check conditions at their destination. 'At least the weather'll be nicer in Provence.' His attempt to break the ice drew only a non-committal nod.

Before long, they were directed aboard. They passed through several transporter carriages, stopping at the tail of the line of cars. Another vehicle pulled up behind them. Trapped again, and literally boxed in. Reeve knew they wouldn't have been allowed to board had they raised any suspicion. Despite that, he still felt rising claustrophobia . . .

But nothing happened. The train was soon fully loaded. Recorded safety warnings played, then, without fanfare, they set off.

The truck was windowless. They only knew they had cleared the tunnel when the train slowed. A few minutes later, it stopped. The doors ahead opened, and Connie followed the other cars through the train's length.

And out. 'Welcome to France,' said Reeve, as the tyres met tarmac.

She managed a half-smile. 'We made it this far, then.'

'We'll make it all the way. And back. Trust me.'

Signs guided them out of the Eurotunnel complex. 'Drive on the right, on the *right*,' Connie muttered. He smiled.

The route was programmed into Jammer's phone. Reeve directed her on to a slip road to the A16 autoroute. Nervous now for entirely different reasons, she increased speed. The time difference meant it was after eight o'clock, but the road wasn't busy. 'I should have got you to drive off the train,' she said, knuckles white.

'You're doing fine,' he said. 'We'll change over when we stop.'

'When will that be?'

'Whenever we need to. It's just over a thousand kilometres, so we'll need to refuel at least once.'

'Where's the *first* place we can stop?'

He laughed, then checked the phone. 'There's an *aire* – a service station – on the A26. Just over twenty kilometres.'

'Great. Sorry, but you'll be doing most of the driving.'

'I don't mind. Follow this road. When you see signs for the A26, head right. And remember, in rain the speed limit's twenty kph lower.'

As in England, it was still raining, but the clouds here seemed lighter. Reeve regarded the phone again. The estimated journey time was nine hours and thirty minutes. Longer in this weather; they would probably arrive around six. And then they still had to find a hotel . . .

The motorway rolled by. Before long, signs appeared. *A26/E15, Reims-Paris.* Connie followed them. They merged on to a new autoroute.

The long journey south through France had begun.

And at its end was the man who had ordered Reeve's death.

CHAPTER 32

Reeve took the wheel at the first *aire*. The sky brightened as they drove south. After an hour, the rain finally stopped. By the time they passed the city of Reims, the clouds had lifted. For what felt like the first time in years, he saw the sun.

Connie's mood improved too. By a third of the way through the journey, she was her usual cheery self. Little red-roofed villages slipped by, quaint churches at the heart of each. 'It's really beautiful,' she said. Rolling green farmland dotted with wind turbines was interspersed with woods.

'Yeah, it is,' Reeve replied, stifling a yawn. Despite its attractiveness, the landscape made for a monotonous drive.

She noticed, despite his attempt to hide it. 'I'll drive again at the next *aire*.'

'You sure?'

'You're tired. Probably,' a cheeky smile, 'because you're so old.'

He belatedly remembered he was still disguised. 'Maybe I *do* need a refresher.'

Rest stops were frequent on French motorways. Reeve pulled in to the next. It was little more than toilet facilities surrounded by trees, but would do. Connie went to a cubicle while Reeve used a washbasin. 'Amazing the difference a bit of sun makes,' she joked, when they met again. 'It's taken years off you.' He had washed away the bags and wrinkles. 'You look good.'

He smiled. 'Thanks. Are you sure you want to drive?'

'Sure. You need a break. And I should practise.'

The journey resumed. With the rain gone, they could travel at the full speed limit. At 130 kilometres per hour, even the little Saxo ate up the distance. They chatted about everything, and nothing. Reeve found that oddly liberating. It had been a long time since he'd just *talked* to someone. No ranks and hierarchy, no instructions and orders, no competitiveness over training – no *seriousness*. He enjoyed it. That in itself was a feeling he hadn't had for a while.

The conversation came around to Connie's family. Both her parents were dead, he learned. Her father in her teens, her mother a few years ago. No siblings, but she had cousins in Italy. Also an Italian grandmother, Constantia . . .

That prompted him to pick up her passport. 'What are you doing?' she asked – followed by a more urgent, 'No, wait!'

Too late. He had opened it. 'So Connie's short for Constantia? And your full name is—' It was listed in the passport as *Grace Constantia Jones*. He couldn't help but smile. '*Grace Jones?*'

'Give me that!' She snatched away the passport, half-annoyed, half-amused. 'My parents didn't think things through. They named me after both my grandmothers. I've heard *all* the jokes. Go out dancing? "You're a slave to the rhythm!" When I learned to drive, it was always "pull up to the bumper, baby". So I started calling myself Connie.'

'Not Constantia?'

A resigned sigh. 'Constantia Jones,' she explained, 'was an infamous eighteenth-century prostitute. My parents didn't have Google when I was born. But it's the first thing that comes up now. Hence, Connie. You have no idea how good it felt to get a new identity.'

'Actually . . .' He hesitated. But now Connie was regarding him with curiosity. 'Actually, I do,' he pressed on. 'Alex Reeve isn't my original name.'

'It's not your real name?'

'It is – now. But I changed it after I joined my new unit. All the recruits did.'

'Why did you choose Alex Reeve?'

'It was just top of a list of options. I could have made something up – some of the others did. But I wasn't bothered about sounding like some movie tough-guy.' He knew that was exactly why Mark Stone had picked his new moniker. 'As far as I'm concerned, it's my real name now. I never liked my old one anyway.'

Connie's interest was piqued. 'What was it?'

'I . . . can't tell you.'

'What? Oh, come on,' she protested. 'You can't lead me on like that.'

'It's for security reasons. One of the rules.'

'The rules of the people who are *trying to kill you*?'

Reeve remained silent. He *wanted* to tell her, but SC9's regulations were firmly engrained. On the other hand . . . he couldn't dispute her point. His loyalty had definitely not been returned. And she was an ally, a friend. She had gone above and beyond to help him.

What could it hurt?

'All right,' he said. 'I used to be called . . .' A moment to overcome his instinctual secrecy. 'Dominic Finch.'

Connie looked at him. 'Yeah . . . you don't seem like a Dominic. Were you named after a relative?'

'No. It was a name my mum liked. I think it was a character on television.' The thought of his mother changed his mood, as if the grey clouds had returned. The open landscape suddenly felt threatening.

Connie picked up on the shift. 'Are you okay?'

'I'm fine. Just . . . thinking about my mum.'

She correctly inferred his meaning, while wrong about the specifics. 'I think about my mum a lot too. I miss her.'

'Me too.'

She nodded in sympathy. A pause, then: 'We can talk about something else. How about . . . politics? *That* won't cause any problems.'

'Politics isn't really my thing,' he said. She smiled again. 'What?'

'It's funny,' Connie replied, 'but it's something I've learned as a nurse. People who claim they aren't interested in politics usually have *very* strong opinions on things.'

'So are *you* interested in politics?'

'Very much. In parts.'

'Which parts?'

'Well, the NHS, obviously. I work inside it, so I feel my view's as valid as any politician's.'

'And what's your view?'

'That it's being deliberately starved of funds so it can be privatised. Targets are set that can't be met on the money we have. Then we're accused of being "inefficient" – and only the private sector can fix it.' She gave him a probing look. 'And your view is . . . ?'

'I can't argue,' he replied. She was pleased, and a little relieved. 'Same thing in the military. All the money goes to companies who build the big, expensive toys. Carriers, stealth jets, submarines. They won't spend anything on the *little* things, though.' His sarcasm was acidic. 'The things soldiers on the ground actually *need*.'

Connie nodded, then smiled. 'See? We did politics, and nobody got hurt.'

'We did. So what other parts are you interested in?'

Her deep breath suggested she had a lot to say. 'The country's falling apart. It's getting . . . nastier. More divided. People with money are hoarding it, and the ones who don't have less than ever. There's a *lot* of anger. I'm worried something's going to spark it all off. Maybe something good would come from that eventually, but lots of people will get hurt.'

'We wouldn't let that happen,' he said.

'We?'

'The system,' he backtracked, not wanting to mention SC9. 'The British establishment. They won't let things get that bad.'

'They're a big part of the problem,' Connie countered. 'They want things to stay the same, with them on top. But the country's changing – the *world's* changing. If they don't change with it, something's going to give. We need politicians who're willing to move forward instead of looking back.'

Reeve tried to temper his discomfort at the conversation's turn. 'That's assuming you can trust any of them.'

'I think there are a few who are genuine. Like Elektra Curtis,' she said, animated. 'I like her. She's progressive, and she really believes what she's saying.'

'I don't know much about her,' he said. 'But isn't she more "kick everything down" than "move forward"?'

Connie pulled a mocking face. 'Ooh, get you, Mr Reactionary! Shall we go back to England for your copy of the *Daily Mail*?'

'I'm not a reactionary,' he objected. 'I just prefer stability over chaos.'

'Or change?'

'They're the same thing – at least for me at the moment. I'd *love* some stability after the last few days. Maybe after I meet Scott, I'll get some.'

'Scott?'

Another slip. Christ, tiredness was making him sloppy . . . 'The man I need to talk to. If I prove to him I've done nothing wrong . . .'

He let the words hang. He'd already had similar discussions with her *and* Maxwell. This would end the same way. 'Anyway, let me know when you want to swap.'

'Typical man,' Connie said. 'Soon as they're finished, they roll over and go to sleep.'

He smiled back. 'I'm just enjoying the scenery.'

'How much further?'

Reeve consulted the phone. 'We're coming up on Dijon, so . . . about five hundred kays. Halfway there.'

'I could use another break.'

'Me too. There's another *aire* not far away.'

This stop was home to a service station. They used the facilities and bought food. Reeve took the wheel once more, and the journey continued.

CHAPTER 33

The hours rolled by with the landscape. It gradually changed as they continued south. Uplands rose to the east: the foothills of the Alps. Their destination was tucked against their southern edge. Montsalier was a tiny village, too small for a hotel. The nearest town with accommodation was Banon, a couple of kilometres away.

Scott's retreat, the Villa Mielena, had taken some work to find. It was not listed on any online maps. Reeve eventually located it from a passing mention in someone's walking tour blog. A picture contained embedded GPS coordinates. The minor road at that point wasn't included in Google Maps' Street View. However, zooming in on the satellite imagery revealed only one property nearby. It matched what Maxwell had told him; in the hills above Montsalier.

Part of his mind wanted to reconnoitre before finding a hotel. The rest of his brain mentally shouted it down. He had been awake for over fourteen hours, and he was hungry. The junk food sold at the *aires* had left him feeling vaguely sick. He followed the signs for their destination instead.

They entered Banon from the south. Like the other villages in the area, it was both quiet and beautiful. The sun gave the stone buildings an almost golden glow. The oldest structures defensively topped a small hill. The centre, below, was relatively newer, but still timelessly and distinctively French.

The town square housed a car park. 'It's free?' Connie remarked as they got out. 'France really *is* civilised.'

'It makes up for all the toll roads,' Reeve pointed out. 'Still, Jammer paid for them.' His stolen credit card was contactless. That it hadn't been cancelled suggested Jammer hadn't left hospital.

He checked the phone to locate the hotels. Two were at the end of the square, a third in the old town. He slowly turned, taking in his surroundings. 'What are you looking for?' Connie asked.

'That,' he said. At the car park's far end was a black Range Rover. He moved closer. As expected, it had British plates. 'Wait here.'

Leaving her behind, he walked past the Range Rover. At first glance, it appeared unremarkable. But he knew what he was looking for. A discreet antenna on the roof. Run-flat tyres. A black box on the dash connected to the car's USB slot. Exactly what he'd expect in an MI6 pool vehicle.

SC9 requisitioned mundane equipment from the other intelligence services. Scott's bodyguards had travelled from England in this 4x4. There were two hotels nearby; which were they staying in?

Whichever, it ruled out either for him and Connie. The risk of being spotted was too high. He had taken a chance just by coming this close.

He returned to her. 'Scott has bodyguards. They came in that Rangey.'

She was alarmed. 'Do they know you're looking for him?'

'I don't think so. But if their car's here, we can't stay at the hotels in the centre. I don't know which one they're in.'

'If they're his bodyguards, why aren't they at his house?'

'Scott's a VIP trying to relax. He won't want two guys with no necks constantly looking over his shoulder. Or monopolising his bathroom.' That drew a laugh from her. 'They can reach his villa in a few minutes, though. I'm sure they'll be on his speed-dial.' He checked the phone again. 'There's another hotel up the hill.'

The ascent took them through a minor maze of cobbled streets. The result was worth it, providing a stunning view. Lavender fields nearing bloom blanketed the valley floor below. Connie was entranced; Reeve was more concerned with the hotel. It was open, but did it have any rooms? 'I'll check reception,' he told her.

'I'll enjoy the view,' she replied, letting the sun warm her face.

She entered the building a few minutes later. To her surprise, she found Reeve sharing a joke with the owner in fluent French. 'Oh, there you are, darling,' he said. 'We're in luck. They have room for us! Only bed and breakfast, but beggars can't be choosers, eh?'

'No they can't . . . darling,' she replied, hiding her confusion.

He spoke to the owner again, then led Connie back outside by her hand. 'She's going to make up the room. We'll get the stuff from the car.'

'Okay. What's with the "darling"?'

'It makes us seem obviously a couple if anyone comes asking.'

They started back downhill. 'Do you think anyone will?'

'Probably not, but I'd rather be safe. Also,' he went on, faintly embarrassed, 'the only room has a double bed. We're in a rural part of a Catholic country. I thought it was better to pretend we were married. In case she changed her mind about the room being available.'

They reached the car and collected their belongings. 'So, you speak French?' Connie said.

'Part of my training. I speak four languages fluently, and a couple more enough to get by.'

'You learned all that in a year? Along with all the,' she mimed a couple of punches, 'other stuff?' He nodded. 'God. It took me three years to get my nursing degree.'

'It wasn't like going to university. There was hardly any downtime. If we weren't sleeping, we were training. You can get a lot done if there aren't any distractions.'

'Like a social life?' His reply was a lopsided smile.

They returned to the hotel. Their room was now ready. 'Cosy,' said Connie. There was just enough space to walk on either side of the bed.

'I'll sleep on the floor,' Reeve assured her. 'But before that, we need some food.'

The owner recommended a restaurant not far away. It turned out to have a terrace overlooking the valley. 'Oh, we *have* to,' said Connie, on seeing it. Reeve checked they would be out of sight from below, then nodded.

They ordered dinner, Connie also requesting red wine. The lowering sun's warmth and the valley's calm beauty gradually relaxed Reeve. Cicadas thrummed in nearby trees.

'This is stunning,' she said. 'I'm so glad I forced you to let me come.'

'My pleasure,' Reeve replied, amused.

The food was soon before them. Connie had opted for spicy piperade topped by baked eggs. Reeve went for a traditionally French beef bourguignon. Connie's wine also arrived. 'Sure you don't want some?' she asked.

'I'm good. I'll need a clear head tomorrow.'

'Oh well. *Santé.*' She clinked her large glass against his, then sipped. 'Nice. *Very* nice. But at that price, I'd hope so.'

'Jammer's paying,' he reminded her.

'He's good for one thing, at least.' Another, bigger sip, then she started on her meal.

Main course finished, they contemplated the dessert menu. Connie was now on her second glass. She rested her chin on her hand and regarded Reeve, head cocked to one side. 'You know, you've got a nice glow.'

'This sun'd make anyone look good,' he replied.

'No, you look good anyway.'

'Why, thank you . . . darling.'

She beamed. 'Even when we first met, I thought, "Hmm, not bad." You scrub up pretty well.'

'Well, it was a pretty low bar to start with. I was a mess. I'm glad I met you.'

'Me too. Unusual circumstances, admittedly, but . . . well. Look where we are now.' She gestured at the landscape. 'It's so beautiful. Very romantic.' A meaningful sidelong look.

Romance had not been a major feature of Reeve's previous life. But there was no way to misinterpret *that*. 'It really is,' he agreed. 'And we might be here on . . . business. But that's tomorrow. We've got tonight to ourselves.'

She didn't misinterpret him either. 'We have,' she said, with a cat-like smile.

He grinned and signalled to the waiter. '*L'addition, s'il vous plaît.*'

CHAPTER 34

Connie nuzzled against Reeve, arm draped over his chest. 'Thank you,' she said, drawing a deep, satisfied breath. 'That was very, very enjoyable.'

'Thank *you*,' he replied, with a smile. 'It's . . . been a while.'

Even as the words escaped, he was sure he'd committed a faux pas. But Connie's response was amused curiosity rather than offence. 'Really? A handsome guy like you?'

'I didn't have time for anything except the job.' A half-truth. There *had* been women occasionally, but he'd never let any get too close . . .

The windows were open, wooden shutters ajar to let in air. Somewhere nearby, a cat started yowling. 'Are you kidding?' sighed Connie. 'I like the cicadas, they're exotic. But I can hear noisy cats at home.'

Reeve was glad of the change of subject. 'No, he's fine. I like cats. All animals, really. Had one as a kid. Smudge, she was called. All white, except for a black patch on her back.'

'Did you have to leave her behind when you joined the army?'

'No, she . . . she died before then.' He paused, dark memories drowning nostalgia. Connie registered his change of mood and sat up. He knew she would ask what happened. Normally he would have said nothing. But after what they had just shared, he felt she deserved the truth . . . 'My dad killed her.'

She was shocked. 'What? Oh, my God.'

'He didn't like animals. My mum brought her home. But Smudge clawed things; it's what cats do. My dad left his jumper on a chair, and she tore it. So . . . he kicked her against the wall. Hard as he could.' Images flashed through his mind with awful clarity, even after fifteen years. 'She started screaming. He'd broken her back. So he kept kicking her, and kicking her, until . . . she was dead. I tried to stop him, but he started on me as well.'

Connie's hand went to her mouth, eyes wide. 'Oh, Jesus. Alex, that's – that's terrible.'

'He was drunk,' Reeve replied, feeling a buried rage rise. 'He was a piece of shit. He was – a murderer.'

It took her a moment to take in his words. 'A murderer?'

'He killed my mum.'

A long silence. Connie held him, unsure what to say. Finally, she whispered: 'My God. I . . . I'm so sorry. I . . .'

He held her. 'It's okay. It's not your fault, is it?' He was aware his natural Mancunian accent had slipped back out. Sadness welled alongside the simmering anger. 'I was thirteen. He was horrible to her – he was horrible to everyone. No idea why she married him. They were both young – maybe she thought he'd grow up, get better. But he just got worse. Got involved with the local drug dealers, started beating people up for them. Killing Smudge and beating me up was . . . the last straw. She was going to leave, take me with

her. But he found out what she was doing. And killed her.'
He felt his eyes prickle.

'What happened?' she gasped. 'Did they arrest him?'

'Not right away. He . . . I hated him, but he was smart.
Cunning, I mean. Mum had already packed up some stuff.
He dumped it somewhere, then called around, asking if
people had seen her. Pretending that she'd left – without me.'

'What did you do?'

'Nothing, at first. I was too scared. He said if I told anyone,
he'd kill me too.' The darkest of all memories returned. Cold,
grey, bleak moorland, an open hole yawning before him.
And inside . . . 'He *buried* her. Out on the moors somewhere.
He made me see the body. Then he told me he'd bury me
next to her if I talked.'

'Jesus,' Connie whispered.

'I had to go back home and . . . pretend I didn't know
where Mum was. For weeks. But then a farmer found the
body. Once they realised who she was, the police questioned
my dad. But he'd already set up his story. They'd broken up,
she walked out weeks ago. She'd gone to some friend he
didn't know in London. They didn't arrest him because he'd
done a good job of cleaning up. There wasn't any physical
evidence in the house. So then they asked me, and . . . ' The
shame almost choked him. 'I was so scared of him, I backed
up his story.'

Connie said nothing, horrified. His words kept tumbling
out. 'But eventually they found some evidence that pointed
to him. They finally arrested him. Once he couldn't hurt me,
I . . . I spoke up. I told them I saw him kill her. They charged
him, put him on trial. I gave evidence. They put him away.

He's still in prison. And I hope he fucking *dies* there.' That last came out with a snarl of raw emotion.

'I'm sorry,' she said softly. 'What . . . what happened to you after that? Did you have any other family to go to?'

He shook his head. 'Not in Britain. I've got an aunt and uncle, but they'd moved to Australia. Mostly to get away from my dad. That's how big a shit Jude Finch was. Not even his sister wanted anything to do with him.'

'Jude Finch – that's your dad?'

Reeve nodded. 'Now you know why I was happy to change my name. It finally meant I had nothing to do with him.'

'So where *did* you go?'

'Foster homes. I was with five, six families. And what happened wrecked me at school. I wasn't qualified for anything . . . except the army. Soon as I was old enough to join up, I did.'

'Did you think that was all you could do?'

'It was all I *wanted* to do. It meant I'd have something to focus on. I wouldn't have to deal with other people. Not on a personal level. Just professional. All I had to do was get the job done.'

'You didn't have any friends?'

He shook his head. 'Nobody did anything to help me after Mum was killed. I was just this . . . *thing* that had to be dealt with. Stick me in a foster home. Stick me in a school. Remind me what I'm supposed to say in court. Then after they're finished with me, that's it. Nobody cared. So . . .' A sigh. 'I decided, why should I care about them? And once I was in the army, I didn't need to. I knew what I wanted to do. I was going to push myself. I was going to be a fighter, better than anyone else . . .' His voice cracked. 'Because I didn't want to be afraid of anyone any more.'

He had never admitted that before, even to himself. She held him. 'It's okay.'

Reeve kissed her cheek. 'First time I've ever told all that to anyone.' But it wasn't *all* of it. There was more, but . . .

Connie spoke again before his conscience could reveal anything else. 'And . . . I suppose you *did* become the best. You wouldn't have made it into the special forces otherwise, would you?'

'No, I wouldn't. Because I *did* push myself, SRR eventually approached me.'

'You didn't apply to join them?'

'Not how it works. If you fit the bill, your CO – commanding officer – gives you "the tap".' He tapped the back of her shoulder to demonstrate. 'He told me there was an opportunity in – well, he didn't say the name. But I knew it was special forces. Turned out it was the Special Reconnaissance Regiment. They want people who can act alone under pressure. So I volunteered, went through selection – which was *tough* – and got in. I was in the SRR for five years. Pretty much constantly on assignment.'

'Still not wanting to deal with people?'

'Yeah. Ironic. I probably spent more time undercover with bad guys than with my own side. But then, I got the tap again.'

'From your mystery unit that you won't tell me about?'

A nod. 'I actually thought I was being kicked out of the SRR. I screwed up on a mission – at least, that was the official line. Far as I'm concerned, I did the right thing. But the *right* thing and the *proper* thing aren't always the same.'

'What did you do?'

'I was undercover, abroad. We were tracking people traffickers.'

Connie looked grim. 'They make women work as prostitutes. I've had to treat some of their victims.'

'You don't know *everything* they do,' he said, grim. 'Forced prostitution's just the start. But we were after this gang for national security reasons. We'd tracked down a major mid-level guy. The objective was to capture him. Once we had him, we'd make him give up his bosses.'

Connie couldn't hide a momentary frown. Reeve knew what she was thinking: *you were going to torture him for information?* He pressed on. 'We moved into the target's building. There were only a few of us. I was on my own, we'd had to mobilise fast. Something happened; I don't know what, but he got spooked. He ran from one team – straight into me. He took a hostage. One of the people he was trafficking, a young woman – with a baby.'

Connie's eyes went wide. 'Oh, God. What did you do?'

'The right thing. Not the proper thing. I saved her, and the baby – by shooting him. Single round to the forehead. He died instantly.'

The moment he said it, he knew the clinical extra detail had been a mistake. Connie stiffened. 'But . . . they were both okay?' she asked.

'Yeah. I was . . . not popular, though.'

'But you saved two innocent people.'

'By killing the person we were meant to bag. That was the

objective: the *proper* thing to do. I could have shot to wound, but – to me – it was too big a risk. He could have shot back, killed me, or his hostages. So I took him down.'

Reeve felt her touch lighten, as if she was about to pull away. He knew why. She was a nurse, dedicated to healing, to saving lives. He had just admitted to taking one. It was a kill that he would always argue was justified. His hostage, after overcoming her shock, had burst into tears of joy at being rescued. But Connie didn't know that. To her, *any* life taken was a tragedy.

'The SRR's operation was back to square one,' he went on. 'That's when I thought I was finished. But then . . . someone else approached me. I was exactly what they wanted. I had a solid record – and I'd killed someone.'

Now she withdrew. 'They only came to you *because* you'd killed someone?'

'In the line of duty.'

'But still— What the hell kind of unit did you join?'

Reeve took several conflicted seconds to answer. 'It's called SC9. It doesn't exist – well, not officially. I can't tell you much about it. I shouldn't tell you *anything*, but . . .' Another long pause. 'It's an elite special operations unit. Its members come from all parts of the British security state. Military, the intelligence services, police – anyone who actively defends the country. Once you complete training, you become an Operative. We take on new identities to become deniable assets.'

'Meaning what?' Connie asked.

'If we're caught during a mission, we're on our own. The British government can say it knows nothing about us. So,' he added, 'we're trained not to get caught.'

Her eyes narrowed. 'What kinds of missions?'

You're talking too much. You shouldn't tell her. But one confession was leading to another, as if he couldn't help himself. 'Covert missions at home and abroad, against threats to the state. If action can't be taken through normal channels, SC9 gets it done.' He realised he was parroting something Maxwell once said.

'You mean, against the law?' Connie's voice turned cold. 'And you work in Britain? "Threats to the state", at home – what kind of threats? People who disagree with the government?'

He knew where she was leading. 'I joined SC9 to protect the country – to protect the people,' he insisted. 'People like you, like Jaz and her baby, like Mr Brownlow. There are enemies out there who are trying to kill you. You don't even know about them – because we stop them.'

'Alex, these people are trying to kill *you*. They're . . . I don't know, state-sanctioned assassins – and you're defending them!'

'That's not what they are.'

'Then what are they?'

He rolled away. 'I've – I've already said too much. I can't say any more.'

'To protect me, or because you think I won't like the answer?'

He had no reply. Angry more at himself than her, he got out of bed. 'Where are you going?' she demanded.

'I need to prep for tomorrow. Got to reassemble the gun.'

'Oh. Great. The gun.' She rose herself, pulling the unicorn

T-shirt from her case. 'I'm going for a shower. I need to get clean.' She marched to the bathroom.

'Connie, wait—' The door shut.

'You can sleep on the floor,' she said from behind it.

Reeve stared at the barrier. 'Shit,' he muttered, crushed. He had got close enough to someone to feel a moment of actual joy . . .

And then he had fucked everything up.

He had poured out his heart, made himself vulnerable – then kept talking. Now Connie knew about SC9. Not much, but *anything* was more than she should. *Fuck!*

The shower clanked and hissed to life. A deep sigh, then he dressed and headed for the car.

CHAPTER 35

'I'm sorry, but visiting hours are over,' the staff nurse told Stone and Flynn. 'I can't let you see him.'

Stone frowned, then took out his police warrant card and badge. He held them intimidatingly close to the nurse's face. 'I can see anyone I want, whenever I want, *miss*,' he said. 'He's a witness to a major crime. If I have to piss about waiting for visiting hours, my suspects will be *gone*. You understand?'

'I thought he was mugged,' the nurse protested.

'He *says* he was mugged. Another witness says different. I need his side of the story, right now.'

Flynn spoke up, playing good cop. 'Look, we only need a few minutes. He's not in critical condition, is he?'

'No,' the other woman replied, 'but – it's against regulations—'

'You think whoever broke his leg cares about regulations?' Stone sneered. 'Think the guy who rammed a car with a baby inside cares?' The lie got the shocked reaction he had hoped for. 'I need to talk to him. Okay?'

The nurse looked around for help. It was late, and her superior was nowhere in sight. 'Okay, but – please, be quick.'

'Thank you,' said Flynn.

'Just take us to him,' Stone growled.

The nurse led them to a room off the ward. 'So was that what you were like when you were a cop?' Flynn whispered. Stone nodded. 'No wonder you got fired. All that *Sweeney* shite.'

'I didn't get *fired*,' he hissed back. 'I was about to be suspended pending investigation when SC9 called. I would have been cleared – just like the two other times.'

The nurse opened the door. 'Mr Haxhi? Sorry to bother you, but some police officers need to see you.'

Jahmir Haxhi – Jammer – lay on the bed inside. His broken ankle was tightly bandaged following surgery, little finger splinted. He sat up in alarm, only to wince as his leg shifted. 'What? No, I don't want to see anyone.'

'Just a minute of your time, sir,' said Stone, with a crocodile smile. He turned to the nurse. 'Some privacy, please? This is police business.'

'We'll be finished very soon,' Flynn assured her. The nurse gave Jammer a worried look, but left.

Stone waited for the door to shut, then advanced on Jammer. 'Right then, son.'

'What do you want?' Jammer demanded, trying to cover his concern. 'I gave a statement. I didn't see the guy who mugged me. There's nothing else I can tell you.'

Stone gave Flynn a theatrical look of surprise. 'Strange. Mugging victims are normally *happy* to see the police.'

'They are,' she replied, going to the other side of the bed. Jammer looked warily between them. 'Unless they've got something to hide, maybe.'

Stone leaned closer. 'You got something to hide, Mr Haxhi?'

'No, course not,' he said.

'That's funny, 'cause when we got word about your injuries? We knew you hadn't just been hit with a sock full of snooker balls. A professional snapped your leg, mate. A man who knows how to properly beat the shit out of someone.'

'We want to know who that man was, and where they are,' Flynn added.

'I told you, I didn't see them,' Jammer snapped, agitated. 'That's all I have to say.'

Stone shook his head. 'That's not good enough.'

'I don't fucking care.' The dealer's anger overcame his fear. 'I'm the victim, not the suspect! Am I being detained?' It was a question the police were required to answer. If the answer was no, the interview was legally over. Jammer knew the routine, having used it on many occasions. Without concrete reasons to push further, the cops were then powerless to ask more questions.

'No, you're not being detained,' Stone replied.

'Fine. Then fuck off. I'm tired, and my leg hurts.'

The two visitors exchanged glances. 'That looks like a bad break,' said Flynn, regarding Jammer's bandaged ankle.

'Yeah,' Stone agreed. 'Must have been painful.'

Jammer's eyes flicked between them, uncertain. 'It was. You can go now.'

Another silent exchange – then Flynn clamped a hand over Jammer's mouth. Her other elbow slammed down on his stomach, winding him.

Stone grabbed his broken ankle – and twisted it.

Jammer's back arched in agony. Flynn hit him again to

force him back down. Her hand remained locked airtight over his mouth.

'Now, have I got your *full fucking attention*?' Stone snarled. Jammer stared helplessly at him, eyes streaming with tears. 'I know about you, saw your file. You're involved in dealing drugs. You're just a little bit clever and haven't been caught. Lots of suspicion, never any charges. But I don't give a shit about that. Well, that's not true. I really, *really* fucking hate druggies. I'd cave in your fucking skull and dump you in the Thames given the chance. But I need some information from you.' He released him. 'So I'll ask again. Who broke your leg, and where is he?'

'Make a noise and we'll break your other ankle,' Flynn warned, before easing her hold.

Jammer could barely speak through the pain. 'You – you can't do this, you cunts! I'll fucking sue you!'

Stone laughed. 'We're not ordinary cops, son. We can do whatever we fucking want. Like this.' A glance to tell Flynn to gag him again, then he wrenched Jammer's foot around. The wounded man's howl escaped only as a muted keening. Flynn looked towards the door, but the nurse didn't return.

'You going to talk now?' Stone asked as he let go. Jammer gave an anguished, frantic nod. 'Good boy. Who did you over?'

'I – I don't know his name,' was the breathless reply.

'Describe him,' said Flynn.

'I dunno, about – about six foot. Short brown hair. He had a bandage on his left arm. Here.' He indicated the spot on his own biceps. The two Operatives shared a knowing look. 'I think he had grey eyes. Looked about thirty, maybe a bit less.'

'See? That was easy, wasn't it?' Stone said mockingly. 'So where do we find him?'

'He was in a house in Streatham. Ground floor flat, 37B.' He gave the street address. 'A woman lives there.'

'You know her name?' asked Flynn.

'Connie something.'

'You've been very helpful, son,' said Stone. He rested his hand on the broken ankle. Jammer flinched. 'Now, you keep quiet about this little chat. Otherwise we'll need to come back. And you don't want that, do you?'

Jammer blinked away more tears. 'No. No. I don't.'

'Too fucking right you don't.' He straightened. 'All right. We'll be on our way.'

'Good luck with the leg,' Flynn added as they exited.

The nurse hovered hesitantly nearby. 'We're finished,' Stone told her. 'I'd let Mr Haxhi have a nap now – he's very tired.'

Flynn used her phone to find the address as they left the hospital. 'The flat's right around the corner from where Haxhi was picked up.'

Stone smiled in triumph. 'We've found him.'

They returned to their Land Rover Discovery. Flynn drove while Stone called Maxwell. 'We got something. The guy with the broken ankle? The description he gave of his attacker matched Reeve.'

'Did you get a location?' Maxwell asked.

'Yeah, a flat in Streatham. Right where he beat the guy up. You want us to go around there?'

A reply did not come at once. 'Tomorrow morning,' Maxwell finally said. 'Play it subtle for now.'

Both Stone and Flynn were surprised. 'You sure?'

'I doubt he'll be there any more. He would have left before the cops canvassed the area. But we might get a lead on where he's gone. Keep posing as the police and see what you can find out.'

'What if he *is* still there?' said Stone.

A faint laugh. 'Then kill him, obviously.'

The call ended. 'What do you think?' Flynn asked.

'I think Maxwell's being too fucking cautious,' Stone replied. 'He fucked up after the footie match, so he's not sticking his neck out again.'

She nodded. 'Should we just go around there anyway?' A check of the gun inside her jacket.

'Nah. We'll do what he says. For now. If he fucks up again and we lose Reeve a second time, it's on him.' A humourless chuckle. 'Maybe the boss'll think he let Reeve escape on purpose and Fox Red him.'

'Promotions all round, hey?'

He didn't realise she was mocking him. 'I wouldn't complain about a pay rise in my first week. Come on, let's get back.'

The Discovery drove off into the London night.

CHAPTER 36

Connie woke, blinking in confusion at the unfamiliar room. Then memory returned. She was in France, with . . .

She sat up abruptly. She was alone. 'Alex?'

No answer. She checked the time. Just after eight. Her mouth was dry. Paying the price for two large glasses of wine.

She hunched up, knees to her chin. Christ. Last night had been . . .

Enjoyable, definitely. The first part, at least. Then it all fell apart.

Alex had revealed things she wished she hadn't heard. She couldn't help but regard him differently now. She'd let herself get caught up in the adventure. A handsome man on the run from injustice, dependent upon her healing hands to survive. That was the fantasy she had created. The reality was grubby, sordid. She should have seen it. She *would* have seen it, if she hadn't become besotted. He was running from professional killers because he *was* a professional killer.

God. *Now* what should she do?

Get out while she still could—

Alex had taken the car keys the previous night. She searched her handbag in case he had returned them. Nope.

'Oh, shit,' she sighed. Whatever he was doing, she was now stuck with it.

Reeve had awoken at six. Connie didn't stir as he dressed and slipped away. He took the Saxo and headed north out of Banon.

The disaster of the previous night still preyed on his mind. Any chance of taking things further with Connie was over. Rationally, practically, it shouldn't even have been on the agenda. He was on the run, in danger; deeper involvement would endanger her too.

But . . . he had *wanted* to go further. The closeness, the *warmth* they'd shared was something he hadn't felt for a long time . . .

Then he'd blown it. And it was entirely his fault.

'Fuck!' He banged his fist on the wheel. There was a reason SC9 actively discouraged personal attachments. In his vanity, he'd believed himself immune. Self-isolated, armoured against emotion, he'd thought he was safe. But he was human, just like everyone else. His weakness had been someone else caring about him. That had been all it took to break his shell.

Angry at himself, he checked the phone's map. The minor roads not only weren't on Street View; the satnav didn't know them. He would have to navigate the old-fashioned way. Left, straight on, left, right. His destination should be about half a kilometre beyond the last junction. He set off again.

The drive did not take long. He passed more lavender fields, purple corrugations amongst the surrounding green.

The road weaved down into a narrow valley before rising again. Left here. The broader valley south of Montsalier opened out before him. Now right, then around a tight, steep hairpin. The road took him along the edge of a crest.

His objective should be on the left, a short way downhill.

Reeve slowed, taking in the scenery. Bushes and small trees partially obscured what lay below. He glimpsed an ochre rooftop. That had to be it. A little farther on, and he passed a gate with a mailbox. *Villa Mielena* was written on it.

He was here.

Reeve continued past. Behind the bushes along the roadside was a fence. It turned downhill a hundred metres past the gate. The property's boundary. Beyond it the land was more scrubby, almost wild.

He hadn't seen any cameras watching the road, but that didn't mean they weren't there. Another couple of hundred metres and he was beyond sight of the villa. He pulled over and got out. Cicadas chirped in the trees. The temperature was already in the twenties. It would top thirty Celsius by noon. Considerably better weather than England. No wonder Scott had a retreat down here.

Reeve picked his way through the bushes. Once in cover, he started back towards the villa. Before long, it came into sight.

A farmhouse stood fifty metres down the slope from the road. A south-facing stone terrace at its rear overlooked the valley. A long lawn ran downhill from the terrace. Beyond it was woodland.

No clear points of access that he could see. He needed to

get nearer. Staying in the bushes, he advanced. He was already hot, but couldn't take off his jacket; it was concealing the gun.

Thirty metres from the fence, he saw movement. A dog padded up the lawn; large, yellow. A Labrador or golden retriever. Maxwell had said Scott had a dog. *Dogs*, plural. Another animal, almost white, ambled out of the trees.

He slipped through the undergrowth until he neared the fence. The boundary was a sturdy wire mesh, over two metres tall. It stood out by its mere presence. None of the other properties he had passed were enclosed. You could tell Scott was British, Reeve thought. Everyone has to protect their own little patch of land . . .

Speaking of protection: was there CCTV? He cautiously leaned out to view the house. Yes; a ball-like camera was mounted on the side wall. If there was one, there would be others—

A dog barked. Not one of the two on the lawn. Closer. Reeve ducked back, peering through branches. He spotted the dog on the house's north side, looking in his direction. Another Labrador, yellow like the first. It barked again. If it hadn't seen him, it had certainly smelled him . . .

More movement – but this was no dog.

A side door opened, a figure peering out. A man, wearing light clothing. Scott. He called to the barking dog, then followed its gaze. Reeve froze. Had he been spotted? His hand crept towards the silenced Walther . . .

Scott spoke to the dog again, then retreated. The door closed. One last grumpy *ruff*, and the Lab trotted away to join its fellows.

Reeve waited for it to get well clear before moving again. The dogs would be a problem. Labradors didn't make good attack animals, but would certainly warn of his presence. He would have to deal with them before entering the house.

If he could find a way to reach it unseen. He needed to continue his recce – without alerting the dogs. That meant skirting the grounds at a distance. It would take a while, but he had no choice. He withdrew, angling downhill.

Connie's greeting when he returned to the hotel was icy. 'Where have you been?'

'Reconnoitring Scott's villa,' he replied. He was sweaty and tired, but wanted to stay cool and avoid a fight. 'Looking for a way in without being seen.'

'Did you find one?'

'I think so.' He went into the bathroom to wash his face and neck with cold water. 'Are you okay?'

'I'm fine.' Her tone suggested otherwise.

'I'm . . . I'm sorry.'

'What about?'

'Last night. That things went wrong.'

'It's okay.' It wasn't.

'I didn't mean to upset you, to . . .' He returned to the bedroom. 'Connie, you're the only friend I've got. You're the only person in the world who cares about me. And right now, I think I've even lost you. That's not what I wanted to happen.'

She gave a sad shrug. 'I believe you, Alex. But . . . you're not the person I thought you were.'

Reeve remained silent, emotions churning. 'I'm sorry,' he repeated. 'If you want to go home . . .'

'I'll still help you today,' she said. But afterwards . . . I should leave.'

'Okay. Thank you.' Neither was quite able to look at the other. 'All right. We need to check out.'

They quickly packed. 'I'm ready,' said Connie.

'I need to go to a shop in town before we set off,' he told her. 'And the petrol station.'

'But we filled up after we came off the autoroute.'

'It's not for the car.' He collected his own belongings. 'Let's go.'

Reeve paid the bill, then they returned to the car park. The black Range Rover was still there. He now knew from experience that Stone's minders could reach the villa in six minutes. Less, if they broke the speed limit.

He was counting on them doing so.

They loaded the car, then Reeve visited a shop. He returned with something wrapped in brown paper. 'A packed lunch?' Connie asked.

'Not for me.' They got into the Saxo, Reeve driving. He stopped at a small petrol station beyond the town square. The owner ambled out, but Reeve met him at the pumps. A brief discussion in French, then the owner went back inside. He returned with a plastic jerry can, then filled it with diesel.

Connie watched in confusion. 'But my car's petrol,' she said, after Reeve paid.

'Again, not for me,' he replied.

She rolled her eyes. 'Now you're just being secretive to annoy me.'

They set off again. Reeve didn't need to consult a map this time, the route memorised. Once they left the main road, they didn't pass a single other vehicle.

He turned at the last junction, then stopped just beyond the hairpin. 'Back in a minute,' he said, collecting the jerry can.

'Where are you going?' asked Connie.

'Making sure Scott's bodyguards don't turn up unexpectedly.' He descended the hill, disappearing around the corner, then soon returned. He put the can back in the boot. 'Okay, we'll be there in a minute,' he said, as he drove on. 'Are you sure you still want to help me?'

'Well, I'm here now,' she said, faintly testy. 'What do you need me to do?'

The Villa Mielena was a few hundred metres ahead. He stopped by an overgrown gate to the neighbouring land. 'Wait for me here. Keep your phone ready. If I call you to pick me up, stop by the villa's mailbox. If I call and tell you to go, then *go*. Don't wait for me, just get away. If you don't hear from me after an hour . . .' He didn't want to alarm her by saying he would probably be dead. 'Head back home.' He gave her Jammer's credit card and a wad of euros.

She accepted them with disquiet. 'You want me to leave you here?'

'It'll be safer for you. Oh, and if you hear gunshots? Get out of here *immediately*. Because they won't be mine.' He drew the PPK to show her the silencer.

'Oh, shit,' Connie gasped. 'You're not going to kill him, are you?'

'If he's dead, he can't tell me anything,' Reeve assured her.

He opened the door. 'Okay. I'm going.' He hesitated, then put his hand on hers. She twitched, but didn't pull away. 'Thank you. For everything.'

She nodded. 'Just . . . stay safe, Alex.'

'I'll try.' A half-smile, then he collected the package and left the car.

Reeve looked towards the villa. The car was hidden from it by trees. He climbed over the gate. A last look back at Connie, then he started downhill.

CHAPTER 37

'Doesn't look like much,' said Flynn, regarding the rain-slicked terraced house.

'Doesn't need to,' Stone replied. 'Roof over his head is all Reeve needs.'

'You think he's here?'

'Soon find out.' They both checked their concealed weapons, then got out of the Discovery.

Stone tried the buzzers by the front door. Nobody responded in flat B. He pushed the top button. A woman soon answered. 'Hello?'

'Metropolitan Police,' Stone said brusquely. 'Can we talk to you?'

'Uh . . . okay.' A clack, and the door's lock released.

'She sounded worried,' he said, as they entered the shabby hall. 'Maybe she knows something.'

They climbed the stairs. A young black woman holding a baby peered from a doorway. 'Hello?' she said. 'Is something wrong?'

Stone took out his warrant card. 'Detective Inspector Stone. This is DS Flynn.' Flynn produced her own ID. 'There was an incident here last Friday. A Mr Jahmir Haxhi was beaten up and hospitalised.'

Both watched her reaction closely. The woman was concerned, even fearful. A blink of confusion at the unfamiliar name, then realisation. 'Oh, you mean Jammer? He's the rent collector. No, I . . . I don't know what happened to him. Sorry.'

Stone produced a notebook. 'Can I have your name, miss?'

'It's Jaz. Jasmine. Jasmine Prince.'

'Jas. Mine. Prince.' He overenunciated each syllable as he wrote, not taking his eyes off hers. 'The thing is, Miss Jasmine Prince, I'm pretty sure that you *do* know.' He leaned closer; she shrank back. 'Now, lying to a police officer is obstruction of justice. That's a major charge. Could get you five, six years in prison. You wouldn't want to not see your baby for six years, would you?'

Jaz looked at her child in alarm. 'No, no! Of course not!'

'Then tell us what you know,' said Flynn.

'It was—' Jaz stopped, conflicted. Fear overpowered loyalty. 'It was Alex. Connie's friend. He – he helped us. My ex hit me, and Alex made him leave. Then Jammer hassled Mr Brownlow in the bottom flat, so Alex sorted him out too. Jammer came back the next day with some guys, and a gun. But Alex just—' She tried to think of a suitable word. 'Demolished them.'

Flynn and Stone exchanged glances. 'What happened to the gun?' Stone asked.

'I don't know. Jammer ran off with it, I guess. Alex went after him.'

'Jammer won't be running anywhere for a while,' said Flynn. 'What can you tell us about Connie?'

'She's nice, she's a nurse. Older than me, about thirty?'

'Do you know which hospital she works at?' A shake of the head.

Stone snapped his notebook shut. 'Okay, Miss Prince. That'll be all for now. But remember,' he added as she turned away, 'lying to the police is a crime.' He jabbed a finger at her. 'Don't do it again.'

'No, I – I won't,' Jaz gabbled. 'I'm sorry. Sorry.' She hurriedly closed the door.

Flynn shook her head. 'You enjoyed that, didn't you?'

'You have to remind these people who's boss. All right, so Reeve *was* here. Kick the flat open and see if he still is?'

'Maybe see if this Brownlow's at home first,' she suggested.

They trooped down to the bottom flat. A middle-aged man answered their knock. Like Jaz, he seemed startled, then worried at seeing the police. Stone got straight to the point. 'We need to ask you about Alex Reeve.'

'I, ah . . .' Brownlow seemed about to deny any knowledge, but thought better of it. 'Yes, Connie's friend. What about him?'

'He's alleged to have violently assaulted a man. Do you know where he is?'

'No, but – but it was self-defence,' Brownlow insisted. 'Jammer was going to kill him! Alex helped me. Jammer was smashing up my flat, and Alex stopped him.'

'Why was he smashing up your flat?' asked Flynn.

Brownlow immediately became evasive. 'It was, er, an argument over the rent.'

Stone decided not to waste time. He pushed past Brownlow. 'Mind if we come in?'

'What?' the older man spluttered. 'No, wait, you – you can't just barge in!'

Stone gave him a menacing look. 'You going to stop me?' Brownlow shrank back. The Operative surveyed the flat, then spotted something. 'Bullet hole,' he told Flynn.

She looked for herself. 'Been playing with firearms, have we, sir?'

'That was Jammer!' Brownlow protested. 'Alex beat him up even though he had a gun.'

'So where's Alex now?' demanded Stone. 'Is he still in Connie's flat?'

'No, he's gone. They both came back on Saturday, but just for a few minutes.'

'And do you know where he went?' asked Flynn.

'No – no,' he repeated, more firmly. Defiantly? 'I don't know where he is.'

Stone advanced, intimidating Brownlow with his size. 'Concealing information can be regarded as obstruction of justice.'

'I really don't know!' the older man insisted. 'The last time I saw them was Saturday.'

Stone was about to push further, but Flynn spoke first. 'What's Connie's surname, please?'

'Jones, I think. Yes, I'm pretty sure. I've seen her post in the hall.'

'Okay. We'll be going now,' she told Stone pointedly.

He followed her out. Once they reached the hall, Stone expressed his displeasure. 'What the fuck are you doing? He was obviously lying. He knows more about Reeve.'

Flynn checked the pile of mail on the windowsill. Junk,

some addressed to G. C./Connie/Constantia Jones. 'He was telling the truth – that he doesn't know where Reeve is *right now*. He's gone off somewhere with this nurse. Which explains why he didn't show up at any hospitals. She must have patched him up.'

Stone frowned. 'How the fuck did he persuade her to do that?'

'His natural seductive charm.' They both chuckled sarcastically. 'She's helping him, and they've gone . . . somewhere. But we've got her name and address. We can find out if she's got a car. If she has, the number-plate cameras will have tracked it.'

'If they're still in London.'

'Where else would he go?' The question made them both uncomfortable. If Reeve was no longer trying to reach Maxwell, what was his new objective? 'Anyway, let's report in.'

They went back to the Discovery and updated their superior by phone. 'Okay, I'll see what comes up for this Connie Jones,' said Maxwell.

'What should we do now?' asked Stone. 'Stake out the house?'

'No,' Maxwell replied. 'From what you said, I'm sure Jasmine or Brownlow will warn him you called. He won't come back if he knows we've tracked him there. I'm surprised he went back at all.'

'Maybe he left something he needed,' suggested Flynn.

'So why not just ask Connie to bring it?' None of them had an answer. 'I've got to report to the boss later today. I can ask him to get GCHQ to track any calls they make.

Might give us Reeve's location. For now, though . . .' Maxwell let out a concerned breath. 'We need a new plan. We've lost him.'

CHAPTER 38

Staying in cover, Reeve made his way downhill to the villa's southern boundary. That morning, he had found a tree with a bough extending over the fence. He located it and scaled the trunk. His wounded arm throbbed as muscles stretched, but he ignored it. Cicadas chirped above, but the only creatures concerning him were the dogs.

None were in sight. He sidestepped along the branch, then dropped down. Inside the fence, there was less under-growth – less cover. Scott must have had it cleared. He looked uphill through the trees. One of the dogs lay in shade at the bottom of the lawn.

He would have to pass it to reach the house. Long before then, it would smell him – and bark at the intruder. Scott's appearance earlier meant he trusted his pets as early warning systems. They had to be silenced . . .

Reeve unwrapped the parcel. Inside were what he had bought from a *boucherie*: several pieces of raw beef.

The dog raised its head. It had heard the paper crackling, or picked up the scent. Either way, it would soon investigate—

Soon was now. The Labrador jumped up and barked, then started through the trees towards him.

Reeve stayed in cover, watching the villa. The dog came

closer – then a figure appeared in a doorway.

Scott. He was shaded, hard to see clearly – but definitely staring downhill. Reeve remained stationary. The dog barked again. Another animal responded from somewhere out of sight.

He took out a piece of meat, then tossed it a short way uphill. The dog approached. Its attention had gone to the beef. 'Good dog,' Reeve whispered. 'Have a treat.' It sniffed the slice, then started to eat. He looked past it. Scott was still in the doorway. Two more Labradors trotted down the long lawn. One barked questioningly. Reeve sent two more pieces after the first, spacing them out. The newcomers investigated, beginning their free meal.

Their owner remained in place. Reeve began to worry. He'd hoped Scott would dismiss the barks as a false alarm. He had three more pieces of meat, but wanted the Labs to come to him. That would have let him befriend them. But if Scott kept watching, he would become suspicious of their behaviour . . .

The figure shifted – then finally retreated indoors.

Reeve reacted immediately. 'Come! Come!' he said, rustling the paper. All three dogs congregated around him. 'Good boy. Good girl.' He handed out the remaining pieces. From the wagging tails, the animals were delighted by the gifts. He stroked them. Labradors weren't used as guard dogs for a very good reason: they were too friendly.

He waited, giving Scott time to resume whatever he had been doing. Then he made his way to the edge of the trees. One dog followed, the others sniffing the discarded paper. No movement at the house.

Go.

His recce had picked out the route least exposed to cameras. Hunched low, he scurried uphill to the terrace's lower wall. He found cover against it. The dog lost interest and ambled back down the lawn to rejoin the others. Reeve glanced up the stone steps, checking the house. A white globe on one wall overlooked its corner. He sidestepped to halfway across the terrace, then climbed up. Another camera on the house's far side. He was between their fields of view. Bent low, he moved to the villa's wall and waited. Seconds passed. No alarms, no sounds of movement.

Reeve moved cautiously to the open door and drew his gun. A peek inside. White walls, tiled terracotta floor. Several interior doors, and a flight of stairs. Scott could be anywhere. Walther ready, he slipped inside.

The house was pleasantly cool. A faint thrum from a doorway to his left; a fridge. The kitchen was empty. He moved on, checking each door in turn. A dining room overlooking the terrace, a small bathroom, a library—

Light in the next opening. Not noonday sunlight, but artificial. He crept to it. An office; filing cabinets, bookshelves. Some sixth sense warned he was not alone. He raised the gun – then swept fluidly around the door.

Sir Simon Scott sat before him.

Reeve kept the weapon fixed upon him as he approached. The head of SC9 was in his sixties; balding, paunchy, pink rather than tanned. Far from the fearsome figure he had imagined. He was behind a desk, a large laptop open. 'Hands up,' Reeve ordered. Scott obeyed, raising them to shoulder level. 'Move away from the desk.'

Scott warily rolled back his chair. 'Well, well.' His voice was clipped, expensively educated, condescending. 'Alex Reeve.'

Reeve gestured with the gun for him to stand and retreat. The older man was a full head shorter. Once the way was clear, Reeve went behind the desk. A glance at the laptop – just in time to see an application close and vanish. Scott had shut down his work before it could be seen. He had known Reeve was coming. Another program revealed how. The villa's CCTV cameras were streaming straight to Scott's computer. The Labradors' barks had made him suspicious. Reeve realised at a glance that there were more cameras than he'd thought. The obvious ones were backed up by concealed devices at every entrance. He had walked right under one.

A rapid check of the desk's drawers turned up a Glock handgun. Reeve thumbed the magazine eject. The loaded mag clunked out. 'You didn't use it?'

'There wouldn't be much point, would there?' Scott replied. 'I know exactly how good you are. And that you'd kill me if I posed a threat.'

'I'm not here to kill you.'

'Then what are you here for?' The older man scowled. 'How did you find me?'

'Like you said, you know how good I am.' Maxwell had helped him; Reeve decided to return the favour by hiding the truth. 'I'm here for answers. Why are SC9 trying to kill me? Why did you declare me Fox Red?'

The response was not what he expected. Scott grew visibly more angry, sun-pinkened face reddening. 'You know *damn* well why,' he spat. 'You're a traitor! Don't even try to deny it. The evidence was incontrovertible. Someone at Mordencroft tried to hack into SC9's servers in London. Tried, but failed. Our security was up to the task. But that started us looking at the recruits. You covered your tracks well, but not well enough.'

'I didn't "cover my tracks", because I didn't do it,' Reeve insisted.

Scott ignored him. 'You used Russian software to help with the hack. Unluckily for you, it also told us who was backing you. The program is apparently very distinctive. Have you been working for the Russians the whole time, or were you recently turned?'

'I'm not working for the Russians,' he snapped. 'I work for SC9 – for Britain.'

The older man's fury rose. 'Don't you *dare* try to claim you're a patriot, you treacherous little bastard.' That he had a gun pointed at him did not lessen his outrage. 'It took a couple of weeks to pin you down as a mole. All the data we accumulated during training narrowed down the suspects. As well as the instructors' reports, the computers compiled your psychological profile.' He glanced at the laptop as if the information were on-screen. Perhaps it just had been. 'Anti-authoritarian tendencies. Anti-*establishment* tendencies. Solitary and secretive. Coldness of behaviour. You say you work for Britain, but you never expressed any particular love for it.'

'Says the man with a second home in France,' Reeve shot back.

Scott's eyes blazed. 'And then there was the deciding factor. The polygraph test.' Reeve remembered it; a surprise sprung on the trainees two weeks prior. 'The others probably thought it was just another exercise. But we were using it to catch *you*. And we did. The results confirmed you were hiding something. That you'd been concealing something from us the whole time, even in the army. Were you working for the Russians even back then?'

Reeve's anger grew. 'I am *not* a fucking Russian spy.'

'So you deny you were hiding something from us?'

'Yes.'

'Untrue. You probably thought you could fool the test. Polygraphs aren't perfect, we all know that. But there are some things you *can't* hide. We *know* you lied to us, Reeve. You are hiding a secret so ingrained that duplicity about it is automatic. *But it is still duplicity.*' Each word came as a sharp, accusing bark. 'And that is how we knew we had our traitor.'

Reeve couldn't respond immediately. He knew what the polygraph had really uncovered. But he couldn't bring himself to tell Scott. The secret he had never revealed to anyone; the necessary lie . . . 'Someone altered the profiles,' he finally said. 'They hacked them to make it look like I was the mole.'

Scott let out a sarcastic laugh. 'The hack *failed*, Reeve. It's how we caught you.'

'But you need to talk—' If he revealed how he knew about the amended profiles, it would expose Maxwell. 'Talk to the instructors, rather than relying on what the computers say,' he managed instead. 'Get them to check their own notes. They'll see things have been changed. Whoever did it is trying to frame me. I want to prove that I'm innocent.'

'And *then* what?' Scott mockingly exclaimed. 'Do you *really* think I would let you back into my agency after all this?'

'How else am I supposed to prove my loyalty? Let SC9 kill me?'

The answer was presented as if it were self-evident. 'Yes.'

CHAPTER 39

All Reeve could manage in reply was a despairing laugh. Scott's eyes narrowed with a cruel half-smile. He was about to say more when both men heard a noise. Distant, a sudden, scraping thud . . .

Reeve's heart rose as he realised what it was. Scott, however, continued. 'Do you know the significance of the term "Fox Red"?' he asked, almost conversational. Reeve shook his head. 'As you no doubt noticed, I breed Labradors. My family always has, actually. Marvellous animals. Not much use as guard dogs, as your presence attests. But strong, dedicated, intelligent, reliable – and loyal.' A pointedness to that last word.

Not knowing where he was leading, Reeve said nothing. Scott gave him a disparaging look and carried on. 'The traditional Labrador colours are yellow, black and chocolate. "Yellow" can mean from white to butterscotch, but within a certain range. *Proper* breeders,' a faint emphasis, 'recognise these colours as signs of a strong, pure bloodline. The best lineages can be traced back to the early nineteenth century. But the so-called "fox red" Labrador,' his disdain was audible, 'is relatively new. It's the result of crosses with other bloodlines. It's impure, and for some breeders, unacceptable.'

'And that's where SC9's code comes from?'

'Our dark little secret. Fox-red pups are killed at birth so as not to further pollute the bloodline. And also to preserve the financial value of the whole litter.' A humourless smile. 'My private joke. Anyone declared Fox Red is a threat to SC9's integrity. They're eliminated to protect the whole.'

'It's hypocritical,' said Reeve, frowning. 'You're killing the ones that stand out – the obvious targets. But the fox-red genes are still in the whole litter.'

'Hypocrisy is a necessary survival trait in society,' was the pompous reply. 'But the point stands. Traitors must be dealt with before they infect others. And in this business, *any* suspicion of treason must be regarded as proof. We can't take any risks.'

Scott's confidence rose as he spoke, almost to the point of smugness. Reeve decided it was time to turn the tables. 'That's all really interesting. And a nice long speech to keep me occupied. I suppose you're expecting your minders from the hotel to arrive any minute.'

Scott reacted with surprise, then unease. 'Meaning?'

'Meaning, I poured a load of diesel on that hairpin between here and town. Very slippery. That bang was their Range Rover skidding off at high speed. I expected you'd have some kind of emergency alert to call them.'

Scott's mouth opened in shock – then his anger returned. 'If there was any doubt you were a traitor, that just ended it.'

'I just wanted to talk to you. Undisturbed.'

'There's nothing to talk about, Reeve. I know you're working for the Russians. The technical aspects of your hack prove it.' He glared at him. 'Was that your goal? To worm your way into SC9 as the seemingly perfect recruit? Then hack our systems to steal records of our operations?'

'Someone's *framed* me. Why won't you believe me?'

'Because the evidence is overwhelming. If you'd succeeded, what would your next step have been, hmm? Leak our stolen files to the media? They'd have a field day. And Britain's reputation would be catastrophically damaged. The diplomatic fallout from the revelation of a state-backed assassination unit would be enormous.'

'That's not what we *do*,' Reeve protested. 'I joined SC9 to *protect* Britain and its people.'

Scott almost laughed. 'Is that what you tell yourself so you can sleep soundly at night?'

'What do you mean?'

'You know full well what SC9's true function is. Or were you asleep on the day of no return? You and the others were asked, very clearly, if you wanted to know the truth. You were also warned that, afterwards, there was no backing out.'

'I remember,' Reeve growled. It had come over six months into his training. Maxwell had been the one to ask the question. He had accepted without hesitation.

'And what were you told?'

'That SC9 eliminates threats to the British state, by any means necessary,' he recited. 'At home, or abroad. Even if this means breaking the law. And also that if we failed . . . we were on our own. We were all deniable assets. And I accepted that.'

'So you *were* listening. But not clearly enough.' Scott's smugness returned – with a nastier edge. 'Operatives must be willing to break any national and international law, yes. You were all recruited because you were proven killers, beyond conventional legality. But SC9's purpose is to eliminate threats to the British *establishment*. Not the British *state*.'

'They're the same thing.'

'They most certainly are not.' Scott seemed almost offended. 'The establishment *is* Britain, heart and soul – mind and money. Politicians are ephemeral, they come and go. The political pendulum swings from right, to left, and back again. Usually in balance, but sometimes, events push it to one side. The further the pendulum swings, the harder it eventually swings back. Unless someone puts their hand out to stop it. That's my job. I send SC9 to correct matters. To protect the way things should be.'

Reeve felt his confidence crumbling. 'That's not what SC9 is about.' Outside, the dogs barked again. Were Scott's bodyguards here? No; they couldn't have arrived on foot so quickly.

Scott's sarcasm was palpable. 'Oh, isn't it? Let me tell you *exactly* what SC9 is about, Reeve. We deal with "turbulent priests" – I hope you understand the reference? You did go to a state school, after all.'

The snide comment prompted another shot of anger from Reeve. 'Yeah. Thomas Becket. The king said, "Who will rid me of this turbulent priest?" He was speaking hypothetically, but some knights went out and killed Becket.'

'Good. We deal with turbulent priests so our political *masters*,' more sarcasm, 'keep their hands clean. There are things it's best mere fly-by-night politicians don't know. The right kinds of politicians, that is. The wrong kind become our problem – our targets. And I don't just mean in Parliament, either. The rot can set in at any level. Communists, socialists, Irish republicans, grubby little fascists, Muslims, peaceniks, feminists, tree-huggers . . . Now it's these so-called "progressives".' Scott almost spat the word.

'But they're not a threat.'

A stern look. 'Who are you to decide? But we'll deal with them like all the rest. Take out a keystone, and the whole edifice crumbles. The threat is removed. The great British public can continue ambling peacefully through their sub-urban lives. And the politicians keep their hands clean. All thanks to SC9.'

The implications coalesced for Reeve. 'The politicians don't know what we do?'

'The politicians don't even know we exist. We are the blackest book of all, hidden inside the other black books. We realised the need for a completely deniable covert operations unit after Gibraltar, in 1988.' Reeve knew the event. An undercover SAS unit had shot several IRA members suspected of planning a terrorist attack. Civilian witnesses revealed the suspects had been given no warning or chance to surrender. The British government was, as a result, accused of executing them without trial. 'I proposed the creation of what would become SC9. All its funding was secretly syphoned off from other agencies. I've been in command since its formation in 1991.'

'So who chooses the targets?'

'Why, *I* do, of course.' Scott's hands had gradually lowered; he now clapped them to his chest. 'I *am* SC9. I see the collated reports of all Britain's other intelligence agencies.

I see the growing threats, before they can flower.' His voice hardened. 'I decide which of these threats must be eliminated. At home or abroad.'

Reeve remained still, gun level – but internally he was reeling. He had known none of this. SC9 took extra-legal actions, yes – to defend and protect the country. Britain's enemies weren't hamstrung by laws. So nor were the Operatives. They fought fire with fire. That was what he had been told, what he believed . . .

But a new truth now stood before him. This unprepossessing man held the power of life or death. On nobody's whim but his own, he could declare someone a threat to Britain. Not even to the country as a whole, just the establishment. And on that whim, SC9's Operatives would hunt down that person – and execute them.

'I'm not the traitor,' he said at last. '*You* are. I'm defending the country. You're . . .' A moment to find the right word. '*Debasing* it.'

Despite the gun aimed at him, Scott actually laughed. 'Do you expect me to believe you joined SC9 to become a noble white knight? A protector of the innocent? You're an *assassin*, Reeve. A *killer*. You defied orders to kill a man in cold blood. That was why you were selected in the first place.' His expression darkened. 'But that was the secret you were hiding from us, wasn't it? You presented yourself as the perfect recruit so you could infiltrate SC9 for the Russians.'

'That's *not* what I'm hiding.' It was the one thing he had sworn never to reveal. But now he was out of options. 'What I've been hiding is . . . I lied in court to put my father in prison.'

Reeve briefly froze, shocked by his own confession. 'I told everyone that I saw him kill my mum. I didn't,' he continued. 'He *did* kill her; he made me see her body in the grave he dug. But I didn't tell anyone until much later. And by that time, he'd made up an alibi. The police weren't sure they could make the charge stick. So . . . I gave them what they needed. And they accepted it. I was thirteen, and I'd been so scared of my dad I hadn't spoken up. Until I finally found the courage. At least, that's how they took it.' His gun hand quivered, slightly. The revelation had taken a physical toll on his emotions.

Scott regarded him impassively. 'Ironically, that's Operative-level thinking. But . . . it changes nothing.' Reeve looked back in dismay. 'If anything, it explains your actions. The British system failed to protect your mother, so you perverted it to get revenge. I would almost praise your ingenuity and determination. Unfortunately, it made you a prime recruitment target for our enemies. Did they blackmail you? Or did you volunteer for another chance to attack the system from within? If you assassinated someone and then were deliberately caught, you could expose SC9. Was that your plan?'

Before Reeve could respond, he heard movement, close by. He whipped around. But it wasn't Scott's minders. 'Alex!' Connie said from the hall.

'In here.' She appeared immediately. She'd been outside the doorway. The look she gave him was hard to read: shock? Disgust? How much had she heard?

Enough.

But she had more urgent concerns. 'Two men are running

up the road! I drove here as fast as I could – but they'll be here any minute.'

'Operatives 53 and 57,' Scott informed them malevolently. 'Proven men.'

'We've got to go.' Reeve kept his gun trained on Scott as he backed out. Then they both ran for the front door.

Connie's car was at the gate beside the mailbox. 'I'll drive,' Reeve said. He glanced down the road. Two figures pounded along it, three hundred metres away.

'In, quick,' he called. Connie jumped in beside him. He set off with a rasp of tyres. A glance in the mirror. One man stopped, arm coming up—

'Duck!' he yelled, pushing her down. A shrill *clank* as a bullet struck the Saxo's tail. He hunched lower, expecting more shots, but none came. The car was beyond a handgun's effective range, even for an Operative.

'Jesus!' Connie shrieked. 'Did they just shoot at us?'

'Yeah.' He concentrated on driving. The roads ahead were unfamiliar; tight turns could catch him out at speed.

'Where are we going?'

A brief, grim look. 'I don't know.'

The two Operatives reached the house and raced inside. The dogs greeted them excitedly. 'Sir!' one man shouted, ignoring them. 'Are you okay? Sir!'

'I'm fine,' Scott snapped, emerging from the office. 'It was Alex Reeve. He's Fox Red. Get after him – and kill him.'

'Our car's wrecked, sir,' the other Operative admitted.

Scott glared at him. 'Take mine. It's in the garage.' He

tossed over a set of keys. 'And there's a woman with him. She's a witness. Kill her too.'

'Sir,' the first man replied with a nod. They both hurried out.

The garage was beside the house. Inside was Scott's vehicle: a powerful Jaguar XF Sportbrake estate car. They got in and started it.

Scott had chosen the top-of-the-range model. The engine roared, shaking nearby windows. The Jag tore out of the garage, through the gate, and on to the road. It snarled past the 60mph mark less than six seconds later.

The gap to the escaping Saxo was already closing.

Fast.

CHAPTER 40

'You shouldn't have come in,' Reeve said, as the car sped down the narrow road. 'Now Scott's seen you.'

'But he doesn't know who I am,' she protested.

'He can describe you. That could be enough to have you stopped at customs.' A flash of reflected sunlight in the mirror caught his eye. A red car was racing down the road after them. 'They're coming.'

Connie looked back in alarm. 'Are you sure it's them?'

'There hasn't been a single other car on this road. And it's speeding – *really* speeding.'

The pursuing vehicle disappeared behind trees as they rounded a bend. Reeve braked sharply for a junction. Left or right? He had no idea where either road led. 'Hold on!' he said, going right. The Saxo threatened to roll, Connie yelping as it lurched back upright.

The road weaved uphill. More junctions. Some led only to dirt tracks. Not an option; he couldn't risk a skid. He shot straight through the first two, going right at the third. To his relief, the road widened. The landscape levelled out, lavender fields whipping by. Was the other car still following? He couldn't see it, but vegetation could be obscuring it.

Past farmhouses, open fields – and he saw a main road

ahead. Going right, a tighter turn, would require him to slow. He swept left. Trees lined the roadside ahead as it curved. If he reached them, they would be hidden from view—

The red car reappeared in the mirror, powersliding on to the road after them.

It had closed the distance enormously. A Jaguar – the little hatchback couldn't outrun it.

So it had to evade it.

Reeve powered into the bend, losing sight of the Jag. But it would be back in sight in seconds. Through more curves, the surroundings trees a blur. Then the valley opened out ahead. A sign warning of a junction was there and gone in a split-second. One more sweeping corner and the road forked. The left route led downhill, the narrower right staying level. Two signs, one pointing each way. He registered their words almost subconsciously – as he went right.

'What did that other sign say?' Connie asked.

'*Itinéraire recommandé poids lourds*,' he replied. 'Or "recommended route for heavyweights" – trucks. So it won't be as steep or twisty as this one.'

She looked at him in alarm. 'Then why are we going *this* way?'

'Your car's not as fast as theirs. But it's smaller, more manoeuvrable. If I can keep our speed up through the turns, we might lose them. Or they might crash.'

She was not reassured. 'So might we.'

Reeve could do nothing but focus on the road. Driveways shot past; they were nearing a village. The other sign had said *Simiane*. Simiane-la-Rotonde, he remembered from yesterday's journey, was a few kilometres west of Banon. But he knew nothing about it. Would it offer an escape route – or be a trap?

They were about to find out. A last couple of increasingly tight turns, and he saw a large building ahead. A castle, a grey stone cylinder overlooking the valley. Mirror. Red flicked between the trees. The Operatives were only a couple of hundred metres behind.

A few vehicles dotted a small car park along the roadside. The village had drawn tourists. The main road turned sharply right, a track descending to the castle's left. Reeve almost took the latter – until he glimpsed rooftops below. The hillside was steep, and in a village this old probably inaccessible to cars. Instead he braked and flicked the Saxo to the right, tyres shrieking. Connie joined them as she was thrown sideways.

The road dropped towards a tight hairpin a few hundred metres ahead. Reeve accelerated and checked the mirror, hoping the bigger Jag had been forced to slow. To his dismay, he saw it round the corner in a screaming rally-style drift. High-speed pursuit was apparently a speciality of the Operative driving. He had actually gained ground.

'Shit!' Reeve gasped. The other car would soon catch up. 'Plan B.'

'What's plan—' Connie began – before screaming as Reeve yanked the handbrake and turned hard.

The Citroën's back end swung around in a barely controlled skid. Ninety degrees, more, the valley spinning before them – then handbrake off. His right foot stamped down. The Saxo lunged forward . . .

Off the road.

The ground between the hairpin's legs was rough scrub, speckled with small trees. He spun the wheel in a desperate attempt to follow its contours. A pounding *bang* rattled his teeth as the front suspension compressed to its limit. Connie wailed, but he barely heard her over the raucous roar of flying stones. The car slammed over a bump, briefly airborne, then pitched nose-down—

It hit the ground like a plough. Both airbags fired. The impact was like a punch to Reeve's face. A hideous tearing crunch as the front bumper was ripped off. Dizzied, he hauled at the wheel, sliding the Saxo about. It jolted as it ran over its own debris. The deflating airbag flapped over his legs. He saw the road below angling towards them. Another turn, revving hard to keep the side-slipping car from rolling. It pounded back on to asphalt. The suspension hit its limits again – and went beyond them. Metal sheared apart.

Another blow, this to the base of Reeve's spine. A moment lost to pain, then he recovered. The battered car reeled drunkenly across the road. He tried to correct, but the wheel was slack in his hands. A steering arm had snapped. He turned harder, finally dragging the Saxo about. Buildings loomed ahead. They were nearing the village.

'Oh my God!' Connie cried. 'You've wrecked my car!'

Reeve accelerated as best he could. A dying shrill came from the gearbox. 'Only way I could stay ahead of them.' The Jaguar wasn't following his insane shortcut. It would take thirty seconds to round the bend and catch up.

That was all the time they had to escape.

The road dropped into a right-hand hairpin. A smaller

street ahead led past houses. Reeve guided the crippled Citroën towards it. Red flashed in the mirror. The Operatives rounded the turn. He shot between the buildings, the new road narrowing—

Steps led uphill. He braked hard, stopping at an angle blocking the confined street. 'Up there, quick!' Connie blinked at him, dazed; he jabbed her seatbelt release, then jumped out. A look back. The Jag powered towards them. He vaulted the buckled bonnet and yanked open her door. 'Come on, run!'

She scrambled out with her handbag. 'But we've left our stuff!' she protested. The rest of their luggage was still in the boot.

'We'll come back for it,' he said, as they reached the steps. They ascended to an even narrower cobbled street. It led left and right. Right meant away from their pursuers; he took it. A couple of tourists outside a café reacted in surprise as they raced past. This was not a village used to excitement.

It was about to get it. Tyres screeched below as the Jaguar stopped. The Operatives were coming.

Reeve pulled Connie around a corner. A paved path weaved uphill between the warm stone buildings. Another route angled right. He made the turn. The more twists they took, the better the chances of losing their pursuers.

But he knew those chances were still terrifyingly small.

Both Operatives charged up the steps, guns in hand. They didn't care about their weapons being seen. In rural France, the police would take several minutes to respond. By then, their job would be done.

They reached the top of the steps. Their targets weren't visible in either direction. No need for consultation; Operative 57 went left, Operative 53 right. One of the tourists cried out in alarm as he saw the latter's gun.

Operative 53 was a rangy, jut-jawed man with thinning blond hair. He went by the name West. No sign of his prey on the street continuing onwards. Instead he turned uphill. The steep path winding up through the village was also empty. The targets hadn't been far ahead. If they'd gone that way, they would be in sight. Instead he rounded a corner to the right—

A brief glimpse of movement where the new street curved past a church. Someone running. Reeve and the woman. West charged machine-like after them.

Reeve and Connie hurried past a small church. A fork ahead; the route split on either side of a little shop. Reeve angled left, uphill. 'Wait, wait!' Connie cried, panting. 'It's too steep, I can't run up there.'

He looked back at her. 'You have to. We—'

One of the Operatives ran into view by the church.

His gun came up—

The ivy-covered building to Reeve's left housed an art gallery. Beyond it was a side path. He tackled Connie around the corner as the Operative fired. The bullet cracked against a high stone wall just behind Reeve.

He released Connie and snatched out his own gun. Their hiding place *wasn't* a path, but access to another property behind the gallery. Dead end. A wooden bridge crossed over the nook to the gallery's upper floor. He could climb up to it – but Connie probably couldn't. Not in the time they had.

Which was almost nothing. He heard running footsteps—

A large potted bush sat on a low wall at the building's corner. Reeve whipped out from behind it, weapon raised.

West was almost at the fork. He saw his target's gun and ducked against some railings as Reeve fired. The suppressed round twanged off flagstones. The Operative returned fire. Several shots tore up the hill. The bush shuddered, leaves flying as Reeve ducked. Someone in a nearby house screamed.

Reeve switched the gun to his left hand and fired blind around the corner. Two shots struck stone. He risked a peek. His opponent had retreated to the gallery's entrance.

'Connie!' Reeve barked. 'Run, now. Up the hill!'

Though reluctant, she hurried past him. She still trusted him enough to keep her safe, at least. Reeve fired another two shots to hold the Operative back, then glanced after her. She hared breathlessly up the slope and rounded a corner to the left.

She was clear – for now. Now he had to get away himself. The Walther's magazine only contained another two rounds. He unleashed one in West's direction, then turned to run. If he could reach the corner before the Operative reacted—

The other man had the same training. He was just as capable, just as quick. West was already leaning out of cover to locate him. Two rapid shots, but Reeve had jumped back into the nook.

He was pinned.

Unless—

*

West waited for a few seconds, poised and ready to fire. His target didn't reappear. Reeve couldn't run uphill without exposing his back. That more suppressing fire hadn't come implied he was almost out of ammo. And since he'd told the woman to run, his hiding place had no other exits . . .

He had him.

West bent low, gun trained on the corner as he advanced. He reached the end of the building. A glance at the bush. Nobody lurking behind it. He readied himself – then snapped around the corner.

Reeve wasn't there.

What—

A noise – and his target leapt down at him from above.

Reeve had scaled the wall and grabbed the little bridge above. No time to climb on to it as he heard movement. Instead he threw himself back at the other man.

A painful, bone-jarring collision. They both fell. West's gun went off. Then it flew from his hand as he crashed down.

Reeve was on top of him. He slammed his right elbow into the other man's face. West's head cracked against the paving. Reeve had been forced to pocket his own gun as he climbed. He fumbled for it while the Operative was briefly stunned—

Too briefly. West's hand caught his right wrist. Reeve strained to twist the PPK towards him. He was too close; the suppressor caught the side of West's head. Reeve tried to point the muzzle at the back of his skull. The other man realised what he was doing and pushed with his legs, rolling sideways. Reeve lurched and went with him. He pulled the trigger. A thud of tearing flesh and a shrill crack as his last round hit stone. The Operative screamed.

But he wasn't dead. The round had shredded his right ear and carved through his scalp. But it had not penetrated his skull. West flailed at him in raw fury. A knee pounded against Reeve's back. He fell against the low wall.

The Operative pushed out from under him – and sent a punch at his face. Reeve had nowhere to go. The blow struck with heavyweight force. The back of his head smacked against rough stone. Dazed, he swung the now-useless Walther at West, but scored only a glancing blow.

The SC9 man pushed himself up – then lunged. Reeve tried to deflect him, but West's hands clamped around his throat. Thumbs dug hard into his trachea. Reeve choked. He struck back, gouging at his attacker's wound. West cried out again, but squeezed harder. He pulled Reeve upwards – then pounded his head against the wall.

Colours exploded in Reeve's vision. Intense pain almost overcame him. West rose higher, adding his weight to the force crushing the other man's neck. Reeve strained to throw him off, but had no leverage. The Operative loomed over him, silhouetted against the bright blue sky—

Greenery above him. The bush.

Reeve desperately reached up – and grabbed the plant pot.

He jerked it from its roost with all his remaining strength. West looked up – and the heavy piece of earthenware struck him in the face.

He jerked back, releasing his grip. Reeve slammed the pot against him again. It cracked, spilling soil. Reeve closed his eyes as it spattered him. He threw the plant at West. Another solid impact, the pot shattering. He rolled clear and looked around. The Operative was on his knees, wiping dirt from his face, temporarily blinded—

Reeve sprang up and grabbed him – then smashed his head against the wall's corner.

Again. And again. Bone cracked. One final blow, then he let go. West collapsed, blood gushing from his pulverised face. Reeve drove a heel into the back of his neck. Vertebrae crunched sickeningly.

Gasping, swaying, Reeve staggered back. If his opponent wasn't dead, he was definitely no longer a threat. Where was the Operative's gun? He turned, spotting it a few metres away. A man watched fearfully from the shop doorway as he collected it. The police would have been alerted by now. He had to move—

A gunshot.

Connie. She had run on ahead – and now the other Operative had found her.

Despite the pain, despite his lack of breath, he ran after her.

Connie fled up an ever-steepening path, breath burning in her throat. Long hours, stress and lack of exercise had all taken their toll.

But the gunshots behind her provided a fearsome jolt of adrenalin. She kept running as the pathway curved upwards. Nowhere to hide, walls penning her in. Terror threatened to swallow her. She had once been mugged, a youth snatching her phone from her bag. The fright she had felt was nothing compared to this. The men chasing her were going to *kill* her . . .

A side alley led back downhill. She reached the turn and looked down it—

A man rounded the corner at its foot.

Her heart froze. He saw her – and stopped, snapping up his gun—

The terror now drove Connie onwards, survival instincts taking control. A bullet exploded against a wall just behind her, spitting stone chips.

The hill continued towards the castle. All she could do was run.

Operative 57, who called himself Hayes, didn't pursue her. Instead he reversed direction at full speed. In his dash through the village, he had seen another path heading upwards. He was sure it would intersect the higher route near the hilltop. If the woman kept ascending, he would still reach it not far behind her. But if she turned down it, trying to evade the man she thought was following . . .

She would run right into him.

Connie saw the castle looming above. If she continued past it, she would be back on the main road. Out in the open, exposed. Nowhere to run – or hide.

A glance back. Her pursuer was obscured by the path's zig-zags. There was another downward path ahead, past a tall, run-down building. If she got to it without being seen, she could double back, maybe lose him.

She looked behind again as she reached the corner. Still no sign of him. Eyes front—

The man was right there.

He had run much faster than her – so fast even he seemed taken by surprise. His gun wasn't readied. Instead he lashed out, his forearm striking her face. She fell backwards, nose bleeding.

Hayes stepped forward. He aimed his weapon down at her head. 'Where's Reeve?'

Connie couldn't reply, fear clenching her throat. The Operative frowned, then his face became terrifyingly emotionless—

A gunshot – and one side of his skull burst open.

He crumpled to the ground like a broken puppet. Blood and the glistening grey of brain matter was sprayed over the wall beside him. Connie gasped, desperately scrabbling from the twitching corpse. The shot echoed in her ears. Even now, she thought it was meant for her—

'Connie!'

Reeve ran up the path she had taken. Smoke streamed from his gun. He raced to her. His face was dirty and bloodied. 'Are you hurt? Did he shoot you?'

'No, no,' she managed to reply. 'He – he hit me.' She put a hand to her nose, finding blood of her own.

He helped her stand. 'We've got to get out of here,' he said, quickly checking the dead man's pockets. No car keys. Either the other Operative had them, or they had been left in the Jaguar. 'Come on.'

He took her hand. She numbly followed him downhill.

CHAPTER 41

They returned to the bottom of the hill. The Jaguar's front doors were open, the engine still running. A look inside; the key fob was in the centre console. 'Get in,' Reeve told Connie.

'What about our stuff?' she asked. Her voice was oddly level. She was still in shock.

Reeve was about to return to the Saxo when he heard a siren. Some way off – but getting closer. Their wrecked car had stopped at an angle, blocking the tailgate. Retrieving their belongings would mean clambering into the back and pulling out the parcel shelf. It would take too long – he needed every second. 'We'll have to leave it,' he replied.

'But—'

'The police are coming. We have to go. Now.'

They got in. A fast reverse to make a skidding J-turn, starting back up the hairpin hill. 'You're going this way?' she asked in surprise.

'The cops are coming from the valley, and I don't know the roads.' He switched on the navigation system. 'Find the nearest big town.'

She had an answer by the time they passed the castle. 'Looks like somewhere called Apt.'

He glanced at the digital map. About fifteen kilometres south-west as the crow flew. The current road led northwest, but he was sure there would be connections. 'Okay, put it in as a destination.'

'Why are we going there?'

'A bigger town'll have other transport options. We don't want to stay in this car. Even if nobody from the village saw it, Scott'll report it stolen sooner or later. He'll realise his men aren't coming back.'

She said nothing for some time, then, in a near-whisper: 'You killed that man.'

'He was going to kill you.'

'What . . . what about the other guy?'

'He tried to kill me.'

'You killed him too?'

A small nod. 'Yeah.'

Connie fell silent again. Reeve knew there was no point justifying his actions. All he could do for now was leave her alone. Another glance at the map. The satnav had been trying to make him turn back south, through Simiane-la-Rotonde. Now they were clear of the village, it finally decided on a new route. Left in five hundred metres. He reached the junction and made the turn. The new road wound through open countryside, a patchwork of grass and lavender fields. He lowered the window. Not for ventilation, but to listen for sirens. All he heard was the wind and the engine's low snarl.

He followed the satnav. They eventually reached a main road, the D30. A sign told him he was twenty-three kilometres from Apt. The computer agreed. He cruised south, sticking to the speed limit. Scott's car was distinctive enough without drawing attention.

They entered another swathe of lavender fields. The scent of flowers filled the cabin. Reeve had still been on full alert; he finally began to calm—

'Stop the car,' Connie croaked.

There was nowhere to pull off the road unseen. 'We need to—'

'Stop the *car*!'

Reeve obeyed, halting on the verge. Connie flung open the door and leapt out, running to the roadside. He emerged just in time to see her vomit. She coughed, then slumped back against the Jaguar. Her hands were shaking.

'You're all right,' he assured her. 'It's just the adrenalin.'

'I *know* what it is!' she yelled back. 'I'm a fucking nurse!' More coughs, then she spat out a thick string of saliva. 'Jesus Christ. He was going to kill me. That man was going to kill me!'

'You're okay, though. We both are.' He stepped closer, raising a hand to comfort her.

She moved sharply away. 'Nothing is fucking okay, Alex. I . . . I heard you and that man at the villa talking.'

Reeve felt a leaden lump form in his stomach. 'How long were you listening?'

'Long enough.' Her eyes were locked accusingly on to his . . . then they turned towards the ground. 'Is what he said true? About SC9 – about what it does?'

'He thinks it is,' he replied. 'But that's not why I joined.'

'He's the boss. I think he has a better idea of what it's about than you.' She walked shakily into the lavender field.

Unsure what to do, Reeve followed in the neighbouring row. 'I heard what you did, Alex. In court.' Connie looked back at him. 'You lied.'

'I lied to put my father in prison. He killed my mum – if there was any justice, he'd be in the ground.'

'Is that why you joined SC9? To kill bad guys?' Her disgust was clear.

'No,' he protested. 'I told Scott the truth. And I'm telling *you* the truth. I joined SC9 to protect the country.'

'Protect the country?' she cried. 'You joined a *death squad*. That's their job – to kill anyone Scott doesn't like. I heard him reel off his enemies list.' She faced him over the purple dividing line. 'Feminists, peaceniks, progressives – I'm all three of those, Alex. Does that make me an enemy of the state?'

'No, of course not.'

'But if Scott decided I was a target . . .' She spread her hands wide, as if exposing her heart. 'Would you kill me?'

'I'm not in SC9 any more,' he countered, not wanting to answer. 'Right now, they're my enemy. And after what Scott said, I don't see that changing.'

An unexpected emotion on her face: sadness. 'And if one of the others had been declared a traitor instead of you? Would you be trying to kill *them* right now?'

'I—' He had no reply. All he could do was stare helplessly at her. She turned away. 'Connie, I . . . '

A sound from the car caught them both off-guard. 'That's my phone,' said Connie. A warning glare at Reeve as she returned to the Jaguar. He remained still. She took the phone from her handbag. 'Hello? Jaz, hi.' A look of surprise that her neighbour was calling. 'What is it?'

She listened. Reeve saw her concern rise. 'Wait, wait,' she said, hurrying back to him. 'Let me put you on speaker.'

'Alex, are you there?' said Jaz's amplified voice. 'Look, we had a really weird visit from the police this morning. I would have called sooner, but . . . to be honest, I was a bit scared.'

'How come?' asked Connie.

'They were really aggressive. They asked about Alex – and you. They talked to Mr Brownlow as well. He said they just barged into his flat.'

'What were they asking about?'

Reeve had a more urgent question. 'What did they look like?'

'A man and a woman, both white,' came the reply. 'The man was really big. Sort of dirty-blond hair. Really horrible guy. The woman was a lot smaller. Quite a thin face. Short reddy-brown hair. I think she was Irish.'

'It's SC9,' Reeve mouthed to Connie, before speaking to the phone again. 'Okay, Jaz, if they come back, can you let us know?'

'Yeah, of course.'

'Thanks for telling me.' He tapped the screen to end the call.

'Bye,' said Connie, a moment too late. She looked at Reeve. 'It was definitely them?'

'Mark Stone and Deirdre Flynn. Jaz described them pretty much dead-on.'

Her alarm rose. 'So – so SC9 were at my *house*?'

'Yeah. That means I can't go back there. They might be watching it.'

'But what about me?' she said, dismayed. 'I *have* to go back – it's my home! What if they're there? Will they arrest me for helping you? Or – or something worse? What do I do?'

'I . . . don't know.' It wasn't only Connie he couldn't help. He had no idea of his own next move – if there even was one.

The sound of an approaching vehicle brought him back to immediate concerns. 'We need to go,' he said.

The car was just a Peugeot with a family inside. Reeve waited for it to pass, then pulled out. They continued south towards Apt.

Twenty-five minutes later, they arrived. Reeve stopped in a large car park opposite one of the mediaeval town's old gates. He opened his door. Connie remained still. 'Are you okay?' he asked.

'No, not really.' She didn't look at him. A deep sigh, then she got out. 'Where are we going?'

'Away from the car, for now.' He gestured towards the archway. 'We'll go into town and look for buses, trains, whatever. Might be worth buying a change of clothes as well.'

'You know what you're doing.' Her voice was dejected, resigned.

They entered the old town. Reeve slipped into the first bar they passed, washing his bloodied face and hands. Once clean, they continued. Apt at lunchtime on a beautiful day was busy. They easily vanished amongst the people milling through the narrow streets. Quick purchases gave them new clothes, different in colour from the old. 'We'll need to eat,' he told Connie. She reluctantly followed him to a café. Not a word was exchanged during the meal.

Reeve used Jammer's phone to locate Apt's bus station. Annoyingly, it was back the way they had come, beyond the car park. He checked routes and timetables. One bus went to Avignon; the city had a high-speed rail link to Paris. From there, they could return to England. Once Connie finished picking at her food, he led her back through the town.

She finally spoke as they reached the car park. 'Oh, shit.' Numerous cops, both municipal police and gendarmes, stood around the Jaguar.

'Just keep walking,' Reeve whispered, turning past a hotel towards a pedestrian crossing. 'Nobody would have noticed us arrive. Even if they did, we've changed clothes.' Connie followed him, though kept shooting nervous glances towards the police.

They soon reached the bus station. Reeve checked a timetable. The next bus to Avignon was due in forty minutes. They sat down on a bench to wait.

'You've still got your passport, haven't you?' he asked.

'Yeah,' Connie replied. 'In my handbag.'

'Good. I'll give you more money. Once we get to Avignon, catch a TGV to Paris. Get the Eurostar to London from Gare du Nord. I'll find another way back. We'll need to travel separately; the authorities will be looking for a couple.'

'Don't worry,' she said, with sudden anger. 'We're definitely not a couple. You won't see me again. *Don't* see me again.'

He was startled by her hostility. 'Connie, that's not what—'

'You've ruined my life, Alex!' she cried. 'I'm on the run from the police after you killed two people!'

'Keep your voice down,' he said urgently.

She dropped it to an angry growl. 'Ever since I met you, I must have gone crazy. I helped a fugitive with a gunshot wound. I let you stay even though you kept getting into fights. You made the local drug dealer personally threaten me. You've wrecked my car – shit, my laptop was in my suitcase as well. You've got the police after me. You've got *international fucking assassins* after me. And on top of all that . . .' She hunched up, arms and legs clenched defensively. 'You're one of them. You're part of a death squad.'

'I told you, that's not what I thought it was. That's not why I joined.'

'And why should I believe you? You lied, Alex. You've lied about everything. You lied about your name, who you are, what you do. You lied about your dad murdering your mum.'

'I *didn't* lie about that!' he snarled, barely holding his voice down. Connie flinched at his abrupt anger. 'He *did* kill her. He forced me to see her body. I lied to make sure he didn't get away with it. I lied to make sure she—' His voice unexpectedly cracked. 'To make sure she got justice. Do you know why? Because I could have stopped it happening.'

'What do you mean?'

'I should have been at home, when it happened. If I had been, he wouldn't have done it. I should have finished school and come home. But—' Sickening guilt roiled within him. 'I skived off school that afternoon. I was pissing about smoking and drinking at a mate's house. I should have come home. I could have saved her. *I should have been there.*' The sudden unleashing of truth and emotion long held contained – concealed – left him shaking.

'Alex . . .' He drew in a trembling breath and turned towards her. Sympathy in her eyes, her voice. But . . . not enough to change things. 'I'm sorry, I really am. About what happened to your mum. You – I get that you believe you were joining SC9 for good reasons. But that doesn't . . .' Connie lowered her head. 'Everything's fucked, Alex. It's your fault for dragging me into this.' She looked back up at him. 'But it's my fault for going along with it. I let myself get taken in by the thrill – of who I *thought* you were. You're the super-spy saving the country. Protecting the innocent. But you're not. You're just . . . a killer. You're no better than your father.'

That last struck Reeve like a blade to the heart. He opened his mouth to reply, but no words emerged. He slumped back, gazing miserably at nothing. Connie sat beside him, equally silent.

Finally, the bus arrived. 'Here,' said Reeve, speaking at last. He passed her two wads of notes; one euros, the other pounds. How much exactly he wasn't sure, but at least a thousand of each. 'You take this bus, I'll get a different one. Go home. Stay safe. Try to . . . try to fix everything I've broken.'

For a moment she seemed about to give him a scathing reply. But then her face softened. 'I'll try.'

'I'm sorry,' he said simply.

Connie put the money in her bag, then went to the bus. One final saddened look back, then she was aboard.

Then she was gone.

Reeve stared after the departed bus. What now? He was completely alone. No support, no allies, and the only friend he'd had was now utterly alienated. And his objective, his hope – of convincing SC9 he was no traitor – lay ruined. There was no way back: for anything.

What to do?

Cold pragmatism gradually overcame loss and dejection. He was in France; that opened up the whole of Europe to him. He could travel to anywhere in the Schengen area. As a white European, the odds of his being stopped in transit were slim. And he could fluently pass himself off as French or other nationalities if challenged. Once he changed his appearance, he should be able to slip into hiding.

But . .

There was something else beneath the pragmatism. A deep, simmering fury. Someone had forced him into this situation. Somebody had set him up, framed him as a traitor. Someone within SC9 itself.

He was going to find them.

Reeve channelled the fury, controlling it. Using it. He had a new objective. He could never return to SC9, but he *could* find whoever had destroyed his life.

And make them pay.

CHAPTER 42

Jahmir Haxhi limped painfully on crutches from the taxi to his building. His broken ankle was immobilised in a cast. He hadn't wanted to leave hospital so soon, but its policy was clear. Deal with patients as quickly as possible, kick them out, empty the bed. His protests that his leg still hurt had been met with a prescription for painkillers.

He had needed to stop by the letting agency. The bastard who broke his leg also stole his keys. Replacements in hand, he fumbled to open the lobby door. Nobody offered to help him; there wasn't even anyone *to* help him. He had grown up on an east London council estate. A shithole, yes – but at least family and friends would assist when needed. Here, he didn't even know his neighbours' names.

He eventually got in and reached the lift. There was so much to fucking *do*! Cancel his cards and get a new phone, for a start. So many people to call, and he'd been unable to do so at the hospital. All his contact numbers were in the phone.

At least they were backed up to the cloud. Once he bought a new phone, he could get things rolling. And there were a few people he could talk to right away. The flat had a land-line, his most important contacts programmed in.

He hobbled to the flat, unlocked the door – and froze. Someone had been here.

'Oh, shit,' he gasped. Things had been moved, the blinds closed. His attacker hadn't just taken his keys, he'd raided his home.

'Shit . . .' The word *raided* made him think of his most important possessions. He stumbled to the kitchenette.

'*Shit!*'

The cupboard containing his safe was open. He leaned down to look inside.

The safe was open too.

Jammer felt his heart thud in fear. The money was gone over sixty grand. And most of it wasn't his. How the fuck was he going to repay it?

But the money's absence was not what filled him with the most terror. The iPad was also gone. 'Fuck, fuck, *fuck*,' he whispered, dropping to his knees. He clawed through the safe's remaining contents, hoping the tablet would magically reappear. It didn't. '*Fuuuuck* . . .'

He pulled himself back up. The landline's handset was on the kitchen counter. He thumbed through its few contacts. The one he wanted was listed simply as 'Uncle'.

Scrub that – it wasn't a call he *wanted* to make. But it was one he *had* to make. Delaying would only make matters worse. Sweating, he pushed the button.

The man who answered wasn't the one he had to talk to. Only a select few people had his direct line. Even though he was related, Jammer was not one of them. 'I need to talk to Mr Bato,' he said, trying to sound calm. 'It's Jammer. It's very urgent.'

The reply chilled him to the marrow. 'He's been waiting to hear from you.'

Seconds passed, Jammer's nervousness rising. Then finally he heard a new voice. Deep, languid – dangerous. 'Yes?'

'Uncle Valon, it's Jahmir. Jahmir Haxhi.' He used their family connection in the desperate hope it would gain him some leniency. 'I just got back from hospital.'

'I heard you had been hurt.' No sympathy in the words. The older man's English was perfect, but he still had his native accent. 'Your friends Konstantin and Joseph as well. Why did you not call me before now?'

'I couldn't. The guy who put me in hospital stole my phone.'

'Have there been problems with the police?'

Jammer hesitated. His encounter with the psychopathic cop had been agonising. But he and his bitch partner hadn't seemed interested in him, only his attacker . . . 'I told them I'd been mugged,' he said. 'Said I didn't see who did it. They didn't ask anything about my business.'

'But there is a problem, yes? I can hear it in your voice. Do you have something to tell me, Jahmir?'

A deep breath, then: 'Yes. I . . . kept all my business records on an iPad. It was in my safe. But . . .'

'Go on.' The two words were laden with menace.

'But someone's been in my flat. They broke into the safe. And they've got it. They've got the iPad. And all my – our – money.'

A long silence. Jammer almost hoped the line had gone dead. But eventually Bato spoke again. 'You kept records on a computer.' Not a question; a criticism, an accusation. 'And now it is gone.'

'It's secure,' Jammer said frantically. 'Only I can get into it.'

'I imagine you thought the same about your safe. If the police were to obtain it . . . what would happen?'

'It would be . . . bad,' he admitted, aware how grossly he was understating. 'All my deals are in there, for the past year. Contact names, phone numbers.'

'*My* name?'

'No, of course not! I would never use your name. I'm not stupid.'

'But could the police follow the trail to *find* my name?'

'I wouldn't grass,' Jammer said, pleading. 'I'd never tell them about you.'

'That is not what I asked, Jahmir. Could they find my name?'

'I . . . I don't know. Maybe if they did a full investigation. But they wouldn't do that, would they? I'm a nobody!'

'A nobody living in a luxury flat with no apparent source of income. No, I am sure they would not consider you worth investigating.' There was no humour behind Bato's sarcasm, only cold anger. 'This is very serious, Jahmir. I am . . . disappointed.'

Jammer felt as if his bowels were about to release. People who 'disappointed' Valon Bato would generally not do so again. Ever. Shaking, he forced out a reply. 'It – it's not my fault.'

'No?'

'There's this guy, the one who broke my leg. He must

have broken into my safe. He was staying with someone living in one of your flats. He decided to play hero over a cuckoo who was giving me shit.' A look down at his immobilised ankle. 'Things escalated from there.'

'I would say they did.' Bato drew in an aggravated breath. 'Come to my house, Jahmir. Tell me everything that has happened – everything you know about this man.' His tone somehow became even more threatening. 'I will take care of this myself.'

Maxwell put down his phone. 'Well,' he said, addressing the others in the safe house. 'That was a hell of a development.'

'What did the boss say?' asked Parker.

'He said Alex Reeve turned up at his villa in France.'

Eyes widened. 'What?' said Blake. 'How the hell did he find him?'

Maxwell ignored the question. 'He killed the boss's bodyguards. Two of ours – Operatives 53 and 57.' More shock from his team. 'He was with a woman. They escaped in presumably her car; after it was wrecked, they stole the boss's car. It was found in a town called Apt by the French police.'

'When did this happen?' asked Flynn.

'Late this morning, our time.'

'So what did Reeve want with the boss?' said Locke. 'Not to kill him, obviously.'

'From the sound of it,' Maxwell told him, 'he wanted to plead his innocence.'

Stone snorted mockingly. 'Good luck with that.'

'The boss certainly wasn't convinced. He kept Alex talking until the Operatives showed up.'

'They weren't with him?' said Parker.

'They were in a hotel nearby. Alex booby-trapped the road to the villa somehow. The boss didn't go into detail. But we do have *some* details, which we need to follow up. The woman's car was registered here in London. To a Constantia Jones.'

Stone and Flynn exchanged looks. 'Jesus,' the latter muttered. 'She's the nurse – the one who was looking after Reeve.'

'And he convinced her to go to France with him?' said Stone. 'Fucking hell. Maybe he's better at chatting up women than I thought.'

Parker opened his laptop. 'I'll check the Border Force records. There can't be many Constantia Joneses.' He started to type. 'We might find out what name Reeve's travelling under. If we do, we can flag him for arrest when he comes back.'

'If he comes back,' said Blake.

Flynn turned to Maxwell. 'Is the boss okay?'

He nodded. 'Shaken, understandably. But he's not hurt. He's furious, though. Wants to know how the hell Reeve got to him.'

'A good question,' said Locke, eyeing his superior. 'We don't even know his name, never mind how to reach him.'

'However it happened, we know where Alex just was,' Maxwell said firmly. 'Let's find him.'

'I've got something.' Parker said urgently. 'Constantia Jones went through Eurotunnel customs at Folkestone early on Sunday morning. Travelling in a Citroën Saxo—'

'That's the car that was found,' Maxwell confirmed.

'—with a man, Philip Brownlow.'

'Brownlow's Connie's downstairs neighbour,' said Flynn.

'That's what he was hiding when we talked to him,' Stone growled. 'He'd given Reeve his fucking passport.'

'He must have done an amazing disguise job. They don't look anything alike.'

'Alex was always good at that,' Maxwell reminded her. 'And the Channel Tunnel car shuttle is the weakest link for passport checks.' He looked at the screen. 'Okay, so we know what passport he's using. Maybe he's got another identity for the return, but I'd be surprised. If he's resorting to borrowing from a neighbour, he must be desperate. I'll notify the Border Force. They can flag Constantia Jones and Philip Brownlow at all ports of entry. When they come back into the country,' he smiled coldly, 'we'll have them.'

CHAPTER 43

A knock on the door jolted Jaz Prince from a half-sleep. Hallie dozed on her lap as the television burbled banalities. She held in an obscenity, carefully lifting the baby. 'Who is it?' she called. It had to be Connie or Mr Brownlow; the front door buzzer hadn't sounded.

No answer. She went to the door. 'Hello?'

'May I speak to you, Miss Prince?' A man's voice, with an odd accent.

'Who is it?'

'Your landlord.'

Was this because of the fight the other day? 'Just a sec.' She put the chain on the door, then opened it a crack.

A man in his fifties stood outside. Quite tall, broad-chested, silver hair swept to one side. His face was hard and deeply lined, mouth downturned and cheeks sunken. Intense blue eyes stared unblinkingly back at her. He wore an expensive dark suit. His black leather shoes were polished and spotless. 'Hi,' she said, still wary. 'What is it?'

The man tilted his head to see through the gap. 'Oh. Your baby is asleep. I am sorry to disturb you.' He looked to one side and nodded slightly.

'That's okay,' said Jaz, thinking he was about to leave.

'If you want to come back—'

Another man stepped into view – and kicked the door open.

The chain ripped from the wood. She stumbled back with a scream. Hallie woke, crying. The second man came in. He was even bigger than the landlord, clothing tight on an over-muscled frame. 'Over there,' he said, jabbing a fat finger. His accent was pure east London. Jaz fearfully retreated.

The landlord followed him inside. A tut at the damaged door, then he moved clear. Three more men entered behind him. To Jaz's shock, the first was Brownlow, looking scared. Pushing him was another hulking young man, this one with a beard.

The final person was someone else she recognised. Jammer struggled through the doorway on crutches. 'Hi again,' he said, with a malevolent smile. 'Didn't think you'd see me so soon, did you?'

'I'm surprised to see you at all,' she said, trying to sound defiant. 'Get out of my flat!'

'This is *my* flat,' said the landlord calmly. The bearded man shoved Brownlow alongside her. His boss regarded them both with his icy stare.

'What do you want?' asked Brownlow, breathing heavily.

'My name is Valon Bato,' said the landlord. 'I am involved in many businesses; property is just one. I am very successful, very rich. I feel . . . secure.' A meaningful glance at the broken chain. 'Your friend – Alex, I believe?' Jaz nodded involuntarily. 'He is threatening that security. He has taken something that belongs to my nephew.' He indicated

Jammer. 'I want it returned. I also want to meet your friend Alex. In person.'

Hallie was still crying, Jaz struggling to calm her. Brownlow spoke up instead. 'I don't know where he is. He came round for a few minutes on Saturday, then left. I told the police the same thing.'

Bato's stone face twitched slightly. 'The police?'

'They were looking for Alex too.'

'I see.' He turned to Jammer. 'Did they come to you as well?'

Sweat glistened on the younger man's face. 'They, uh – yeah. At the hospital. But they didn't ask about you! They were only interested in this guy Alex. They were fucking insane!' he added, outrage overpowering fear. 'They held me down and twisted my broken leg – they tortured me!'

Bato was surprised. 'Excessive, even for the Metropolitan Police.'

'They *really* wanted to find this guy.'

'So do I. And I would like to find him first.' His gaze came back to Jaz and Brownlow. 'I will ask again. Where is this man?'

'I don't know,' replied Jaz. 'I last saw him when he beat up Jammer and his friends.' Jammer glared at her.

'And you?' he asked Brownlow.

'Like I said, I saw him briefly on Saturday,' said the nervous man. 'I haven't seen him since.'

'Hmm.' Bato pursed his lips as if deep in thought. Then: 'I shall tell you something. My becoming involved personally in a matter such as this is rare. My time is very valuable. So when it is wasted . . . I become angry. Those who know me,' his eyes flicked to Jammer, 'know this is a dangerous thing.'

The way Jammer blanched warned that he was not bluffing. Brownlow took a half-step forward, positioning himself before mother and baby. 'Look, we're not wasting your time. We really don't know where he is.'

'They're covering for him because he helped them!' snapped Jammer. 'They *must* know.'

'We don't!' Jaz protested over Hallie's cries.

Brownlow advanced on Bato again, this time a full step. He took a breath, chest swelling. Despite his fear, he also felt a courage he had long thought lost. Alex Reeve had helped him; he would do the same in return. 'Look, we can't help you,' he said. 'Please, leave us alone. You're scaring the baby.'

Bato regarded Hallie. 'We can't have that, can we? Not with such a pretty baby. Okay. We will leave.'

He turned towards the door. Jammer shot him a disbelieving look. 'You're just *going*?'

'Are you arguing with me, Jahmir?'

The young man shrank back. 'No, course not.'

'Good.' Bato exchanged muted words in Albanian with his minders. He then gestured for Jammer to leave. Still incredulous, Jammer clattered out. Bato followed, the two hulks falling in behind him. One put a hand in his pocket. Brownlow half-turned, giving Jaz a relieved look—

The big man pulled his hand back out. Wrapped around his fingers was a set of brass knuckles. He marched back at Brownlow before the other man could react. His fist came up – and he drove a metal-hardened punch into Brownlow's kidneys.

Brownlow fell with a strained shriek. Jaz screamed, jumping back and clutching Hallie tightly. The bodyguard bent lower and smashed his fist into Brownlow's face. Two punches, three. Blood sprayed with each blow. The other minder joined in, delivering merciless kicks. A steel-edged heel stamped down on the squirming man's hand. Bones snapped. 'Oh God, oh my God!' Jaz wailed. 'Stop it, stop! You'll kill him!'

'If I wanted him killed,' said Bato calmly, 'he would already be dead.' A click of his fingers, and the brutal assault instantly ceased.

Tears streamed down Jaz's cheeks as she looked at Brownlow. His face was barely recognisable, covered in blood, flesh torn. A wet gurgle came from his mouth as he struggled to breathe.

Bato moved closer and took hold of her chin. He forced her head upwards until their eyes met. 'If you talk to the police, I *will* have you killed. All of you. Your baby as well.' Jaz's legs quivered, and she almost fell. 'Now. Tell me. Where is this man? *Who* is this man?'

She could barely get the words out in her terror. 'He – his name – Alex. Alex Reeve. He's – a friend of Connie's. I don't know anything more. Please, please, I don't know. I don't know where he is. Please don't hurt my baby. Please.'

Bato's stare drilled into her soul for endless seconds. 'I believe you,' he finally said. He withdrew, nudging Brownlow with his foot. 'You. Talk. Where is Alex Reeve? Answer, or they will beat you again.'

'No, no,' Brownlow wheezed, blood running from his mouth. 'I don't know where he is, I don't know. But – my passport. He took my passport. He must have gone abroad.'

Bato frowned. 'Where?'

'I don't know. He didn't say. I don't know!'

The frown deepened. Bato stepped back. Brownlow cringed. 'I believe you too,' the landlord said at last. A gesture, and his bodyguards retreated. He took out his phone and made a call. 'Inspector? This is Valon Bato. Yes, good evening. Listen, there has been a . . . home invasion at one of my properties. A man is badly hurt. Can you please call for an ambulance? No, I thought it best to call you first. I am sure you will want to handle the investigation.' He looked back at Jaz with a thin, lizard-like smile. 'After all, we are friends.' He gave the address, then hung up.

Jaz stared at him in appalled realisation. 'Someone in the police works for you.'

'A mutually beneficial relationship,' he replied. 'The advantages of wealth.' He spoke to his bodyguards in Albanian. They hustled out. 'You go too,' he added to Jammer. The young man gave Jaz and Brownlow a gloating look, then limped away.

'I shall wait here.' Bato sat on the sofa. Another reptilian smile. 'To look after my tenants until the police and the ambulance arrive. Please. Sit.' He patted the space beside him. 'I insist.' With fearful reluctance, Jaz sat down, holding Hallie as far from him as she could. 'Now, you understand that I am a man who means what he says, yes?' He waited for Jaz and Brownlow to nod. 'So you will not do anything . . . silly. Do I have your promise?'

'Yeah . . .' Jaz whispered, lost.

'And you, Mr Brownlow?'

'I . . . won't say a word,' the battered man replied. 'I promise.'

'Good.' He stretched out, filling his space. Jaz recoiled. 'Then if you see or hear from Alex Reeve, or Connie? You will tell me at once.'

CHAPTER 44

Reeve had left the warmth of Provence far behind. The northern French port of Cherbourg was grey and damp. It was as if its proximity to Britain's miserable weather had infected it. Gulls squalled in the slate morning sky, mournful horns bleating in the harbour. It was not a town presenting any obvious delights to visitors.

But it was his last step on the journey home.

He had bought a ferry ticket with no difficulty. Foot passengers making spur-of-the-moment trips across the Channel were not rare. Of more concern was the French border check. His disguise kit had been in Connie's car. A visit to a twenty-four-hour supermarket near the port provided a limited replacement. He ensconced himself in a toilet cubicle at the ferry terminal. Using a hand mirror, he did his best to replicate Brownlow's appearance. The results this time were less impressive. He would have to rely on bluff and institutional weariness to get through.

He headed for the boarding gate. Passengers were already queueing. That was good; the officials would have less time to examine each face. He stood in line, exaggerating his yawns as he neared the front. His tiredness was no act, though. The trip from Avignon had been tense yet tedious.

Several train changes, and the night in a shabby but overpriced hotel in Le Mans. The knowledge that the police were hunting for him hung overhead the whole time.

But he had made it this far.

The employee at the gate checked his boarding card and passport. Brief smalltalk as she did so. He replied with eyes downcast, shoulders slumped. Just another tired traveller wanting to get home. It seemed to work. She returned his documents and directed him through, already turning to the next passenger.

Passport control was next. The security check wasn't a concern. The gun had been dumped, and his remaining money was below the notification limits. But a lone man travelling on short notice with no luggage, paying in cash? That could raise flags. If he was taken aside to be searched, his already weak disguise would fall apart. And if he was arrested, he was doomed . . .

He reached the checkpoint and presented his passport. The officer in the booth looked up at him. The moment of truth—

A sleepy-eyed flick between photo and face and back again, then the man shrugged. The passport was returned with a laconic '*merci*'. Another *rosbif* leaving France, so no longer his problem. Reeve caught his own reflection in the glass before moving off. His exhaustion had made him resemble Brownlow more than ever.

Finally, the security check. The phone and his few metal items went into a tray. Through the detector. No bleep. Would the officers pull him aside?

No. Like the man at the passport booth, they didn't care.

British tourists leaving the country were low priority for additional checks. He collected his belongings and moved on.

A bus took everyone to the ferry. The journey to Poole would take four and a half hours. Reeve's choice of destination had not been random. Information on Connie's car would have reached SC9 by now. Flynn and Stone had been to her house. The link between Connie and Brownlow therefore wouldn't take long to discover. Ferry companies routinely forwarded each passenger list to the UK's Border Force. Brownlow's passport would almost certainly be flagged for detention on arrival.

But arriving in Poole had advantages. It was far enough from London that the Operatives might not arrive before the ferry. And even if they did, he had been there recently. He had seen the area. There were other possibilities for escape . . .

Connie. He had hardly thought about her, his mind on more immediate concerns. But her passport would be flagged too. Would she be detained? Would Operatives be waiting for her? Scott knew she had heard some of the discussion at the villa. *Any* knowledge of SC9 was a dark secret. Would they consider her a threat?

Guilt welled once more. She had done nothing but help him. But now her life was at risk. Someone else he'd failed to protect . . .

Locked in maudlin thought, he barely registered when the ferry started to move. The blast of its horns brought him back to full awareness. France slipped slowly away. In four and a half hours, he would reach England.

To face his pursuers.

*

'Whoa, hey,' said Parker, as a notification popped up on his laptop. 'We've got something.'

His call brought all the other Operatives. 'What is it?' Maxwell asked.

'Philip Brownlow's passport just got flagged. Departing Cherbourg . . . no, *departed* Cherbourg. The passenger list only just came through. Heading to Poole by ferry. The ship arrives at 14:45.'

Maxwell checked his watch. 'That's in three and a half hours. Can we get there in time?'

'Fucking right we can,' growled Stone. 'Flag our car with a national security notification so we don't get pulled over. We'll be there in *two* and a half.'

'What about Connie Jones?' asked Blake. 'We know she's arriving on the Eurostar. Do we still bag her?'

'Yeah,' Maxwell said, after brief consideration. 'John, Harrison, meet her at St Pancras. Mark, Deirdre, get to Poole.' Another moment of thought – then he smiled. 'I know why he's heading there. He's going to jump off the ship! The entrance to Poole Bay is narrow; he'll easily be able to swim ashore.' Realisation from the others as they too remembered their recent visit. 'Change of plans. John, go with them. One of you goes to the ferry terminal. If Alex is detained by the Border Force, make sure he doesn't escape. The other two cover each side of the harbour entrance. Whichever way he goes, we'll have him.'

'Shall I still meet the woman?' asked Locke.

Maxwell nodded. 'We need to question her. The boss thinks she heard him and Reeve talking. We have to find out how much she knows.'

'If she knows anything, she's a potential threat,' Locke said. 'She should be eliminated.'

'Like I said,' Maxwell replied firmly, 'we'll question her.' He turned to Parker. 'Craig, I know you've got your own assignment. Will you be available if we need you?'

Parker nodded. 'I have to recce a location. But if it means taking down Reeve, I'll do what I can to be there.'

'Good. Okay, everyone get moving.' Maxwell clenched a fist. 'Alex is coming home. Let's give him a welcome.'

CHAPTER 45

The ferry ploughed across the Channel, grey waves smacking against its prow. England's southern coast grew larger on the horizon. Reeve regarded it through the windows of the ship's buffet restaurant. He was glad the saying 'Never swim after eating' was only an old wives' tale. In about thirty minutes, he would be putting it to the test.

He finished his meal, then headed aft. He had already worked out his plan. Poole Bay was one of the world's largest natural harbours. Despite that, its mouth was less than three hundred metres wide. There was an exterior stairway near the stern. He would leap from it as the ship entered the bay. Land was a short swim away. Once ashore, he could head around the bay to Poole. From there, he was only a train ride from London.

If SC9 wasn't lying in wait.

Someone would be watching for him at the port. But had they also predicted his escape plan? The odds were worryingly high. He knew how they thought; they knew how *he* thought. Operatives could be positioned on each side of the harbour mouth, armed and ready—

Armed and ready.

The words hit like a thunderbolt. They had roiled in his

subconscious ever since he had fled Mordencroft. His mind had been trying to tell him something. But he hadn't known what.

Now he did.

He knew who had framed him.

Reeve flashed back to his fateful meeting with Maxwell. His mentor had drawn a gun to shoot him in the back of the head. He had sensed the movement and instinctively dodged. A fight, then he had run from the room. Parker had been right outside . . .

Armed and ready.

Why would he have been armed? Weapons were not routinely carried at the training facility. And Parker had been ready for trouble. Why? As far as he knew, Maxwell was telling Reeve if he had become an Operative. Yet he had reacted to the gunshot within moments.

He could have been working with Maxwell, Reeve knew. He had been the first to meet him; they could have planned the kill together. But Maxwell had said nothing about it on the Tube. And everything he *had* said was true. There was no reason for him to conceal that one point . . .

Parker was the mole.

He had set Reeve up. If Maxwell failed, he had been ready to make the kill himself.

Certainty, as solid as the steel bulkheads around him. Parker, the quiet, amiable one. The observer, always watching, listening. The computer expert. The one with the skill to break into SC9's servers undetected and alter the profiles. And the finesse to deliberately *fail* another hacking attempt to frame his patsy.

He had aimed SC9 at Reeve like a rifle bullet to divert attention from himself. Why? What was his goal?

Reeve thought back to Scott's accusations. The hacker had been helped by Russian software. The Russians would gain enormously if SC9 was exposed and Britain revealed as a hypocrite. The country claiming to be an exemplar of law and order, carrying out extrajudicial assassinations? Of its own citizens, as well as those of its enemies – and allies?

The diplomatic damage would be huge, humiliating. An already weakened power would become a pariah. *Divide and rule,* break up opposing alliances piece by piece. Russian orthodoxy. Britain was already out of the European Union. This might see it driven from NATO, from other organisations. Rather than protecting the country, SC9's own actions would cripple it.

Why Parker had done it, he didn't know. Were the attitudes attributed to Reeve in the profiles really his? An anti-authority streak, a hatred of the British establishment? Reeve had no particular love for the so-called ruling classes himself. But nor did he actively seek to destroy them; he felt antipathy, at most. They were just *there*. But Scott represented one extreme end of the spectrum of feeling about them. Perhaps Parker was secretly at the other . . .

It didn't matter. He would force the truth from Parker if he found him. *When* he found him. More hard-cast certainty. He had a new mission, a new target. He was going to hunt down Craig Parker – the traitor.

But first, he had to escape the rogue Operative's comrades.

The coast was now ten minutes away. He resumed his journey towards the stern, heading downwards. Deck five marked the top of the ferry's hull, everything below enclosed. He went to the starboard-side aft stairs, at the superstructure's rear. They were directly behind one of the funnels, foul diesel fumes wafting over him. Trucks and cars were parked on the open main deck beside their foot. He faced away from the vehicles, towards the sea.

The coastline stretched away eastwards. The Isle of Wight was a featureless grey mass in the distance. Closer was the town of Bournemouth, pier jutting into the Channel. Nearer still was the elongated spit of Sandbanks, sheltering Poole Bay. It was home to some of the country's most expensive real estate.

It was also where Reeve intended to make shore. A beach ran almost to the natural harbour's mouth. The ferry followed a dredged channel through its centre. When he jumped, his swim would be at most a hundred and fifty metres. Despite the conditions, he could do it in three minutes, even injured.

Enough time to make shore before SC9 reached him? He would be a helpless target in the final metres before reaching the beach.

But he had to try. If he stayed aboard until the ship docked, he would need to pass through customs. A confined space, with blanket CCTV coverage and armed guards. With SC9 waiting, a death trap.

It was swim – or die.

The coastline rolled closer. He saw the expensive houses and apartments along the spit and on its wider end. Pricey architecture wasn't what interested him, though. It was the stretch of concrete extending into the harbour mouth itself. One terminus of the chain ferry crossing the gap, saving drivers a twenty-mile detour. It was also the closest point of approach for his own ship. The quickest place for him to get ashore – and an obvious lookout point for SC9.

Reeve weighed his options. Every metre closer would save precious seconds in the water. But he would be more visible. Even in this weather, tourists would be waving at the passing ferry. Someone jumping off would be instantly spotted.

He watched the approaching spit. The sea was choppy, striated with whitecaps. Three minutes now looked like a minimum, not a maximum. The water should be calmer within the bay. But waiting until he entered it would take him further from land. More time swimming. More vulnerable. Shit. What to do . . .

The ship slowed, following the narrow channel through the gap. Small craft, yachts and motorboats, cleared from its path like scattering bugs. The terminus came into clearer view. The chain ferry itself was out of sight, somewhere to port. Reeve could see cars lined up waiting for their crossing. People too, as the ship drew ever closer—

A sudden chill. Even from a distance, he recognised someone.

Only a handful of people were on the ramp leading into the water. All but one wore hi-vis vests. The only man who didn't was big, straw-blond, eyes fixed on the incoming ferry.

Stone.

Reeve guessed he had waved some fake ID to enter the restricted area. He wanted to be at the ship's point of closest approach, correctly guessing Reeve's intent.

Stone had a long bag slung from one shoulder. It would contain a rifle. The Londoner was as blunt and brute-force as ever. Was he willing to open fire on his target in front of civilians?

If he wanted Reeve dead badly enough: yes.

The bow drew level with the beach. The ramp was two hundred metres away, less. Reeve looked past it. A row of waterfront mansions, some with their own jetties. Tightly packed, no public roads or paths between them. The shore curved around, Poole Bay opening out beyond. More small boats and even windsurfers dotted the shallows. The ferry approached the ramp. Reeve pulled back into cover, peering out at Stone. The Operative was scanning the ship's flank. Anyone going overboard would become his immediate target.

The ship passed the chain ferry terminal. Stone watched it go. The mansions slid by. Reeve judged distances, times. How long dare he wait before jumping? Too soon, and he would be an easy target . . .

The shoreline started to curve away. Out of time.

He climbed up on to the railing – and leapt off.

The drop was about ten metres. Reeve had tried to throw himself clear of the ship's wake.

He didn't make it.

CHAPTER 46

The bow wave's rolling turbulence snatched Reeve up and flipped him over. Churning bubbles stung his eyes. Disoriented, blinded, he kicked, trying to find the surface. The noise of the ferry's engines became a metallic roar. And there was something else – a hissing thrum, growing louder—

The propellers.

He felt their suction pulling at him. A rush of fear. This threat he couldn't outwit or outfight. All he could do was avoid it.

Reeve aimed away from the force dragging him down. Powerful strokes with his arms, strong kicks with his legs.

No effect. It was like trying to swim up a waterfall. The propeller's vortex relentlessly sucked him towards the whirling blades. He could *hear* them scything through the water. Cavitation bubbles hissed like steak on a skillet. And he would also be dead meat any second—

The hiss became a shriek – then the ship passed him.

The suction abruptly reversed, prop wash blasting him away. He tumbled again, flailing helplessly.

Finally, the swirling current eased. He managed to stabilise himself, then swam for the surface. His wounded left arm ached. Dizzied, his head broke the water. He looked around, panting. The shore of Sandbanks reeled into view. He was over a hundred metres from land, beyond the spit's curving end.

Stone. Where was the Operative?

He looked back towards the chain ferry. The ramp was three hundred metres away, the people on it mere dots.

Reeve could see them clearly enough to pick out the one without hi-vis, though. He couldn't tell if Stone was drawing his rifle – and wasn't waiting to find out. He swam again, wounded arm aching. The shoreline was cluttered with jetties and boats and trees. If he could get further into the bay, Stone's line of fire would be blocked.

A horn sounded. Three long blasts: *man overboard*. The ferry slowed, froth churning beneath its stern. His fall had been seen; people on deck were pointing in his direction. The ship's crew would try to rescue him.

That was the last thing he wanted. He would be rushed to the terminal on arrival – straight into SC9's hands. He angled away from the ship. A glance to his right. The ramp was still visible, but no gunshots had come from it. Stone had lost sight of him. That, or even he was reluctant to blast away in front of dozens of witnesses.

But he would come after him.

Stone had been about to turn away when a figure leapt from the ship. *Reeve*.

His instant thought was to take out his rifle and shoot him when he surfaced. But he held off. Reeve had splashed down three hundred metres away. Only his head would be visible, bobbing in the waves. A tough shot. And right behind Stone were a couple of dozen cars waiting for the chain ferry. Lots of tourists; lots of phones and cameras. There was only one road out of Sandbanks. Even with his credentials, the police wouldn't let him through. Not after opening up with an automatic weapon in front of civilians.

Instead he ran back up the ramp. The waterfront was inaccessible, high fences and walls blocking his path. He would have to go around the road inland of the millionaires' mansions.

Stone leapt into his Discovery, parked on double yellow lines. He tore out of the ferry terminus on to the road. Expensive houses whipped by on both sides. He quickly reached the point where the road curved away from the harbour mouth. The Discovery skidded to a halt at a mansion's gate. Bag in hand, he jumped out and vaulted the barrier. A large modernist house stood before him. He tore down its side to a waterside garden.

The ship was a great slab of steel beyond. It had stopped to search for the man overboard. Stone joined the hunt. People on the ship pointed into the water. He followed their lead, eyes scouring the waves—

There. Reeve had survived his jump. He was swimming – not for shore, but into the bay's shallows. Stone realised why. Several small motor boats floated ahead of him. If he commandeered one, he could escape across the bay.

'No you fucking don't,' the Londoner growled. He swung the bag from his shoulder and opened the zip—

'Hey!'

An angry shout from behind. Stone turned. A man with flowing silver hair strode down the lawn towards him. 'What

are you doing? Get off my property! I'm calling the police!'
He raised his phone.

'I *am* the police!' Stone yelled back. 'Go back inside!'

The house's owner was not deterred. 'Let's see some ID,
then!'

'*Here's* my fucking ID,' said Stone, pulling out his HK416.
The other man fled – though he was already making a call.

That would complicate things, but right now killing Reeve
was his priority. He raised the gun to find his target.

Reeve swam towards the small boats. Fishermen, catching
shellfish or crabs in the bay's shallows. The commotion on
the ship had caught their attention. The nearest man rose
to watch his approach. 'Hey!' Reeve shouted. 'Help! I need
help!'

The fisherman hurriedly started his outboard and swung
his craft around. Reeve kept swimming to meet it. The
engine slowed, the boat drifting closer. Its occupant stretched
out a hand—

Sharp cracks as wood splintered under sudden impacts.

An assault rifle clattered. Stone was firing at him from a
mansion's garden. More rounds pounded the boat. Reeve
dived, swimming under the keel. He surfaced on the other
side. A flat *thwap* from above, followed by a scream. The
fisherman fell into the water with blood streaming from his
shoulder.

Reeve could do nothing to help him. His own survival
took priority. He grabbed the boat's gunwale and pulled
himself higher. The craft tipped towards him under his
weight – acting as a shield. Stone kept shooting. The wooden

hull was thick, but some rounds still punched through. As soon as it rolled level again, it would take on water.

Reeve didn't care. It just had to carry him far enough. Supporting himself on his right arm, he strained for the outboard with his left. The throttle lever was mounted on the tiller. He found it and squeezed. The engine rasped, the propeller churning through the waves.

The boat immediately swung around, exposing him to the shore. He forced the tiller over to compensate. More bullets smacked against the hull, and now the stern. Reeve held on, dragged through the water – then hauled himself aboard. The boat rolled back upright. Spouts of seawater erupted through the bullet holes. Staying low, he aimed the boat towards Poole. Full throttle, and the boat powered across the bay. The gunfire continued, but impacts on water quickly outnumbered those on wood.

Then the shooting stopped.

Reeve kept his head down. He was beyond Stone's effective range, but Flynn might be on the other headland. A sniper rifle could easily reach him. He held course for a couple of minutes before risking a look back.

No shots came at him. He was safe.

For now. He still had to get away once he reached shore. And then he had to get back to London.

But he was back home.

Ready to begin his new mission: hunt down Craig Parker.

CHAPTER 47

The Eurostar pulled into St Pancras station. Connie wearily joined the crush of disembarking passengers. Her journey from Avignon, stopping overnight in Paris, had been fraught, paranoia her only companion. Were the French police looking for her? Were more killers on her tail?

Her tension didn't ease as she left the train. She was on home soil, but so were SC9. Would someone be waiting for her?

Only one gate was open. No choice but to go through it. A lot of police around. Was that normal for the Eurostar? She didn't know. All she could do was keep walking. Everyone slowed as they neared the gate. More cops stood at it, all armed. Fear returned. She fought the urge to push through the crowd and run. *Just keep going, stay calm, keep going . . .*

She reached the gate. Stony faces under black baseball caps watched the passengers exit. Were they staring at her? She didn't dare look around, lowering her head. Keep moving, almost through—

'Constantia Jones.'

Raw terror at the sound of her name. She looked up. Two armed cops – and a civilian standing between them. A man, fine side-parted blond hair, intense blue eyes. They were fixed unblinkingly upon her. 'Constantia Jones,' he repeated, one hand gesturing at her. His other arm was in a sling.

Her knees almost buckled, nausea swilling in her stomach. It took all her effort just to stay upright. 'Y-yes?'

The blond man held up an identity card. A blue logo with the crown and portcullis of the British government. Beside it, the words *Security Service*; *MI5* was appended on the line below. The man's picture was on the card, but in her fear she couldn't register his name. She looked back at him. His expression was cold — no, worse than that. It was as if he had no feelings at all.

He spoke. His voice was calm, urbane – yet frightening. 'Come with me, please. We need to talk to you.'

'What about?'

Now a tiny hint of emotion flickered across his face. It was not a pleasant one. 'Alex Reeve.'

Reeve himself was on another train, heading towards London.

He had made shore near a park on Poole's outskirts. Once clear, he walked purposefully towards the centre. The incessant rain meant his soaked clothing drew little notice. He found shelter and took stock. Jammer's phone case was thankfully waterproof. Everything else was wet. Luckily, many of his sterling banknotes were polymer rather than paper.

He bought a coat and new, dry trousers and trainers in an outdoors shop. He also bought a baseball hat, more to cover his face than keep it dry. A pharmacy provided painkillers and replacement dressings for his injured arm. Once changed, he searched for transport. Rather than go to

Poole's railway station, he took a cab to nearby Bournemouth. The odds that Operatives would be watching for him there were lower.

Now, he was halfway through the two-hour journey. Wet green countryside rolled past. He used the time to think about his objective. Deducing that Parker was the real traitor was one thing. Finding him was something else.

Where was he, and what was he doing?

Reeve's mind returned to Mordencroft. Not to when Parker had been waiting for him, armed and ready. Before that. On the way to Maxwell's office. Parker had said he was carrying out background research for his first assignment. Maybe he hadn't seen Parker while tracking down Maxwell because Parker hadn't *been* there. If he was on a mission, he would have other priorities.

There had been a picture of someone on his screen. A female politician. Elektra Curtis, Reeve remembered: the woman Connie admired . . .

A progressive. The antithesis of the British establishment, wanting to overturn the old guard. The kind of person Scott had moved to the top of his enemies list.

He used the phone to find out more about her. Words like 'firebrand' and 'radical' appeared regularly in the search result summaries. She was young, passionate, charismatic – and an expert at utilising social media. The hashtag *#MakeThemPay* was hers. 'Them' included offshore tax dodgers, exploitative bosses, corporate polluters, greedy bankers, lying newspapers. Targets to excite the ordinary citizen – and horrify the establishment elite. Small wonder she aroused support and vitriol in equal amounts.

What doubtless concerned Scott was that the vitriol wasn't sticking. Reeve knew friendly media outlets were a first line of attack against 'troublemakers'. SC9 was the deadliest instrument in the security state's toolbox, but there were others. Coordinated smear campaigns would squash low-level problems. Few people could withstand concentrated attacks by the more rabid parts of the press. Stress and fear would quickly force them to cave. Never mind that their reputations might be unjustly destroyed. What mattered was that criticism of the state had been neutralised.

Elektra Curtis, however, was having none of it. Clearly nothing illegal or immoral had been uncovered about her past. That would have been front and centre in a media 'monstering'. Instead, criticism focused on salacious trivia and fearmongering insults. Dated insults, at that. Nobody of her generation's knees jerked to terms like *red* or *socialist*. If anything, she had embraced them. Her message was that forty years of fundamentally the same politics had broken the country. Now, it was time to break those politics – and the powers behind them.

No wonder Scott despised her. But enough to set SC9 upon her? If he did, and Parker had been assigned the task . . . how would he do it?

How would *Reeve* do it?

Uncover the method, and find the man.

He read more, building up a target profile. Young, from a deprived background, overcoming adversity through intelligence and willpower. Active in her community, champion of underdogs of all stripes. Quick-witted, quotable, but always on-message. That message was: she would never sell out.

#MakeThemPay.

Martyring Curtis would be the last thing Scott wanted. So no overt assassination. An 'accident' instead. She was the face of a movement, one of Scott's 'keystones' to be taken out. If she could be discredited in the process, the whole edifice would fall. Not drugs; she was openly pro-decriminalisation, so no chance for charges of hypocrisy. Corruption would be preferable. 'Proof' would emerge that she had taken payments from some business she supposedly opposed. For all her words, she had been working within the system. She knew how the game was *really* played; everything else was just for show.

That would be the background. What about the actual killing itself? Hit and run? Too messy, too many questions raised. Curtis could be the only person involved. Something like a carbon monoxide leak or a fall down stairs. That was what Reeve himself would do—

He realised with a flash that he was completely, utterly wrong.

That was what Scott *expected* Parker to do. Deal with a problem so carefully that nobody even realises it's been dealt with. Sometimes SC9 sent blunt messages: that was what Operatives like Stone were for. But political issues, especially at home, needed to be handled subtly.

Except Parker was a traitor. He was working against SC9 – against Britain. If he publicly exposed SC9's existence and methods . . .

Scott could have been right about the traitor's intent. Just wrong about his identity. Murdering a progressive Member of Parliament, then exposing SC9, would not just destroy the agency. It would be a bomb beneath the entire British establishment.

Parker would assassinate his target in full public view. Before as many cameras as possible. And then . . . he would tell them why.

A new search on the phone. What were Curtis's upcoming public engagements?

The leading result leapt out at him.

Curtis had angered the government by challenging its policies on the Islamic Republic of Iran. The official line was that Iran was a menace that had to be contained. By sanctions, pressure on its allies, military action. Curtis, however, believed in opening dialogue. To that end, she intended to meet the Iranian ambassador.

The government, and most of the press, was furious. But they couldn't stop her. The Institute of Middle Eastern Studies at King's College in London was holding an event. The ambassador would be a guest. So would she. She would both raise her profile, and give the government the finger.

The event was that very evening.

Reeve leaned back, staring at the little screen. Was that where Parker intended to strike?

If so, he had to be there as well. To prove his innocence, he had to stop Parker – and save his target.

The train would reach London in less than an hour. He began a new search. He had to find out all he could about King's College.

Internally, Connie was close to tears. But she used all her remaining strength to maintain a poker face. She sat in a stark interrogation room at St Pancras's security headquarters. An armed officer stood guard. The MI5 man, whose name was Locke, had taken a phone call. From his tight-lipped reaction, it had not been good news. Something to do with Alex? Rather than talk in front of her, he left.

Now Locke returned. He got straight to the point. 'Do you have relatives or friends in Poole?'

'What?' she replied, confused and tired. 'No, I don't. I've been telling you for the past hour, I don't know where Alex is.' He had already extracted the story of how she met him, and events in France. Now she just wanted everything to be over.

Locke stared icily at her in unnerving silence. She tried to match his gaze, but quickly withered, looking down. At that moment, he spoke again. 'You can go.'

She was startled. 'What?'

'I said you can go. We're finished here.' He walked out.

Connie looked at her guard, expecting some trick. But he was just as surprised. 'Okay, I . . . I guess you can go, ma'am.' He stood back to let her leave.

Even on the way out, she still expected a double-cross. But nothing happened. As she emerged into the station, she scrutinised everyone nearby. Was she going to be followed? But nobody paid her any attention.

Unsettled, bewildered, she headed for the Tube. If anyone *was* following her, they would be disappointed. The only place she could go was home.

Locke waited in a side office for Connie to leave, then made a phone call. Maxwell answered. 'Jones has left,' he told him.

'Okay,' Maxwell replied. 'John, Deirdre and Mark are on their way back to London.'

'What about the search for Reeve?'

'Local police are handling it. I doubt they'll find him. He's gone.'

'Where?'

'Good question. Did you get anything else out of Connie?'

'No. And I don't believe she knows his location. She was tired, upset – angry. To quote her, "He's ruined my life." They did not part on good terms.'

'Explains why they took different routes home. She probably couldn't handle being with him any more. Not after what happened in Provence.' A pause, then: 'Did she in any way imply that she knew about SC9?'

Locke's eyes narrowed. 'I believe she knows more than she was willing to say. She never mentioned us by name, though. Either Reeve didn't tell her, or she's clever enough not to reveal it to us.'

'I agree; she probably is hiding something. The question is, is she scared enough to keep it to herself?'

'Are we going to take action against her?'

'No . . . not yet, anyway. We'll keep an eye on her. Not a stakeout,' Maxwell added. 'I doubt Alex will go back to her flat. But GCHQ can monitor her communications. If she says anything suspicious, I'll reconsider.'

'So what do you want me to do now?'

'Now?' Maxwell said, with a sigh. 'Until we get a lead on Alex, there's not much *anyone* can do. Facial recognition is running on all gateways to London. We need to be ready to move the moment he's spotted.'

*

Connie finished the long, wet trudge to the house. She unlocked the front door and checked the mail. Several letters, nothing interesting. They could wait. She was about to go to her flat when she heard a noise. She looked up. Jaz peered from her door. 'Hi,' said Connie, waving.

'Hi,' came the hesitant reply. Connie was about to ask if she was okay when she withdrew. The door closed, lock clacking.

That was odd. Had she been expecting someone else? Maybe her ex had threatened trouble again. A shrug, and she went into her own flat.

Everything was as she had left it. Yet even without Alex there, it seemed somehow . . . smaller.

That made her wonder what had happened to him. *Don't start thinking about him*, she warned herself. Her kindness had been repaid with a wrecked car and an MI5 interrogation. And beyond that . . .

The image of the gun swinging towards her came unbidden to her mind. She shuddered, trying to stop the mental playback. What came next would, she was sure, haunt her nightmares for years. As a nurse, she had often seen the gory end results of violence. Witnessing the actual moment was something else entirely.

She needed something to occupy her mind. It was getting late, and she was hungry and thirsty. The fridge was sadly devoid of wine. Damn. Tea would have to do.

Ingredients were thrown together to make a meal. The resulting vegetarian chilli wouldn't win any culinary stars, but at least it was filling. And cheap. She needed a new car, so no more calling out for pizza. She flopped on to the sofa. A deep sigh. God. What the hell had happened to her life? But at least now it was over . . .

A sound from the main hall. Someone unlocking the front door. Philip, she guessed; Jaz was already home. Should she go and say hello—

Oh, Christ – Alex still had his passport. Connie got up. She had to break the bad news. She went to her door.

It opened before she reached it.

She froze in surprise. She had locked it. But a large, bearded man pushed into the flat. He had a key in his hand. 'Hey, hey!' she cried, suddenly afraid again. 'What are you doing? Get out!'

He said nothing, merely giving her a menacing look. Another man, just as big, followed him in. Now truly scared, she backed away.

A third man appeared. He was older, wearing a smart suit. Neat silver hair was swept above a hard face, lines as deep as tree bark. His eyes gave Connie another chill of fear. They were as cold and pitiless as the MI5 man's. He stopped between the two other men and stared at her.

'Who are you?' she demanded, finding some spark of courage.

'I am your landlord, Miss Jones.' His accent was Eastern European. Albanian? She thought she recognised it from patients at the hospital. 'Valon Bato. At your service.' He smiled, without warmth.

'Oh. But – but that still doesn't mean you can just walk in here,' Connie protested. 'You're supposed to give me advance warning of any inspections.'

'I am not here to inspect the property. I am here to see you.' He stepped closer. 'I need to talk to you about Alex Reeve.'

She made an exasperated sound. 'I don't know where he is. Last time I saw—'

Bato drove a brutal punch into her stomach.

Connie folded and fell, gasping in pain. He stood over her, fist still clenched. 'I do not know if you know where he is, or not. But I do know . . .' He crouched, grabbing her by the hair. She cried out. 'That you are going to bring him to me.'

CHAPTER 48

Reeve pulled his cap low as he left the train at Waterloo. It was the busiest station in the country – and bristled with security cameras. Most were accessible by the security services. Facial recognition software would be monitoring live feeds. Sooner or later, he would be spotted.

The best he could do was postpone the inevitable – and make himself hard to track.

That meant travelling on foot, in crowds, through places with multiple exits. Basic tradecraft, learned even before he was recruited by SC9. He looked down at the phone's map. King's College was less than a mile away, across the Thames. He needed to reconnoitre it. See the layout, find entrances and exits, assess the security—

The phone buzzed. A notification dropped down: a text message.

ALEX REEVE. ANSWER THE PHONE.

A jolt of fear, and confusion. Who would be sending him messages through Jammer's phone? Even from just five words, he knew the text wasn't from Connie . . .

Before he could do anything more, the phone rang. The

caller's name appeared: *Uncle*. Someone in Jammer's contacts. But how would they know who he was?

Connie. Shit—

He hurriedly answered. 'Hello?'

'Mr Reeve.' A man's voice, accented; Eastern European. The controlled arrogance of power behind it – and also restrained anger. 'My name is Valon Bato. You took something from my nephew, Jahmir Haxhi. You will bring it to me. Now.'

'I'm busy,' Reeve replied, navigating the crush at the platform's end. He surveyed the station's concourse. No police in sight. 'You give me any trouble and the iPad goes straight to the cops. We're done.'

'If you hang up, I will kill Connie.'

The words were like a physical shock. Reeve spoke in a taut whisper. 'If you hurt her, I'll kill *you*.'

'I have already hurt her. And I will hurt her again.' He spoke to someone in Albanian. Sounds of movement nearby. 'Here. Talk.'

'Alex?' Connie. She was scared, voice quavering.

'Connie?' said Reeve. 'Are you okay?'

'No. He hit me, they – Alex, they've kidnapped me. I'm at a big house somewhere, I don't know—'

More Albanian – and she screamed.

He flinched at the awful sound. 'Listen, you fucking—'

Bato returned. '*You* listen. Bring the iPad to me. I hope you are in London, because you have until midnight. If it is not in my hand by then, she dies. My house is on The Bishops Avenue, in Hampstead.' He gave the exact address. 'Do not involve the police. My people will kill her later if I am arrested.' In the background, Reeve heard Connie sob. 'You have made a mistake by interfering in my business, Mr Reeve. You have one chance to correct it. If you care about your girlfriend, do not waste it.' The call ended.

Reeve stared at the silent phone. It trembled; he realised he was shaking. Fear – and fury. At Bato, and at himself. It was his fault Connie was being hurt. He had to save her . . .

But he also had to find Parker. If he really was targeting Elektra Curtis, there was only a limited time to stop him.

The Bishops Avenue. He looked it up. Over seven miles away. The Tube was the quickest way there – but he couldn't risk using it. More chance of his being spotted, and tracked. The thought prompted him to move faster. He had to get out of the station.

And then what? Save Connie, or stop Parker? His friend, or his country?

He made his decision.

'Alex has been spotted,' Maxwell announced urgently, lowering his phone. 'Facial recognition caught him at Waterloo four minutes ago. He was tracked leaving the station, but then the cameras lost him.'

Locke hurried to the map on the safe house's wall. 'So where's he going? Back to Connie's?'

'Maybe.' Maxwell joined him. 'But she hasn't called him; she hasn't called *anyone*. GCHQ would have alerted us. You spoke to her. Do you think she was genuinely pissed off at him?'

Locke nodded. 'I would say so, yes. She may have concealed information, but she couldn't hide her emotions.'

A moment's thought. 'Reeve would surely think we were watching her flat. Would he risk it?'

'Would you?' The other man shook his head. 'I agree.'

'Then what do we do?' said Locke.

Maxwell stared at the map. 'As soon as we get an idea of where Alex is going . . . we move.'

Craig Parker paused at the street corner to don a hi-vis jacket. Under it, he wore an off-the-peg dark grey suit. A private company was handling security for the Institute of Middle Eastern Studies. Their website helpfully featured pictures of its 'operatives' on duty. He was now dressed like them.

A mocking smile. *Operatives*. He knew who the security personnel would really be. Ex-squaddies, burned-out cops, losers who couldn't even qualify for the police. Compared to a real Operative, they were jokes. But he still had to be careful. They had the advantage of numbers. And if they called the real cops, things could escalate quickly.

The finishing touch was an identity card on a lanyard. It had been fabricated and delivered to him by MI5. Ironic; an agency protecting the state he hated was helping him bring it down. He had taken full advantage of the broad leeway given to complete his mission. SC9 had access to the services of all the other British intelligence agencies. MI5 didn't know why he needed the card, only that he was authorised for it. So they had given him what he needed, no questions asked. SC9's behind-the-scenes power would bring about its own downfall. And with it, the entire rotten British system.

Another irony was that he would have sided with Elektra Curtis. Not on everything, admittedly. She was soft, way too touchy-feely. But bringing down the establishment? The politicians and the judges and lawyers and all the other rich, public school cliques? He was all for that. Drag the posh bastards from their mansions and burn them down. Burn it *all* down. She would help bring it about. It was almost a shame she wouldn't live to see it happen.

He started down the Strand. King's College sprawled through numerous buildings along the famous London street. The event was being held in the Great Hall of the King's Building. It was not directly accessible from the Strand. He had to go through an adjoining building, or the courtyard of nearby Somerset House. The latter was where the VIP guests – including the Iranian ambassador – would arrive. The ambassador was his secondary target. If he could be eliminated too, great . . . but Curtis was his primary objective. She had to die.

Just as he had been ordered. But things would not go the way his superiors expected.

Parker reached the university's Strand Building. It was an unattractive concrete block, obscuring the more impressive architecture behind. He made a show of hurrying in, shaking water from his jacket. The uniformed man at the security desk looked up. 'God, bloody hell,' said Parker. 'Is this rain ever going to stop?'

The guard smiled. 'Doesn't look like it. The great British weather, eh?'

'Tell me about it. I'm with security for the do tonight.' He held up his ID. 'I had car trouble. Had to get the bloody bus. Are my mates here already?'

The guard inspected the card, then nodded. 'Yeah. Some

of them came in about twenty minutes ago. Think the rest went through the courtyard entrance.' He gestured vaguely over one shoulder.

'They all go to the Great Hall?' Another nod. 'Oh, I'm going to get a bollocking for being late. Still, at least the guests won't turn up for a while. Do I need to sign in?'

'Not here. I think your gaffer's handling all of that. Down through there.' He indicated a corridor at the lobby's rear.

'Cheers, mate.' Parker set off deeper into the building. His smile vanished the moment his back was turned.

He had explored the building on a prior visit, passing himself off as a student. Seeing the university's layout had let him devise a plan. The security company would establish a perimeter to protect their VIP charges. But he would already be inside it. Just another anonymous figure in hi-vis.

Then, by the time the event began . . . he would be someone else.

CHAPTER 49

The black cab pulled up outside Connie's house. 'Wait here,' said Reeve. 'I'll be right back.'

He was taking a huge risk coming here – SC9 could be staking the place out. But he had no choice. A light was on upstairs, so Jaz was home, at least. He ran to the front door and pushed her buzzer. To his relief, she answered. 'Who is it?'

'It's me, Alex,' he said. 'I need to come in.'

'Alex? Oh, my God.' Was that fear in her voice? 'Are – are you okay?'

'Yeah, I'm fine. Can you open the door?'

Silence. Seconds passed. He was considering kicking it open when the buzzer sounded. He entered, going to the radiator. The iPad was still behind it. He started to fish it out.

Jaz's door opened. He glanced up as she rushed out, carrying Hallie. 'What's wrong?' he asked.

'You – you shouldn't have come back here,' she said, hurrying to him. 'The landlord beat up Mr Brownlow. He's in hospital.'

Reeve felt another wave of appalled guilt. Someone else had been hurt because of him. 'Will he be okay?'

'I don't know.' She sucked in her lips, tearful. 'They were

going to hurt me too. And Hallie. I had to tell him about you, I had to. He wanted—' She saw what Reeve was retrieving. 'Oh God. That's what he was after, isn't it? That's why he beat up Mr Brownlow.'

'He's hurt Connie too,' he said, to her shock. The tablet finally came free of its hiding place. 'If I don't give this to him, he'll kill her.'

Jaz looked sick. 'Oh, God. Oh my God. And – you're going to do it?'

'I have to.'

'But he'll kill you.'

'He'll try.' He tucked the iPad into his coat.

'There's . . . there's something else.' She couldn't quite meet his eyes. 'He told me to tell him when Connie came home. It's – it's my fault that he's hurt her, isn't it?'

Reeve put a hand on her shoulder. 'No.' She looked up at him. 'It's *his* fault. I'll make sure he doesn't hurt anyone else.'

'You're going to kill him?'

He didn't answer. Instead he went to the door. 'I've got to go. Stay safe, Jaz. Look after your baby. I'll be in touch.' Then he was gone.

Parker stood in the long courtyard beside the King's Building. A stone archway led to the much larger quadrangle of Somerset House. Through it, the VIPs would soon arrive. Parking spaces had been set aside for their vehicles – once they cleared security. With several ambassadors attending, everyone coming in was carefully checked.

They were looking in the wrong place. The threat was already inside.

He had spent his time 'patrolling' the secured zone. All entrances now had hired guards stationed at them. The company providing security was a well-known multinational, often used by the government. Its reputation and size had made it an obvious choice.

It also provided a weakness that Parker had exploited. It had over twenty-five thousand employees in the UK alone. On a job like this, the odds of one guard knowing every other were minimal. He'd counted at least thirty people handling ground-level security. None had realised he wasn't part of the team. He had the right clothing, the right accessories, the right badge. Just another one of the lads.

Nor did the university staff pay him attention. As far as they were concerned, he was invisible. A hireling in hi-vis; their eyes slid right past him. As he'd hoped.

A queue had formed at the archway. Not important guests; they wouldn't have been made to wait in the rain. There was also a hardscrabble scruffiness to them. The press.

He knew why they were here. Love her or hate her, Elektra Curtis made headlines. He suspected most of those waiting worked for the hater side of the media. They would be salivating for a photo of her shaking the Iranian ambassador's hand. On a slow news day, accompanied by outraged headlines, it would dominate the front pages.

But tomorrow would definitely not be a slow news day.

The reporter at the queue's head was summoned to the security checkpoint. He was scanned, had his identity checked against a list, then was let through. Parker waited until half a dozen people were cleared, then headed inside. He had checked the itinerary. The event itself started at nine o'clock.

Beforehand, the organisers would address the press in the lobby outside the Great Hall. Certain attendees would also speak. Elektra Curtis was one. That was when she would greet the ambassador.

That was when he would strike.

He entered the lobby. The doors to the Great Hall were at the far end. A red carpet ran to it. Broad stone stairs doubled back upwards on each side of the large space. University employees were setting up a lectern and microphones. A few people milled around, chatting in anticipation. He passed them to ascend the stairs, looking back at the entrance.

Before long, the press began to file in. Parker regarded each one in turn. He needed a suitable candidate . . .

There. A man bearing a camera, a large shoulder bag and a smaller case. His face was creased by perpetual sneering cynicism. He was roughly Parker's height, brown hair unkempt. Little facial resemblance, but that didn't matter.

The photographer staked out a spot alongside the red carpet. Others moved in around him, but no pleasantries were exchanged. Good; he wasn't with friends. Parker descended the stairs again. He crossed in front of his target, glancing at the badge he wore on a lanyard. His press card. *Paul Babcock, photo-journalist.* Parker memorised the name, then continued on.

He waited unobtrusively at the room's side for a few minutes, then returned. 'Mr Babcock?'

Babcock reacted in surprise. 'Yeah?'

'There's a telephone call for you, sir. They said it was urgent.'

'Who is it?'

'I don't know, sir. But they asked for you by name. If you'll come with me?' He gestured towards the stairs.

Babcock followed with bad grace. 'Keep my spot for me,' he snapped at his neighbours. Neither journalist seemed inclined to help him out.

Parker led the way upstairs, the laden photographer lumbering after. He turned at the top and headed down a corridor. He had surreptitiously picked an office's lock earlier. 'In here, please.' He ushered Babcock inside.

Babcock strode in and looked around as Parker closed the door behind them. 'So where's this pho—'

The Operative moved up behind him and with a single swift movement snapped his neck.

The photographer crumpled, rasping for breath through a collapsed airway. Parker lowered him to the floor. 'Nothing personal,' he told the dying, terrified man. 'By the way, that was the first time I've done that for real. It's not something they let you do in training.' He gave Babcock a crooked smile.

It lasted only a moment. Professional hardness replaced it. He waited for the photographer to fall still, then took his equipment. He removed the man's damp coat as well. If he looked too smart, he would stand out. He shed his hi-vis vest and the suit jacket, then donned the coat. A quick rub of the hand to mess up his hair. Done. He now looked the part.

The last thing he needed was the dead man's press card. Parker took it, then produced something from his wallet. A passport-sized photo of himself. *Thanks, MI5*. He peeled off its protective backing and stuck it over the ID's picture. It wouldn't pass a close inspection – but inside the perimeter, there wouldn't be one.

He dragged Babcock's body behind a desk. The corpse hidden, he collected the camera gear. SLR around the neck, large bag over one shoulder. He decided to leave the case. It was placed alongside its late owner. Parker wanted both hands free at all times.

One last thing. His gun was in a shoulder holster. He drew it and gave it a final check. Fully loaded, one round in the chamber. Safety off. He returned it to its hiding place. Ready to rock.

Parker opened the door slightly and looked out. Faint murmurings reached him from the lobby; more people had arrived. Good. Extra cover. Nobody in the corridor. He quickly slipped out and shut the door, heading back to the stairs.

The murmur became a buzz. Most of the press from the queue were now present. Other visitors had joined the crowd. From the attention given to them, some were VIPs. They weren't his targets, though. He still had some time to wait.

He didn't mind. He knew the value of patience.

Parker descended and slipped into the crowd. He over-heard some of the photographers talking. As he'd suspected, they weren't there to celebrate international relations. 'A handshake'll be good, yeah,' rasped one beaky-nosed man. 'A kiss'd be better, though. That commie bitch planting a smacker on the fucking Ayatollah? I'd get usage fees for *years* for that. Every time some Muslim shithead stabs someone? Boom, here's the terrorist-lover again! Get more mileage out of it than that picture of Maddie.'

'He's the ambassador, not the Ayatollah, you fuckwit,'

said an older, haggard man. 'And she won't kiss him. He's an Iranian. They hate women. We'll be lucky to get a handshake.'

'Thought the Saudis hated women?'

'I don't fucking know.' A shake of the head. 'They're all the same to me. Long as I get the shot, I'm happy.'

'Me too. Where do you reckon they'll stand?' The beaky photographer surveyed the area before the Great Hall. 'I don't want some stupid cunt in a dinner jacket blocking my shot.'

'I wouldn't worry about it,' Parker chipped in. He felt the comforting weight of the gun, and smiled. 'I think we'll all get the shots we want.'

CHAPTER 50

Valon Bato leaned back in his leather chair and checked his watch. 8:15PM – less than four hours before Reeve's deadline expired. He had not lied on the phone. If the stolen iPad was not in his hands by midnight, the woman would die. He would kill her himself. He had not personally taken a life for almost two years. But a message had to be sent.

Nobody fucks with Valon Bato.

He had come to Britain over twenty years earlier. Officially, he had been a refugee, fleeing the ethnic cleansing in Kosovo. In reality, he had never set foot in the former Serbian state. Ethnic Albanians received fast-track immigration status in Western Europe; he had taken full advantage. London or Paris, he had decided. London simply became available first. That he was denying a genuine refugee an escape from violence did not trouble him.

He had always had criminal connections, his family working with the Italian 'Ndrangheta syndicate. Moving to the UK allowed him to expand on those links. Drugs and enforced prostitution via people trafficking were his stock in trade. The opportunities for profit were vastly higher than in his impoverished home country. And he had taken every opportunity that came.

Ten years after his arrival, he was a millionaire many times over. Respected by those who mattered, but, more importantly, feared by potential enemies. Increasing crackdowns on organised crime, however, forced him to diversify. To become . . . legitimate.

Property had been his route. London was an ever-swelling bubble that seemed impervious to puncture. He snapped up relatively cheap housing, former council properties bought by their tenants. Sweeteners helped him win bidding wars. Few sellers refused an extra five or ten thousand in cash, tax-free. The money was quickly earned back from rent. Properties built for one family could be divided into three or four units. All paying London's inflated rates. After a few years, his legal empire was almost as lucrative as his other concerns.

The law was always a worry. He took care of that from the top and the bottom. As a now-respectable businessman, he could enter certain social circles previously barred to him. The lower echelons of the British establishment. Councillors, solicitors, barristers, judges, police officers – even an MP or two. He would never be one of them; his birthplace alone ensured that. But he was rich and powerful enough for them to crave his 'friendship'. And once they had it, he had them. A mark against him would sully themselves. To be exposed as a friend of an Albanian gangster would be embarrassing. And embarrassment was something these people sought to avoid.

At the bottom end, simple, brutal violence did the job. If you crossed Valon Bato, you would pay. Severely. His reputation was enough to deter people from doing so. But it seemed this Alex Reeve hadn't heard of him.

He was about to regret his ignorance.

Bato stood, going to the window. His expansive lounge was on the first floor of his Hampstead mansion. The Bishops Avenue was nicknamed 'Billionaires' Row', containing some of the capital's most expensive houses. His home had been a relative bargain. Its Saudi owner had fallen on hard times, needing cash urgently. He had also been a client of both arms of Bato's less-legal business. A deal had been easy to strike.

Below were the front garden and driveway. High walls surrounded the property. Right now, his desire for privacy was greater than usual. Trusted men were stationed around the house. All were armed with silenced weapons. He was taking no chances. Reeve was clearly not just some thug. From what Jahmir and his friends had said, he was more likely ex-military. Tough, capable, violent – and ruthless.

But so was Bato.

Satisfied that his home was secure, he went to an adjoining room. The woman was inside, guarded by two more men. Her arms were folded tightly around herself, legs closed. A dark bruise marred her cheek. Also there was Jahmir himself. He sat glaring mockingly at the prisoner, broken leg supported on a stool.

'Your friend is still not here,' Bato told her. 'He is running out of time to save you.' Her only reply was a sullen, fearful glance.

'He's not coming,' said Jammer dismissively. 'He'd be insane! He must know you're going to kill him. I wouldn't come.'

'That is because you are a coward,' Bato growled. 'Reeve is not. He will be here – but he will not walk meekly to the front gate. Why do you think I have so many men on guard? He is a soldier, I am sure. He *will* try to rescue his girlfriend.'

'I'm not his girlfriend,' Connie said, quietly but with defiance.

'But you *do* think he will come for you,' Bato replied. He crouched before her, basilisk eyes fixed upon hers. 'I can tell. You still have hope. And I can tell when a woman has lost all hope, trust me. It is when I know they belong to me.' She looked away in disgust – and fear. 'You know what he can do to a man.' He indicated Jammer's ankle. 'And you hope he will do the same to me.'

'You don't have a clue what he can do to a man,' was her reply. Her tone unsettled Bato.

But only for a moment. He stood again. 'You *should* have hope. The only way your life will be saved . . . is if he loses his.' He loomed over her. 'Pray that he comes for you. Because if he does not, you will die.'

Reeve was already there.

The taxi had taken him to Winnington Road, paralleling The Bishops Avenue. The satellite view on Jammer's phone showed him which houses backed on to Bato's. He strolled past, observing them. One seemed to have nobody home, windows dark. Its front gate was open. He nonchalantly walked through as if visiting. Hat on to block security cameras, he went around the house's side. The expansive rear garden opened out before him. Bato's property – a full-on mansion – was beyond a high wall.

He climbed to its top. He didn't drop down into the

bushes below, though. Instead he surveyed what he suspected would soon become a combat zone.

Bato was ready for him.

He counted three men in the garden behind the mansion. All had weapons. Compact Skorpion submachine guns, with suppressors. They were patrolling, moving slowly through the incessant rain. He watched them, tracking their routes. One disappeared around the house, but a different guard soon emerged from the other side. Assuming the mansion's front was equally well guarded, he guessed at least seven hostiles. And that was just in the grounds. There could be many more inside.

He looked for a route to the house. There was a separate, blocky building behind it. A garage? He picked out a CCTV camera with infrared illuminators on its wall. It covered most of the rear lawn. Another was on the back of the house itself. That limited his options for a stealthy approach.

But there still *were* options. There was a feature partway down the lawn. A circular fountain surrounded by a divided ring of low walls. The bushes along the northern boundary wall, to Reeve's left, ran close to it.

He scoured the rest of the property for cameras or other security devices. None visible. As he'd learned at Scott's villa, that didn't mean there were none there. But he couldn't waste any more time.

The overcast sky had darkened as evening drew in. He waited until the nearest man was facing away, then silently dropped down. The wet bushes gave him concealment. He crawled behind them to the north wall, then turned along it. Gaps in the foliage gave him occasional glimpses of the guards.

Bato's men were amateurs, Reeve saw. Fingers rested on triggers, the guns themselves being waved around. Several guards were smoking, and there was a lot of chat. Had he still had Jammer's gun, he could have killed everyone in sight within seconds. But without a weapon, he would have to be more subtle—

Floodlights on the house burst to life.

Reeve froze. Had he been seen? But the guards merely reacted with annoyance as they were dazzled. Someone had turned them on to counter the growing darkness. He waited to see how the men would adjust their patrol routes. They didn't. They stayed in the light, ignoring new swathes of shadow.

He moved on until he neared the fountain. The low walls now cast black voids over the lawn's floodlit sheen. The nearest was three metres away. A guard ambled past, more focused on his cigarette than his task. Reeve looked down the house's side. Another man was approaching from the front. But he was on his phone, unconsciously gesturing with his gun hand. Reeve slipped into a gap between the plants and waited, poised . . .

The man on the phone laughed, turning his head. Reeve sprang out from the bushes and rolled to flatten himself against the low wall. If the approaching guard had noticed the movement, the alarm would be raised *now* . . .

It didn't come.

He stayed still. Would the man follow the same route? If so, he would pass on the other side of the fountain. If he changed his mind . . .

The man's voice grew louder; he was still on the phone.

Footsteps became audible over the soft hiss of rain. Unhurried, swaggering—

Fading. Another laugh, then he continued past the fountain.

Reeve cautiously raised his head. The man's back was to him. He rose and darted to the house. The floodlights were above the windows; the walls directly beneath were in shadow. He crouched in a dark corner behind a circular metal table. Anyone looking his way from the lawn would be part-blinded by the glare. Unless someone came right up to the table, he would be hidden.

More confident, he took out Jammer's phone. His plan had formed during the taxi ride. Two objectives, several miles apart. He had brought up the phone's map to check routes, distances, times. The pulsing dot representing his position sparked an idea. He could pinpoint his exact location using the phone. But others could do the same . . .

He opened the internet browser, about to enter an IP address. Then he hesitated. The phone was linked to the 5G network, an icon confirming the connection. But Jammer was Bato's nephew. Had he been here before?

Reeve had turned off the phone's Wi-Fi to save power. He reactivated it. The symbol replaced the 5G icon. The phone had automatically logged on to Bato's wireless network. Even better than planned.

He entered a memorised address: not a name, but a series of numbers. It was not a server that advertised its existence. But it was one he had used frequently over the past months.

A login screen appeared. Would his code still work? It

might not matter. Just trying to use it could be enough. He entered it. A pause . . .

And he was in.

He shielded the screen as another guard rounded the house. In cover, in shadow, he wasn't seen. He waited for the man to walk on, then continued his work.

His enemies were about to become his unwitting allies.

CHAPTER 51

Maxwell's phone rang. He knew the ringtone. 'Sir?'

'Maxwell.' Scott. Excitement in the older man's voice. 'Reeve's logged in to SC9's main server. We left his access open as a honeypot – and it worked.'

'Can he reach anything beyond his authorisation?' Maxwell asked.

'Security was increased, so he shouldn't be able to. But what matters is that we have his location.'

Maxwell collected his laptop. 'Where is he?'

'I'm sending the details to you. He's not far from you. Eliminate him.'

'We will, sir,' Maxwell assured him. Scott disconnected. The laptop woke; Maxwell accessed SC9's network. Scott's message had already come through.

'Have we found him?' asked Flynn, recently returned from Poole.

'The boss thinks so. Let's see . . .' He typed rapidly, transferring the incoming information to database searches. Results quickly appeared. 'He's in Hampstead. The IP address he's logged into our servers from is a private residence. Owner is . . . one Valon Bato.'

Stone reacted with surprise. 'Bato? I know the name.

Albanian gangster, and a right piece of shit. Nobody's ever managed to pin anything on him, though. Friends in high places.'

Maxwell accessed a security file on the man in question. 'Suspected of involvement in drugs, prostitution, human trafficking. There's a whole lot of "released without charge" here, though. And the police haven't even sniffed at him for a few years.'

Locke peered at the screen. 'If he can afford to live on Billionaires' Row, that's perhaps not surprising.'

'So what's Reeve doing there?' asked Blake. 'Why would he be accessing our systems from an Albanian gangster's house?'

Maxwell's eyes widened in realisation. 'The Albanians have been known to do proxy work for the Russians . . .'

'Maybe Bato's his contact,' said Flynn. 'He might have given Reeve the software he used for the hack.'

'And he's hacking in again for him,' Stone said in alarm. 'We've got to stop him.'

'Agreed.' Maxwell memorised Bato's address, then shut the laptop. 'This isn't a time for subtlety. We arm up and get over there, full speed. Simple objective. Find Alex Reeve – and kill him.'

Reeve spent several minutes lurking in the dark corner. He used the phone to flit through SC9's server. If his access had been curtailed, there was no sign. But he was certain his presence was known.

He was counting on it.

But now he had to move. The other Operatives would

be coming. How long before they arrived was a question he couldn't answer. If they were based in west London, they could be minutes away. South-east London, they might take an hour to battle through traffic.

Either way, he had to make his move. He put the phone screen-down under the table, leaving it running. Then he waited for another guard to pass before slipping across the house's rear. A door led inside, one of three access points he had seen. He peered through the glass. A kitchen, unlit. He tested the handle. It turned. He ducked inside.

Reeve listened, unmoving. Faint voices reached him. Nobody in sight, though. In a house this sprawling, they could be anywhere.

He moved through the kitchen. Spill from the floodlights illuminated it. Large, expensive, spotless, an ode to stainless steel. The hob was gas-fired. Reeve regarded it, then turned all the knobs to full before continuing. The more chaos he raised, the better his chances of escape.

He spent the next few minutes exploring the ground floor. At least two more men on this level. One near the front door, smoking. The other he heard rather than saw, having a phone conversation in a dining room. The mansion had two staircases. A large, sweeping one in the main hall, a smaller one near the rear. He added them to his mental map.

Bato was not on this floor, he realised. Nor was Connie. He returned to the back stairs. Paintings lined the hallway leading to it. Battle scenes, a moustachioed warrior on horseback facing various enemies. He glanced at one's title. *Gjergj Elez Alia.* An Albanian folk hero? Whoever he was, Bato obviously admired him.

He silently ascended. More voices became audible. A mixture of English and Albanian. He moved towards the front of the house. He wasn't sure how many men were talking, but knew one thing for certain.

Valon Bato was amongst them.

Reeve recognised his voice from the phone call. Precise English, but strongly accented. But was Connie there? He didn't want to reveal his presence until he found her—

As if on cue, he heard her. Another voice he recognised: Jammer. He couldn't tell what they were saying, but Connie sounded scared. He moved closer. A set of double doors were open ahead. He crept over to them and peered in.

The large room was a luxurious lounge. Marble floor, black leather furniture, lots of gold and gilt. A bearded man at the expansive windows watched the street outside. Bato? No. Too young.

Where was Connie? A side door led to another room. She had to be in there – along with Bato and Jammer. At least one more bodyguard too; he glimpsed another big man through the doorway.

Reeve took a breath. How long should he wait? Several clocks were ticking. Not just here; he also had Parker to consider . . .

Connie spoke again. 'If – if you kill me, the police will find you. I don't care how much money you have. You can't get away with murder.'

Bato's reply was chilling enough to Reeve. It would terrify Connie. 'I already have. Many times.'

Even if it was too early, he had to act now. He entered the lounge. 'Mr Bato. I'm here.'

The bearded man reacted in shock, fumbling out a pistol. Two more men hurriedly emerged from the side room. It was easy to guess which was Bato. He was older, weathered, cruel. Eyes that had seen too much, and been responsible for much of it. 'Mr Reeve!' He was surprised, but quickly covered it.

'Alex?' said Connie, from the other room. She was equally shocked – but also afraid.

'I'm here, Connie,' Reeve replied. He advanced until he could see her. She was in a chair, another large man guarding her. 'It's going to be okay.'

'No, it's not! Alex, he's going to kill you.'

Reeve didn't reply. Both Bato's companions now had their guns fixed upon him. Bato himself regarded his guest. 'I expected you would come here,' he said. 'But I did not expect you to reach me without being seen. Impressive.'

'I brought what you want,' said Reeve. 'Let Connie go, and you can have it.'

Bato gave him a tight smile. 'I will have it anyway. The woman? We shall see.'

Reeve's voice hardened. 'Let her go.'

The smile vanished. 'You do not tell me what to do. Especially in my own home!' Bato held out a hand to one of his men, who gave him his gun. He aimed it through the doorway – at Connie. Her breath caught in her throat. 'In my life I have killed twenty-seven people, Mr Reeve. I can make it twenty-eight with a squeeze of my finger. Shall I?'

The other bodyguard's gun was still locked on Reeve. He couldn't attack Bato without being shot. But even knowing he would eventually have to give in, he still did so reluctantly. 'Okay. *Okay*. Don't hurt her. I've got the iPad.' He slowly reached into his jacket. The bodyguard's finger tightened on the trigger. He brought the tablet out. 'Here.'

'Jahmir,' said Bato. Jammer hobbled into the room on crutches. 'Is that it?'

'I, uh . . . I don't know,' the young man replied, worried. 'Show me the lock screen.'

Reeve tapped the power button. The screen lit up. The background image was a mound of hundred-dollar bills. 'Yeah, yeah,' Jammer said, relieved. 'That's mine.'

Bato aimed the gun at Reeve and advanced. He was careful not to cross into his bodyguard's line of fire. 'Give it to me.'

'Alex, if you do, he'll kill you,' Connie said, voice quavering.

'If I don't, he'll kill *you*.' Reeve handed the tablet over.

Bato backed away, passing it to his nephew. 'Check it.'

Jammer awkwardly supported himself on the crutches as he unlocked the machine. He opened the spreadsheet app and swiped through pages. His relief was palpable. 'It's here! It's all here.'

'It is all there,' Bato echoed. He was not being complimentary. 'Have any copies been made?'

Jammer's joy was very short-lived. 'I . . . I don't know. I don't even know if there's a way to find out. He could have sent copies to anyone . . .' His face fell further with each word.

'I only took it so you'd stay away from the people in the house.' Reeve shot an angry look at Bato. 'You didn't have to do that to Brownlow.'

'I have done worse to people for less,' was the uncaring reply. 'And I can still reach him. And the girl, and her baby. Did you send copies to anyone? To the police?'

'No.'

'And why should I believe you?' The icy eyes drilled into him.

Reeve's gaze remained firm. 'If I had, the police would already have arrested Jammer. And since he had all those helpful names and addresses, everyone else as well.'

Bato gave Jammer a cold glare, then turned back to Reeve. 'You underestimate how many friends I have in the Metropolitan Police. But . . . I believe you.' He returned the gun, and held out his hand to his nephew. Jammer hesitated, then passed the iPad back to him.

The gangster was briefly still – then with shocking force smashed the tablet against Jammer's face. He fell with a shriek. Connie screamed. Bato hurled the iPad at Jammer's bloodied head. It struck with a solid thud, the screen breaking. The young man cried out again, raising his hands to defend himself.

It made no difference. Bato kicked him, again and again, yelling in Albanian. Reeve watched. His face was impassive, but internally he was preparing for the same – or worse.

Finally Bato paused the assault. He stepped back, leaving Jammer writhing and groaning on the floor. A huff of breath from his exertion. 'If we were not joined by blood, Jahmir, I would have killed you,' he growled. 'You made a stupid mistake. *Stupid.*'

'I'm – I'm sorry,' Jammer whimpered. 'I'm sorry!'

Bato glared at him – then delivered one final kick. 'I accept your apology.' Another exhalation, then he rounded on Reeve. 'But you . . . we have no blood in common.'

Bato's fists clenched – and he lunged.

CHAPTER 52

Maxwell pulled over on The Bishops Avenue, fifty yards from Bato's mansion. 'What have we got?'

His team were spread through three vehicles. He was in a Discovery with Locke. Blake and Stone were in an identical Land Rover ahead. Flynn drove an anonymous dark Transit van, which halted behind Maxwell's 4x4. 'Not much,' Stone replied over the phone. The other Discovery had driven past the house to reconnoitre. 'Walls are too high to see inside.'

'Okay. Come back and stop fifty yards from the gate. You should be out of sight. We'll use the drone. Deirdre?'

Flynn was also linked in on the call. 'Setting it up now.'

The Operatives had brought everything they needed – or *might* need. The drone was one of their contingency items. A modified civilian quadcopter, it could provide real-time video surveillance in almost total silence.

Maxwell watched the van in the mirror. A hatch in its roof soon opened. A brief matt-grey blur in the streetlights, then the drone was gone.

He took out a small tablet computer. A few seconds to load an app, then the feed from the drone appeared. His own vehicle was visible as the little aircraft climbed. Then it turned, gliding across the road towards the mansion.

Figures came into view in the grounds. 'Looks like they're giving Reeve an honour guard,' said Flynn.

Maxwell's eyebrows rose. 'You're not kidding.' Several men stood in the rain outside the house – and all were armed. 'Can you zoom in?'

She complied. The camera fixed upon one man. 'Suppressed Skorpion,' Maxwell noted. 'They've all got the same weapons. They're expecting trouble.'

Flynn zoomed back out and continued the survey. 'More men at the rear. Seven in the grounds, at least. There could be more inside.'

'I'd put money on it,' Maxwell replied.

'I've seen wankers like this on busts,' said Stone dismissively. 'Fucking Albanians. Macho arseholes, with no training. They're only tough guys if they have a gun and you don't. Go in heavy on them and they piss their pants in terror.'

'So what do we do?' asked Blake.

'What we're trained to do,' said Maxwell. 'Alex is still in there, and he's still connected to our servers. Whatever he's doing, it stops now.' He straightened. 'Vests on and arm up.'

'How long will we have?' asked Locke.

Stone had the answer. 'Unless a Trojan happens to be driving right past?' *Trojan* was the Met's code for an Armed Response Unit. 'We'll have five minutes before one gets here from the nearest station.'

'Then let's be done in three,' Maxwell announced. 'We go in and kill every living thing we find.'

Bato's fist rushed at Reeve's face. He easily dodged it. The Albanian was tough, brutal – but also predictable, telegraphing his moves. Another strike. Reeve's right forearm swatted it aside.

Anger flared on Bato's face. He barked an order – and one of the bodyguards joined the fray.

Reeve's immediate thought was to get his gun. But the big man shoved the pistol into the back of his waistband before engaging. He had some martial arts training, Reeve instantly saw. Not to a high level, but enough to complicate things. And the bearded bodyguard, holding back, was still armed. If Reeve broke away, he would be shot.

He jerked clear of a punch, sidestepping a kick at his knee. The bodyguard circled around him. He now had attackers in front and behind. If he didn't deal with them quickly, he would be trapped—

The guard was the bigger threat. Reeve swung to face him. He waited for his next strike, dodging – then snapped out a counterattack. The heel of his palm crashed against the man's jaw. The Albanian staggered back, rattled.

Reeve pressed his attack. A heel-kick to his shin, then, as his target cried out, a second blow to his head. The bodyguard reeled—

Sound behind: footsteps, the hiss of fabric. Reeve turned his head. Bato was charging. He pulled sharply away, expecting a punch. Instead a kick landed hard on his hip. It was Reeve's turn to stagger. Connie gasped.

The man watching her came to the doorway, gun in hand. Bato shouted another command. The gun rose to track Reeve. The bearded bodyguard pocketed his own weapon and advanced. Reeve moved clear of Bato to face him. The newcomer clenched his fists, weight on the balls of his feet, left foot forward. Orthodox stance – a boxing move. His right hand jabbed at Reeve. He blocked it, but the impact still delivered a fierce blow to his forearm.

Three against one, and all were at least competent fighters. Thoughts of his plan were replaced by reactive survival instinct. He had to get a gun. The first bodyguard was recovering. Reeve whirled and ploughed a fist into his stomach. He stumbled backwards. Reeve tried to angle around him. The pistol's grip protruded from his waistband. He snatched at it—

The bearded guard rushed at him from the side. Reeve had no choice but to pull away – only for Bato to attack from behind. A stone fist slammed against his kidneys. Pain exploded in Reeve's lower back. He held in a yell. He would be pissing blood for a week . . .

If he lived that long.

He *sensed* more than saw Bato pressing his attack. Reeve's right arm lashed downwards as he spun, deflecting another punch. Bato lurched, momentarily unbalanced. Reeve continued his turn. Pain flared in his injured arm as his left fist lanced at the gangster's face. The older man jerked back – not quite fast enough.

Reeve's knuckles caught his cheekbone. Bato let out a grunt. Fury rose in his eyes. It had been years since he'd been on the receiving end of an attack. His bodyguards were momentarily shocked. Then their assaults resumed, more forcefully, fuelled by anger – or fear.

Reeve fought to defend against attacks from two directions. The gun was still his objective. He ducked beneath a sweeping haymaker, whipping around on one foot. His other smashed against an ankle. The bodyguard cried out, almost falling. Reeve sprang back up. His hand slashed, fingers extended. They raked across the bearded man's eyes. He leapt back with a yelp, one eye squeezed shut. Reeve whirled back to his companion. The gun was exposed. He snatched for it—

Bato's balled fist crashed against his left biceps.

An explosion of agony almost overpowered Reeve. Bato had hit the bullet wound. This time he couldn't contain an anguished howl. Before he could recover, one of the bodyguards body-slammed him. He fell. 'Fucking *yes*!' Jammer exulted, laughing. 'Make that cunt scream!'

A foot thudded into Reeve's stomach. The other man went for his head. Blood welled in his mouth. His vision blurred. Another kick hit home. He heard Connie begging for his attackers to stop. They didn't. His wounded arm was hit once more. He screamed again—

Bato snapped an order. It wasn't one Reeve expected. 'Stop! Stop, hold him down.' The bodyguards obeyed. He was in too much pain to resist. The gangster moved closer, frowning – but also curious. 'You take so much without a sound. But then . . . here?' He tugged Reeve's clothes from his left shoulder. A bandage was revealed. A fresh oval of bright red blood blossomed on it.

Bato pulled it down. Reeve gasped as the injury was exposed. 'This is a bullet wound,' the Albanian exclaimed. He looked at Jammer, who had struggled to a sitting position. 'You did not say you had shot him.'

'I didn't,' Jammer replied. 'Wish I had, though. It wouldn't have been in his fucking arm, either.'

'Shut up.' Bato turned back to Reeve. 'Not many men can fight so well with a wound like that. Who are you?' Reeve didn't answer. 'Who are you working for? Are you a cop?'

'Keep hitting his bullet hole,' Jammer suggested, with sadistic relish. 'He'll talk.'

'No.' Bato stepped back, staring intently at Reeve. 'Something is not right.' An order, and the two bodyguards hauled Reeve to his feet. 'We kill him, now, and dispose of the body.'

'No!' cried Connie. She ran into the room. The third bodyguard grabbed her.

Bato took a gun from one of his men – then addressed his nephew. 'Jahmir. You can kill him. For *kanun*.' Reeve didn't know the Albanian word, but guessed it involved honour, or revenge. 'You say you are tough and strong. Prove it. Take his life. Show your worth, and I may even forgive your stupidity.'

'Oh, I'll fucking kill him, yeah,' said Jammer, trying to stand. The third man released Connie to help him up.

'Good.' Bato waited for him to hobble closer, then gave him the gun. 'Do it.' He stepped clear, his guards following suit.

Jammer faced Reeve. He clumsily propped himself on one crutch to raise his right arm. Reeve kept his eyes fixed upon the gun. The bodyguards had readied their own weapons. He would never reach Jammer before being gunned down. But if he could bring him closer . . .

'You look a bit shaky, Jammer,' he said. 'Sure you can hit me from there? Only way to be sure is do it point-blank.'

The younger man didn't take the bait. 'Fuck off.'

Then he took aim.

'Alex!' Connie wailed.

Reeve tensed. He could dive clear – but the bodyguards would kill him anyway. A sick, leaden feeling ran through his veins. The realisation that he was about to die—

A thunderous *bang* came from outside.

CHAPTER 53

Blake and Stone took their Discovery some way back along the street. Then they returned, at speed – and swerved to ram Bato's front gate.

It was a heavy barrier, but couldn't withstand the force of two tons of metal. It smashed open. A guard leapt clear to avoid being mown down.

Blake had disabled the airbags. Even braced, the impact threw him and Stone hard against their seatbelts. The Discovery reeled on its suspension, front end caved in. Blake recovered, straightening out. The mansion loomed ahead. He skidded to a halt near the front door.

Stone was already moving. 'Get 'em!' he yelled, scrambling out. He raised his suppressed UMP-9 as the guards responded.

All heads – bar one – in the lounge snapped around at the unexpected noise. The bearded bodyguard on Reeve's right darted to the window. 'Valon! It's—'

Reeve moved.

He had kept his eyes fixed on Jammer's gun. He lunged, swinging leftwards away from the muzzle. Before the other man could react, he grabbed the gun with his right hand. His left hit Jammer's wrist. The pistol was wrenched free.

Reeve's foot swept at Jammer's broken ankle. His heel connected solidly. Jammer fell with a piercing shriek.

Reeve turned the gun and clamped his fingers around the grip. The bodyguard to his left was the most immediate threat. Reeve spun and shot him twice in the chest. Before he even hit the floor, Reeve had continued his turn. Two more shots slammed into the bearded man's back. One went straight through, shattering the window. He toppled over the sill and fell to the driveway below.

Reeve's spin brought him back around to Bato and the last bodyguard. His entire movement had taken under two seconds. The third bodyguard finally broke through his shock, gun rising—

Reeve fired first. Another two bullets found their mark. The man fell backwards on to a glass table. It shattered beneath him.

Bato hurled himself over the back of a large sofa. Reeve tracked him, firing again. The round struck the leather with a flat *whap*. The upholstery burst open – but the bullet didn't penetrate the seat's back. Bato hit the marble floor behind it with a thump.

Reeve was about to go after him when muted gunfire came from outside. The Operatives were here. He had to escape the house before they found him. He ran to Connie and grabbed her wrist. 'Come on!' he said, pulling her with him. 'It's SC9 – we've got to move.'

She was too stunned by the sudden eruption of violence to resist. They ran past Jammer into the hall.

Bato rose, glaring after the departed couple. He moved to

retrieve the nearest fallen gun – then changed direction. Another, boxier sofa was against one wall. He reached down into the gap behind the seat cushions and pulled. It hinged open, revealing storage space beneath.

Several weapons were stashed inside. He grabbed an AM-17: a state-of-the-art upgrade of the venerable Kalashnikov rifle. A laser sight was mounted on its accessory rail. There were several standard magazines inside the sofa. He ignored them, collecting something larger. A 76-round drum magazine clacked into place.

Ignoring his wailing nephew, he ran in pursuit of Reeve and Connie.

Stone saw a guard running towards him. No need for armed police warning procedures any more. He fired a three-round burst into his target's chest. The gunman tumbled to the ground.

More gunshots, unsuppressed, but these came from above. Stone looked up. Flashes in a first-floor room – then a man crashed through a window. His body hit the driveway nearby. 'Reeve must be up there!' called Blake from the Discovery's other side.

'Guess he and Bato fell out. Ha!' Someone in the front garden opened fire. Bullets clanked against the battered Land Rover. Like many MI5 vehicles, it had a degree of bullet-proofing. Both men shot back. Another guard fell. The remaining defenders scrambled for cover. 'Let's get inside and nail the bastard.'

Tyres shrilled. The second Discovery, Flynn at the wheel, screeched through the wrecked gate. Maxwell leaned from a window, sending bursts of fire at the guards. A man screamed. The 4x4 tore past Stone and Blake, following the driveway along the mansion's south side. The plan of action was straightforward. Stone and Blake took the front, Maxwell and Flynn the rear. Locke, not yet combat-ready, would oversee from the van using the drone.

'Two men on the north side,' Locke warned the others through their earpieces. 'Coming to the front. South side is clear.'

Neither Stone nor Blake acknowledged. They simply acted on the new information. Two men ran around the corner. Before they even took in the scene, they were dead. 'Moving in!' shouted Blake, running for the front door. Stone followed.

'The other men from the rear went into the house,' continued Locke. 'Watch out.'

'Nah, I thought we'd just fucking wander in there without looking,' Stone sniped. He reached the door as Blake readied a stun grenade.

He pulled the pin. A brief count, then Blake opened the door and tossed it inside. 'Flash out!' Both men's right ears were shielded by their radio earpieces. They ducked, palms clapped against their left ears—

A dazzling flash and an ear-splitting *bang* inside the house. Blake and Stone moved even before the echoes faded. Blake threw the door fully open. Stone whipped through, gun raised. Two men staggered in the grandiose hall beyond, stunned by the flashbang.

The Operatives made sure they would never recover. Stone gunned one down, Blake rushing in behind him to shoot the other. Nobody else in sight. A broad marble staircase curved upwards. 'Going up,' Blake announced. Stone covering him, they quickly ascended.

Flynn powered along the mansion's side. The drive led to a large detached garage behind it. 'Turning!' she shouted. Maxwell held on as she threw the Discovery into a shrieking 180-degree skid. It stopped in front of the garage entrance. Anyone trying to escape in one of Bato's vehicles would be blocked in.

Blake's warning in their earpieces was followed by the flashbang's detonation. 'Is the back garden clear?' Maxwell asked, sweeping his gun from the 4x4's window.

Locke's reply was immediate. 'Yes. Go now.'

Maxwell jumped out. Flynn followed, leaving the engine running. They would be making a rapid escape; even a few seconds' delay could be critical. He signalled for her to head to patio doors nearby. His own destination was farther away, near a fountain.

Flynn reached the doors. She tried the handle. It didn't move. A single bullet shattered the double-glazed pane. She went inside. A large dining room. She headed for a doorway in the far corner.

Maxwell was still running along the mansion's length when Locke spoke again. 'Tony. One man coming back towards you on the north side.'

The house presented no immediate cover. The low walls circling the fountain were the only protection in reach. Shit! He'd made a mistake. The floodlights were now dazzling him—

Movement in the glare. Someone rounded the house's

corner. Maxwell snapped his weapon towards him – but a gunmetal glint warned he had already been targeted.

He dived. A flat rattle from the Skorpion's suppressor as rounds tore over him. He rolled across the wet grass and flattened himself against the little wall. More bullets cracked off the stonework.

The noise stopped. Maxwell crawled forward a few feet. His bulletproof vest made the movement awkward. He risked a peek over his cover. The glaring floodlights obscured everything. He dropped again – as more rounds hit the wall above.

He was pinned down.

Stone and Blake reached the first floor. Stone got his bearings. 'All that shooting was over there.' He pointed at a hallway leading off the landing.

Blake hustled to it. 'Clear.'

Stone joined him. Another passage led off the hallway towards the house's rear. An open doorway caught his attention, though. 'In there.'

Blake took the lead, Stone giving him cover. They reached the entrance. Blake gestured with one hand. *On three*. A silent countdown – then both rushed through, guns up—

'Well, balls,' said Stone, as he took in the scene. 'Looks like we missed Reeve.'

Two dead men greeted them, blood oozing across the marble floor. Another had made his exit through the broken window. 'This one's still alive,' said Blake. A young man with a cast on his ankle was sprawled over his own crutches.

'Oh, I know him,' Stone said, almost cheerfully. 'Jahmir Haxhi, innit?' Jammer looked up in surprise at the sound of his own name. The pain on his face was replaced by terror when he saw who had spoken. 'It's not your week, mate.' Stone fired a single shot at the injured man's head. Blood and broken bone burst across the polished floor.

Blake gave the carnage only a glance as he checked the adjoining room. Empty. He moved to the open sofa. 'Christ, there's an armoury in here. Think Reeve took anything?'

Stone went back to the door. 'Let's find out.'

Flynn moved deeper into the house, checking each corner. She reached a hall lined with paintings. Battle scenes. Maybe Bato fancied himself as a general. Stairs nearby led upwards. She listened for activity above. Nothing that she could hear. Blake and Stone had gone upstairs; they could deal with that part of the mansion—

A sole squeaked on marble. She turned – as a man ran around a corner. He looked at her in surprise.

Then his gun came up—

Flynn's weapon was already fixed upon him. Fear erupted on his face. His hands opened to drop the gun in surrender. She fired anyway, stone-faced. Three rounds punched into his heart. He flailed backwards and fell.

She kept the gun aimed down the hallway in case he had company. Nobody appeared. She moved on, passing the twitching body . . .

Another noise, more footsteps. Multiple people, running. Above.

Reeve hurried with Connie towards the mansion's rear. She was still in shock, trailing slightly. He looked back as he pulled at her arm. 'Down these stairs, then through the kitchen—'

Bato came around the hallway's far end.

Carrying an assault rifle. It swung at them—

Reeve dived for the staircase, desperately hauling Connie with him. They crashed against its side wall as Bato fired. The AM-17 blazed on full-auto. Bullets ripped through plaster and wood and breezeblock. Flying debris showered over them. Reeve had to drop his gun to grab the banister as he fell downstairs. He caught himself a few steps down, yanking Connie to a stop.

Bato ran after them, teeth bared in a snarl of blood-lust.

CHAPTER 54

Flynn was running back to the stairs when an automatic weapon opened up above. The Albanian's house was turning into a war zone. If armed police hadn't been alerted already, they soon would be. SC9 needed to finish the job and get out—

She reached the staircase – as a man ran from a doorway to her left.

Flynn spun to face him. Too late. His gun was up.

He fired.

The rounds hit just below her sternum. Even with the vest, the impact felt like a sledgehammer. She fell hard on her back. Her UMP was knocked from her hands. She clawed breathlessly for it. But the man was already looming over her. Hesitation, confusion – then his face hardened—

Another gunshot. She flinched. But it wasn't from his weapon. The man crumpled, blood gouting from a ragged neck wound.

Alex Reeve descended the stairs. His face was bloodied and bruised. Behind him was a woman whom she guessed was Connie Jones. Flynn glanced towards her UMP. It was three feet away. She would never reach it before he shot her.

Reeve's own gun was locked upon her head. No vest to protect her. She was dead—

'Alex . . . ' Connie's voice, quiet, scared – pleading. Reeve didn't look at her – but Flynn knew he was listening. Not so much to the single word as what she *hadn't* said. Gun still fixed upon her, he kicked her weapon away – then they ran.

No time to think about his decision. Still straining to breathe, Flynn crawled for her weapon—

She froze at another burst of fire from upstairs.

Much closer than before.

Bato reached the bullet-shredded stairs. He swept around the corner, AM-17 aimed down. Nobody there. *Mut!* He started to follow—

Running feet on marble. Behind him. Not his own people – they were all dead. He whirled. Two armed men charged around the hallway's end. Bato's fury grew. Whoever these bastards were, they weren't the police. Cops would have shouted warnings, demanded surrender. These had come in shooting.

If they wanted bullets, he would *give* them bullets.

Stone and Blake saw the AM-17 swing towards them. Both men dived back into cover as rounds shattered the walls.

'Jesus Christ!' shouted Stone, scrambling clear of the corner. 'Who's he think he is, fucking Scarface?'

The gunfire stopped. Blake brushed splinters from his sleeve and squinted through the plaster dust. 'We'll take him on three. Ready?'

Stone raised his UMP. 'Yeah.'

Another silent countdown – then they darted back out.
Bato was gone.

More bullets cracked off the wall shielding Maxwell. He crawled forward to reach its end. A brief glance. The fountain was now between him and the gunman.

Firing in the house. Heavier weapons, unsuppressed. Bato and his men were fighting back. Time was ticking away, fast. They had to find Reeve and escape before Armed Response arrived. But first, he had to deal with this idiot—

The idiot ran around the fountain to look for him.

Maxwell instantly put three rounds into his chest. The man tumbled to the ground. Stone's assessment of the Albanian gang seemed spot-on. High on machismo, low on ability.

He checked nobody else was coming, then ran for the kitchen entrance.

'Through the kitchen,' Reeve ordered.

Connie recoiled. 'I can smell gas.'

'I know. Hold your breath.' They reached the doorway. Nobody in the steel-and-tile room. 'Come on.' They ran for the door—

Its window shattered.

Reeve saw the running man outside a split-second before he fired. He threw himself sidelong, pulling Connie down with him. The bullet cracked past his head.

They landed hard behind a counter. In cover, protected – but trapped. And Reeve knew who was in the garden. Maxwell. A blink had been enough to recognise his mentor.

Maxwell had let him escape once. But Reeve doubted he would do so again. Not with other Operatives so close. Flynn was probably already coming after him—

Someone else was closer. Bato's AM-17 roared again – from the bottom of the stairs.

Bato pounded down the staircase. Where were Reeve and the woman?

He couldn't see him – but he *did* see a different woman. Black clothes, bulletproof vest – one of the attackers. Another surge of anger.

She saw him just as he targeted her, and dived headlong through a doorway. Wood exploded in her wake. He was about to pursue when a window shattered in the nearby kitchen. Reeve! He ran through the doorway, looking for his prey.

And finding them.

Reeve heard Bato coming. He was sure Maxwell was closing from outside. Even holding his breath, the stench of gas made his nostrils tingle. Three ways he could die in the next few seconds.

The only way out was to use them all against each other . . .

He pulled Connie with him and rushed for the exterior door. Bato charged into the kitchen. His machine gun swung towards them. Reeve shoulder-barged the door open. Maxwell was near the fountain. His gun also found its target.

Reeve dived—

Maxwell fired. The round tore over Reeve's head as he

fell. Behind him, Bato pulled the trigger—

Flames erupted from the AM-17's barrel – and ignited the leaking gas.

Bato recognised the acrid smell a moment too late. He opened his mouth in a cry of fear. The sound never emerged.

An explosive inferno swallowed him. The fireball ripped through the kitchen. Every remaining window blew outwards.

The whole house shook with the detonation. Fire erupted from the doorway and gushed down the hall. A vortex of flame whirled up the back stairs. Stone and Blake, reaching them, hurriedly retreated.

Maxwell saw the flash just in time to hurl himself backwards. The explosion burst out through the door and windows, roiling upwards. He landed hard beside the fountain, cracking his head on the paving.

Even flat on the wet lawn, Reeve felt the heat singe his hair. Connie was beside him. He rolled to shield her as smashed glass and burning wreckage rained down.

The fireball's orange flare faded, replaced by the harshness of the floodlights. A couple had broken, but there was still plenty of illumination.

Enough to see Maxwell on his back, six metres away.

His silenced UMP-9 lay an arm's-length from him. Reeve realised he had lost his own weapon. The garden was strewn with flaming debris. His pistol was somewhere under it. A glance back. The kitchen was a gaping mouth in the mansion's wall, fire swirling between broken teeth. Bato was dead.

Maxwell was still alive, though. He stirred. Reeve forced himself to rise, starting shakily towards the other man.

Maxwell blinked into the floodlights' glare – and saw the

silhouette stumbling towards him. He rolled, searching for his gun. Spotting it. He lunged—

Reeve threw himself at the weapon. The landing was hard – but his hand found it first. He snatched it up. Maxwell clawed for the UMP-9. Reeve twisted around to point it at him. The older man tried to force it away, but lacked leverage. The suppressor swung at his head.

Maxwell finally found grip on the gun and pulled. But to his dismay, he only managed to yank out the magazine. Reeve swatted it from his hand – and pressed the muzzle against Maxwell's forehead.

His former instructor froze. 'You've lost your mag.'

'Still a round in the chamber,' Reeve rasped.

'I know. So why's it staying there?'

Reeve tore out Maxwell's throat mic's connection before replying. He didn't want anyone else in SC9 overhearing. 'Parker's the traitor.'

Despite the gun jammed against his face, Maxwell managed to express surprise. 'Parker? Why do you think that?' The question was more probing than disbelieving. Had Maxwell had suspicions of his own?

'Doesn't matter. But he's working for the Russians. He's going to assassinate Elektra Curtis – tonight.'

Surprise turned to shock, then caution. 'She's his target, yes. But he's working on an accident. Not a hit. And definitely not tonight – too public.'

'That's why he's doing it. He's going to kill her in front of everyone, then expose SC9 to the media. To the world.'

'You got proof?'

'Not yet. But I will. If you let me.'

Maxwell's dark eyes fixed intently upon him. Gears whirled behind them, then: 'That's my car,' he said, glancing towards the Discovery. 'Engine's running.' He looked back at Reeve. 'There's a drone overhead somewhere. So make it look good. Draw blood. Just . . . not too much.'

Despite everything, Reeve couldn't hold back a smile. 'Thanks.'

Maxwell carefully withdrew his hands. Keeping the gun fixed on him, Reeve pulled back—

Then smashed the UMP against his temple.

The blow indeed drew blood. Maxwell's face contorted in pain, and he slumped. Reeve didn't think he had hit him hard enough to knock him out. But he didn't have time to confirm if Maxwell was faking. He had to leave.

They had to leave. Connie had risen. 'Alex? What . . . what's—'

'I'll tell you in the car.' He quickly led her to the Land Rover. As Maxwell had promised, the engine was still running. He tossed the gun inside and took the wheel. She clambered in beside him, still dazed. 'Buckle up. We'll be driving fast.'

Connie fumbled the seatbelt into place. 'What do you—'

Reeve saw movement beyond her. Stone and Blake ran around the mansion. They had found another exit on the north side. Blake hurried to Maxwell—

Stone saw the figures inside the Discovery.

Reeve jammed down the accelerator. The 4x4 leapt away from the garage. 'Duck!'

Stone opened fire on full-auto. Bullets clanked against the Land Rover's flank. The window beside Connie crazed—

But didn't shatter. The bullet-proofing held.

Reeve tore down the drive. Another Discovery, front end mangled, stood near the mansion's front door. He jinked to avoid a body on the driveway and sped through the smashed gate. A hard, skidding turn, going right.

One mission accomplished, but he still had another. And the clock was running out. He pushed the pedal down. 'Are you okay?'

Before she could answer, the Land Rover shot past a parked Transit van. The drone's operator was probably inside. Locke. If it had been Parker, Maxwell would have told him his theory was wrong . . .

'Yeah, yes,' Connie finally replied. She looked at him. 'Alex, you – you came for me.'

'Of course I did.' She reacted with surprise. 'Everything that's happened to you is my fault. This too, I'm sorry. Bato said he'd kill you if I didn't turn up. I wasn't going to let that happen.'

She shivered. 'What happened to Bato?'

'He blew himself up.'

A sharp laugh, a release of fear and tension. 'And those . . . other people? Were they SC9?'

He nodded. 'That was Tony Maxwell in the garden. He let us go.'

'Why?'

'Because I think he wants to find the traitor as much as I do. Just for different reasons.'

'What reasons?'

'I don't know.'

'Do you trust him?'

A brief glance at her. 'The only person in the world I trust right now is you.'

Surprise flashed on her face again. 'Alex, I . . . I'm sorry.'

'For what?'

'For what I said to you. About your father. You're . . . not like him. Someone like him wouldn't have rescued me. You did.'

'Thanks,' he said, with gratitude. The end of The Bishops Avenue was not far ahead. He slowed. 'Okay, left or right from here?'

'Where are we going?'

He noted the pronoun, but there wasn't time to argue about it. 'King's College. The Strand.'

'From here? Left. I know King's – I had friends who went to uni there.' He swept the Discovery through the turn, tyres squalling. The movement tipped her sideways. 'Whoa! Jesus.'

'Sorry.'

She managed a faint smile. 'It'll take at least half an hour to get there.'

It was Reeve's turn to smile. The expression did not reassure her. 'I think I can beat that.'

CHAPTER 55

'*Fuck!*' Stone roared as the Discovery disappeared. 'Missed him.'

Blake helped Maxwell stand. 'We need to get after him.'

Maxwell shook his head, wincing at the stab of pain from his temple. 'No. We get out – the police will be here any minute.' He checked his watch. Barely three minutes had passed since SC9 crashed through the gate. 'Deirdre, you hear me?'

'Your mic's disconnected,' Blake told him, noticing the loose wire. 'I'll tell her.'

'Good. Let's move.'

'He stole your fucking car,' Stone told him angrily. 'He could be going anywhere.'

They ran around the mansion. 'It's an MI5 pool vehicle. It's got a tracker,' Maxwell reminded him. 'We can follow him. But right now we need to go. Before any of your old mates turn up.'

By the time they reached the second Discovery, Flynn had emerged from the house. She hurried to meet them. 'Nobody still alive inside, far as I can tell.'

Maxwell saw her damaged vest. 'You're hit.'

'I'm okay. The guy who shot me's dead.' She hesitated, then: 'Reeve killed him.'

413

'What?' snapped Blake as he took the wheel. 'And he didn't kill you?'

'No.'

'Not to look a gift horse in the mouth, but: why not?'

Stone laughed as he climbed into the passenger seat. 'Fucking fancies her, doesn't he?'

Flynn scowled at him. 'Wouldn't touch him any more than I'd touch you.'

Maxwell got into the back beside her. 'That's enough. John, go.'

Blake brought the battered Discovery around. 'The car'll attract attention in this condition.'

'Dump it near the closest Tube station. I'll get MI5 to recover it.'

Blake drove through the gate. A siren rose in the distance. 'We picked the right time to leave.'

'Drop me at the van,' Maxwell ordered. 'I'll see you back at the safehouse.'

Blake halted beside the Transit. Maxwell hopped out, and the Discovery headed off. He climbed into the van's cab. Locke was already in the passenger seat, arm in its sling. 'I'm glad you remembered me,' he said spikily. 'It was hard enough operating the drone with one hand. A manual is, quite literally, out of my grasp right now.'

'Did you bring the drone back?' Maxwell asked, starting the engine.

'There wasn't time. I triggered the self-destruct. It's a good thing the house was already on fire. I imagine fifty grams of thermite would burn straight through the roof.'

Maxwell pulled away. The gunfire and explosion had

drawn onlookers from neighbouring homes. He would have to ditch the van in case its number had been noted. But there was something he needed to do first. 'I'll drop you at Highgate station. I'll get rid of the van, then meet you at the house.'

'Understood.' A pregnant pause; Maxwell could tell he was eyeing him. 'I saw the explosion from the drone,' Locke eventually said.

'I saw it from a lot closer.'

'Amusing.' No humour in his voice. 'I also saw Reeve get the drop on you in the aftermath. Your microphone was cut off.' The cold eyes turned fully towards him. 'What did he say to you?'

'Nothing of importance,' Maxwell replied.

'It's hard to judge that without hearing for myself.'

'I *am* the judge.' He took his eyes off the road long enough to give Locke a stony stare. 'I'm in charge here.'

'Of course.' The faintest hint of insolence.

Maxwell didn't care. 'If you must know, he was pleading his innocence again. Claiming he was framed, trying to pass the buck on to someone else.'

'Who?'

'Maybe it was you.' Locke drew in a sharp breath, sounding almost offended. Maxwell let him stew for a moment. 'It wasn't.'

'Then who did he accuse?'

'Does it matter? You're convinced he's guilty.'

'Are you?'

Maxwell ignored the question, driving on.

*

'Oi, oi,' whispered a photographer. 'Here's that fucking bitch.'

Cameras came up to track Elektra Curtis as she entered. Parker joined in so as not to stand out. He couldn't deny she had a physical charisma most politicians lacked. Tall, confident, long dark hair drawn back in a loose ponytail. Eyes flashing with idealism and energy. She hadn't yet been ground down by the system. It was almost a pity she never would.

Almost.

She strode past, giving even the men there to vilify her a bright, genuine smile. Such shots would not be used, of course. The picture editors wanted sneers, scowls, jabbing fingers. The more unscrupulous would fire up Photoshop to make her seem even more threatening. Curtis, as her first name suggested, had Greek ancestry. Certain newspapers routinely darkened her naturally olive-tinted skin still further. Anything to otherise her: *she is one of Them. Not one of Us.*

The newspapers. He held back a scowl of his own. They were all part of the same rotten system. He remembered the picture they had used of his father. Always the same one. Eyes wide in anger, a snarl forming on his mouth. One moment, frozen in time for ever. And now it always represented him. An animal about to bite, a monster. One of Them. Not one of Us.

But now one of Them was about to burn the whole country down. His revenge had finally come.

Curtis was welcomed by men and women near the Great Hall. Some of the photographers kept shooting, hoping for the perfect unflattering image. Parker instead lowered his camera and took out his phone. The screen lit up as its facial recognition system identified him. He selected a mail app.

Two emails were queued, ready to be sent on command – or at a specific time.

He selected the first. It had a large attachment, close to the email's limit. If he could have, he would have made it much larger. But it contained enough. More than enough.

Send.

A progress bar began its crawl as the mail was sent to multiple addresses. Some recipients were in the UK; more elsewhere around the world. All were major media outlets.

The other email, from a different account, would have to wait. He couldn't risk setting the timer until all his targets were here. Once they were, though . . .

Britain would catch fire.

CHAPTER 56

'Go right,' said Connie, pointing. 'Once you're around the corner, the uni's on our left.'

'You're better than a satnav,' Reeve told her. She had identified several shortcuts, shaving precious minutes from their journey.

'I've lived in London all my life. Plus, my uncle was a cabbie. I think some of the Knowledge rubbed off.'

He brought the Discovery around the Australian High Commission on to the Strand. Somewhere behind, he heard police sirens. Another thing shaving minutes from the trip had been his driving. Their speed had rarely dropped below fifty, the oncoming lanes used to overtake traffic. 'Just in time. We need to get out.'

He flashed past the brutalist Strand Building, then braked hard. The Land Rover skidded on to the pavement near the entrance to Somerset House. They both jumped out. 'You don't have to come with me,' he told Connie as they ran.

'Alex, you saved my life,' she replied. 'I want to help you stop this guy.' He had summarised his theory about Parker during the journey.

Reeve had objections, but there were bigger issues. 'Shit.' Somerset House had three arched gateways, two for pedestrians and one for vehicles. All had security in place. He stopped. 'They'll never let me through – not looking like this.' He was covered in blood and dirt and soot. 'I need another way in.'

He looked up at the neighbouring buildings. One a hundred metres away had scaffolding covering its front. If he scaled it, he could run around the roof—

Connie had a better idea. 'Back here, quick.' She pulled him by the arm past the abandoned Discovery.

'Slow down, don't draw attention,' Reeve cautioned. A police car rounded the embassy. It flashed past and made a skidding stop to block the Discovery's possible escape. 'Where are we going?'

'The Strand Building,' she said. 'You can get into the King's Building through there.'

They reached the entrance. Reeve looked through the glass doors. A reception-slash-security desk inside, two uniformed men at it. Past them, a corridor led deeper into the building. 'Which way?'

'Straight down there.' She indicated the corridor.

It was close to a flight of stairs. 'Can you get to it from the floors above as well?'

'I think so.'

A plan came to him. 'Okay, you distract the guards.'

'How?'

'You're an attractive woman in distress. They'll come and help you. Just think of a reason.' He pushed through the revolving door.

'Alex, wait—' But he was already inside. Distress rising for real, she followed him.

Reeve hurried across the lobby, adopting a stagger. He put a hand over his mouth. 'Oh, God!' he wailed. 'I'm going to be sick, gonna be sick!'

'Help us, please!' Connie cried. 'Someone's been run over! A car came up on to the pavement!'

The men glanced at the security monitors. One showed the Discovery on the kerb down the street. 'Oh, Jesus!' a guard gasped. 'Call an ambulance, and get the first aid kit.' He hurried out from behind the desk. 'Are you okay?'

She followed Reeve's lead and put a hand to her head. 'I don't know. I – just help, please!'

By now Reeve had reached the staircase. The second guard was caught between stopping him and following instructions. He did the latter, going to a telephone. Reeve glanced down the corridor. A couple of men in hi-vis gilets were visible some way down it. Instead he hurried up the stairs.

As he'd hoped, the first floor's layout was broadly the same as that below. Another hallway led into the King's Building. He ran down it.

Parker mimicked his companions and raised his camera as the Iranian ambassador entered. He was accompanied by his wife and a couple of besuited assistants. They marched down the red carpet, ignoring the press to greet other diplomats and officials.

The head of the Institute awaited them at the Great Hall. But all eyes were on the woman beside him: Elektra Curtis. She had a brief whispered exchange with her host. He nodded, a little reluctantly. She smiled, thanking him, then faced those approaching.

The ambassador reached the group outside the Great Hall. The Institute's head spoke to him, indicating Curtis. The ambassador nodded. He stood beside the Member of Parliament.

Parker took more pictures as the photographers shifted position. Was she going to give a speech? Even better than he'd hoped. There were a couple of television crews present. The kill would be captured live. And the recipients of his first email would realise it was no fake.

The message rolled through his mind. *Attention. A major media event will soon occur. Attached are numerous top-secret files from a clandestine British intelligence agency. They are encrypted; the password will be released imminently. These files detail numerous assassinations carried out by the British government. It is time to expose these illegal acts to the world. The one I am about to carry out must be the last. You will know I am genuine in the next few minutes.* Not great prose – but it would make the point with chilling clarity.

Other intelligence agencies would have intercepted the emails. Keyword warnings would already be flashing at GCHQ. But the accounts he had used were anonymised, impossible to link to him. By the time anyone made the connection, it would be too late.

The Institute's head finished a brief address to the on-lookers, then moved back. Curtis took his place. She smiled to the cameras, then faced the Iranian. 'Mr Ambassador, it is a great honour and pleasure to meet you.'

'Fucking traitor,' muttered a photographer. Parker ignored him, raising his phone again. He set the email app's scheduler to send his second message. Six minutes should be enough. The countdown began. He returned the phone to his pocket, then looked back at Curtis.

'It's regrettable,' she continued, 'that I can't speak here on behalf of my government. I may be an MP, but I am also in Opposition. I have no say in government policy.'

'Thank fuck,' growled another journalist. Some of the non-press attendees glared in his direction.

Curtis heard him too. A sharp glance, then she went on. 'However, I hope that will change. The tides of public opinion are turning. People are sick of the current status quo. Politics has become about creating division, stoking hatred. With the collaboration of certain elements of our *free*,' biting sarcasm, 'press.' Hostile rumblings from the media scrum.

She brushed it off and continued. 'Those currently in power have a vested interest in declaring other nations our enemy. Fear of entire peoples gives them a way to keep us scared. To control us. But now is the time for the people to take back control. And the first step must be to end the policies of knee-jerk, unthinking hostility. We must stop looking for excuses to go to war. We must embrace what we have in common, not exaggerate what keeps us apart.'

She turned back to the ambassador. 'I'm not saying this will be easy. There are major issues, like political prisoners, to overcome. And as any Middle Eastern history student knows, Iran has little reason to trust Britain. If we hadn't overthrown Mohammad Mosaddegh, the Middle East would be very different today.' Quiet, faintly awkward laughter from some guests. 'But every journey starts with a first step. Mr Ambassador, not every British politician considers your nation a threat. This one hopes that, in time, we can become friends. If you will, let's take that first step together.'

She held out her hand to him. He regarded it almost with surprise. But then his own hand came up to meet hers.

Parker had already lowered his camera. His right hand went into his coat as he pushed towards the front. Fingers closed around the gun.

It was time to kill Elektra Curtis.

Reeve ran through the first floor of the King's Building. Bookcases and murals of important dates in the college's history flicked past. The Great Hall, he remembered from his online research, was just ahead, one floor below. Two staircases led down to a large lobby. Either would make a good vantage point for Parker to carry out the hit.

But there was an obstacle to deal with first. A security guard at the top of the stairs. He turned at the sound of running footsteps—

Reeve slammed into him, knocking him down. The nearest stairs were right beside him. A few people stood on them, one looking up at the unexpected noise. None were Parker. Reeve ran down, pushing past the onlookers.

The lobby opened out below. He looked across to the other staircase. Still no sign of Parker. A red carpet divided the room along its centre. The people on its far side were smartly dressed, watching with respectful interest. Those nearer to him were more mixed. A lot of younger people – students. But there was also a scruffy, older scrum at the front. The press. Cameras and microphones pointed like guns towards the red carpet's end.

There was Elektra Curtis, sharp and professional in black dress and heels. She held out her hand to a dignified-looking man in a dark suit. The Iranian ambassador. His own hand came up. Cameras clicked and flashed in anticipation.

This was the moment Parker was waiting for. He would strike now for maximum impact.

But where was he?

The press pack. It was the only place an unknown face could blend in. Reeve looked down at the crush. Everybody was jostling for position.

But someone was pushing through with extra force.

Parker.

Reeve recognised him instantly, even from behind. His build, his hair, his movements all gave him away. His left hand was outstretched to cut through the crowd like a plough.

His right was inside his coat.

No time to run down the stairs. Reeve vaulted on to the stone balustrade.

Parker pushed out into the open. A security guard stepped forward to intervene – then froze as Parker drew his gun. He swung it towards Curtis. The ambassador reacted in shock. Curtis's head turned towards the assassin—

Reeve hurled himself over the crowd.

His outstretched hands caught Parker's back. He clenched his fingers tight, tugging at his coat as he fell. Parker lurched backwards. The gun went off, the echo piercing. The round cracked loudly off stonework above.

Reeve hit the floor hard. Pain exploded in his knees. He lost his hold on Parker. The Operative almost fell, catching himself on his gun hand. The weapon was jolted from his grip.

Reeve raised his head. Curtis was looking directly at him, stunned. '*Run!*' he yelled. The gun was just a metre away. He scrambled towards it—

Parker swung his camera. Metal and glass and plastic smashed against Reeve's head. He cried out, dizzied. Chaos erupted around him as people overcame their stunned paralysis. Screams and yells filled the chamber. But to his horror, Curtis wasn't running. She was pushing the ambassador into motion.

The Operative snatched up the gun. He located Curtis. The pistol rose.

The ambassador finally started to run, Curtis going with him. One of his aides rushed forward—

Another gunshot. The round hit the younger Iranian's chest. Blood exploded over his white shirt. He fell. Parker searched for his target again.

Too late. Curtis and the ambassador passed behind a thick pillar. Parker started to pursue – but Reeve grabbed his leg.

Parker hadn't seen his attacker. All he knew was that someone had tackled him. He kicked the person gripping his leg and pulled free. Fleeing people now obscured his targets. He swore, then glanced back as the press pack broke and ran. Even as self-preservation instincts kicked in, a few photographers took pictures as they retreated. The television cameras weren't following suit, though. Shit! Without a live feed, he couldn't reveal the encrypted files' password to the media. He had meant to do so immediately after assassinating Curtis, before anyone overcame their shock.

It didn't matter. His backup plan was still in effect.

The rest of his plan needed to adapt. Armed police would be on the way. He had tried to assassinate an MP within a mile of Parliament. Even though he had failed, they would be out for blood. He had to escape before he was killed.

Luckily, he had a route.

The lobby joined with corridors running the length of the King's Building. He ran down the one leading south. Curtis had gone north. He would have pursued, but time was now critical. He had to reach his egress point before the police arrived. If he was spotted, his chances of escaping were almost zero.

Fleeing people filled the hallway. He fired a shot at the ceiling. 'Move!' More screams, and they flattened themselves against the walls. He charged past. Another exit to the courtyard was ahead. But he wasn't going outside – not yet. Instead he reached a staircase and raced upwards.

CHAPTER 57

Reeve painfully stood. The lobby was now largely clear. Stragglers still crowded the exits, desperate to escape.

The Iranian aide lay dead before him. Reeve looked towards the hallways. Curtis and the ambassador had fled north. Parker had run the other way. Why hadn't he followed to finish the job?

Because he had failed – and was now trying to escape. If he had assassinated Curtis, he would have voluntarily surrendered. All for a moment before the cameras to expose SC9. But the cameras were gone. His message would never be heard. So he was running.

Reeve ran after him. Frightened people hunched against the walls. 'Where did he go?' he shouted.

'He went upstairs!' someone replied. The stairs were not far ahead. Reeve halted to check, wary of an ambush. But Parker was not in sight. He ascended, two steps at a time.

A shadow swept across a wall above. Parker. He was almost at the top floor. Reeve kept climbing—

The faint echo of Parker's footsteps abruptly stopped. Reeve looked up – and saw the Operative leaning over the railing, gun in hand. He threw himself against the wall as a bullet chiselled a chunk from the polished concrete. Parker swore, then a door banged above.

Reeve ran again. The fifth floor was the top. He paused at a fire door, taking cover against the wall before shoving it open. No gunfire. He rushed through. Parker was not in sight. Where had he gone?

A crash of glass. Reeve whirled to find the source. Another door. He kicked it open. An office, tall windows overlooking the courtyard. All were intact. He turned. Another window on the side wall. It was broken. He darted to it and cautiously looked out.

The window overlooked a rooftop. The Thames was visible beyond, the lights of the South Bank shimmering through the rain. A dark figure clumsily navigated the sloping tiles. Reeve leaned out for a better look. Where was Parker going? He couldn't jump down from this height—

He saw the other man's plan. An extension linked King's House to the neighbouring, palatial Somerset House. From there, Parker could reach the rooftops along the Strand. The scaffolding would let him reach street level and disappear into the crowds.

Reeve climbed out after him. Parker reached the corner, vaulting on to the next roof – then looked back. He saw his pursuer. Reeve ducked, but the expected shot didn't come. Parker's footing wasn't secure enough for him to aim accurately. Instead he ran along the roof's crown.

Reeve scurried in pursuit. The tiles were wet, his soles barely finding grip. Parker was twenty metres ahead. He leapt across to the extension's roof. Numerous chimney stacks rose beyond where it met Somerset House. The

Operative veered away from them, wanting an unobstructed run.

However, Reeve angled towards them. He had seen something Parker hadn't. The rooftop between the two ranks of tall stacks was flat. He could move much faster along it – and catch up. He hurdled an air-conditioning duct and landed on the level surface.

Reeve kept running. Chimneys flicked past. He vaulted another section of ducting. Ahead, a structure blocked his path. A large dome, green copper shimmering wetly in the floodlights below. He would have to go back on to the sloping roof to get around it—

Parker had realised the danger and stopped. His head turned, searching the shadows.

Spotting movement—

The gun barked. A bullet smacked into brickwork just behind Reeve. He slithered to a halt against a chimney. Another shot whipped ahead of him. If he had kept running, he would have been hit.

Scrabbling sounds over the slates. Parker was coming. He couldn't run without exposing himself to fire. Which side would the Operative come from: left or right?

He readied himself—

Left arm extended for balance, Parker advanced. Reeve was behind the chimney stack ahead. The lights of London, reflecting from the low clouds, provided plenty of illumination. Whichever way Reeve tried to break, he would be visible.

But would he come from the left side, or the right? Forwards or backwards? Forwards. Reeve wasn't the kind of man to retreat. How he had found him, Parker had no idea. But it didn't matter. In a few seconds, he would be dead.

Gun raised, he rounded the chimney—

Reeve wasn't there.

Impossible—

Left or right? Reeve rejected both choices, remembering Simiane-la-Rotonde. He picked a third: up. He scaled the chimney stack. The low clunk of footsteps on slate came closer. Reeve glimpsed Parker approaching the obstacle, rounding it—

He launched himself at the other man.

Bodies collided. Prepared for the impact, Reeve came off better. His elbow smashed against Parker's temple. The Operative fell backwards with a cry. Reeve landed on top of him. A clatter of metal from the shadows as he dropped his gun.

Reeve pushed himself up, balling his right fist for a punch—

Parker's own fist swung – and hit his bullet wound.

It was Reeve's turn to yell in pain. His arm gave way. Parker pushed and rolled out from under him. His foot lashed at Reeve's groin. Reeve twisted just in time. The blow landed hard on his hip.

Parker forced himself upright. He turned to find the gun. No sign of it. He darted to the next pair of chimney stacks. It was not behind them either. An angry glance back at Reeve, then he ran.

Reeve rolled over – and saw the gun underneath some air-con ductwork. He snatched it out and leapt up.

Parker neared the base of the dome. A copper-sheathed section of roof angled upwards ahead. Reeve ran in pursuit. London spread out before him. The other man was almost at the metal roof. An access ladder led to a balcony below it. But the Operative was going up and over, following the most direct route—

'Stop!' Reeve yelled – as he fired.

The bullet struck the copper sheeting ahead of Parker. Reeve's aim was off; he'd meant to clip his arm.

But it had the desired effect. Parker stopped sharply. Caught on the slope, he was completely exposed. The dome's base was a featureless, curving wall providing no cover. He raised his hands and slowly faced his pursuer.

Reeve advanced, the gun fixed upon him. He crossed the catwalk leading to the access ladder and started up the copper slope. Parker remained still, but Reeve knew he had not surrendered.

They measured each other up. Reeve broke the tense silence. 'Why did you frame me?'

Parker cracked a thin smile. 'It wasn't personal. We had similar backgrounds, similar attitudes. So when I hacked SC9's files and pinned my actions on to you, they fitted.'

An open confession. Both men knew how the situation would end: with one of them dead. 'There's one big difference between us,' said Reeve. 'I'm not a Russian spy.'

'You figured it out? I'm genuinely impressed.' The compliment still sounded mocking. 'The rest of SC9 didn't. But then, they'd put all their effort into chasing the wrong guy.'

'Why did you turn traitor?'

'The same reasons you would have, if you'd opened your

eyes.' All humour was abruptly gone, his Liverpudlian accent returning at full force. 'Britain's a fucking disgrace! If you're not born into the right class, then that's it – you're fucked, you're scum. You're just there to be exploited by posh bastards. Your life means *nothing* to them if they can make more money.' There was genuine anger in his voice, a passion Reeve had never heard from him. 'My mum died on a trolley in a hospital corridor. There weren't enough beds or enough doctors. Why? Because of cuts so some rich *cunts* could pay less tax!'

'And you wanted revenge by assassinating a politician who's *opposed* to all that?'

'I was *ordered* to kill her, Alex. She's a threat to the establishment. They want her dead. I was going to do their dirty work – and then *expose* them for it. I'm going to show the world how corrupt this country is.' Even with the gun on him, Parker couldn't help gesticulating in anger. 'The more I learned about it, the worse it got. We're as bad as any fucking banana republic. No, we're worse: we just have better PR! Cool Britannia, didn't we put on a good Olympics show? But it's all just a front! We're arms dealers, warmongers, fucking robber barons. The British Empire never ended, it just went corporate. And all the money they steal goes to the same people – at the top!'

'And Russia's any better?' Reeve shot back.

'I don't give a *fuck* about Russia. Yeah, they recruited me, helped me become a prime candidate to join SC9. As they said, "You want to bring down the British establishment? The walls are too thick to break from outside – we've tried. But if you plant a bomb *inside* . . ."' He mimed an explosion.

'They gave me the hacking tools. But I would have taken the same from fucking *Botswana* if they'd offered. This *is* about revenge, Alex. I want those posh bastards to pay for what happened to my mum and dad!'

'And what *did* happen to them? Your mum died in hospital – what about your dad?' Reeve felt a growing unease. Parker had been desperate to escape. Why was he now willing to stand there venting long-concealed rage?

'My dad died in prison. He beat the shit out of our landlord. The bastard evicted us so he could turn our home into flats. Dad was trying to protect his family and keep a roof over our heads! But the establishment couldn't let that stand, could they? So all these posh bastards in wigs and gowns spouting fucking Latin stitched him up. The newspapers joined in too. Some photographer got a picture of Dad telling him to fuck off. So that was on the front pages. Look at this working-class thug – he's angry! He's a killer!'

'Your dad killed this guy?'

'It was an accident! He hit his head when he fell – he didn't die until days later. But no, that got turned into fucking *murder*.' Parker's fists clenched in fury. 'They found him guilty, he was sent down for life. Six months in, he was stabbed in a fight. He died, and they didn't even fucking *tell* me! I got pulled out of class on the Monday. "Bad news, sorry, your father died in prison at the weekend." That was all they fucking said. I was left with nobody. *Nobody*.'

'So you wanted revenge on the system.'

An unnerving smile. 'Yeah. I didn't realise it at first. I joined the army because I was angry. I wanted to *kill* people. But even there, it was always posh bastards telling me what to do. Fucking Ruperts everywhere. You know the type.' Reeve did; a 'Rupert' was squaddie slang for a public school-educated officer. 'I don't know how the Russians found me, but they did. A guy called Morozov gave me some . . . career advice. I took it. Pushed myself hard, got into the SAS. Did the right things, and eventually got the tap. I'd made myself look perfect for SC9. And now . . .' The smile widened, wolf-like. 'Everything's paid off.'

Reeve's disquiet increased. Parker now sounded almost victorious. Maintaining his distance, Reeve angled up the slope to stand level with him. 'It hasn't, though. I stopped you.'

Parker laughed. 'You stopped me from killing Elektra Curtis – but I still won. Or I will do, in . . .' He turned his left wrist to view his watch. 'Just over two minutes.'

Reeve took a step closer. 'What do you mean?'

'I stole a load of files from SC9's servers when I hacked them. The *real* hack, not the one I botched to set you up. I was in their system *months* ago. Found all the juicy details of SC9's greatest hits, at home and abroad. Some famous names in there! I sent them out in a password-protected file.'

'To who?'

'To *everyone*. The papers, TV, internet news. All over the world. So the government can't just slap a DSMA-Notice on the media to suppress it. I was going to announce the password to the cameras after assassinating Curtis. You messed that up. But it doesn't matter. If anything went wrong, another email with the password gets sent automatically on a timer.' He lowered his hands, palms upturned, challenging.

'I'm not going to stop it. And you sure as fuck won't be able to make me.'

Reeve frowned. 'You think?'

A disdainful snort. 'SAS versus SRR? Proper soldier versus glorified boy scout? Who's going to win?'

'SC9,' Reeve countered. 'Because that's who we both are. Who we both *were*.' He realised he had one chance to stop Parker's plan. Another step closer. 'Take out your phone.'

'Why?' But he knew Parker already suspected the reason. 'Just do it, or I *will* shoot you.'

Parker reluctantly produced his phone. 'Unlock it,' Reeve ordered. Parker looked down, tapping slowly at it with his thumb. The first two digits were zero and two. 'Use the facial recognition.'

'I haven't set it up.'

'Then why are you keeping it away from your face? Look at the fucking screen!'

Parker hesitated – then whipped his arm back, about to throw the phone—

Reeve shot him.

Parker lurched back against the dome's base. But his arm had already started its forward movement. The phone flew from his hand.

Reeve lunged for it – but missed. It spun past him. He whirled, seeing it arc towards the roof's edge—

Parker's throw fell short. It hit the copper sheeting just short of the brink . . .

And skittered over it.

CHAPTER 58

An involuntary cry of 'No!' burst from Reeve's mouth. He ran to the edge. A *clack* from below. A balcony ran across the building five metres beneath him. A small rectangle of light shone from the wet shadows. The phone had survived.

How well, he didn't know. But he had to find out. Parker's timer was still ticking down.

A glance back. Parker had collapsed against the wall, clutching his bloodied abdomen. Reeve scurried down the slope to the ladder. It led to the top of the building's façade. From there, more steps descended to the balcony proper.

He took them. The phone had gone dark. Where was it? Everything was wet, reflective . . .

There. A faint sheen on a curved corner. He hurried over and retrieved the phone. The screen lit up as he raised it. Several cracks lanced crookedly down it. The glass was damaged; what about the sensors beneath?

No warnings that the cameras were broken or obscured. The facial recognition might still work. He just needed the right face. Reeve turned and ran back up the stairs—

Parker hurled himself down them.

The two men collided again. This time Parker came off

better despite his wound. The impact hurled Reeve backwards. He landed hard on top of the balustrade . . .

And rolled over it.

Gun and phone clattered to the balcony's floor as he clutched desperately at the stone. Primal terror as he fell – then his left hand caught the stonework's edge.

He jerked to a stop. His shoulder crackled, agonising spikes driving through bone. The bullet wound seared as if oozing with lava. Torn muscle strained, stitches snapping . . .

He swung his right hand up – and clapped it against the balustrade.

Reeve dragged himself higher. His toes scraped the wall below, searching for purchase. Finding none. His entire weight was being taken on his hands. Mostly his right; his left arm was weakening, quivering in agony. He swung a leg higher. If he found a foothold, he could lever himself back on to the balcony. The muscles in his right arm started to burn—

His sole pressed against solid stone.

He forced himself upwards, reaching across the balustrade's top—

Parker rose beyond it.

One of the Operative's hands still clutched his bleeding wound. The other held the gun. Both men's eyes locked.

A sadistic smile – then Parker pounded the gun down on Reeve's hand.

Bone cracked. Reeve yelled. Raw instinct jerked his hand back. His mind and training regained control – but too late. The movement had unbalanced him. His foot slipped – and he fell.

Another jolt of pure fear—

His left hand still had grip. It caught him again. The survival urge overcame pain and fatigue and injury. His fingers closed vice-tight on the balustrade's edge.

But he was now dangling twenty metres above the ground. His reserves of strength would only last for moments.

And Parker would not even let them hold out that long.

Reeve could see the other man through the balustrade's carved pillars. He sidestepped to stand in front of him. Reeve tensed, waiting for the gun to smash his fingers—

Movement. Beyond Parker, back the way he had come. Someone was on the rooftop.

Connie.

A new fear filled Reeve. The moment Parker killed him, he would turn on her. It didn't matter who she was. She was a witness – a complication.

And Operatives were trained to eliminate complications.

'Connie!' he yelled. '*Run!*'

Parker hesitated, surprised. Then he let out a brief laugh. 'The "look behind you" trick, Alex? I expected bet—'

'Alex!'

Reeve's heart plunged. Connie hadn't heard him, or hadn't understood—

Parker reacted automatically to the unexpected threat. He spun, seeing the figure on the rooftop – and fired.

Connie fell. She slithered limply down the tiles and disappeared behind the balustrade.

Parker turned back to finish Reeve—

His target was waiting for him.

Reeve's pain was overpowered by fury. He pulled upwards with all his left arm's remaining strength – and lunged with his right. His hand clamped around the collar of Parker's coat. He yanked downwards. Parker lurched forward. His wounded midsection hit the balustrade. An agonised cry – then Reeve pounded his forehead against the stonework.

Parker reeled. Reeve didn't release him, smacking his head down again, and again. Blood splattered the balustrade. The gun dropped from his hand. One last impact, then Reeve used the other man to haul himself up. His weight almost pulled Parker over. The stomach wound ground against the edge, making him howl. Reeve didn't care. One knee reached the stone surface. He levered himself on to it, then rolled over, releasing Parker.

The other man gasped in fear as his legs slipped over the parapet. He clutched frantically at its inner edge. One hand caught it. He slewed around.

Reeve dropped to the floor. He snatched up the phone and painfully stood.

Parker's free hand clawed for grip, found it—

'Craig.'

The Operative instinctively looked up – and saw the phone right before his face.

It recognised his features. Blood and bruises meant nothing, only the shapes beneath them. The phone unlocked. Parker's eyes went wide in realisation—

Reeve punched him, hard.

Parker lost his hold. His weight snapped him backwards, over the edge. He fell with a scream – that ended abruptly on hard stone several floors below.

Panting, Reeve pulled back. Connie's slumped form was partly visible beyond the access ladder. He had to help her—

The phone glowed in his hand. If it went back into rest mode, he would never be able to unlock it. Even in death, Parker would win.

He summoned the list of recently-used apps. One was an email program. He opened it. It resumed where Parker had left off. Two items. The first was marked *Sent*. The other was scheduled to be sent at 21:07.

The clock at the screen's top read 21:06.

He had under a minute. Maybe just seconds. How to cancel it? A three-dot icon next to the waiting mail. He touched it. A new screen appeared. The scheduler itself. Where was cancel—

There. He thumbed the button. Relief . . .

Was premature. A pop-up. *Are you sure?* 'Yes!' he roared, hitting it—

The pop-up vanished. A moment later, the clock ticked over to 21:07 . . .

Nothing happened.

The email remained queued. No progress bar appeared, no list of recipients ticking off one by one. Reeve gasped, relief *now* flooding him. He had done it . . .

'Connie!' Victory already forgotten, he staggered to her. He pocketed the phone and crouched. Blood glistened on her clothing. 'Connie, can you hear me?'

Silence for a long moment . . . then she moved. 'Alex?'

'I'm here. Where are you hit?'

Teeth clenched, she looked up at him. 'My arm . . .' She tried to move; he helped her sit up. Her upper left sleeve was torn. She regarded the wound – then released a pained laugh. 'Oh, that's ironic. I got shot in the same place as you.'

'At least nobody hit you with a car,' he replied. 'Let me check—'

Footsteps nearby. He turned in alarm, looking back along the rooftop.

Maxwell advanced on them, gun in hand.

CHAPTER 59

'Stay there, Alex,' Maxwell snapped. He aimed his weapon at Reeve. 'Raise your hands, slowly.'

Reeve obeyed, palms open. 'I'm unarmed.'

'You were trained by SC9. There's no such thing.' He stopped a few metres away. 'Move away from her.'

'She's hurt,' Reeve protested.

'I'll see to her.' The statement was chillingly ambiguous. 'Don't make me shoot you.' Reeve reluctantly stepped back.

Despite her fear, Connie spoke. 'Isn't shooting him what you're here to do?'

Maxwell gave her an almost amused look. Then: 'Where's Craig?'

'Down there,' Reeve replied, glancing towards the plaza below.

'Dead?'

'Hopefully.'

'Saves me the trouble. You were right. He was the mole.' A wry smile. 'His trying to assassinate an MP on live television was a bit of a giveaway.'

'He told me the Russians backed him,' said Reeve.

'Did he say why he did it?'

'Revenge against the establishment for his parents. He

wanted to burn everything down.'

Maxwell nodded. 'Releasing SC9's records to the media would have done that, yes.'

'You know about that?'

'The boss phoned just before I got here. So many alerts went off at GCHQ I'm surprised you didn't hear them from here. Craig's email went to over a hundred media outlets worldwide. But not the password to unlock the files. Thanks to you.'

'Do I get a medal?' was the mocking response.

'What happens now?' Connie asked quietly. 'Are you going to kill us?'

Maxwell pursed his lips. 'My orders concerning you still stand, Alex. And I'm going to carry them out.' Reeve and Connie exchanged glances; hers fearful, his defiant. But he knew he couldn't escape Maxwell in his battered, exhausted state—

The older man continued. 'Starting in . . . three minutes.' He gestured at the rooftop beyond the dome. 'I think there's a way to climb down to the Strand. I suggest you take it.'

Reeve stared at him in surprise. 'You're letting me go?'

'As you said all along, you weren't the traitor. That won't change your Fox Red status, unfortunately. After what you did in France, you can't come back to us. But as far as I'm concerned? You've done SC9 – the whole country – a great favour.'

'I didn't do this to protect SC9,' Reeve replied. 'I did it to save an innocent woman *from* SC9. You know, maybe Parker was right. A country that allows something like SC9 to exist really *is* corrupt. Maybe it *should* be exposed.'

Maxwell merely shrugged. 'Then innocent citizens would pay the price of the diplomatic fallout. Is that what you want?' Reeve had no reply. 'Didn't think so. Your profile suggested you had an idealistic streak, Alex. I guess Craig didn't need to fake that part.' He pointedly checked his watch. 'Two and a half minutes.'

With reluctance, Reeve backed away. 'What about Connie?'

'I said, I'll see to her. Don't worry, I won't hurt her.' That was said almost with exasperation. 'I trusted you, Alex. Do me the same favour, huh?'

Reeve grudgingly nodded. 'Connie – go with him.'

'But what about you?' she protested.

'I'll be fine.' He started past the dome.

'Go somewhere we'd never look for you,' Maxwell called after him. 'And don't give us a *reason* to look for you. I'm giving you a chance. Don't waste it.'

'What if Scott sends more Operatives after me?' Reeve asked over his shoulder.

'Then you have to be better than them. Which . . . well, remember what I told you at Mordencroft.'

'Thanks.' He looked back at Connie. 'And thank you, Connie. For everything.' With that, he disappeared over the crest of the copper roof.

Connie watched him go in dismay. Despite his promise, she didn't trust Maxwell. She looked up at him. '*Are* you going to kill me?'

'No. Here. Let me help.' Maxwell holstered his gun and raised her gently to her feet. 'You're hurt. I'll get you to a hospital.' He led her back towards the King's Building.

'You're not going to arrest me, or anything?'

'I don't think either of us want to involve higher authorities right now. Do you?'

They reached the broken window. A security guard and two police officers were waiting inside. Connie stiffened in fear, but Maxwell was unperturbed. 'Jason Trent, Security Service,' he said, presenting an MI5 identity card. The cops reacted in surprise, but accepted his credentials. 'The assassin's taken a dive off the roof. Secure this area until an investigative team arrives. I'm going to find the body.'

'What about the other man?' one officer asked. 'The one who ran after him?'

'I didn't see anyone else out there.' He started past them.

'Who's this woman, sir?' said the other cop, probing. 'We'll need to know for the report.'

'Bystander,' Maxwell replied firmly. 'She went out there to help and got shot for her trouble.' He pointed at the security guard. 'You, take this lady to the ground floor. If there isn't an ambulance there already, call one for her.'

'Er . . . yes, sir,' the guard replied, cowed by Maxwell's instant assumption of authority. 'If you'll, ah, come with me, ma'am?'

Connie followed him to the stairs. Maxwell had already hurried ahead. 'Thank you,' she called after him.

He didn't break stride. 'Remember what I said.'

'Which part?'

'About not wasting chances.' He continued his rapid descent.

The guard brought Connie to the ground floor. She was

soon in an ambulance. It sped from Somerset House with lights and siren on. On its way along the Strand, it passed the building covered in scaffolding. Connie looked out at Reeve's escape route.

If he had taken it, there was no sign of him. Nor was he amongst the crowd at ground level.

He was gone.

Maxwell made his way to the Thames side of Somerset House. Parker's body was easy to find. A police cordon had already been set up around it. He used his MI5 credentials to pass through.

Parker was definitely dead. His skull was smashed, bloodied face grotesquely deformed, limbs twisted at unnatural angles. The fall had probably broken every major bone in his body.

Maxwell found the most senior officer present, a uniformed inspector. Higher ranks would be on the way; he needed to act before they arrived. 'Has he been searched?'

'Not yet, sir,' the inspector replied. 'We're waiting for the CSIs.'

'This can't wait. I need to check him now. My authority, on national security grounds. File a report with Thames House if you have any objections.' Thames House was MI5's headquarters.

But again, nobody challenged his apparent seniority. 'Yes, sir,' was the only reply.

Maxwell donned gloves and quickly went through the broken corpse's clothing. Most of what he found belonged to whomever Parker had killed to get press access. But a wallet contained several credit cards, all in different names. Some fake IDs, ditto.

There was something conspicuously absent, though . . .

'His phone,' Maxwell muttered. He half-smiled, shaking his head. 'Oh, Alex. You cunning little bastard . . .'

Time to go. He waited until the inspector was occupied, then quickly departed. Once clear, he took out his own phone.

His call was answered almost immediately. 'Well?' Scott barked. 'What happened?'

'Craig Parker's dead,' Maxwell replied.

'And Reeve?'

No hesitation in the reply. 'He'd already gone by the time I arrived. They must have had a fight on the roof. Parker lost.'

There was no immediate response. But Maxwell could hear Scott breathing heavily in his anger. 'At least SC9 is protected, sir,' he continued. 'Parker didn't send the password for the stolen files.'

'That might still happen if he set the email on a timer,' said Scott.

'I think it would have already happened by now. If something went wrong, he would have timed it to go almost immediately. And something *did* go wrong. Alex Reeve stopped him from killing Elektra Curtis in an extremely public assassination. That was very much against the intent of your orders, sir. I think we can safely assume Parker was the mole, not Reeve.'

'Reeve.' The name sounded almost like a curse. 'How the hell did he track Parker down?'

'No idea. But in this case, he helped us.' Maxwell paused, choosing his words carefully. 'Sir, with that in mind . . . are you going to rescind his Fox Red status?'

'Don't be absurd,' came the sharp reply. 'He's more of a threat to SC9 than ever. He knows too much. For all we know, he intends to carry on where Parker left off.'

Maxwell knew there was no point arguing. Anything else he said might raise questions about his own actions. 'Very well, sir. Am I still in charge of the operation to track him down?'

'For now.' Distinct petulance behind the words. 'Although you've hardly covered yourself in glory.'

'We'll get him, sir. It's just a matter of time.'

'It had better be, Maxwell. It had better be.' Scott ended the call without another word.

Maxwell lowered the phone. His expression was blank, placid; the emotions beneath were anything but. He drew in a deep breath, looking back towards Parker's body. A long moment of thought. Then he turned and walked away into the night.

CHAPTER 60

Connie looked out at Paris as the Eurostar slowed. She was excited – but also nervous. She didn't know what to expect.

Nine months had passed since the night Alex rescued her. Since the night she last saw him. She had tried to return to her old, normal life. It had been impossible.

Even as her wound healed, she knew she wouldn't be the same. Not physically, but mentally. Nightmares had been frequent companions, and sudden bursts of heart-clenching anxiety. Over time they reduced in frequency, and intensity. But every so often, something would trigger a memory. Valon Bato's lizard face would reappear, promising sudden, brutal violence. Other men loomed behind him. Jammer, sneering and smirking. Bato's thugs, fists clenched.

And a stone-faced assassin, pointing a gun down at her.

That was the most terrifying memory of all. Not just for the event, but for what it represented. She had glimpsed something meant to stay unseen. Something rotten, dirty. Corrupt. A part of the system the state wanted to conceal, even from itself.

SC9. A death squad.

And Alex had been a part of it.

That was one fear which never faded. SC9 knew who she

was. Knew she had seen the face of the man controlling it. If he thought for a moment she could expose him . . .

It felt as if the entire weight of British state security was upon her. Unrelenting, remorseless, uncaring. It would crush her without a thought. Unless she moved.

So she had.

She made the effort, found the time. Found the money. Literally. Returning from work one day, she discovered a package addressed to her in the hall. It contained over ten thousand pounds in cash.

The package hadn't borne a stamp. Alex had been there.

She knew the risk he had taken. Her flat could have been under observation, agents watching for him. But nothing came of it. She knew that, because a week later, a letter arrived for her at the hospital.

Hope you got my present. It might help you follow your dream of a change from this island life. If it does, I'll see you again at the star's end. Love, A.

She knew instantly it really had come from Alex. *Island Life* was a Grace Jones album. A smile at the memory of their night in Banon.

The good part, at least – not the awkwardness that followed. She had come to terms with why things unravelled. Alex had been clinging to the hope that SC9 would take him back. That had been dashed with force. Because of that, he had realised the agency's real nature. He had saved Elektra Curtis – he had saved *her*. Had he truly been the merciless killer of his training, he would have done neither.

The real man was still there, under the protective shell.

The man she wanted to see again.

So long-held idle dreams were finally pushed to fruition. She applied for an Italian passport. It had at last arrived. From what she'd heard about Italian bureaucracy, nine months was considered a rush. She made use of her new identity to book a train journey to Paris. As an EU citizen – once more, post-Brexit – all Europe was open to her.

The Eurostar pulled into Gare du Nord. End of the line: the star's end. She hoped that was what Alex had meant. How he could even know she was coming, she didn't know. But she knew how resourceful he could be. If there was any way for him to meet her . . . he would find it.

She could be wrong, of course. She could have made a huge mistake in coming – in abandoning her old life. Her flat's lease was about to expire. She hadn't renewed it. She had handed in her notice at the hospital. She had sold anything she didn't truly need – which had been a surprising amount. Even her phone and replacement laptop had gone. They could be traced, she now knew; tracked. That was not paranoia, but necessity. Whatever promises Alex's mentor had made, he wasn't in charge of SC9. They would still be looking for him. She had to be sure she didn't lead them to him.

The other passengers moved for the exit. Connie waited for the aisle to clear, then retrieved her wheelie case. It was not large. She followed everyone off the train. Crisp late-morning light shone through the station's glazed roof. It was chilly, midwinter, but the sky was clear and blue. She walked down the platform. Wariness at the uniformed men near the exit. But nobody stopped her, or even paid her any attention. She passed through the glass gate without trouble.

Now what?

Part of her had the romantic hope that Alex would be standing there waiting. She knew that was unrealistic. She was right. He was nowhere in sight. But she still felt a flutter of worry. What if he wasn't coming at all?

The flutter grew to a flap as the minutes passed. The Eurostar arrivals concourse gradually emptied. The gate shut. Everyone was off the train. Connie felt exposed and vulnerable, standing alone in the echoing space. The fear grew that she had made an awful mistake. God, what had she done? She had given up everything, walked away from her life – to what? She must have gone insane . . .

But she still held on to the bead of hope. *I'll see you again at the star's end.* She hadn't seen Alex – but he might have seen her . . .

That thought buoying her, she headed for the main atrium. The crowds thickened again, people hurrying for local trains. She glanced back. Nobody followed her from the Eurostar terminal. Was anyone watching for her ahead? She picked a course through the throng almost at random. Part of it was out of concern that she was being tailed. The other part was simply that she didn't know where she was going. She descended an escalator to a lower level, crossed it, then came back up. Her concern grew. She really had come to Paris for nothing. She'd been wrong, stupid. He wasn't here—

'*Bonjour. Suivez-moi.*'

A man in a dark hoodie walked past her. Connie stared after him, momentarily frozen. Was it Alex? She wasn't sure.

He was the right height, but she hadn't seen his face.

The man didn't look back. She drew in a breath – then followed him, as asked. She glanced around as she walked. Was anyone paralleling her movements? Were Operatives all over the station, hoping she would lead them to Alex?

She didn't know. But she was sure that *Alex* would. If she was being followed, he wouldn't have come to her.

The man went through an archway, disappearing from sight. She went after him—

He was gone.

Connie stopped in alarm. She saw only harried travellers. Where was he? He'd only been metres ahead of her—

'*Bonjour.*'

The same voice, now behind. She whirled – to face a smiling, bearded Alex Reeve.

Reeve was relieved when Connie returned his smile. 'Alex!' she cried, hugging him. He embraced her too. 'Are you okay?'

'I'm fine,' he said. 'You got my message, then.'

'Yeah.' She released him, and looked up into his face. 'But how did you know I'd be here?'

'Trade secrets,' he said, with a grin. 'Sorry.' In truth, Jaz had told him she was about to leave the day before. He had stayed in occasional contact with the young mother by email. Both she and Brownlow had also received gift packages.

'I see.' Concern crossed Connie's face. 'But . . . you weren't worried about me being followed?'

'You weren't,' he assured her. All the same, he gave his surroundings another check. Nobody triggered his internal radar. 'Shall we go?'

'Where to?'

He smiled again. 'Let's find out.'

Reeve and Connie headed for the station's exit. Paris lay beyond, and all of Europe. They walked out into the light, together.

Discover more from bestselling author

Andy McDermott . . .

We hope you enjoyed reading *Operative 66*.

Rogue Asset is Andy McDermott's next pulse-racing and action-packed thriller featuring Alex Reeve.

Coming July 2021 . . .

Available to order now

HEADLINE

www.headline.co.uk
www.hachette.co.uk

Have you discovered the latest novel in Andy McDermott's bestselling Wilde and Chase series?

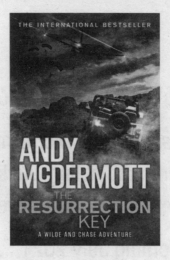

Their days of death-defying adventure seemingly behind them, acclaimed archaeologist Nina Wilde and her husband, ex-SAS soldier Eddie Chase, live like any normal family. However, when a mythical civilisation is unearthed deep in the Antarctic ice, they are drawn into a battle for control of its astonishing power.

Dashing from New York to New Zealand, from futuristic Chinese cities to the outback of Australia, they soon confront the gravest threat they've ever faced. Pursued by ruthless mercenaries and a secret special forces unit, Nina and Eddie discover the clock is counting down to the extermination of all humanity . . .

Available to order now